Blind Obsession

ELLA FRANK

Edited by Jovana Shirley
www.ellafrank.com

Special Acknowledgments

The author acknowledges the copyrighted or trademarked status and trademark owners of the following word marks mentioned in this work of fiction; William Shakespeare ~ A Midsummer Night's Dream. Helen Keller. Thais:Meditation ~ Massenet, Canon In D Major ~ Pachelbel, Adagio for Strings ~ Samuel Barber, Air ~ Johann Sebastian Bach, Lux Aeterna ~ Clint Mansell, Winter (The Four Seasons) ~ Vivaldi

Also by Ella Frank

The Exquisite Series
Exquisite
Entice
Edible

Masters Among Monsters Series
Alasdair
Isadora
Thanos

The Temptation Series
Try
Take
Trust
Tease
Tate

Sunset Cove Series
Finley
Devil's Kiss

Standalones
Blind Obsession
Veiled Innocence

The Arcanian Chronicles
Temperance

Sex Addict
Co-authored with Brooke Blaine

PresLocke Series
Co-Authored with Ella Frank
Aced
Locked
Wedlocked

Dedication

This book is dedicated to one of the most supportive partners-in-crime I have ever had while writing a book. She does so much to assist and support, that I truly cannot believe I have only known her for such a short amount of time. You know who you are and I appreciate every, read through, picture choosing, music playing, dirty word discussion we have had. Without you, this book would still be in my head and nowhere close to finished.

And as always, for my husband. There are no words to express what you mean to me. I love you.

Xx Ella

First Impressions

Chateau Tibideau. I've heard so much about this place and the man who lives here.

Nestled against rows of lush, plump grapevines, the sprawling old manor is slowly crumbling into the ground a little more each day. As the sun begins to dip below the hills of Bordeaux, France, a stunning golden hue sweeps across the skyline, highlighting the magnificence of the chateau in all its fading glory.

It's fading because the owner has closed the gates. He's stopped producing the wine that was once exported from here, and he's refused visitors ever since—well, ever since his world exploded all over the media front.

Standing beside my little rented Toyota with my laptop bag slung over my shoulder, I look up at the second story window of the main house. I notice a heavy black curtain shift and move almost as if someone has taken a step away from peering out of it.

Taking a calming breath, I remind myself, *I was invited here. He reached out to me.*

He is a man so private and so isolated from the outside world that no one has seen or heard from him in months, ever since he was hounded relentlessly about his involvement in the tragic events that had unfolded here. That, of course, all came on the heels of the acclaim he had received over his artwork, which had catapulted him into the public eye in the first place.

His artwork includes a series of paintings that have been revered as, and I quote, "an alluring mixture of dark eroticism enhanced now by its devastatingly haunting sadness," end quote. With all of that praise, one would think that the artist would be available and forthcoming for interviews, but Mr. Phillipe Tibideau has disappeared. He's vanished from the spotlight.

It's easy to understand why. Rumors have swirled about the man whenever he is in a room. They have even surfaced when he is nowhere in sight. Peace seems to be a very distant friend for this man who was once one of the most public and famous faces in the world.

Gathering up my courage, I walk forward and knock twice on the large wooden door. Taking a step back, I wait patiently for someone to answer. I glance over to the left where a black plaque is mounted on the wall with a quote written in intricate gold paint.

It reads, *Les vrais paradis sont les paradis qu'on a perdus.*

My French is certainly nowhere near good enough to translate that, so I pull out the little notepad from my overstuffed laptop bag and write down, *Ask about plaque.* Just as I put the notepad away, the old door opens, and a small white-haired lady steps forward with a smile.

"Mademoiselle Harris?" she questions.

My American last name sounds so foreign with the French accent.

"Yes, ma'am. I'm here to meet with Mr. Tibideau," I inform her.

She stands aside, ushering me in. Taking a step forward into the large foyer, the first thing I see is the grand staircase to my left. It wraps up the curved wall, which is what I presume is the turret I could see from outside.

What an amazing place to live, is my initial thought. As my eyes glance around the room, they take in several pieces of artwork hanging from every wall. They are so stunningly breathtaking that I start to feel as though I'm in a museum.

Waiting for me to finish my obvious admiration of the place she calls home, the little lady beside me clears her throat, regaining my attention.

Gesturing up the stairs I was just admiring, she informs me in her strongly accented voice, "Mr. Tibideau is waiting for you upstairs in his studio."

She turns and walks away in the opposite direction, leaving me to look around the room again as I make my way to the staircase.

Reaching out, I place my hand on the old worn banister, tracing the cracks in the wood, as I slowly take the steps one at a time. On the wall closest to me is a painting I've seen before but only in prints. As I stand before what I believe is a life-size replica or perhaps the original, I am instantly compelled by it. Although the room I am standing in is completely silent, there's something about the image that screams out to me. In fact, the only thing I can consciously hear is my breathing and the slight creak of the floorboards every time I take a step.

The painting is absolutely captivating. I can't even begin to describe how the artist has managed to make each brushstroke feel as though you are actually touching the woman in pose. Instantly, you're aware that the person who painted her so lovingly had stroked his hands over the naked flesh he so beautifully captured.

Shifting my feet a little, I find myself almost uncomfortable to be standing in someone's house—no, not someone's house, *his* house—staring at this image, and feeling so moved and completely mesmerized by it.

Slowly looking over the painting, I tear my eyes away from the supple perfection of her nude posterior, stopping at the curve of her right cheek where it meets her thigh. Reaching out, I move to trace it with my fingers, but at the last minute, I pull my hand back. Admonishing myself, I turn on the step, determined to be on my way, although I can't help but take one more quick look at the painting. I wonder about the violin that is being held by the woman to cover a portion of herself. *I know it is hers, but what message is the artist trying to convey?*

Pulling out my notepad, I write that question down, too. *Does the violin represent more than* just *a violin?* Putting the pad back, I make my way up the final steps. I look around and notice the door to the left is open. Taking a deep breath while I move toward it, I step inside and find a room shrouded in darkness. Narrowing my eyes, I search the space.

When my eyes finally focus, they are drawn to a man sitting in a small chair in the corner of the room. It isn't easy to spot him right off, and I understand why.

From what I can make out, he's dressed from head to toe in dark clothing. One of his long legs is bent, with his ankle propped up on the knee of his other leg. Stepping into what I have now determined is his studio, my eyes squint as he flicks on a lamp sitting on the table beside him.

While my eyes adjust to the soft glow of the light, I'm suddenly face to face with a man the world dubbed nearly a year ago as the most beautiful man. That headline, however, has been replaced with ones that read along the lines of, *Beautiful? Or Beautifully Terrifying?*

"Mademoiselle Harris?" he inquires.

His voice heats me like the burn of smooth whiskey.

I watch carefully as he unfolds his large body from the plush-looking chair. As he moves toward me, I track him crossing the studio space. Instantly, I forget my own name.

It isn't hard to know why. He moves with such elegance for a tall man. He easily tops six-foot which places him perhaps at around six-foot-four.

When he stops in front of me, he holds out his hand. This is a natural introduction for two people about to begin a business relationship. *So, why am I holding my breath?* Reaching out, I slide my hand into his, marveling at the paint flecked on his fingers and embedded under the blunt nails on his hands.

"Yes, Mr. Tibideau, but you can call me Gemma," I reply.

A small smile barely touches his lips as he nods.

For a moment, I try to push aside all I have heard, and I look at him objectively. The man has the most sensual eyes I've ever seen. They have a come-to-my-bedroom quality all on their own. Once you add in the full, pouty lips and sexy little dimple on his chin—not to mention, the dark brown hair that falls haphazardly like he has run his hands through it—then you have the most beautiful man in the world. Or, if you believe the other stories, you have a beautiful monster.

"Well, in that case, Gemma, I insist you call me Phillipe. After all, you are about to know me very well, no?"

Heat rises in my cheeks as I try not to act embarrassed. I remind myself, *I'm a professional.*

"I suppose you are right," I manage to say, unable to think of anything else at the moment.

He lets go of my hand and turns silently, walking over to the only window in the studio. I'm left standing in the doorway, feeling oddly bereft.

The window with the French provincial shutters is closed and I watch intently as he unlatches and pushes them open. He then takes a moment to slide his hands into his perfectly tailored pants as he looks out of them.

Looking around, I spot a small table and chair over to the left. "Should I set up over here then?"

Turning, he looks to where I'm standing. "Yes. I had the table brought up here for you. I figured this room is probably the best place to conduct these sessions." He pauses as he turns back to look out at the now darkened sky. "This is where I am most comfortable."

Walking over to the small desk, I place my bag down and remove my laptop from its case. Turning back around, I see he still has his back to me. I try to control my erratic heartbeat as it thumps nervously in my chest. *I need to calm down. This man can either make or break my career.* As I stare at him, trying to forget all the things other people have warned me about, I can't seem to stop my heart from racing.

For several months now, journalists from every form of media have been trying—and failing—to get Mr. Tibideau to tell his side of the rumored story as well as share the inspiration behind each of his paintings. Somehow, I, Gemma Harris, have been chosen.

I finish setting up my things as he finally turns back to face me, moving to the chair that's situated under the soft lamplight. Taking a seat silently, his eyes never waver from mine. He's intimidating as hell, but instead of making me nervous, it makes me more determined. I'm determined to get the story I came looking for.

Looking away from him, I pull out the chair he's provided, turn it to face him, and sit down.

"Thank you for allowing me to do this."

"Thank you for accepting my terms. Not everyone would have packed up their lives and moved to France for a couple of months."

I laugh to hide my first-day nerves. With a smile, I tell him, "Really? Well, those people are crazy. This is a wonderful opportunity. France is beautiful. It will give me an authentic feel for your story and your life. After all, it did take place here, didn't it?"

He forms a steeple with his hands in front of his nose, and I watch as those serious green eyes move to mine.

"It did happen here, yes." Closing his eyes, he leans his head back on the chair. "The important parts anyway."

Regarding him carefully, I probe. "When would you like to begin? Tonight or in the morning?"

His eyes open as he raises his head. I can feel the full impact of that penetrating stare.

"Tonight. Let's start now," he replies.

Clearing my throat, I grab the notepad and pen from my bag. When I look back at him, he is leaning forward, holding out a bound leather book to me. Glancing down, I reach forward and take it as he settles back in the chair. He tries to appear calm, but he doesn't succeed. Instead, he just looks uncomfortable.

"What is this?" I ask the obvious question.

"It's a journal. You'll need that for any of *this* to make sense."

He doesn't seem to want to say more, so I nod while I move to open it.

"No, not yet," he instructs.

I find it hard not to flip it open just for a peek, but I'm here to listen. I want to learn about his paintings and what really happened that night, but since he says not to look at it yet, I place the bound journal on the desk.

"Okay, let's start at the beginning."

He takes a deep breath, and for some reason, I hold mine before he finally blows his out.

"Go ahead."

Shifting in my seat, I begin. "What inspired you to paint your critically acclaimed series?"

He lifts a hand to stroke the stubble lining his cheeks and chin, and then he replies so softly that I almost miss it.

"Beauty." There's a pregnant pause before he repeats himself louder. "Beauty inspired me."

Scribbling this down, I ask my next question without looking up. "Beauty of the world?"

Not missing a beat, he replies, "No, beauty of a woman. One woman."

Looking up at him, I instantly know he means *her,* and I swallow deeply. I now understand the reason for his focus on every intense stroke of the painting that hangs center stage on the wall by the staircase, lit up as though it is the pride and joy of the house. *That painting is beauty, and she is the one woman.* She is the woman that has captured the attention of the entire world, bringing probing questions to this man's door.

Urging my brain to catch up, I remind myself to be professional, to ask only what I need to, and to build up to the parts of the story I so desperately want to know from this very private man. Instead of following my own directions, I blurt out, "What moves you?"

He seems to think about this question longer than I expect him to before he deflects with one of his own. "You don't want to ask me the most obvious question first, Miss Harris?"

Immediately, I know what question he means, but I'm not ready to ask that yet. I'm here to learn about the vision behind the images and his side of this terrible nightmare. *So, no, I don't want to ask him the obvious…yet.*

"I thought we decided on you calling me Gemma," I point out, trying to keep our conversation light.

Narrowing his eyes, he tilts his head in a mock bow. That's my signal to continue.

"What moves you?" I ask again.

For some reason, I anticipate him having an answer ready. Instead, he sits there in thought while I picture the woman in the painting, knowing he is thinking of her.

"What moves me?" he repeats my question.

I nod and wait, gripping the edge of my seat, and this is only my second question.

"The answer to that is the same to your first question, Gemma. Beauty moves me."

After scribbling that down, I bring my eyes back to his. "And beauty is one woman?" I clarify just to be sure.

His eyes remain steadfast on mine, and without a shred of doubt, he tells me, "Beauty is Chantel."

Finally, the woman in the painting, Chantel, has been invited into the room.

Chapter One
FIRST SIGHT

First Sight ~

I need to type something, and I need to type it now.

Something happened to me—a moment, I believe.

I've always held on to the idea that moments happen to shape who we are and who we will become, and I'm almost one-hundred percent positive that I had a moment of clarity today.

In wine country in Bordeaux, France, I met a man.

Yes, today out in wine country, I met a man, and something about that man moved me.

Something about that man changed me.

* * *

Closing the journal, I look out the window to the sun that's now shining brightly, casting a beautiful morning glow over the vineyard.

Phillipe instructed me to read no further than the natural end of each journal entry. Every page is a time capsule of precisely inked words typed meticulously letter by letter, old-school style. All of the words have been methodically tapped out by the hands of a very unique individual. It's obvious by the way he had the pages bound together that they mean the world to him and now he is entrusting it to me.

Honestly, I know there's no way Phillipe would ever know one way or another, but I can't stop remembering the firm tone in his voice and the steely determination in his eyes when he handed me the journal with strict instructions and a request that I meet him this morning.

Looking at the clock, I watch the hand as it slowly moves to nine, and then I turn and head up to the studio to wait for Mr. Tibideau.

* * *

Today is going to be painful, like opening an old wound.

Phillipe stands in the drafty kitchen with a cup of coffee, listening to Penelope, his housekeeper, hum as she bustles about making pastries.

Today, he's going to allow himself to look back, remembering a time he'd rather lock away and keep to himself. He knows that if he doesn't tell the story the way he wants it to be told, he'll forever be judged. He'll never be left to live his life in peace—*well, at least be left to live it alone. Peace is just a selfish illusion now.*

He notices it is 9 a.m. Turning on his heel, he brushes a kiss on Penelope's cheek, and then he makes his way up to his studio.

When he arrives, he sees the assiduous Gemma Harris sitting at her desk with her notepad open.

She put on a courageous face yesterday. He saw the apprehension in her eyes when they first met. She probably remembered all the things she had read in the tabloids about his artistic temper or the even worse headlines that he couldn't bring himself to think about.

Well, no matter what she had heard, Gemma is presenting a steady and strong composure, and he has to admit that he is impressed.

She set up her laptop, but the screen is blank. He has a feeling that she takes notes first, and then she goes back to write her story. He respects that. He understands an artist's mind, and in a way, Gemma is an artist, just like he is.

As he makes his way into the room, she looks up at him. He detects the slight tightening of her fingers around her pen.

Ahh, not so calm.

"Good morning, Gemma. I trust you slept well?"

She monitors him closely as he moves into the room. "Like a baby. This place is so quiet at night."

Nodding his agreement, Phillipe makes his way over to the chair he favors and sits down. "So I've been told."

Gemma turns in her chair to face him, pen in hand and notepad on her lap. When it's clear he isn't going to say anything, she licks her bottom lip before speaking. "I read the journal entry this morning. I have to admit, from a journalistic point of view, it will be extremely difficult for me to stop reading and wait until our next meeting."

Phillipe smiles briefly. "But did you?"

"Did I what?" she responds, staring at him with wide, guileless eyes.

"Wait?"

She shifts in the chair and nods. "Oh. Yes. Yes, I waited."

"Good, Gemma. That's good. Trust me when I tell you that waiting is often the best part of a story," he explains. "After all, once you know the story, it's over."

Leaning back in his chair, he waits as she scribbles something down.

"I'm ready when you are," she says.

Looking her over, he feels his heart actually start to ache as he closes his eyes.

* * *

It just wasn't happening for him today.

No matter what he did or didn't do, he couldn't seem to find inspiration in anything. Sighing, he threw the rag down onto the drop cloth beneath his bare feet. Some days, he really felt like giving up on the whole fucking thing.

Maybe he wasn't supposed to have a masterpiece. Maybe he was just supposed to be a mediocre painter who would sell his pieces in a little gallery for ten dollars each, so people could hang them over their mantles and never even look at them.

Fuck that, *he thought in disgust.*

He didn't want to paint something for some suburbanite to hang up and dismiss every time she walked into her living room. He wanted to create something that moved people—a piece so fucking brilliant that people would cry when they looked at it. He wanted to alter their emotions and to touch their soul.

A little over a year ago, when he'd been living back in the States, he'd found out through his father's will that he had acquired an old family vineyard in France. Having lost his mother at an early age he had seen no reason to remain in America and decided he might as well try his luck in France.

He had somehow stupidly assumed that he'd move over there and suddenly create the next world-renowned artistic piece. What he hadn't expected was to feel absolutely nothing.

Walking over to the window in his studio, he watched the workers who were picking the grapes from the vines. He'd decided that if he was going to take over this property, he wanted to revitalize the vineyard that made Chateau Tibideau.

At least I did that part right.

As his eyes moved over his workers, he was surprised to spot a woman with Beau, his foreman. He'd never seen her there before. From where he was standing, all he could make out was long black hair. He could see she was wearing some kind of flowing white peasant skirt and a blue blouse that kept shifting with the slight breeze.

Almost as if she could feel his eyes on her, she turned around, looking up to the window where he was standing. As their eyes met, he felt something in the air change.

Desire, *he thought as he gripped the window frame.* Strange, intense, and unexplainable desire.

Before another moment passed, he turned and made his way to the stairs, determined to get to her. He was determined to meet her.

Taking the steps two at a time, he became almost desperate to get outside. He needed to meet the woman who had felt his stare and had turned to meet his gaze as if he had called out to her.

Rounding the corner of the kitchen, he pushed open the door and made his way out to where he had seen her. As he hurried around the side of the west turret, he literally ran into the woman he had been searching for.

"Well, hello." He chuckled, raising his hands to grip her shoulders.

Unable to brace herself, it seemed as though she hadn't seen him at all.

"Please let me go," she replied almost instantly.

"Oh, good. You're American."

Removing his hands immediately, he took a step back as eyes the color of misty gray looked beyond him. He glanced over his shoulder and then turned back to her.

"I'm sorry. I didn't see you there," he explained, hoping to get her attention. "Actually, no, I'm not. You're even more spectacular up close."

Her face was spellbinding. Her beauty was stunning, not in a Hollywood kind of way, but more natural. Like nothing he had ever seen before.

A contrast of shadows and sharp angles. Strength and softness. Those eyes of hers…wow.

As she tipped up her chin a little, he smiled, hoping to dazzle her with what he'd been told was an irresistible grin. She didn't seem impressed; in fact, she seemed to not notice at all.

"Is that supposed to be funny?" she questioned.

He frowned for a moment, as he asked, "Is what supposed to be funny?"

The woman in front of him merely shook her head while she let out a huff of breath.

"Never mind." She sighed, exasperated. "My uncle told me to come in here and find Mr. Tibideau. I'm supposed to tell him that they're done for the day."

He thought the whole exchange was slightly bizarre. Everyone knew that only he and Penelope lived in the house.

Doesn't this woman know that I am Mr. Tibideau?

"Well, mission accomplished. He now knows, and he's now intrigued," he told her, taking a step closer.

Her aggravation only enhances her beauty, *he thought as he ran his eyes over every detail of her face.*

He had to admit that he found it unusual she hadn't yet commented on the fact that she knew who he was. "You don't recognize me?"

An ironic smile finally tipped her rose red lips as her uniquely colored eyes blinked once. "No, I'm sorry. I didn't recognize you by sight,*" she replied with sarcasm. "I'm starting to think* you *might be blind, Mr. Tibideau."*

As she turned away from him, she raised her arm and flicked her wrist, extending a retractable cane from her palm.

How did I not notice that before?

All of a sudden, everything about the exchange made perfect sense. Every word and gesture she had made now shined through with amazing clarity. All he could think was perhaps he was the blind one because everything else had disappeared with one look at her face.

* * *

Out of the corner of my eye, I'm aware of Phillipe as he walks over to where I'm madly scribbling in my notepad. When he's finally standing near, I glance up at him, frowning.

"You're leaving?" I ask. "We only just started."

He points to the journal. "I'll be back in a little bit. The next part you need to know is in there."

Turning, he walks to the door and then stops to look back at me. The man is beautiful. That's the only word to encompass his appeal, and I am *still* staring at him, holding my pen midair.

"Do you want a coffee, Gemma?"

I shake my head. "No, but I'd love some tea."

"Tea, it is. See you in a few," he replies before disappearing out the door.

Finishing off my final note, I put the pen and paper down, reaching for the leather journal. It's a bulky thing bound by a leather strap. I unwind and open it to the page directly after the one where I left off, and I run my fingers over the typed entry. It's hard to imagine her sitting at her braille typewriter, punching out each word smoothly and efficiently, but she did it with constant dedication for quite some time. Now, here I am, reading her most private thoughts.

Sitting back in the chair, I look down at the typed words and start reading.

* * *

His voice was what moved me—the sound of it when he spoke to me.

It was deep and smooth, and it reached inside and calmed me to my very core.

Phillipe didn't even realize that I'm blind. When was the last time that had happened?

He treated me like he would anyone else. He made me feel…normal.

I didn't want to come to France. I admit that I was more than a little bit annoyed and offended when my mother had suggested I "go and live a little, and see the world."

Was that some kind of ironic blind person joke? No. That was my mother's way of saying, stop living in fear.

That makes me wonder. Is that what I've been doing? I don't know. I don't think so.

But here I am, staying with my Uncle Beau and running into a man in a French vineyard.

Not exactly where I saw my life going.

Life, I have discovered, has always had a different idea in mind for me.

Oh, but his voice. "You don't recognize me?"

He asked that like it was an everyday God-given right to be able to see someone and know who he was.

If only it were that simple.

He called me spectacular *as though he had never seen anything like me.*

I find myself wanting to go back to the chateau tomorrow.

Wanting to talk to him.

Wanting to be moved.

* * *

I stop for a moment and look around the studio where I'm sitting.

The space isn't overwhelming in size. On the other hand, it isn't exactly small either. It seems to have a personality all on its own.

When I first arrived, it was cloaked in darkness until he illuminated a small slice of his personal space to my eyes. Now, as I sit here on my own, I really have the chance to see his studio, and I realize that it's a room that captivates me.

Splattered on the rough hardwood floors are obvious reminders of his profession. There are speckles of brown, white, and black mottled across the original wood floorboards. The floor marked up in such a way must not bother him because he has left it as is. Maybe it's even his way of making it his own.

The desk he has set up for me is old and wooden. It creaks every time I apply any kind of pressure to it, but like the room itself, it seems to fit. Pushed up against the right wall, it's situated so that I can either face his chair, which is nestled into the corner, or I can turn to the window and the easel that is set up on the opposite side of the space on the far left.

The walls of the west turret have been built from brick that's the color of burnt cooper. It's been left exposed on the interior of the studio, which I'm sure in the sunlight gives the room a spectacular glow. Right now, with the shutters closed and the room in shadows, it just makes the studio seem dark and volatile. Like a dormant volcano in nature, the room is silently smoldering but almost certain to one day explode in a blazing fiery rain of heat.

I don't sense that this is a place of joy for him. Even with the lights on, the room doesn't feel bright or happy. No, it actually feels intense and somewhat intimidating.

In the soft glow of the light, this room seems to shimmer with an underlying passion I have yet to understand. *A passion for art or a passion for her?* I cannot tell which one it is yet.

At the moment, I am seated facing his chair, which looks soft and cozy. It's covered with an ivory-colored fabric that seems so neutral for this space. Maybe that's what he needs to help calm him.

Beside the chair is a set of shelves. Atop one of the lower shelves, are several paintbrushes of all different sizes stuffed into a jar. The brushes appear to have clean bristles, but the wooden handles have dried-up paint spotted around them. On the shelf above them is a stereo. *Maybe he likes listening to his music when he paints. It's inspirational, I'm sure.*

It's obvious this is where he spends most of his time. His subtle fingerprints appear on nearly every surface throughout the room.

Turning around from where we have set up, I look again at the easel that's been covered with a sheet since I arrived. *Perhaps it's something he is working on?*

I'd love to go and look, but I know that would be a major invasion of privacy. Instead, I turn back to the journal in front of me.

What must it be like not being able to see? As I reflect, I'm struck with another completely inappropriate and selfish thought. It has to do with the man I'm working with. *Imagine not ever knowing how attractive he is?*

It doesn't seem fair that this woman, Chantel, missed out on that. It doesn't seem fair that she didn't know what the man—a man she inspired—looked like.

Glancing back at the journal, I decide to continue reading, starting at the second entry on the same page. Pushing aside my worries that Phillipe will suddenly appear to stop me from going further, I sit back, determined to finish this small typed entry before he returns.

* * *

Second Opinions ~

I went back today, just like I had said I would. I needed to talk to him again.

It took me a while to track him down.

He wasn't where we had last run in to one another. This time, he was down behind the chateau. He was by the old arbor—well, that was what my uncle told me when he led me down the pebbled path to what felt like a shaded area. My uncle greeted his employer, the man I now knew as Phillipe, and then he told me he would be over in the vineyard if I needed him.

I stood there silently, waiting for Phillipe to speak, but he didn't. Instead, I heard him moving around. It sounded like he was shifting his stance from foot to foot. Each time he changed the weight of his footing, I heard the pebbles crunch. When I heard a swivel sound in the gravel, I knew instantly that he was facing me.

I have to admit that I felt a little apprehensive. I'm not good with strangers, and I don't handle change well. That was why I put on my sunglasses today. Yes, I know how ridiculous that seems, but I enjoy the privacy they afford me and the courage they seem to instill in me.

"You came back," he said to me.

I swear that I felt his voice travel up my body, taking my breath away. I took a step closer.

"Do you need some help?" he asked.

Immediately, I sensed him beside me.

I turned in the direction where I felt him move, and I took a deep breath. Suddenly, I was surrounded by the smell of him, and it was so intoxicating. I remember consciously licking my lips because it made me hungry—hungry for him.

"No, I don't need any help," I responded.

Then, I berated myself because he moved away from me.

"Tell me your name," he demanded softly. "I didn't get it yesterday."

I smiled for the first time in months, as I flirted with him. "Well, you didn't ask."

If I thought his voice was sensual, his chuckle was wickedly hypnotic.

"You're correct, so let me rectify that. Mademoiselle, please tell me your name."

That was the moment—the moment I went back there for. That was the moment I knew that this man was going to change my life forever. Suddenly, I found myself wanting to change his.

"Chantel," I informed him. "Chantel Rosenberg."

I felt him step up close to me.

Not many people do that. I think my handicap scares them, but it didn't seem to bother him as he whispered, "Chantel, you're beautiful. I think I'll call you...Beauty."

* * *

I close the journal in a room that is still empty. The clock has just turned 11 a.m.

I have been sitting here for two hours. One of those has been on my own, and I have a feeling that for the rest of the afternoon, I will be hard-pressed to find the man who doesn't want to be found.

Chapter Two

CURIOSITY

As I make my way down to the main dining room later that night, I find myself stopping in front of the painting by the stairs. Again, I discover that I want to reach out to stroke my fingers along the round curves. This time, I actually make the move toward the image, and just as I raise my arm, I hear the sound of a throat clearing from the landing below.

Almost as though I'm being pulled from a dream, I turn and find Phillipe standing at the foot of the stairs. Unflinchingly, his eyes lock with mine. This is the first time that I've seen him since he left me this morning. That's how it had felt. He *left* me. *What an odd way to feel.*

"She's magnificent, isn't she?" he asks me.

I have no idea how to answer him. I'm so entranced, and at the same time, I'm shocked by the image because I never expected to feel so many emotions from observing the female form.

He saves me from having to answer him by making a move. He grips the wooden banister and takes each step one at a time, slowly ascending to where I am paralyzed. When he finally reaches me, he moves into the space between the railing and my body. At this stage, I'm sure I should feel uncomfortable, but all I feel is anticipation.

Anticipation of what, I'm not sure.

"It's her skin." His smooth voice wraps around me. "She's so fair and so plump."

I'm not sure that's it. Just as I'm about to ask what he means, I feel him shift, and a shiver races up my spine as he proceeds to answer my unasked question.

"It's the way she seems to be lit from the inside out. She looks like God gave her skin that glows." He pauses for a moment before whispering my unspoken thoughts out loud. "So, it's completely natural that you'd want to touch her."

As his intoxicating description ends, I move to turn and face him, but I feel two large palms come up to rest on my shoulders. I swallow deeply as he pushes me gently, urging me to take a step forward, closer to the artwork we are both facing. When we're only a couple of feet away from the painting, he halts our movement, squeezing my shoulders. I feel his breath against my ear as he asks the number one question I can't seem to answer for myself.

"You want to touch her, don't you?"

Do I? I don't know. I am definitely intrigued by her. *Is it the painting I want to stroke or the woman portrayed in the painting?*

He assures me. "It's okay to say yes."

His lips are so close to my ear that they are now brushing up against it. Turning my head to the left, I'm shocked when he doesn't move away. Instead, his sage green eyes are focused intently on me, waiting for me to react. His lips part ever so slightly, and I feel my heart start to flutter as his right palm traces over my shoulder, coming up to cup my neck.

For a moment, I feel as if I should be frightened. In recent months, this man has been described as a wolf in sheep's clothing, but like a silly rabbit, I stay inert, enraptured by the predator before me. My eyes start to feel heavy while desire pools in my stomach.

What is he doing to me?

"So? Do you, Gemma? Do you want to stroke your hand over her to feel how smooth her skin is?"

Sighing softly, I let myself finally give in to his spell, falling prey to the perfect seduction. "Yes," I confess, not even understanding everything that I'm feeling.

All I know is his hot palm is sliding down my neck, stopping at the base of my throat right above my heaving breasts. His eyes are still focused on mine, and his sensual mouth is only inches from my own.

"So did I. I would have done anything, *anything*, to touch her," he admits as his eyes leave mine.

The spell is broken as his gaze drifts to the painting on the wall.

With complete reverence, he tells me, "So I did." Dropping his hands from my shoulders, breaking the last of the provocative web he has spun, he says, "Dinner's ready. I'll meet you in the dining room."

* * *

Confession ~

I know I haven't typed much over the last few days, but I have so much to say.

I need to confess something.

I'm stalking Phillipe Tibideau.

I'm not sure if it's really stalking when he keeps insisting that I return, but whenever I'm away from him, I feel an anxious need to go to him, to be near him, to hear his voice.

So, I went back to the chateau today, just like I had done yesterday and the day before that.

There's something about him that speaks to me. As insane and unreal as it sounds, I feel like I can hear him before he makes a sound. I don't understand it, but that's exactly how it feels.

He told me yesterday that he would show *me something if I came to him today.*

I questioned his choice of words because most people slip at one point or another when they talk to me, but he just laughed and repeated that he wanted to show me something.

Should I be scared of the way I'm feeling? Probably.

Am I? No.

I find I'm, eager, and absolutely impatient to see *what he feels he can* show *a blind person.*

* * *

I shut the journal as I lie in bed the following morning, resenting the silent command I find myself now following. He really is bossy in a quiet, insistent way. I wonder for a moment if Chantel felt that way about him, too.

As I think back to last night, I'm surprised that I don't feel at all uncomfortable about what occurred on the stairs. I actually feel the opposite. All of a sudden, I feel like I know so much more than I did the day before, but in actuality, I know *nothing* more than I already did. It's public knowledge that Phillipe was involved with the woman in the paintings, but having it confirmed makes me feel more—*what do I feel? More accepting of the fact that she brought out so many emotions in me? Maybe.* Maybe it is natural to feel desire when you look at a moment in time that has been captured by someone who was full of that same emotion while painting his masterpiece. *Is that the definition of good art? Creating a piece that makes you feel exactly the way the artist wants you to feel.*

In any case, the episode on the stairs has not made me uncomfortable by any means. Instead it has intrigued the journalist in me.

Who is Phillipe Tibideau? Is he just a misunderstood sad artist who now hides himself away? Or is he something much darker than that?

I desperately want to know.

Almost like Chantel in her journal, I find that I want to know more about him. He seems to have that effect on people in general, considering the tabloids and magazines that have featured him since he was discovered in that little French art gallery where he first sold his work.

From the moment his picture had been taken, sold, and then splashed all over the front pages for the world to see, women have been romanticizing him, and men have been speculating about the enigma that is Phillipe Tibideau.

As of right now though, I have another burning question that is chasing on the heels of all of that. *What did he show Chantel?*

* * *

Phillipe moves around his studio quietly.

He wasn't able to sleep last night. Dreams and nightmares plagued him equally. It didn't matter which way the dream took him. Inevitably, when he awoke, one fact remained. *She* is gone.

Making his way over to the shelves that housed his stereo, he reaches out and hits play. Suddenly, the room is filled with the haunting and melancholic rhythm of a violinist playing *Méditation* from *Thaïs*. Phillipe closes his eyes, picturing her.

* * *

"I want you to play for me," he told her as he passed the violin back.

Her elegant fingers gripped the neck of her Stradivarius as she gently pulled it up and rested it on her left shoulder. She turned her chin, so it sat perfectly in the chin rest at the base of the lower bout.

"What would you like me to play?" she asked, closing her eyes.

"Something you want me to hear."

Her eyes opened but focused on nothing. "That's not very specific."

Moving around behind her, he encouraged her, whispering softly against her right ear. "Okay, how about something that will haunt me?"

He listened closely as she took a deep breath.

"That I can do."

To this day, *Méditation* from *Thaïs* haunts his very soul.

* * *

When I arrive at the studio at 10 a.m., I detect the distinct smell that comes from oil-based paints. *He must have been working this morning,* I surmise as I make my way into the sun-filled room. There's no sign of him yet, so I go ahead and sit down in my chair. I pull my notebook out and wait for him to appear.

I don't have to wait long. Not even five minutes later, he enters with two cups in his hand. His eyes hold mine as he makes his way toward me. I find I can't smile or do anything but stare until he finally stops in front of me, offering me one of the porcelain mugs.

"Tea?"

Finally, I muster a half smile, reaching out to take it.

He seems different this morning, agitated in some way. I wonder if he's feeling uncomfortable from last evening's encounter on the stairs. Just as I'm about to ask if he's okay, he sits down and explains.

"I didn't sleep very well last night. I suppose I should apologize in advance for any—what should we call it—asshole episodes I might have."

Shaking my head, I consider that before I take a sip of tea and then place the mug on the desk beside me. "Do you have them often?"

Finally, I get a somewhat hesitant smile from him as his eyes narrow and his mouth shifts. Truly, the man's face is not like any I have seen before. While it's rugged and masculine in its own way, he is so intensely alluring in other ways that it's hard to tear your eyes from him.

"Do I have what often?"

Cautiously, I remind him of his own words. "Asshole episodes?"

Arching a brow, he seems to think it over for a second. "I'm not sure. You'll have to tell me."

"We could just start later."

He shakes his head. "No, no. Let's start now."

As I cross one leg over the other, his eyes drop down to my legs. I have to remind myself that now is not the time. *He is not an option. He is a job—an intimidating and intriguing job.*

"Okay, so tell me. What did you show her the day she came back to the chateau?"

This is the first time I get a full-on wouldn't-you-like-to-know smirk as he settles back in his chair.

"Would you like to rephrase that question and be a little more specific?" he questions, shutting his eyes.

I take the opportunity to watch his throat and mouth as he explains further.

"There were plenty of things I showed Chantel in the chateau, Gemma. So, depending on where you want to be, you need to be much more specific." His tongue comes out to moistens his full bottom lip. "Then again, perhaps that's exactly where you want to be after your indecision last night on the stairs, hmm…between Chantel and me?"

As my heart starts a rapid tattoo rhythm in my chest, I allow my eyes to move up to his face. I find he has one eye open, watching me.

He closes it and queries again. "No?"

Clearing my throat, I think quickly and rephrase my question. "Chantel writes that she is coming to see you the next day because you want to show her something. So, what did you show her when she arrived?"

* * *

She's right on time, *he thought as he heard a sharp rap on the front door.*

Chantel Rosenberg was punctual. He liked that about her.

Actually, he was starting to obsess about everything related to the intensely serious, gray-eyed woman he'd run into only days earlier.

He made his way down the large staircase and over to the door.

Opening it, his breath was once again taken away by her. Her raven hair had been left out today, fluttering around her shoulders. With legs displayed in black shorts, she was wearing a red blouse with short sleeves that cupped around her upper arms, leaving her neck and shoulders bare. He was struck with the sudden urge to reach out and stroke his finger across her naked collarbone. Her skin was incandescent.

"Right on time," he said, dismissing his need to touch her.

"Well, you did tell me 10 a.m. Uncle Beau made sure I arrived on time."

He smiled, moving aside. When she remained where she was standing, he berated himself silently. There were so many things he did unconsciously without realizing that she was not able to see him or understand his meaning. Luckily, this also meant that when he made these mistakes, he could quietly fix them.

"Will you come inside?" he asked, waiting as she moved the cane out in front of her.

Once she was happy, knowing the path was clear, she made her way to move by him. When she was directly beside him, she stopped and turned.

He didn't know why, but he found himself holding his breath.

Those compelling eyes locked onto his face, and he wondered if she could see anything at all. He wanted desperately to ask her, but he had no idea if that was considered rude. So, he stood there, frozen.

She took in a deep breath and then let it out gently. "I like the way you smell."

He grinned at her strange, soft confession as she took another deep breath. He leaned in, so his mouth was by her ear. "I like the way you look." He blew a hot breath gently against her. "And the way you smell."

She turned her head, so they were nose to nose. She breathed out, and he could taste her on his lips and tongue.

"You're going to destroy me," he admitted with a sigh.

"You don't even know me."

"Don't I?" he responded, watching her pulse beat at the base of her throat.

She was nervous but excited, and he was ensnared.

Taking a small step back, she continued past him. He swallowed and closed his eyes as she stopped in the center of the foyer. He shut the door and carefully moved around, standing beside her.

She turned in his direction. "How old are you?"

Her hearing seemed to be extra sensitive. No matter where he was in the room, she moved in that direction, appearing to somehow sense him.

"Does it matter?" he asked, knowing that he wasn't really being fair.

He could see *her, so he knew her approximate age. She, on the other hand, had no idea what he looked like or how old he might be. He got the impression that she liked it when he treated her as he would anyone else, so that was exactly what he planned to do.*

"Well, no, I guess it doesn't." She paused, thinking about it. "Actually, yes. Yes, it does matter."

He stepped closer to her. Reaching out, he moved to touch the ends of her hair, but he thought better of it, not wanting to startle her. "May I touch you?"

He watched closely as a smile tugged at her lips.

*"You may…*if *you tell me how old you are."*

Hesitantly, he stroked the pads of his fingers across her naked collarbone. She took a swift breath.

"How old are you?" she asked again.

"I'm thirty-two. How old are you, Chantel?" he questioned, looking down to see her sightless eyes focused on his face. He knew instantly that if she could, she would be looking right at him.

"I'm twenty-six."

Running his fingers along the bare skin across her shoulder, he inquired softly, "Am I too old for you?"

She chuckled, shaking her head. "No."

"No?"

"No, you're not too old," she confirmed.

Stepping back, he dropped his hand and immediately missed touching her. "Why did it matter?"

Tilting her head to the side, she pursed her red lips as though she was about to answer him. However, at the last minute, she lowered her head.

She's shy.

Placing a finger under her chin, he told her softly, "I feel it, too."

Her mouth parted as she blinked up at him. "You do?"

Silently, he nodded and then realized she couldn't see him. "Yes. I feel you."

A smile lit up her face. It was so radiant that it looked like it had burst from her soul. He couldn't help but think that he was looking at an angel because she sure as shit didn't seem to be real.

"What did you want to show me?" she asked, smile still in place.

"Are you okay to go up some stairs?"

Nodding, she stepped forward, closer to him. "Once I know my surroundings in a room, I don't even need my cane. I use it just to get from point A to point B and, of course, to guide me through unfamiliar territory."

"Well then, we'll have to work on getting you familiar, won't we?"

She shied away, and for the moment, he let her.

"Okay, come with me." He urged her, leading her up the stairs.

* * *

He stops.

I look up at him from my notepad. "Why did you stop?"

Phillipe glances over at me as he asks a completely random question. "Is that your natural hair color? That honey blonde? It almost looks like you streaked the brown through it."

Taken off-guard, I raise one eyebrow as I straighten my back. "You want to know if I streak my hair?"

He picks up the glass of water sitting beside him and takes a sip. "Well?"

"I really don't think that has any relevance. Do you?"

Standing, he makes his way toward me. All of a sudden, I start to think that maybe I should have just answered his question. He leans down until we are eye to eye.

"Actually, it holds a lot of relevance. Why are people so offended when asked such a simple question about appearance?"

Straightening back up, he walks by me and makes his way over to the window.

"Looking at someone's appearance is a privilege we take for granted, Gemma. Describing yourself to a person who cannot see you is difficult to say the least."

He turns back to face me, stuffing his hands into his pants pockets. Leaning back against the window frame, he crosses one leg over the other.

My eyes roam from his long legs up to the white button-up shirt he's wearing. Phillipe is right. Seeing is something I take for granted, and I have to admit that it's an absolute pleasure to see him. He seems to know my thoughts because he grimaces. He pushes himself away from the wall, turning to look back out the window.

"I racked my brain for days, trying to think of a way to let her *see* me, so she could know me. I even looked it up online, and finally, I came up with an idea."

I sit silently, waiting for him to tell me. *Please tell me,* I internally plead.

He looks back at me over his shoulder. "She'll tell you what she saw," he informs in a cool tone as he makes his way past me toward the door. Just before he reaches it, he explains, "I think I'm done for the morning. Maybe we can meet again tonight? Let's say eight?"

I nod before I realize that he's not even looking at me. "Eight sounds good."

Without another word, he continues out the door.

I quickly grab the journal and flick through it. I see there are several pages before the next stopping point, so I pick it up and move over to his soft chair in the corner. Curling into it, I can still feel the body heat he left behind. I snuggle back and open the book, eager to discover what Chantel saw.

Chapter Three
VISION

Vision ~

Today, I saw *Phillipe.*

That sounds so crazy, but it's true.

When I arrived at the chateau today, I had no idea what it was he wanted to show me. In all honesty, I couldn't even imagine what Phillipe could show *me.*

So, when he finally explained—well I'll just type it here.

After leading me up a staircase with fifteen broad steps curving around a wall—which my uncle now tells me is a turret—through a part of the building on the west side of the house, Phillipe guided me by the hand, always gently, into a room off to the left.

Immediately, I was hit with smells that were foreign to me. The scent was strong, almost alcoholic in nature. It wasn't drinking alcohol. It smelled more like rubbing alcohol.

We stopped walking, and that was when I asked, "Where are we?"

I felt him brush by me, walking farther into the room.

"My art studio."

He's an artist. How did I not know this about him? Why didn't anyone tell me?

I had just assumed he ran the vineyard. From then on, I was very hungry for answers. "What do you paint?"

He chuckled, and the wicked rumble of it teased my skin.

"Pictures."

Frustrated, I stepped forward and then stopped, not knowing what was in front of me.

"It's okay," he told me. "I cleared the space. There's nothing to trip over or bump into."

My heart sped up at the thoughtfulness of his gesture. "You did that for me?"

"Yes. I wanted you to feel comfortable and at ease here."

Strangely, I did. Stepping closer toward the direction of his voice, I asked again, "What do you paint?"

This time, I heard him move. His feet shuffled across some fabric, maybe a drop cloth on the floor, before he stopped in front of me.

"I've been looking for something, something that will inspire me, Chantel. Something the world will look at and want to cry because it's so fucking beautiful your body just can't help but weep."

I stood there speechless as his voice, coupled with the words he was telling me, pulled at my soul. From somewhere deep down inside of me, I realized what he wanted. I knew as he moved closer still that I *was what he wanted to paint. I wasn't sure how that made me feel.*

Tilting my head to him, I stated softly, "The world is a big place. That's a lot of people to touch and a lot of people to please."

Absolute silence filled the space we were standing in, and he reached out, taking my hand. Tugging gently, he urged me forward, and I complied. I could hear the cloth as I now stepped onto it as well.

"Okay, how about this? For right now, I just want to please you."

I frowned for a moment and moved my eyes to where I was sure his face would be. "You have pleased me. Thank you for showing me your studio."

He laughed softly as he moved even closer, and I felt his hands grip my arms lightly.

"This isn't what I wanted to show you," he assured me, leaning down to press a soft kiss against my left cheek.

At the first touch of his mouth against my skin, I sucked in a quick deep breath and stiffened as he let me go.

He didn't move far. "Hold out your hands for me?"

Confused but curious, I raised my arms and held them out.

"Palms up," he instructed.

Flipping my hands over, I was surprised when I felt a cool glob of liquid hit the palm of my hand.

"What are you doing?" I asked nervously. "What is this?"

"So many questions, Beauty. Relax. Trust me," he teased, his voice taking on a seductive timbre.

I heard a rustle of movement and knew immediately that he moved away from me. I could hear him doing something but what, I wasn't sure. I didn't understand what he had planned until he stepped back in front of my raised hands. Taking me by the wrists, he tugged me forward. I stumbled a little, nervous and uncertain of what was going on.

He whispered, "I want you to see me."

My heart was now galloping in my chest, and my breathing was coming fast.

"How?" I questioned, but I knew how. It was how the blind always see *people, but I wasn't sure I was ready to touch him that way. I was already under his spell just by his voice alone. Touching him would make it impossible to ever surface above it.*

Pulling my right wrist up, he placed it, wet palm down, on a very naked chest. He must have removed his shirt when he stepped away earlier. His chest was a little higher than my own breastbone, and his muscles were hard and solid.

He released my wrist. "I know you use touch to learn a person's features. I thought it would be fun for you to paint me."

Swallowing deeply, I let out a fit of nervous giggles. "So, I'm just going to...paint you?"

I knew that if I could see him, he would have a smile on his face. I could hear his happiness in his voice.

"Yes. Don't worry. They're watercolors," he confirmed. "Then, maybe one day, you'll let me paint you."

* * *

Wow. Sitting in Phillipe's chair, I stop for a moment, finding I need one. *Hell, I might need several.* I'm trying to imagine how Chantel must have felt. She stood in this very studio with paint on her hands and *him* naked from the chest up in front of her as he gave her permission to touch his body.

The fact of the matter is that I don't have a clue how she felt.

Last night on the stairs, I froze like a statue, allowing him to do whatever he wanted with me, and he was fully clothed during our encounter. She had been standing before him with the knowledge that he had removed clothing. *Yes, my first conclusion is sound. I have no idea how she felt.*

Staring down at that last line—*then, maybe one day, you'll let me paint you*—I'm struck at the simplicity of that moment in time. He made a request. Obviously, somewhere along the way, she granted him permission. *And now?*

Shaking my head, I am amazed by how much one moment can change your life forever. That moment certainly changed theirs.

Looking down at the journal in my lap, I pick it up and continue reading.

* * *

I could feel his heart beating under my palm—thump, thump, thump.

It was steady and calming, but by that stage, I was feeling anything but calm. I spread my fingers wide. The heel of my palm brushed against a pointy nub, his nipple. I moved my hand slowly, so my palm was covering his strong pec. His nipple was now pushing against the center of my hand.

"Touch me all over," he offered suggestively.

No, *my mind was screaming. I had no idea what I was doing. Instead of telling him that, I responded shyly, "Yes. Okay."*

I actually felt the rumble against my palm this time as a low laugh bubbled out of his chest and throat.

"Don't stop now, Beauty. Learn about who sees you. See me," he encouraged.

The paint was dripping beneath my palm. It was probably sliding over his stomach, so I slowly started to move my hand down the side of his body. I kept my left hand palm up, so the paint stayed in my hand. I concentrated on smoothing my other fingers down his ridged ribs. Tracing every single groove, I licked my lips before flattening out my wet palm, caressing his corrugated abdominal muscles.

He shifted, and I felt his body shudder as he sucked in a deep breath.

Stopping my exploration, I tilted my head up to where his eyes would be. "Should I stop?"

I waited for an answer to come. Instead of a verbal response, he reached out and gripped my left hand, pulling it forward with a bit more force than necessary, to place it on the neglected half of his body.

"Definitely don't stop, Chantel," he ordered.

I felt him raise his hands up behind his head.

Taking my own calming breath, I took my bottom lip between my teeth and concentrated as I mirrored the same path my first hand had followed.

With my right hand still on his lower abdomen and my left hand reaching his navel, I found myself becoming more aggressive. I stepped forward and let my fingers trace each abdominal muscle individually before dipping my wet finger into his navel. A loud groan slid free from his mouth. It thrilled me somewhere deep—somewhere I was not familiar with.

His body was amazing, a true work of art in every sense of the word. In my mind, I could see the dips and shadows, the valleys and sharp ridges, and the more I touched him, the bolder I became.

I took the final step toward him, closing the distance between us. I left enough space, so I could still move my hands as I guided both index fingers down to his naked hip bones. His hands came to rest on mine and that was when my breath caught. He hauled me forward and slammed his mouth onto my own.

Our first kiss was a brutal onslaught. I moaned as he slid his tongue in to rub up against mine. I dragged my paint-covered hands up his arms and slid them over his muscular neck. As he pulled his mouth away, he swallowed, and I could feel his Adam's apple move. That's when I began touching his face voraciously, like a starving woman.

His hands were in my hair, and I could feel them gripping tightly as I stroked my fingers over his strong masculine chin and jaw. My finger dipped into a cleft at the center of his chin. Tracing over light stubble, I dragged my nails lightly over his cheeks, moving up to his high cheekbones. I smoothed four fingers of each hand across the sides of his broad face. Breathing deeply, my index fingers traced his beautiful strong nose.

My sensual exploration ended with my fingers gliding up between his brows, smoothing them across his forehead. His face had to be covered in paint by now, but he didn't seem to care.

Feeling his breath whisper across my parted lips, I closed my eyes, letting my head fall back into the cradle of his hands.

Softly, I asked him, "What color eyes do you have?"

"Green," he replied quickly. "Have you seen green before?"

"No," I told him.

"Then, why ask?" he questioned curiously.

"Seemed like the right thing to do." Before he could ask me anything else, I queried, "What color hair?"

"Brown." He chuckled.

I felt him lower his head down until I could taste the breath he was breathing out. He was addictive. This feeling of intoxication was addictive.

"Do you see me?" he asked.

I rested my hands on his cheeks and opened my eyes.

It was an odd question to ask of a blind woman, but as I stared directly into what I now knew were his green eyes, I replied, "Yes, I see you perfectly."

* * *

Day Four

Phillipe wasn't able to go back to see Gemma last night, and now, it's morning.

He knows what part she has been reading, and no matter what he agreed to, he cannot subject himself to the fucking heartache that would come from remembering that first meeting with Chantel.

Christ, he thinks as he stares at the ceiling. Just thinking about Chantel and the day she painted him has his cock hard enough to drill holes.

Sighing, he rolls over to stare out the window opposite his bed. His room is situated on the first floor of the chateau, and he always sleeps with the shutters open at this time of the year. This morning, the sun is shining down over his vineyard, spilling into his room.

Reaching under the covers, he smoothes his palm against his erection. Groaning softly, he rolls to his back and closes his eyes. Bringing his hand up, he spits into his palm and curses himself as he shoves it back down between his thighs. Gripping his cock in his fist, he squeezes it tightly and tries to dampen the desire that's bubbling up inside him.

Damn her. Chantel still *had a way of crawling inside of him.*

He isn't sure if it's the topics they are discussing or the lingering shadow he constantly sees out of the corner of his eye, but whenever Gemma gets too close to a shared intimacy of his and Chantel's, Phillipe finds himself getting antsy, and his cock starts to twitch, just as it is doing now.

Flinging back the covers, he looks down his body that is now mottled with the light of the sun. He watches his own fist as he pulls on his now straining hard flesh. Closing his eyes, his free hand reaches back over his head and clutches the bottom of his headboard.

He feels his whole body grow taut. His muscles strain as he strokes his hard on with his fist once again, moving up and down the angry flesh that is now throbbing with insistence between his thighs.

Squeezing his eyes tight, he pictures Chantel standing in his studio.

* * *

The sun streamed through the open window as she slowly unbuttoned the bright yellow dress she'd worn to see him the first time he painted her.

Her hair was down, spilling over her shoulders. She captured her bottom lip between her teeth and worried it as she concentrated.

"Just act as if you are alone," he told her.

Her eyes rose to his. "Like close-my-eyes-and-pretend-you-aren't-here kind of thing?" she asked with a twitch to her lips.

* * *

Phillipe starts to stroke harder, recalling that first moment of revelation. She watched him with every button she undid. There were twelve—twelve black round buttons. Every time she undid one, Phillipe's heart hammered faster, just as it is doing now.

Raising his right leg, he places his foot on the mattress, lifting his hips into each stroke. Groaning softly, his lips part as he holds on to the headboard again, tighter this time.

Why can't I find release from this world we created?

It doesn't matter how many months have passed. The minute he thinks about her, everything tumbles back—the desire, the pain, the soul-destroying love. It all ends the exact same way. *She is gone, and I am alone.*

Alone and desperate, he thinks angrily, now really squeezing and fisting the stupid cock that got him into this fucked-up situation in the first place. Now, it wants to take him there again. *Perhaps with the journalist? Fuck that!*

Shutting his eyes tightly, he feels his knuckles start to ache while his fingers try to bore a hole into the wood of the bed. His right wrist is pumping so hard that he's surprised he hasn't hurt himself. Yet there he is—still hard, still pissed off, and nowhere near close to being satisfied. *Fuck!*

Agreeing to this whole ridiculous biography about his paintings and what took place that night was his own choice. *Get to them before they get to you.* No matter what happened, he knows that some prick would come up with a story about that night, and it would be full of shit.

So, in the end, he caved. He is the one who sought out a journalist. He is the one who wanted it to be a woman. He is the stupid fucking idiot who picked Gemma Harris because she in no way resembles Chantel Rosenberg.

Finally knowing he is getting nowhere close to a satisfying sexual release, he lets go of his cock with disgust. He whacks his palm against the headboard hard, and he sits up, letting his legs fall over the side of the bed.

Shaking his head in annoyance, he gets up and makes his way over to the window. Standing there with a raging hard erection, he's naked, angry, and annoyed. He takes a deep breath and tries to push it all aside.

He is close to calming down when he hears some gravel crunch to his left. He turns his head in the direction where the noise came from. It takes him a moment, but then he sees her.

Gemma is standing just outside his window under one of the trees behind the chateau. Her eyes are focused on him, looking like a gazelle that has just been spotted by a hungry lion.

His anger and frustration quickly melt away. Instead, curiosity and intrigue surface as Phillipe tips his head to her, leaning forward into a mock bow.

Hope you enjoyed the show, Mademoiselle.

He watches unflinchingly as her flight instinct kicks in, forcing the gazelle to run away.

Chapter Four
CRAVINGS

To say that I ran back to my room is stating it mildly.

Entering my bedroom, I turn around, leaning my back against the door. Lowering my right hand down between my thighs, I cup my aching sex. My body is vibrating with tension, both sexual and nervous.

I'm trying to wrap my mind around what I just witnessed and—well, honestly, I can't. I know exactly what Phillipe was doing to himself as he lay there in all his magnificent naked glory, but the harsh and almost brutal way he was touching himself is what has my mind in shock.

What would make a man treat his body that way? What would cause him to almost inflict injury upon himself while still striving to reach some kind of satisfaction?

And why, oh why, did I find it so erotic to watch?

The minute my eyes peered through that open window, spotting him, my attention was riveted. When the covers were pushed aside, I was bound. My feet refused to go where my brain was telling them to—away. Away from the window. Away from what I was witnessing. Away from his seductive presence. Instead, I stayed and watched. I watched a show so sinfully depraved that I felt myself getting more aroused with each rough and wicked stroke of his hand.

Just thinking about it now has my palms tingling, and I can feel moisture dampening my panties. Making my way across the room, I enter the bathroom with one thing in mind, easing my own sexual need. Moving into the small white ceramic space, I firmly shut the door, locking it for good measure. *Wouldn't want someone watching me, right, Gemma?* What a hypocrite I am.

Looking around the room, I walk over to the built-in shower and tub. Taking a deep breath, I quickly unsnap my black slacks and push them down along with my soaked panties.

Shaking my head, I try and remind myself that this is a healthy response. It's natural to feel intense desire for someone so unbelievably attractive, who just displayed such unbridled self-pleasure. Right after that thought, I also admit that it isn't exactly natural to stand, uninvited, and watch a man abuse himself, all the while finding it intensely erotic.

No matter which way I look at it, what I witnessed has now resulted in me standing in this small room with my arm against the wall and my left leg raised on the edge of the tub.

Biting my bottom lip to keep silent, I reach down between my thighs and stroke the soft flesh that is now alarmingly wet. Closing my eyes, I picture him as I just saw him, lying on his back with all his strong muscles straining. His neck was arched back, into the pillow, with one leg bent and raised as he reached down between them to grip his cock.

Moaning at the image, I press the pads of my fingers against my now swollen clit. The sensations that rock up through me are unreal. I'm so undeniably turned on. I make each stroke of my fingers a little firmer, pushing a little harder, as I swirl them through my wet juices.

Slowly, my mind starts to merge images and memories as my thoughts drift to the painting by the stairs, focusing on the woman's nude behind. I remember the suggestive way he stood behind me, touching my shoulders, as he insisted it was natural to want to touch her.

Was it? Or was it the power of his voice and the sexual haze he created, making me question the desire I was feeling?

Sliding my fingers back and forth through my plump folds, I brace myself against the wall with my left hand and push against the tiles hard. I try to keep from moaning out loud while I continue to rock my hips.

How is he infiltrating my mind this way? How is it that after seeing him down in his room with his naked body, pulsating and strong, that I am now standing in a bathroom with my fingers seeking entrance into my greedy body?

I have never in all my life reacted with such intensity before. I've been stimulated and made love to, but never have I craved the darkness that I witnessed in him. Never have I felt such raw lust from watching someone purposefully hurt himself.

Oh, but watching him in the throes of his own painful pleasure was so erotic and so darkly seductive that I am wishing he was here now, doing it in front of me all over again.

Finally, I push my finger deep into my own tight warmth while I picture the way he looked at me the moment he caught me. Remembering that mocking bow, the insolent arched brow, and a tiny hint of a caught-you smirk, I feel my pussy clench. It spasms around my finger, and suddenly, his voice is in my head. *The again, perhaps that's exactly where you want to be after your indecision last night on the stairs, hmm…between Chantel and me?"* That final memory—that's enough. His deep voice and sexual suggestion penetrate me, and a climax so powerful that it almost takes my breath away washes over me and drags me under.

* * *

Later that night, Phillipe makes his way up to the studio. He sent a message to Gemma to meet him at 7 p.m. He isn't sure where she has been all day, but he knows one thing. He hasn't seen or heard from her since she fled this morning.

As he makes his way into the west turret, he is surprised to see her sitting there, waiting for him. She has her hair tied back in a loose ponytail. She's wearing her usual black slacks and a blue blouse with a black cardigan. She looks every inch the journalist or perhaps a librarian.

He makes his way farther into the room, which is illuminated by the soft lamp behind his chair. He also notes that she has turned on the lamp by her desk. She's trying to send him a message. She's here to work, and what she witnessed this morning is not going to deter her.

Okay, I can play that game—for a little while.

"Evening, Gemma," he acknowledges, finally sitting down in his chair.

He observes her as she studies him from head to toe. As usual, he is dressed in dark colors. Tonight, he's wearing black wool slacks and a hunter green lightweight sweater. When she has finished her inspection, he can't help the next question he asks.

"Is everything appropriately covered, Miss Harris?"

He takes great delight in the blush that creeps over her cheeks.

She lifts her pen and astutely avoids the question *and* his eyes. "I want to ask you about Chantel," she tells him boldly.

Licking his lips, he nods at her once. "Well, I assumed that. After all, isn't she the reason you and the rest of the world want to talk to me?" He stops to cross one leg over the other at the ankles. "Without her, I wasn't anybody." Looking to the open window, he mumbles, "Funny how true that still is."

Turning his head back to face Gemma, he tilts it to the side and raises a hand in a small wave, signaling her to go ahead with her question.

"Okay then…" She crosses her legs, almost like she's trying to quell an ache.

That makes Phillipe wonder, *What exactly has Gemma been doing all day?*

"A lot of recent articles have called your relationship with Ms. Rosenberg an unhealthy one. They report that it was an unusual arrangement with you being center stage in the public eye while she was rather secluded and kept away from the public. They allude to you being too protective. Some even use the word *obsessive*." She ceases in her spiel, her eyes finally glancing up to lock with his.

Phillipe knows she is uncomfortable. *I'll be damned if I'm going to ease her.* If she wants to go down this rabbit hole with him, then she better be prepared for what she will find.

He sits there silently as he waits for the final question.

"Would you say they were right? Were you obsessed with Chantel Rosenberg?"

Phillipe lets the question linger in the air while her foot begins to tap nervously. She starts to flick her pen against the notepad. Finally, he uncrosses his legs and stands, making his way over to the window.

"Do you know why I love this window so much?" he asks as he looks over his shoulder.

"No," she immediately replies.

"This is where I first saw her," he explains, turning back to face the woman who is watching him with intense, smart eyes—the same eyes that saw too much this morning. "This was the window that I looked out of when my life changed."

Crossing his arms over his chest, he closes his eyes and tells her what she wants to know.

"Obsession, as defined by the dictionary, means *the domination of one's thoughts or feelings by a persistent idea, image, or desire.*" Phillipe opens his eyes and focuses intently on Gemma, who now has a crease between her brows as she frowns at him in concentration. "What do you think? Do you think Chantel dominated my thoughts and feelings?"

She swallows once, and boldly, she tells him, "Yes." As she chews her bottom lip more in thought than from nerves, she blinks slowly. "You painted several images of her. You dedicated a whole *collection* to her. If that isn't obsession or persistent desire, I don't know what is."

Pushing away from the window, Phillipe walks over and stops by her desk. He reaches out and fingers the journal that is sitting there.

Gemma turns, glancing down at his hand, before she looks back up to face him.

"A lot of people talk about *my* obsession—my unhealthy need for Chantel. Everyone focuses on the images, the haunting beauty, and the eroticism behind my obsession."

Picking up the journal, he holds it out to her. She flinches back at the unexpected move, and then she reaches out slowly to take it from him. As her fingers grip the leather, he leans down until they are eye to eye.

With firm resolution, he explains, "No one knows that the obsession went both ways. What would they do if they read pages of journal entries where each entry was dedicated in precise detail to a moment in time—*our* moments in time?"

Standing up straight, he releases the book and makes his way to the studio door. "If there was obsession here—a dominant persistent desire—then it was the desire to lose ourselves in one another. The only problem is that one person is now lost, and the other is trapped."

Taking one last look at the now silent Gemma, he turns and walks out. As he leaves, he softly mutters, "Good night."

* * *

I sit in the silence he left behind, shaking slightly, as I hold the journal he just relinquished. He is right, of course. No one knows that Chantel Rosenberg wrote a journal. No one knows that she was just as hungry to know Phillipe as he obviously was to know her.

What must it be like to be craved that way? To return that feeling with such ferocity?

Letting out a sigh, I put the notepad on the desk. I wonder if a time would come when he wouldn't leave after spending thirty minutes in a room with me, but I know it isn't me he is running from. It is *her*.

I look at the empty page that is mocking me. I haven't written down a single thing from this evening's session. In all honesty, I turned on my small recorder because I wasn't sure if I'd be able to function as I sat here and stared at him. After this morning, I can't help from seeing him that way—naked and hard. So, I came prepared, knowing I would be frozen.

Good thing too because this evening's episode was intense. Turning off the lamp, I make my way over to his side table, and I can't help myself from reaching out to stroke the chair he was sitting in. He seemed so lost, yet at times, he was also so present and angry.

Is he what people say he is? Did his obsession ruin a perfect relationship?

I have no clue, but I want to find out. Although he is intense and sometimes frightening in his fierce and passionate nature, I don't fear for my safety.

No, if anything, I muse as I make my way to my room and into bed, *I fear for his.*

* * *

Cravings ~

I want Phillipe. There—I typed it.

Why can't I stop thinking about him? And why don't I want to?

Every minute I'm away from him, I find myself counting down the hours until we're together. I need to be near him again, so I can find a way to somehow touch him. I need to touch his soft but strong skin that is so warm under my fingers. I find myself wanting to stroke those muscles and trace them with my tongue.

I don't want it to be just fantasies anymore.

I want the flesh.

I'm starting to crave it.

He told me yesterday that he wants to paint me in some kind of series. He also told me it would be something so beautiful that the world would weep. He told me it would be perfect—perfect like I am. Ha! *I laughed at that. I'm not perfect, not in any way.*

When I pointed out that I am greatly flawed, he insisted that I was crazy and that was only one of the things that made me beautiful.

So, I agreed with the condition that he called his series Beautifully Flawed *and not some cheesy, sad* Beauty Is Skin Deep *garbage. Again, he just laughed, and I knew whatever he ended up naming it, would fit perfectly.*

I told him that I want to show him something tomorrow. He acted like a petulant child all day, trying to get me to spill my secret, but I told him that he must wait.

Tomorrow, I'm going to introduce him to my best friend, Diva.

He seemed worried. He shouldn't be.

In fact, I think he's going to love her.

* * *

Closing the journal, I lean over and place it gently on the bedside table. Switching off the lamp, I lie there in silence and try to picture the playful and pouty man Chantel describes. While Phillipe is not rude or mean, he certainly doesn't laugh or joke in the way she portrays him.

I guess that's something that belongs to just you, Miss Rosenberg. That is yours alone, along with his flawed heart.

I find myself also wondering about Chantel.

With every journal entry, she is becoming increasingly intoxicated by Phillipe. The more time she spends with him, the more she seems to be falling under his spell. Just like me, she can't seem to explain why.

I close my eyes, and once again, I picture Phillipe naked and hard, violently trying to pleasure himself. Reaching under the covers, I cup my sex and roll over, squeezing my thighs tight.

No. I will not fall prey to a second session of confusing fantasies that involve Phillipe Tibideau and the woman who is his dark obsession.

Chapter Five
REVELATIONS

Day Five

I have been instructed to meet Phillipe down at the arbor this morning.

This is a part of the chateau that I have yet to visit. As I walk down the pebbled path, I find myself instantly enchanted by the birds I hear singing. *This place really is a slice of paradise.* It seems so untouched, yet at the same time, it has footprints—footprints of the past—all over it.

As I reach the end of the path, I find a bench nestled up against one of the large trees. Its branches are leaning over to cover the sitting area. I make my way over to the stone bench and notice there's a passage engraved on it. When I'm finally close enough to read it, I notice it's in English.

Love looks not with the eyes
but with the mind,

and, therefore, is winged cupid painted blind.

My heart clenches as the meaning and impact of the words hit me. Chateau Tibideau is full of Chantel. It's bursting at the seams with the imprints and images of a woman who is no longer here.

I look up into the branches and spot several little yellowhammer birds hopping around from branch to branch. I catch myself smiling as they twitter and jump back and forth. The sun is shining down and filtering through the leaves, warming me as I take a seat on the bench. I don't know what to expect today, but I do know one thing for certain. I need to make Phillipe understand that for me to write this story—*his* story—he needs to trust me, and that means not leaving every time things get difficult, or in his case, personal.

The crunch of the gravel alerts me to look down the path where I see him striding toward me. He has his usual wool slacks on today. This time, they're navy in color, and he's matched it with a cream knit pullover. The combination is quite easily the most attractive outfit I've seen on a man, yet it's so simple. So, perhaps it's not the outfit but the man himself.

As he gets closer, he slides his large hands into his pants pockets. I have noticed that this is a habit of his, revealing when he seems uncomfortable or doesn't want to be somewhere. In this instance, he doesn't seem to want to be here with me.

When he stops in front of me, I stand, but he shakes his head gently, indicating that I should stay seated. I settle back down on the bench as he moves to the opposite side of the shaded area.

The air has a nice cool bite to it this morning, but the sun is warm enough, so the wind doesn't chill to the bone. This time of the year seems to be perfect here.

"You found your way down here alright?" he asks with an arched brow.

I cross my leg, one over the other. "Yes, thank you. I just asked Penelope."

Looking right at me, he asks without preamble, "Are you ready to start?"

I narrow my eyes at him. "Are you in a hurry?"

His whole body stiffens as he straightens. "No. No hurry, Gemma. I'd just rather get this over with."

I think about that for a moment as I stand. Placing the notepad on the bench, I clasp my hands in front of myself. "Well, doesn't that defeat the whole point of this?" I ask, starting to get a little bit annoyed by his attitude.

I understand his reluctance to talk to reporters. I'm aware of the delicate nature of the issues we are covering, but this man asked me—*me*—to come here and report the story. It's a little bit hard to do that if he doesn't want to tell me any of it.

"Doesn't what defeat the purpose, Miss Harris?"

There he goes again, referring back to my surname, trying to get a rise out of me. Taking one step forward, I gather my courage. "Isn't the purpose of me staying here and living under *your* roof for me to interview you? To ask what happened in your life? To learn what happened in hers?"

At the mere mention of *her,* his shoulders become even more impossibly stiff.

"I can't tell your story with any kind of accuracy if you do not trust me," I tell him, raising my chin.

When he moves, his eyes narrow on me. Like an experienced predator, he slowly prowls across the pebbled space. With each step, the stones crunch beneath his booted feet, and I have to admit that I find it difficult not to retreat.

I'm not one who is usually shy or withdrawn. I'm by no means prudish by nature or inexperienced. Yet I feel a shiver of apprehension slide up my spine while I stand in front of this man, watching his sensual green eyes look me over from my black flats and slacks to my blue cowl-neck sweater that dips down between my breasts.

Stopping before me, he reaches out a hand toward my face. I swallow and hold my breath as his large fingers brush against my cheek. He hasn't done more than trace his fingers along my skin, but I can feel my breathing deepen as my nipples harden.

I want him.

I want him with such an unexpected ferocity that I barely stop myself from begging him to rip off my clothes and fuck me right where we stand.

What the hell is the matter with me?

I clench my jaw, tilting my face up to look him in the eye.

"You want me to trust you, you say?" he asks.

That deep melodic voice slides inside of me and travels down to the aroused flesh between my thighs.

I swallow again. "Yes." Then, with a little more force, I tell him, "Yes, I want you to trust me. That's the only way this will work."

His eyes scrutinize my face in a way that makes me think he's memorizing every little thing about me. Suddenly, I'm worried that he might find me lacking. I'm frightened that he is comparing me to her, and I might inevitably come up short.

* * *

Phillipe traces his fingers down Gemma's cheek, along her jawline, and finally, he slides the back of his fingers down her throat. When he reaches the neck of her sweater, he slips a finger inside and touches along the curve where it dips down low, leaving the material to hang loosely between her breasts. Suddenly, he wants to see those breasts naked.

Gemma ceases talking. She is standing so still that he can barely tell she's breathing as she lets her eyes drop to his mouth. He can tell she's curious but oh so cautious. Her eyes can't lie though. Her eyes are telling him that she wants to fuck, and she wants to fuck hard.

Well, I can accommodate her, Phillipe thinks as he slides his hand around behind her neck, pulling her forward.

She stumbles and places her hands up on his chest. He can feel her nails as she flexes her fingers for better purchase.

"You want my trust?" he demands.

This time, he slides his free hand down between their bodies to cup her sex. He watches her mouth part on a needy moan, and instead of answering, she nods.

"I don't trust journalists," he tells her, grinding his palm against her hot covered pussy.

"Then, how—"

"Shh, Gemma."

She immediately complies.

"Let's compromise," he murmurs.

Her eyes focus on his mouth before they slide shut. She squeezes her thighs around his hand. "Compromise?"

"An exchange of trust," he explains. He rubs the heel of his palm against the fabric directly covering her clit. "I don't think that's too much to ask. Do you?"

Her green eyes blink once, and when they open, he notices her pupils have dilated.

Gemma is aroused. As Phillipe stands there, cupping the back of her neck with one hand while his other is wedged snuggly between her strong thighs, she moves against him like a cat in heat. He watches the pulse flutter at the base of her throat before his eyes move to her moist pink lips. All he can think of is how fucking perfect they would look wrapped around his cock.

Perfect, plump, fuckable lips.

Lowering his mouth to hers, he suggests against those very lips, "I think for you to understand this story, you must first become a part of it."

He feels her breathe out, and he can't help but bite her quivering bottom lip. She looks close to climax, like she wants to scream for him. As he releases her mouth, she trembles, panting softly.

She tells him, "I don't understand what you mean."

"I want to paint you, Gemma," he informs.

He thrills at the hesitation he witnesses as her brain starts to catch up. She swallows, trying to pull away, but he keeps her where she is with a firm grip.

"No, don't run," he cajoles. "Aren't you curious? Don't you want to know how it feels to be vulnerable yet so powerful at the same time?"

Her breasts start to rise and fall quickly against his chest.

Moving his head so his cheek is resting against hers, he surmises, "Yes, I can tell you are. Don't you want to know that intoxicating feeling of having a man..." He pauses as he strokes his hand harder and faster against where he can feel her juices moistening her pants. "Having *me* under your spell?"

Lifting his head, his eyes connect with hers. "The only way you can understand who Chantel was to me and how she really felt is to become her. You ask me to trust you, and in return, I'm asking you to trust me. Trust me to paint you, Gemma, in the poses of *The Blind Vision Collection*. Then, you will have your story." He lowers his head and takes her mouth with his own.

Sliding his tongue deep between her lips, he rubs it up against hers, their tongues dancing in an erotic mating. He strokes and presses his hand firmly up between her legs. She tightens those thighs like a vise around his hand and wrist and pushes her hips against him, driving herself toward her sexual release.

Pulling back slightly, he slides his hand from her neck to her hair, clutching it hard enough that her eyes pop open. "Tell me yes, Gemma," he demands of her.

Her mouth parts as he strokes harder. She thrusts her hips twice more as he holds her captive. He has her exactly where he wants her.

Not even granting her reprieve to look away, he commands again, "Tell me yes."

Finally, those sexy lips part, and without him even touching her bare flesh, she screams her agreement into the morning air.

* * *

Revelations ~

Today was my turn to show Phillipe something. I knew if anyone would appreciate it, then it would be him.

I arrived at the chateau around noon. The sun wasn't there to warm me today. It seemed the clouds had decided to chase it away, but not even that could take away the joy I was feeling.

When I arrived, he took me straight up to his studio. This was a place I was now very comfortable in, which was what he had told me he'd wanted all along.

I explained to him that I had something to show him, knowing that he must have seen the music case I was holding in my right hand.

"You want to show me an instrument?" he asked, sounding a little confused.

I wasn't offended at all by his confusion. If I were him, I'd doubt me, too.

"Sit over in your chair," I told him.

I had been in his studio several times now. I was well aware of where everything was, so I smiled when I heard him mutter "bossy" under his breath as he moved away.

I opened my music case and pulled out Diva. I made my way over to where I knew he was sitting, and I handed it to him. He reached out and took my Stradivarius violin from me.

"Careful," I whispered. "You're now holding Diva, my best friend."

He remained silent for several minutes.

"Wow, Beauty, I know this is expensive. Do you play?"

I knew he thought he was being rude. He was always so careful about the things he asked or said to me.

"Yes, I've played ever since I was five years old when my mother handed her down to me."

He let out a breath, and I could tell he wanted to ask more.

Instead, he muttered, "Unbelievable."

I was so pleased that he was impressed—well, impressed with the thought of my talent. Now, I just had to show him.

"I want you to play for me," he told me, placing the violin in my hands.

Gripping the neck of Diva, I gently pulled her up and rested her against my left shoulder, turning my chin so it nestled perfectly in the chin rest at the base of the lower bout. "What would you like me to play?" I questioned, closing my eyes.

"Something you want me to hear," he answered in that voice—that voice that had the ability to calm and excite me all at once.

"That's not very specific."

That was when I felt him stand and move around behind me.

He quietly requested, "Okay, how about something that will haunt me?"

Taking a deep breath, I affirmed, "That, I can do."

Closing my eyes, I started to play Méditation *from* Thaïs. *I listened to my body while I played with everything I was feeling. Whenever I played for an audience, I usually found myself forgetting that they were there. However, as the sad melody floated through the air, I was very aware of my one-person audience. I could feel him as he shifted around me, silently watching my performance.*

As I reached the end of the piece, I heard him move in closer to me. He gently placed his hands on my shoulders.

"That was the most heart-wrenching thing I have ever heard," he whispered.

He laid a hot kiss against my neck. I sighed as I tilted my head to the side, granting him the access he was seeking.

"What are you doing to me, Chantel?" he implored.

Sliding his hands down my arms, he took the violin and bow from my fingers. I relinquished my grip on them, listening carefully as he moved away. He placed them softly in their case, and then he moved back to me. His hands gripped my arms, pulling me toward him, so my back was against his front.

His lips were against my ear. "You intoxicate me, you know that?"

I didn't think he actually wanted an answer, so I let my head fall back against his shoulder as he wrapped one arm across my breasts.

"Let me touch you in the way you just touched me," he begged, turning me to face him.

I felt him take a step back, moving his heat away from me.

"May I?"

Immediately, my eyes were drawn down. From the direction of his voice, the man was kneeling at my feet. His hand reached out and cupped my bare ankle. I was wearing a sundress because it was still warm right now, even with the clouds my uncle had told me were scattered across the sky today.

I swallowed and answered, "Yes."

"Hmm, yes what?" he questioned, running his hand up behind my calf.

"Yes, you can touch me."

He groaned as he moved, and both of his warm palms were on the back of my calves. He leaned in, pushing his mouth against my dress into the apex of my thighs.

I swallowed a sigh when his hot breath seeped through the fabric and his hands slid up under my dress to my ass. Reaching down, I gripped his hair and tugged on it gently.

I could tell he was looking up at me when he asked, "What do you want, Chantel? I'll do anything."

I didn't know what to tell him. So I said all I could manage at that moment. Simply, I answered, "You."

Those big hands slid over my lace panties and his long fingers gripped the edges as he dragged them down. I braced myself as his hands tugged them to my feet. He paused, waiting for me to patiently step out of them. He removed his hands for a moment, and suddenly, I felt alone and naked, even though I was still wearing my dress.

"Lift your dress for me," he told me.

I thought not being able to see him would make this easier, but in fact, I really believe it made it more difficult. I couldn't gauge his reaction to anything I did. I just had to trust him to be honest and tell me what he was thinking.

I bent down slowly to grip the edge of my dress and pulled it up to my waist and waited. I didn't have to wait long because he was there immediately as his hands cupped my ass cheeks. His open mouth pressed a hot wet kiss just above my pelvic bone as I sucked in a deep breath.

He told me, "You are so fucking beautiful you hurt my eyes."

He smoothed one of his palms over my ass, moving down my left thigh. He bit the skin gently above the small patch of hair covering my sensitive mound.

When his palm reached the back of my knee, he gently tugged it, so I let him raise my leg, placing it over his shoulder. Gripping his head, I made sure I was steady on my other foot and I moaned as he dragged his tongue in a hot wet caress across my lower stomach.

"Oh god," I sighed, pushing myself against his mouth.

He nuzzled his nose against my throbbing pussy. He inhaled deeply before he let out a loud groan, raising a hand to push a long, thick finger up between my juicy wet lips.

"I want to worship you," he confided as he pushed that finger deeper into my needy body.

"Phillipe," I moaned as I bore down on his hand.

His wet lips traced a sensuous path across my quivering flesh. Holding on tight, I just about flew out of the room when his tongue finally reached my swollen clit. He manipulated it, flicking his tongue back and forth over my wet nub. I couldn't help the way my hips started to thrust against him, almost as though I was fucking his mouth.

That was when I started to beg. "Please," I implored.

I felt him shift and move lower, farther beneath me, so his wicked hot tongue could slide through my sopping folds. His hands held me in place as he flattened his tongue against my aching pussy. He licked at it like it was his favorite dessert before he moved his mouth back to my clit and sucked it between his lips. That was all I needed. I screamed and pulled his hair, climaxing all over his tongue.

Against my abused flesh, he admitted, "I'm yours."

Chapter Six

SOLITARY

Mid-afternoon finally arrives as I sit in my bedroom with Chantel's journal on my lap. Still, I am trying to understand exactly all that happened out in the arbor this morning.

Was I seduced? Is that what happened? Was I seduced into agreeing to pose for Phillipe? Oh, and it's not just for any paintings. I'm posing for Chantel's collection.

There are millions of women who would clamor for the opportunity to sit for Phillipe Tibideau. That's what happens when you are one of the most attractive, and yes, one of the most enigmatic artists.

He is such a difficult man to get a handle on. One minute, he appears sad and reflective, almost alone in the world he now chooses to inhabit, and then in the blink of an eye, his demeanor changes, and he becomes a frustrated rigid shell of a man. *Both sides are now becoming familiar,* I thought, tracing my hands over the leather cover. I can understand his sadness and anguish in the face of all he has gone through.

But what about the seductive side of Phillipe? He seems to slip into that side, using it to get his way. That is a potent force. It's as natural to him as breathing. When he turns that force on me, there is not a hope in the world that I will be able to resist.

When he kissed me this morning, every single thought I had got lost somewhere between my beating heart and my wet, throbbing sex that had started an insistent pulse between my legs. His strong arms felt sublime when he wrapped one around me while he used the other to stroke me to a splintering hot orgasm, without even undoing my pants. *The man is sex—pure, unadulterated sex.*

However, unlike the flawless and almost reverent way he touched and worshiped Chantel, with me, he seems so capricious. I never know how he'll react, which only makes the idea of posing for him in such an intimate way all the more daunting.

* * *

Phillipe moves quietly around the studio, setting up the area he wants to use for the afternoon's session. Down in the arbor this morning, he let his emotions get the better of him, and once again, he now found himself rethinking his actions.

Touching Gemma in the seclusion of the garden felt right. She was warm, she was present, and he wanted her with a hunger he never thought he would feel again.

What is it about her? Maybe the way she looks at me? Her mixture of wonder and fascination is tinged with a hint of fear. She appeared as though she wanted to touch him, but she thought she might get burned.

Perhaps she is right. *Maybe I will end up ruining her, too.*

Sighing, he makes his way over to the shelves where he keeps his paint and brushes. Pulling them down, he heads back toward the easel, and that's when he spots Gemma by the door. Her eyes are watching him closely as he walks across the well-lit area.

"It's okay. You can come in," he acknowledges, feeling like the wolf inviting Red Riding Hood into his den. *Once upon a time…ha—* yeah, well, once upon a time, he would have never viewed himself that way at all. It's funny how things have changed.

"I know," she replies bravely, stepping inside.

She's clutching the worn leather journal. It's ironic how it now seems like a safety blanket for her, yet to him, it represents a tragic nightmare.

"I was just making sure you were finished setting up. I didn't want to distract you."

Phillipe moves behind the easel, placing the items on the small table he situated beside it. He tilts his head, looking over her slowly. "Ahh, but you're such a lovely distraction, Gemma. Why would I mind?"

She doesn't seem to have an answer for him, so she remains silent as she moves farther into the room to where the drop cloth is now spread out on the floor. When she reaches it, she turns back to face him.

"Which painting do you want to do first?"

Now, there is the million-dollar question, he thinks. Phillipe walks over to the lovely Gemma. She is holding herself rigid. She no longer resembles the woman he held this morning when she came with such intense passion.

"Well, first..." He pauses, reaching out to take the journal.

She lets it go reluctantly before she clasps her hands again in front of herself.

"First, you have to relax, Gemma."

"Was *she* relaxed your first time?"

Phillipe stops on his way to the desk where he is going to put the journal down. He looks over his shoulder at the bold journalist. He can tell she is bracing for his answer, so he lets his eyes travel down over her newly donned black pants before bringing them back up to her sweater.

"I made sure she was relaxed her first time, yes."

She takes a deep breath of air, making it immediately obvious that she understands his double entendre. Placing the journal down, he moves behind the easel to see if she is in the space he is going to need her in. She waits so patiently for him. She's so silent that he almost hates to break the peace that comes with it.

"I thought we'd start with *Solitary,*" he informs, waiting for a reaction.

He knows that she studied each piece before arriving here, so she knows exactly which one he is referring to. As predicted, she shifts, appearing uncomfortable with his choice.

"Why that one? Because it was the first?"

Crossing his arms over his chest, he shrugs. "Sure, why not?"

She tilts her head to the side and plainly states, "I think you're trying to scare me off."

Phillipe lets out a self-deprecating chuckle. "If I wanted to scare you, I would have started with *Armor* or perhaps *Rhapsody.*"

Her shoulders stiffen, and he's aware he has hit on one of her biggest fears.

After all, to most people, *those* particular poses would be the most intimate and the most revealing.

"Fine. *Solitary*, it is," Gemma tells him with determination.

Phillipe nods his assent as he walks around the easel and passes her on his way to the window. When he reaches it, he closes the heavy wooden shutters. Automatically, every shred of sunlight is cut off, and the studio is plunged into darkness as though it is night. He had the shutters installed for the purpose of his craft. Sometimes an image calls for darkness, even though it is daylight outside.

That's when Gemma asks, "So, what now? I just take off my clothes?"

* * *

I stand frozen, waiting for him to tell me what to do. This whole situation seems bizarrely unreal and one-hundred percent sexual in nature. *How do life models do this and not feel so exposed and so extremely vulnerable?*

As soon as Phillipe shuts the windows and the sunlight in the room disappears, all of my earlier apprehension returns. I start to reassure myself as I stand there talking to him. *I can do this.* After all, *Solitary* is just the back of me with no face exposed at all. I continue to tell myself that as the darkness starts to surround me. My eyes adjust, but it doesn't help. I'll be fully naked for this pose. I have to take off every single item of clothing and sit down with my back facing Phillipe. I will be exposed with nothing to cover me.

Taking a deep breath to try and calm myself, I almost jump out of my skin when I feel his hands land gently on my shoulders.

"Relax, Gemma." His deep voice slips into my thoughts. "I'm a professional."

He steps around me, and I almost laugh at that ridiculous notion. *Sure, he's a professional.* A professional who made me come without much effort at all. A professional who, with every word this morning, stripped away my armor. A professional who is now wrapping me in a bundle of aroused nerves.

"Oh, and yes, Gemma, you will need to take off *all* of your clothes."

As if I didn't work that out on my own.

Turning my back to him, even though the room is now dark, I unbutton my slacks and swiftly push them down my hips. I figure I should do this quickly, like ripping off a Band-Aid. Once the pants are gone, my sweater is next, so I pull it up and over my head. Just as I'm about to slide my panties off my hips, a soft spotlight flicks on, and I find the space I'm standing in is now brightly illuminated.

Like a fool, I quickly try to cover myself, and that's when I hear Phillipe's deep chuckle.

"Do you find this amusing?" I snap, looking over my shoulder at him. "I thought this was supposed to be an exercise in trust. It's not supposed to be one where I take off my clothes, and you laugh."

He moves around the easel into the soft light, and continues toward me. I have absolutely nowhere to go and no choice but to stand there as he stops a whisper away from me, our eyes connecting. Idiotically, I still have my hands over my bra and panties, which seems ridiculous since he is standing behind me and can see what I am trying to cover anyway.

All thoughts, however, soon leave my mind as I feel his warm fingers reach out. He traces the curves of my shoulder blades and moves down my back to where my bra is held together. He clasps the hook and eye between his thumbs and index fingers as he expertly unsnaps the bra, letting the stretchy lace fall slowly to the sides of my body. Those same fingers then gently slide down my spine until he reaches my panties.

My breathing starts to come faster with each seductive move he makes. When his mouth stops by my ear, I close my eyes.

"Now for these, sweet Gemma," he coerces softly.

The strong timbre of his voice rumbles through my body, calming and exciting me, just as Chantel described. He hooks those talented fingers into the remaining lace on my body, sliding them swiftly down to my ankles. The move is so eerily similar to what I read this morning that I can't help but wish for him to be in front of me, getting ready to kiss and tongue *my* wet pussy.

Stepping out of the panties, I try to remain calm as his hand reaches up to uncoil several loose strands of hair, freeing them to tickle my shoulders. While he's doing this, I've remained silent. I'm afraid that if I say anything, it will break the spell and ruin the moment.

Then, I feel him move away for a second. Taking that moment to look over my shoulder at him, I have the pleasure of watching him as he makes his way back to me. Those sinfully sexy eyes are locked with mine when he stops behind me once more, raising his hand to show me a piece of black silky material in his palm. Arousal swiftly disappears as fear hurries in to take its place.

My eyes widen, and my lips part. "What is that?"

He tilts his head to the side as he looks at the cloth in his hand. He states plainly, "It's a blindfold, Gemma."

Headlines start flashing to the forefront of my mind. Headlines about a man who takes something pure and makes it depraved. Headlines that scream that this is a man who destroyed softness and preyed on the weak-minded. Headlines, which up until around ten seconds ago, I had forgotten existed.

Staring at the material in his hand, I consider the fact that I am now completely naked, and he is still fully clothed. I can't help the jackhammer speed in which my heart has started to beat.

"I'm not wearing a blindfold," I inform him quite adamantly.

Very slowly, he lowers his arm in front of him, clasping his wrist with his other palm. "Why?"

"Why would I?" I demand with as much dignity as I can muster while standing there with my naked back to him. My brain is ordering me to run.

"I don't know, Gemma," he tells me softly. "Maybe to understand how Chantel felt? *Maybe* to grasp the whole concept of being blind? Or maybe..." He pauses, leaning down so our eyes are on the same level and our mouths are only inches apart. "To realize you can trust me not to hurt you. No?"

Blinking once, I open my eyes to find he's gone back to standing upright, and he's holding out the cloth to me again.

I swivel around a little, reaching for it. When my fingers get a firm grip, he tightens his own hold, tugging me forward. My body gives me no other option than to go with it. So, I'm left standing full frontal, staring up at him.

"When I fuck you, Gemma, I want your eyes open, looking right at me. I've never hidden who I am from anyone I've touched, and I won't start with you."

He lets go of the blindfold and walks around me to the drop cloth. "I need you to sit here," he tells me and I move to sit where he has instructed. Voice back to cool and aloof he continues. "Face toward the back wall, curve your torso to the left, and raise your arms up over your head, so your hands come down to cross over by your hair. Angle this right arm, so it is bent up toward the ceiling. Yes, perfect. Just curve your legs out to the side. I'll cover them with the cloth." He looks down at me. "Do you think you can do that?"

I nod silently, feeling completely off balance.

"Good," he replies, acting as though I'm not sitting here completely naked. "Now, do you want me to tie that around your eyes or would you prefer not to?"

I look up at him, noticing his pupils have dilated. Phillipe is aroused, and all of a sudden, I can't think of anything other than pleasing him.

Holding up the piece of material to him, he takes it from me as moves in close. Crouching down in front of me, he gently places it over my eyes, and his handsome and troubled face disappears from view. I feel his arms whisper past my ears as he moves closer to tie the ends at the back of my head.

"I'm sorry."

"Sorry for what?" he asks, his warm breath floating across my mouth.

"I'm sorry that I didn't trust you," I confide. "I'm sorry I doubted your intentions."

The silence seems thicker without my sight. I'm straining to hear him, but there's nothing, and that's when I feel a soft kiss against the corner of my lips.

"I think you're sorry you got caught. Oh, and, Gemma? You should always doubt my intentions."

With that, he moves away from me, leaving me to find my pose.

* * *

Gemma is resplendent in her nakedness, Phillipe thinks as he situates himself behind the easel. He watches her closely where she is seated and in pose. Her hair is the exact opposite shade of Chantel's. As Gemma holds herself in the mirror image he once so lovingly captured, he is struck at the differences in their bodies.

Gemma is curvier than Chantel, her breasts are rounder, and her hips flare out more, creating a shadow of an hourglass on the wall opposite from where the spotlight is hitting her.

Her reaction to the blindfold is interesting. He knows that she immediately thought of everything atrocious she had heard, causing her to rebel against her initial reaction of curiosity. The moment he firmly told her about his sexual proclivities, she seemed apologetic for allowing herself to go where her thoughts had taken her. *Funny really, considering the things I'm thinking about doing to her.*

Blame can't be placed upon her though. After all, one of the most horrid stories he read about himself described him as a man who had *plucked the wings from a butterfly.*

People are so fucking cruel.

"Why did you decide to paint Chantel in this series?" Gemma asked, breaking the silence.

Phillipe picks up a paintbrush and starts to outline her. He finds not having her look directly at him makes it easier to answer her questions.

"I was fascinated by her," he explains. "Everything she did was always executed with so much grace and such poise." He briefly pauses, reaching over to dip the tip of the brush into more paint before tracing it down the canvas to where her hip would be. "It seemed natural to paint her. Her ability to find beauty in everything was such an amazing quality. I wanted to try and capture that, so I could show the world beauty as I saw it." He chuckled softly. "One of her favorite quotes was *Everything has beauty, but not everyone sees it.* Nothing sums Chantel up better than that."

"Wow," Gemma mutters softly. "She sounds like an inspiring individual."

Phillipe closes his eyes for a moment and sees Chantel as she was when *she* posed for him. *Her black hair piled on top of her head and a few stray pieces escaping to flirt with her shoulders.* He remembers the precise moment he fell, the moment his life changed. His whole reason for breathing was sitting in front of him, illuminated by a soft spotlight.

"Phillipe?" Gemma questions.

He focuses back on the woman now seated before him. Other than the glaringly obvious physical differences, two major things altered this image from the original. That's exactly what Gemma is now questioning.

"Was the violin and the music always part of your vision? Or did that come later?"

For someone who is sitting naked and vulnerable with a blindfold over her eyes, Gemma's voice only wavers slightly. That impresses him immensely.

His eyes are drawn to the dip and sway of her lower back. That smooth expanse of skin is perfect in its unblemished state. Just like with Chantel, he finds himself wanting to mark it. *Mark it with paint.*

"It came later," he replies vaguely. He strokes his paintbrush on the canvas, creating the sweet curve of her ass. "Chantel use to sit with me while I painted, and one day, I asked her if she'd play when she visited. She inspired me, making me think of things I hadn't yet imagined. That was when I decided to paint her. It wasn't until after *Solitary* was complete when I thought to add Diva to the mix. Before that I only added the marks I thought belonged on her skin. Quite simply, she moved me when she played." He then confesses, "She owned me."

The silence is so thick and tense that he can almost see it stretched across the softly illuminated space.

Breaking through the quiet moment, Gemma whispers, "She was beautiful."

Phillipe feels a sad painful smile touch his mouth. "She was perfection."

* * *

Vulnerable ~

Today, Phillipe asked to paint me.

Today, I said yes.

When I reached the chateau, Penelope let me in and told me Phillipe was in his studio as she helped me up to the room. When I entered, I could smell the strong distinct smell of his paints.

"Fuck," he muttered.

I let out a small giggle, and he must have turned to look at me because I heard him walk in my direction.

"Chantel. I'm sorry. I lost track of time."

"You were painting?" I questioned him.

"Yes." He replied and paused. "Well, I was trying to. I hate to admit that not much is happening."

I felt him reach out and take my free hand. Diva was in my other. I brought her with me, just as he'd asked.

"Why do you think that is?"

He led me into the room.

"I don't know, but I was hoping maybe you'd play for me today. Maybe if I hear something inspiring, I'll paint something equally astounding."

I grinned in his direction as we stopped at the chair I had been curling up in lately.

"Can I ask you something?"

"Of course," I replied, assuring him. "You can ask me anything."

I'm not sure what I was expecting, but it wasn't what I got.

"Will you let me paint you today?"

At first, I didn't quite understand, so I questioned him. "Like I painted you?"

His fingers reached out and stroked my cheek. "As much as I'd love to do that, I actually meant on canvas. I would love it if you would pose for me."

I thought about that for a moment. "Like a model?"

"Exactly like a model." His strong hand slid down my arm to entwine his fingers with mine. "You're so undeniably captivating that I want to see if I can capture even a tenth of your magnetism with my brush."

Embarrassment flushed over my skin at his words. I'd never been so revered by anyone. I was always that awkward girl or that amazing blind girl who could play the violin, which was almost just as insulting. To be the focus of such attention from this man was altogether intoxicating.

"How would you want me to pose?" I asked cautiously.

I wasn't completely naive. I knew that a lot of paintings of models were done in the nude, and I also got the impression that Phillipe was the kind of man who'd want to paint his model in such a way.

He oozed sensuality with everything he did—from the way he talked to the way he touched to his chosen profession. It made perfect sense that he'd want to paint me—

"Nude. Naked and sitting on the floor, facing away from me, with your arms above your head. Hair pulled up, revealing all of this perfect pale skin," he softly described directly into my ear.

He pressed a hot kiss on my neck, and my whole body shivered as I turned my face in his direction. I knew somehow we were looking into each other's eyes.

"Yes," I murmured.

I gasped as his mouth took mine in a sensual assault. His warm full lips opened against mine as his tongue slid deep into my mouth to rub and flirt against my own. Moaning, I raised my hands to grip his chest, and I felt his strong arms wrap around my waist. One of his large hands cupped my ass, pulling my body in tight to his own. He groaned loudly as I wriggled against the hard press of his cock that I could feel rubbing against the apex of my thighs.

"Undress for me," he ordered against my lips as he reluctantly let me go.

Although I couldn't see him, I lowered my head, closing my eyes.

"No," he said, putting his finger beneath my chin. With firm determination, he told me, "Don't shut your eyes, Chantel. Don't ever hide from me."

Taking a deep breath, I kept my sightless eyes open, focused on the spot where I believed he would be standing. I reached up to the top button of my dress. As I undid the buttons, I could hear his breathing accelerate, creating a small smile of pleasure on my face. I was affecting him. Chantel Rosenberg, the woman from the States who couldn't see, was making Phillipe Tibideau, artist and beyond intriguing and sexy man, breathe a little harder.

This was such an amazing and powerful moment for me.

He stayed silent through my full disrobing, and then he muttered, "Perfect. Absolute fucking perfection."

I bit my bottom lip, waiting for him to tell me what to do.

"Turn around." He instructed.

I found myself immediately obeying. That was when I felt his warm palm on my lower back and his lips on my shoulder.

"Can I do something?" he asked.

Laughing nervously, I turned my head toward the shoulder he was kissing. "Aren't you already doing something?"

"Yes, I suppose I am." He smiled against my skin before gently biting where he was kissing. "But can I do something else?"

I nodded slowly as he moved away from me. The next sensation I felt was a cool wet one against my lower back. I gasped. "What are you doing?"

"I'm painting you."

Giggling, I looked over my shoulder like I would actually see something. "Well, what are you painting?"

As he blew against the paint he'd stroked onto my skin, his breath fluttered against my lower back and ass. He didn't answer me. Instead, he stayed silent as he repeated the same step on the other side. I remained still until he was done.

"What did you paint on me?" I asked again.

His finger stroked a shape next to one of the spots he had painted, and I concentrated as he repeated the stroke.

I smiled. "An F-hole?"

His laugh rolled through me, and I held my breath as I felt his finger drift down to flirt with the top of my ass crack.

"I almost can't believe my luck with the name of those little sound holes," he said.

I couldn't believe I was letting him touch me where he was. As he continued to talk and stroke his finger farther down between my cheeks, I found the sensation arousing, thrilling, and forbidden. I arched back against his touch as his wicked laugh tickled my ear.

"Do you like this?" he inquired darkly. "Do you like my finger here?"

I completely lost my ability to talk. Instead, I nodded my affirmation as he pressed in deeper. Now, I could feel his fingertip rubbing against my dark little pucker.

"You're so hot here." He groaned.

I let out a soft moan of pleasure.

"Yes, that's it, Beauty. Let go. Let me touch you where no one has before. Relax for me."

His mouth was on the curve of my shoulder and neck as I pushed my hips back against him.

"I want to take you here, Chantel," he told me, his voice husky and deep. "I want to crawl inside of you and never leave."

Just as suddenly as it had begun, he stopped his petting and kisses. He stepped away, leaving me bereft and empty.

"But first I want to paint you. Sit down, Chantel. Let me see you."

Chapter Seven
FIRSTS

Day 6

Today, when I awoke, a note was pushed under my door. Phillipe let me know that he had left for the morning and wouldn't be available. He suggested that I go down onto the grounds and take the main path up through the vines until I see a small fork to the right. There, he had told me, I would find a shaded area, the perfect spot to relax and read the next entry in the journal.

Folding the small piece of paper, I place it on the dresser in my room before making my way into the bathroom. Turning on the water to the temperature I desire, I step into the shower and let the stream slide over my skin, washing away my restless night.

I didn't sleep for more than an hour or so at max, and I know why. I was consumed with words.

Words, thoughts, and memories—every single one of them was centered on Phillipe and Chantel.

Sighing, I lean my head back as the water sluices over my breasts before sliding down to my now constantly aching pussy. Sexual frustration seems to be plaguing me where Phillipe is concerned. I can't solely blame him though. Reading Chantel's journal entries is like witnessing each act in explicit detail.

Without sight, she brought the other senses to the experience. She depicted every sound, every touch, and every emotion. She made me want to experience that.

Picking up the bar of soap, I quickly and efficiently wash myself, wanting to get out of the chateau for a while. I want to see the grounds. It's a beautiful day from what I've seen, and I want to make the most of it.

My plans for the morning are to go and find a quiet spot, lie down in it, and read the next entry of the journal.

* * *

After a fifteen-minute walk from the chateau, I find the secluded spot down through the vineyard and a little way off the path, exactly where Phillipe had indicated it would be. The sun is peeking through the branches above, and it is just enough to keep me warm.

Penelope suggested I take a blanket with me, and she also gave me a packed lunch.

So, here I am sitting down in the vineyard while I read Chantel's journal.

* * *

Firsts ~

Today, Phillipe took me outside. He took me and made me his.

He had told me yesterday to dress in something I wouldn't mind sitting on the ground in. Of course, with him, that could mean anything, including maybe posing again. So, I had put on an old sundress and turned up at the chateau at noon, just like he'd asked.

"Always so punctual, Chantel," he told me as he met me at the front door.

He kissed me under my ear on the neck right where he knew it would send shivers through my body.

"I like that. You always come on time."

I blushed, knowing his true meaning, sighing as he nipped at my lobe.

"Come on. I'm taking you down to the vineyard."

He clasped my hand and tugged me along beside him. After looping my arm through the crook of his, I followed.

"The vineyard, huh?" I questioned. "You're not going to make me pose out there, are you?"

"Hmm, now, there's an idea." He chuckled. "Chantel. Naked. The sun shining down. Woman is now one with nature."

I pushed against his shoulder, smiling. "You're an idiot."

We walked a little while until he finally stopped.

"Here," he told me.

The warmth of the sun was intermingled with the shadows as it hit the back of my neck, and I heard birds above me. We were obviously in among the trees.

"Where's here?"

I heard rustling and a branch cracked right before I felt him in front of me again, his lips pressing against mine.

"Right here."

I grinned against his mouth. "Where are we, Phillipe?"

"We're in a little spot away from the vineyards," he explained, pulling my hand gently.

I felt him move to sit down, and I followed carefully. His hands helped guide me, and I was shocked when I felt a soft blanket hit my knees.

"You brought a blanket?" I questioned.

I moved to touch the material under my knees. It was fuzzy but not scratchy. My fingers sank into the plushness as I stroked my hand across the fabric. His hand came down on mine, as he gently entwined our fingers to stroke the blanket's softness together.

"I came down here this morning and set it up."

"Tell me what's here?" I demanded of him eagerly.

He brought up my hand and kissed my knuckles. "Well, there's a blanket. Above us, I hung a piece of cheesecloth from a couple of branches to shade the area a little better."

As I felt him shift, I guessed he was looking around.

"I also brought several pillows."

"You brought pillows?" I smiled. "Why?"

The scent of his cologne became stronger, and I knew he was only inches from me. His hands slid through my hair, cupping the back of my head.

"Because I want to lie down with you." He explained as his lips met mine in a kiss that was as hot and potent as the sun that was shining down on us.

* * *

I have to stop for a minute because I have a feeling I know where this entry is going to go.

Am I ready to read this?

This is going to be their moment. I can tell from the title and the first line in the entry. *Today, Phillipe took me outside. He took me outside and made me his.*

Do I want to read this? The answer to that is almost embarrassingly easy to come by. However, the real question bothering me—the one that I don't have an immediate answer for—is, *Am I ready for how this will ultimately make me feel?*

Looking up at the branches overhead, I close my eyes, take a deep breath, open the leather-bound book, and continue on.

* * *

Phillipe lowered me down onto the blanket and moved one of the pillows to cushion my head. His breath, warm and sweet, whispered against my parted mouth as his tongue dipped inside to rub against my own.

I ran my hands up through his hair and moaned against his lips as he angled in a different direction to deepen the kiss. One of his hands stroked over my cheek as he lowered to the top of my dress. I gasped as his big warm palm continued down to cup my aching breast. Arching up into his caress, I felt him lift his head from mine.

His low voice rasped out a harsh prayer. "Christ."

I almost echoed his sentiment.

His weight shifted as he moved to my right, stroking his palm over to the middle of my torso. I held my breath as his fingers flirted with my top button, and his hair flopped down to tickle my chin as he laid a hot open-mouth kiss at the base of my throat.

Bringing up my hands, I tunneled them into his hair. His tongue came out to lick a hot wet path up the side of my neck until he was at my ear where he bit the lobe gently.

"I want to sink inside of you, Chantel."

"Yes." I sighed.

"Yes?" he questioned.

His fingers started to undo the buttons at the center of my chest.

"Yes," I repeated.

"You want me inside you?"

I was slowly losing my mind as he kissed and nipped my ear while he continued to undo the buttons of my dress. When he had them all free, he parted the material, and I could feel him move. I sensed he was now looking down at me, so I brought my hands up beside my head to give him a better view of what he wanted to see.

"Yes, Phillipe, I want you inside me."

At that exact moment, I hated that I couldn't see him because I had a feeling I would be looking at something spectacular just as that sexy voice skated over my skin. It was almost as good as seeing.

"Mmm, yes, so do I," he said.

His hand flattened between my breasts, and I arched up my back toward him. He smoothed the heel of his palm all the way down the center of my body until he reached my aching mound.

That was where he stopped and pressed firmly, applying a delicious pressure where I needed it most.

My hips pushed up, imploring him to continue. I could feel him still kneeling by my side.

When he told me, "Open your legs," there was nothing I could have done to disobey.

* * *

I should be ashamed of myself. That's all I can think as I tunnel my hand down under my pants into my panties. My fingers are now perilously close to grazing the small strip of hair covering my aroused flesh.

Somewhere between reading about Phillipe undoing Chantel's dress and imagining how he sounded as he told her to open her legs, my hand unfastened my pants and slid inside, seeking a way to ease my own sexual need.

The journal is still firmly gripped in my left hand, and my leg is angled up so the heel of my foot is planted firmly on the blanket.

I can't believe that I'm going to touch myself as I read this, but I know there's no way to stop myself. I'm so turned on, thinking that I might be lying right where Phillipe spread Chantel's dress apart or that I might be on the same blanket he laid on the ground. Instantly, I can feel my juices start to slide between my thighs.

Quickly, I glance around the area I'm lying in. When I'm satisfied that I'm alone, I finally let my fingers delve down between my aching wet folds. My lips part as I shut my eyes for a moment. I imagine Phillipe's face above me, him kneeling beside my body, while he pushes his finger deep inside of *me* and tells *me* to open my legs wider.

Moaning, I grip the journal tighter, flexing my hips up into my nimble hand. Opening my lust-heavy eyes, I focus on the words in front of me and continue reading the book that has now turned me into a voyeur through no fault of its own.

* * *

I opened my legs as I felt him remove his palm from my body, and two fingers pushed my now soaked panties up against my hot flesh. I arched my back, flexing my hips toward him, not quite believing how incredibly turned on I was. He didn't do anything more than undo my dress and tell me to open my legs, yet I could feel myself becoming so wet that my moisture actually seeped through the fabric between my legs. I knew I had to be soaking his fingertips.

Just as that thought left my lust-addled mind, he was above me. I could feel one arm by the left side of my head, and I felt his right fingers pushing against my bottom lip.

"Taste, Chantel," he instructed.

I opened my mouth to taste myself on his fingers.

Lowering down beside me, he rasped into my ear, "You're so fucking wet that you drenched my fingers through your panties. Do you know how fucking sexy that is? Do you know how hard that makes me?"

I panted and moaned when his right hand slipped back down between my thighs. This time, he moved my panties to slide inside of them. With no hesitation, those two clever fingers found their way deep between my aching pussy lips.

"Hmm," he groaned in my ear.

I curved up against his hand on a soft moan. "Oh god! Ahhh, Phillipe!" I cried out.

When his fingers finally penetrated my body, he pushed deeper and angled them.

"Fuck yes." He growled in my ear.

I let out my own harsh breath of pleasure. I raised my arms and placed my palms on his shoulders as I started to really push up my hips against his astute hand. I could feel my juices running down my thighs now, so I knew his hand had to be coated as he continued to thrust two and then three fingers into me.

Parting my lips, I let out a harsh breath. "I never knew it could be like this."

His head lowered, and his teeth sank into my bottom lip. He thrust his fingers in again, flicking my clit with his thumb. "Neither did I."

* * *

As Phillipe returns from Beau's, he runs into Penelope in the kitchen. She tells him that Gemma made her way down to the vineyard around an hour or so ago.

Looking up at the clock, he notices it has just turned 1 p.m., and he figures he should go down to find her.

Grabbing his black jacket from the coatrack, he makes his way outside to head in the direction Penelope told him she had gone. *It's beautiful outside today,* he thinks as he turns down to the right of the vines in the direction of the fork.

Phillipe thinks about the part of the journal Gemma must be at. He pushes his hands into his pockets and looks around. He wonders about his own slightly masochistic tendencies. He sent her down here, knowing what she would read, but she told him that she wanted to tell their story accurately.

What better way to learn about it than to read one of the most pivotal moments at the actual scene?

He doesn't think much after that though because that's when he spots Gemma.

What a fucking sight she is.

She is lying out on the same exact blanket he brought down here with Chantel, but this woman isn't wearing a dress. *Oh no.* She has on snug black pants and currently has one leg bent up at an angle. Her right hand is buried down between her thighs as she flexes her hips, pleasuring herself with sexy determination to find release.

Stepping toward her, he notices that she's holding the journal in her left hand. That's when everything falls into place. She's reading the entry while she finger-fucks herself to Chantel's words.

Phillipe feels his cock harden as he watches Gemma's hand move beneath the fabric of her pants. Her eyes are closed while her mouth parts. With each sinfully forbidden thrust of her hips, he wants her more. Reaching down to the buckle of his belt, he unfastens it, and then he unbuttons and unzips his pants. He's going to satisfy her need and his right now.

Moving to the end of the blanket, he kneels down quietly and marvels at the uninhibited way she's moving her hips against her palm. Her hair is strewn out across the blanket, and the hand gripping the journal is white-knuckled while she seems to be seeking that elusive moment, her thundering climax.

"Gemma," he calls to her softly.

He watches closely when her eyes snap open as her hand stops its frenetic movement. She makes a move to pull her hand from her pants, but he's quicker. He leans forward, placing his palm against the fabric, effectively trapping her hand where it has been working so furiously.

"What..." she starts to ask.

When he continues to just stare at her, the question seems to vanish. He looks over to the journal she is now trying to close with one hand.

"No, don't," he tells her. "Read it to me."

She's still panting with arousal, but as his words seem to filter through to her brain, she blinks her lust-clouded eyes. "What?"

Licking his lips, he pushes his hand firmer against hers, which is still lying flat against her aroused skin. Narrowing his eyes on her flushed face and parted lips, he tells himself that what he's about to do is, in some way, a gross defiling of Chantel. At the same time though, the sheer eroticism of the act is calling to him.

"I want you to read the journal entry to me."

Gemma takes a deep breath that makes her fantastic breasts heave with their agitation. He notices her eyes travel down his coat to the pants that are parted at his hips.

"Where should I read from?" she finally asks hesitantly.

Phillipe now moves and brings up his other hand to grip both sides of her pants. He keeps his eyes on hers as he tugs them gently. She gets the hint and raises her hips, watching cautiously as he pulls her pants and panties down her legs without question.

When she's left bare, she still hasn't removed her hand from where it is laying, her open palm against her glistening wet sex. He knows a feral grin is now on his lips.

"Start where you left off," he orders persuasively as he leans down to drag his tongue across the wet skin he just exposed.

* * *

Fucking hell, I think as Phillipe lowers his head, dragging his hot tongue across my throbbing clit.

How the hell does he expect me to keep reading? And read this, no less?

I couldn't believe it when he said my name, and I opened my eyes to see him kneeling at my feet. I thought for certain I hallucinated him, dreamed him up like some kind of warped sexual fantasy which came to life.

No, he's really here, and he is currently leaning over my swollen pussy, licking and sucking on it, demanding I read to him from his past lover's journal.

This is insane, I think as it becomes increasingly hard for me to even breathe. That's when I notice he has stopped, and he is now looking up at me from between my thighs.

"Just start where you left off. Start at the spot that made you put your hand in your pants and your fingers inside yourself," he tells me as he blows a hot breath across my sensitive skin. "Hmm, yes. Start there, Gemma."

Blinking slowly, I drag my eyes away from his wicked mouth, sexy eyes, and open rumpled pants. *Holy fuck,* I think.

I try to focus on the words—*her* words—and then I start.

* * *

I could hear him breathing hard against my mouth every time he pushed his fingers deeper into my greedy body, and every time he pulled them out, he sighed.

He tasted delicious. His breath was intoxicating, and the way he moved his fingers inside of me felt like nothing I had ever known before.

"I need to taste you," he told me in a voice that sounded desperate with need.

Was he desperate for me? I didn't know.

He moved away from where his mouth had been pressed against mine, and I felt him trail his lips down my neck to my chest.

Raising my hands up, I threaded my fingers through his hair. It was soft and silky, and I heard him groan as I tugged it, lifting my hips.

"Jesus, Chantel," he muttered against my skin.

His teeth gently grazed my nipple, as his hands pulled the lace cup away from my breast. When his clever lips surrounded my sensitive tip, he sucked it hard enough that there was a slight sting of pain to accompany the pleasure.

* * *

Stopping, I look down my body to the man who now has his hands burrowed up under my sweater.

"Take this off," he instructs gruffly.

Putting aside the journal, I keep my eyes on him as I sit up and pull the sweater over my head.

"Bra, too," he adds.

At this point, I can't find one single reason to not do as he requests.

I'm so consumed with my own hot desire that I'm surprised when I can actually *see* the moisture on my thighs. Undoing my bra, I slide it off, throwing it to the side.

"Lie back down, Gemma." His voice floats across the small space between us.

I slowly move back to the position I was originally in. He picks up the journal and hands it back to me with lowered lids. As I take it from him, I suck in a deep breath when he lowers his head and flicks his tongue across my nipple.

"I believe we were right here."

Moaning, I shut my eyes. I'm almost unable to continue, but I know if I keep reading he'll continue reliving the words on the page. I know I'm not the woman he so obviously hungers for and even though I'm not who he wants, I find myself stupidly willing to be her substitute.

* * *

He cupped my breasts in his hands and tongued my nipple—first the right, and then the left.

It felt strange to me, his tongue was hot and wet. While it was unbelievably exciting, it also tickled a little bit. I could feel his breath against my sensitive skin as he breathed out every time he suckled on me.

Then, he was on the move again. Those lips I was now coming to love made their way down the center of my body to my navel where he dipped his tongue in and bit lovingly around the edges. At this stage, I dropped my hands from his hair. They were up by my head because, honestly, I couldn't even think enough to hang on to him.

"Chantel?" he asked.

I tipped my head in his direction. I knew he was looking up at me. "Yes?"

"Touch yourself for me while I undress."

I reached for my breasts and cupped them. "Like this?"

"Exactly like that," he rasped.

He was not gone for long. I felt his hand slip under my panties as he dragged them down my legs. His whole body weight shifted as he pushed himself between my thighs, wedging his now naked hips between my legs.

His hot skin singed into mine, and I could feel his arms by my head as his fingers played with my hair. He kissed my mouth gently.

"You are the most flawless thing I have ever seen."

I didn't know how to answer him. I could have told him that he made me feel cherished, desired, or even wanted. Did any of that really compare to what he was telling me?

Instead, I leaned up and kissed his mouth. I traced my hands over his face, memorizing every dip, each subtle change in texture. As his lips parted above mine, I was struck with a soul-altering moment of truth.

I was his.

He could do whatever he wanted, and I'd still be his.

I was in love with Phillipe Tibideau.

* * *

I shut the journal and reach down to grip the hair that is tickling against my breasts.

"Stop," I tell him as I put the journal to the side.

Immediately, he lifts his head, and as he focuses on my face, I see dark desire smoldering in his deep green eyes.

"Do you even know who you're with right now?" I ask him.

I'm desperate to know he isn't thinking of *her* as he brushes his mouth across *my* nipples.

He gives me a blistering look that tries to make all my doubt instantly disappear, but this time, I hold firm. *This time, I need to know.*

"Of course, Gemma," he assures seductively. He lowers his mouth down onto the curve of my breast. "Your breasts—they're fuller and rounder than what hers were."

I know I should feel disgusted or at least disturbed that he's kissing me and talking about her. But, as he sucks my nipple between his lips, his cheeks hollow out, and I'm reminded of all the beautiful angles of his face Chantel was talking about. Instantly, I'm struck by his sheer attractiveness.

He moves up my body, and he's suddenly right where he was in the journal—between my thighs. The only difference is that I'm naked, and he's clothed—well, except for his open pants. His eyes are looking down into mine, and I'm finding it hard to make any words come out of my mouth. That's when I feel his right hand move down to trace the curve my hip.

"And your hips are curvier. They flare out more, giving you that sexy hourglass figure that men everywhere would beg to touch."

I can't help but arch my hips up against the hard cock I can feel straining inside his pants.

"But the question isn't really if *I* know who I'm with right now," he points out as he flexes his hips against mine, letting me feel the full force and impact of his desire. "The question is...*do you?*"

I think about that for a moment and lift my hands to his hips. *I know who I'm with, and I want him in me now.* Pushing down his pants, I grip his hard cock in my right hand, lining him up with my greedy pussy.

"I know exactly who I'm with," I tell him.

I watch as he lowers his head to the side of mine.

"So, tell me, Gemma. Is it *me* you're with, or are you here with me *and* Chantel?" he asks seductively.

Before I can answer him, he thrusts his cock up inside of me.

I can't help the scream that comes from my mouth as he pushes his hips forward, and suddenly, he's back at my ear telling me wicked and depraved things I shouldn't know.

"This is the same blanket, Gemma. I'm fucking you on the exact same blanket I took *her* on. How does that make you feel?" he asks me as he drags his thick cock in and out of my dripping sex.

I can't seem to formulate an answer, and he doesn't seem to care because he keeps up his seductively warped monologue.

"Do you know that every time I sank my cock into her, she arched her back, just like you're doing? Her eyes—*fuck,* those beautiful and useless eyes—would stare up at me like I owned the whole fucking world."

I pant as his moves become faster and harder, almost brutal. He shifts and puts his left hand under my ass, pulling my pelvis up, so he can burrow deeper inside of me. I feel like he's close to penetrating my very soul as he leans down to bite my bottom lip.

"Does it turn you on—reading and knowing how she felt every time my cock pushed into her? It must, Gemma, because you aren't even using this smart head of yours anymore. Your arousal is making you careless."

"What?" I question. I'm caught up in my own lust as I feel my core flutter around the thickness wedged deep inside of me.

"Your brain—it's not working, or you'd be wondering or concerned if I am safe, if you are safe."

My eyes snap open to focus on him as he stops moving those wicked hips.

He informs me, "I'm safe. Now, Gemma..." His voice floats through the tiny amount of space left between us. "Are you? Because I'm not moving until I hear—"

"I'm safe." I moan, bowing up to him.

He grips my ass, hauling me impossibly closer.

"I'm so glad to hear it because your pussy is a fucking wet dream," he tells me and with a hard thrust, he adds, "And every time I mention her name, it squeezes my cock like a fucking vise."

I close my eyes, ashamed that what he's saying is right. It's true. *What the fuck is the matter with me?* I have no answer I can give him or myself, so instead, I focus on his face. That serious and focused expression looks so fierce as he moves above me and inside of me, stealing something integral from my being with every delicious stroke of his hips.

"I think you're the one getting confused who's here," he explains. "Because I know exactly who I'm inside of."

Reaching up, he pinches my nipple, and I scream out so loudly that I know my voice will be hoarse the next morning.

"Oh, yes, Gemma, scream for me." he mutters as he leans down, biting the curve of my shoulder and neck as he fucks into me like he's never going to stop.

I grip his ass in my hands and push myself up to meet each of his tortuous thrusts. Right when I think it's impossible for my body to hit a second climax, his orgasm slams into me, bathing me in a warmth that is so intoxicating I feel myself fly with him to a second splintering climax.

Several minutes later, I find myself lying in silence on a blanket, the sun shining through the trees. I'm struck with the realization that I'm holding onto a man who, for now, is holding onto me but he has still not let go of *her*.

Chapter Eight

IMPULSIVE

"Have you ever heard *Pachelbel's Canon in D* played live with a full orchestra?" Phillipe asks me later that night as we walk into the studio.

"No, I haven't heard any orchestral pieces live. Isn't that one of the songs people play for the wedding march?"

Looking at me over his shoulder, he moves toward the stereo system on the shelves. He tells me with the barest hint of humor, "I don't know, Gemma. I've never walked down an aisle."

I shake my head at him with a smirk. "You know what I mean."

Nodding, he concedes. "Well, when put that way, then yes, I suppose it is the song that a lot of brides walk down the aisle to."

Pressing what I presume is play, he turns back to make his way toward me as the deep base starts. I keep my eyes locked with his as he crosses the space to stop before me, holding out his hand like a gentleman from a forgotten era. Curious about his mood, I go with it.

I slide my hand into the palm that so expertly touched me this afternoon, and I gasp when he tugs me in close to assume the waltz position. Looking up into his blazing green eyes, I have to admit that I can quite easily understand Chantel's quick fall into love, although Chantel would never have seen those eyes.

Before I have too long to consider that, he slowly starts to waltz me around his studio. Holding on tight, I can't help but smile. It feels wonderful to have a moment of such simplicity when things here have been so intense and so confusing. This feels simple.

Two people dancing. Two people enjoying a moment. Until that moment is gone.

"This piece was originally scored for three violins and a basso continuo. Listen..." He pauses in his explanation as he moves me effortlessly around his studio.

My mind spins with each expertly executed turn.

"All three instruments work together in breathtaking synchronicity, Gemma. The fourth is there just to keep them in order because three of anything is bound to get messy."

I can feel my breath picking up as his meaning takes root, and I'm left wondering, *What is he getting at? He's always playing such head games with me.*

Twirling me away from him, I stare at our joined hands, and I bring up my eyes to meet his, which are now focused on me with absolute intensity. He tugs me back to him, and I go because the music is still floating through the air. It seems this waltz isn't over, not by a long shot.

"They feed off one another," he tells me as his lips brush a kiss against my head. "They're each so flawless in their transitions that you start to believe they're all one and the same."

He stops talking as the music swells, and I close my eyes as I'm pulled under. I'm swept away by the beauty of the piece and again by the seduction that is Phillipe. His arms, strong and solid, wrap around me as I allow myself to really let go. I feel as though he's given me permission in some way, like he's telling me that what I'm feeling is okay—*even when I know that it's not.*

How can I be so fascinated with him and, at the same time, be so captivated by her?

These are questions I have no answers for as the music softens and his lips move to my ear.

"That's right, Gemma. Close your eyes. To really feel the music, you have to listen...blindly."

That's when it hits me. The complete picture unfolds. The moment of joy he's feeling plus the confusion I'm experiencing all mixes together to equal the total mindfuck I'm having.

"This is *her* playing, isn't it?" I ask, stiffening in his arms.

"Yes, she recorded it for me after I saw her play it one night."

He holds me tight, refusing to let me go. As the music rises once again, he spins me away.

"Why are you sharing this with me now?" I demand of him.

I'm more annoyed than I probably should be, but all I can think about is the fact that *she's* here again. *She's always here.*

"Because, Gemma, this is us," he explains in a voice that's now become somewhat detached. "We are three. Can't you see that? Just like any moment of beauty, we're all working in synchronicity to find that elusive moment, like that moment you and I found out in the vineyard...*with her*."

Finally, the music stops, and I'm staring up into a face that seems oddly serene, almost as though he's made some calming realization, just as I'm having a major fucked-up one.

"No, I can't see that, Phillipe," I snap as I step back.

I'm trying to disentangle myself from the web he's once again drawn me into. I'm also silently berating myself. Although I'm outwardly telling him *no*, knowing he's delusional, I realize deep down that he's right. *I'm just as entangled with Chantel as I am with him.*

"Okay, Gemma." His voice breaks through the tense silence, sounding defeated. "Have it your way."

I'm standing only a couple of steps away from him, but as he moves forward, I cross my arms over my chest like a shield.

"Do you want to pose this afternoon and continue with your questions?" He reaches out, touching my cheek gently. "Or do you want to leave?"

Looking up at him, my eyes land on his full sensual lips. I'm reminded of this afternoon and the way his mouth moved over my skin. I find myself wanting to reach out and touch that mouth. He must sense a change in me because one corner of those incorrigible lips tilts up.

He demands quietly, "Undress for me."

God help me, I do.

* * *

Impulsive ~

I asked Phillipe to come and watch me tonight.

When my mother had first mentioned I should go and stay with Uncle Beau, my first thought had been,

Where would I get to play? *I didn't want to be anywhere I couldn't play my music.*

Don't get me wrong. I enjoy losing myself when I'm on my own, but there's simply no better feeling than playing at the front of a full-scale orchestra.

It's hard to explain, but imagine you're in a smooth body of water as you effortlessly swim along. You're just rising up with each movement and then flowing back down. Now, add a stormy ocean, and as each loud and powerful wave hits you, it pushes you up, higher and higher toward the sky, before crashing you back down into the turbulent ocean.

You might be scared and terrified, but you love feeling the exhilaration and power of that ocean along with the sheer force and beauty of it.

Well, that's how I like to think playing in front of a full orchestra feels, like one big powerful wave that crashes down over you.

I use to play as a guest performer with the local orchestra back home. I had told my mother that before I would even consider moving here, we would need to find one close by, and we did.

Tonight, Phillipe is coming to watch me.

* * *

Gemma surprises Phillipe when she silently walks to the drop cloth and removes her clothes.

After the way she pulled away from him, he was positive that she would have tucked tail and run. Instead, she is now sitting in pose, nude, with her back to him and the blindfold firmly in place. *Probably cursing my name.*

He doesn't understand why every move forward they take feels as though it's somehow enhanced by the memory of Chantel.

When he originally went into this bargain with Gemma, he did it with the expectation that she would understand Chantel better, and as their story unraveled, she would get to see a side of him he found so difficult to show. He did not count on the intense feeling of connection to Chantel *through* Gemma. *Perhaps it is Gemma herself?*

Maybe, if she didn't seem so bewitched and curious about Chantel, he wouldn't feel this way. *Maybe* if she just asked him questions in a perfunctory manner, he wouldn't be feeling this aberrant entanglement of desire that he can't seem to shake.

As he looks over to the woman seated on the floor, he remembers the way she came with such force. He can still feel the sweet tight squeeze of her pussy. He knows he isn't the only one baffled by this strange connection that they seem to share.

"You're very quiet," he states, waiting patiently for her reply.

"I'm trying to decide what I want to ask you today."

"Ahh, I see. I thought you might be sitting over there plotting out a way to leave my evil clutches."

When she turns her head to face him over her shoulder, he glances at her over the top of the easel. Her eyes are covered, but he can almost guess that they are narrowed on him. Phillipe has to admit that he enjoys the slight annoyance he can sense in her posture. *It's almost a shame this isn't a frontal pose.*

"Who said anything about leaving?" she queried.

"No one. I see there's no answer about my evil clutches though, hmm?"

She harrumphs softly, but he hears it as she turns back to face the wall.

"Did you enjoy our afternoon together, Gemma?" he finds himself asking her, seemingly out of nowhere. He strokes the paintbrush down the canvas, creating the curve of both her back and hip, making them appear seamless.

"I think you know I did," she whispers so faintly that he almost doesn't catch it.

"Then, why are you acting so ashamed?"

He dips the brush into the color before bringing it back to the material. He isn't here to create a masterpiece. He is using this time to show Gemma how Chantel felt as she sat there in pose.

"I'm not ashamed, and I'm not here to answer your questions. You're here to answer mine."

Phillipe finds himself holding back a smile at her pretentiousness. "Well, maybe you should ask me some."

He turns and puts the paintbrush down on the table beside him, watching as she shifts slightly in her position. *Is she uncomfortable or aroused?*

Either way, he takes selfish delight in telling her, "Try not to move, please."

She blows out a deep breath. "When did you ask Chantel to move into the chateau with you?"

Phillipe was waiting for a question, but somehow, he didn't expect it to be that one.

"Why would you just assume *I* asked her? Unless, you already know better."

Silence, thick and tense, stretches out between them.

"Well, with the way you talk about her and the way she writes about you, it automatically makes me think *you* asked *her*."

Phillipe steps around the easel. He walks over to the perceptive Gemma and crouches down behind her. He must have been quieter than he thought because she flinches when the back of his finger traces down her naked spine.

Without moving so much as an inch, he confesses, "I didn't ask. I begged." He stands, walks over to the journal, and taps the cover. "But this, you already knew."

* * *

Tonight, when I arrived at the Grand Théâtre de Bordeaux, my uncle led me down to the dressing rooms, and I was greeted by the music conductor who would be up front tonight.

I was nervous about playing this evening. It was not because there would be an audience but because he *was going to be there. Tonight, Phillipe was going to watch me play with the local orchestra, and I wanted it to be perfect for him.*

I was led to the stage door to start the warm up.

One of the other violinists I was going to be playing alongside for the opening piece told me, "I'm so excited to play with you tonight. I think you're amazing. To be able to play in such a way and be completely..." She paused as I smiled in her direction. She too was American.

"Blind? It's okay. You can say it."

"I'm sorry. It's not very polite for me to point out something so obvious. I'm sure you get sick of it. When they told us who was going to be playing here tonight, I was thrilled. I know all about you. You inspired me to

play." The girl giggled. "Sorry. I went a little crazy there, didn't I? I'm Jessica. I'll be playing second chair violin."

I liked Jessica immediately. She showed me to my seat, and I began warming up.

Running through the usual warm-up exercises, I felt the music as it flowed through my fingers and vibrated through my ear. It made its way into my heart, and as silly as it sounds, it touched me deep down into my soul.

Thirty minutes later, the orchestra was introduced, and I heard my name along with Jessica's and two others mentioned. We each stood, and applause filled the room as we made our way—me with the assistance of Jessica—to the center of the stage.

The audience hushed and waited in complete silence.

I felt the warmth of the spotlight as it moved to focus on the four of us. This evening, we were going to be playing Pachelbel's Canon in D. Taking a deep breath, I closed my eyes and lifted Diva to my shoulder.

That was when it happened. I felt him.

Somehow, I knew exactly where he was in reference to me. Like a compass being pulled north, I found myself pivoting toward the left, and I opened my eyes. I knew that was where he was. I knew he was sitting up there.

Closing my eyes once again, I listened as the basso continuo started, and I swayed slightly as I let the wave crash down over me.

* * *

"So, you asked her the night you went to see her play?" I ask, knowing he has moved back behind the easel now.

He seems further away each time he speaks.

"Yes. What can I say? The moment I went and saw her play, I knew."

His voice fades out toward the end of his thought, but I'm not letting him get away with it that easily. I need to know exactly what he means.

"You knew what?" I press, finding courage in the darkness I am now inhabiting.

Not having to face him when asking such personal and probing questions makes me bolder. It makes it easier to dig deeper into the heart of a man who I know is wounded. It makes me ruthless in my pursuit of his story. This story is so provocative that it has captured the attention of the whole world. That's when, I hear him confirm what I already suspect.

"I knew I had to keep her."

* * *

She is mesmerizing, *he thought as he watched the spotlight move in and focus on the four musicians now at the front of the orchestra.*

After she had told him she was playing tonight, she had invited him to come, and he had bought a box seat. There was no way he was going to miss out on this.

So, here he was. For some reason, he held his breath when she stood and closed her eyes. She raised her beloved Diva to her left shoulder, and that was when it happened. She opened her eyes, turned her head, and looked up right at him.

Phillipe felt his breath leave his body on a sigh while his chest ached and tightened with the knowledge that she somehow knew. She felt him inside her very being, proving that theirs was a connection he couldn't explain to anyone.

She smiled slightly before closing her eyes once more, and he found himself blocking out the other three people standing by her along with the fifty orchestral members who also disappeared from his view. All he saw was Chantel, standing center stage, playing the most beautiful and spellbinding rendition of one of the most famous pieces ever scored.

He had known the minute he saw her out in his vineyard that first morning that there was nothing he wouldn't do to know her. Just as he knew, right this second, there was nothing he wouldn't do to keep her.

* * *

"So, after the show, you…what? Went back to the dressing room? To the chateau?" I stop and sigh. "Why are you being so difficult about this part in the story? If you didn't want to talk to me about it, then you should have let me finish reading her journal." I pause before muttering, "At least, *she* answers my questions."

"You seem frustrated," he tells me.

"I am frustrated. I want to know what happened, Phillipe."

Pausing, I realize I am still sitting on the floor naked, and he seems to have moved his position. He isn't over where he was when he was painting. No, he sounds as though he's sitting in the chair that's over in the other corner of the room. Reaching up, I remove the blindfold, twisting my body around to see that my suspicions are correct.

"Why didn't you tell me you stopped for the evening?"

His eyes travel over my hair that has now fallen across the shoulder that is twisted toward him.

"Because I was enjoying looking at you."

Completely annoyed at this stage, I reach for my clothes that are strewn across the floor. "Well, isn't that nice?" I mutter while I tug my sweater over my head.

"I thought so."

Bending down, I pick up my panties. "I can't believe you. Well, I'm not going to sit here just for you to look at."

"Well, this view is working pretty well, too."

Looking at him over my shoulder, I turn and attempt to cover myself with the pants and panties bunched in my hands. He stands and slowly walks closer. All the while, he's twirling a paintbrush in his fingers, which seems to be a habit that comes second nature to him.

Standing my ground, I look up at him when he stops only inches from me.

"I keep catching you without your pants on today," he muses.

His eyes look down to where I'm clutching the two items in front of me.

"Both times, need I remind you, are due to no fault of my own," I point out with as much dignity as I can find.

Reaching forward, he takes hold of the material in my hand and tugs gently. I don't want to let it go because I know that if I give in, he's going to do something. Something that will make me forget why I'm annoyed. Something that will turn me into a person I don't quite understand.

"Let go, Gemma."

Reluctantly, I obey, and he drops the clothing on the floor, leaving me in just my sweater.

"I stopped talking because *she* tells it much better, which you will discover when you read it."

I shiver at the mention of her, and I swallow as he brings his hand up, still holding the paintbrush in it.

"And I stopped painting because I realized you are missing something important."

My heart almost stops at the thought that this man finds me lacking in anyway. As ridiculous as it seems, I now want him to want me, no matter how wrong it is.

"Well, I'm sorry you felt that way." I stand there, staring up into eyes that are daring me to run.

I try not to flinch when he reaches down with the paintbrush, running the soft bristles across my vulnerable mound that is still naked and on display for him. I bite my bottom lip to keep from moaning, as he raises a brow and moves his hand lower, letting the brush bristles tickle and flirt their way down between my thighs.

Looking down our bodies, I find my eyes transfixed by the scene I'm witnessing. With his big fingers wrapped around the paintbrush, he gently continues to stroke it against my clit. I can't help but reach up with one hand to grip his inactive arm, steadying myself.

Widening my stance, I raise my eyes to his as he leans his head down and traces my bottom lip with his tongue.

"Gemma." He sighs against my mouth.

"Yes?"

"You like this, Gemma? The soft tickle of the brush against your clit?"

I don't know what he expects from me at this stage because I seem to have lost the ability of speech. All thought disappears as the brush dips lower, and I feel it stroke between my tender folds as he slides it through my juices. I wonder if he's going to do what I think. *Will he take it there?*

Panting heavily, my lips part against his, and I can't help myself from taking a bite of his full bottom lip. That's when I feel his depraved smile appear. He shifts his hand, and the brush disappears deep inside of me.

Gripping his arm tight, I know I'm going to leave nail marks. I moan and open my eyes to stare into green ones filled with decadence and desire. His desire is so hot that it's literally burning me, melting me from the inside out.

"Now, this is much more fun. Don't you think, Gemma?"

I blink at him, my breathing accelerating. He starts to slowly pull the paintbrush from my body, the bristles tickling me on their way out.

"This is the way I think I should always paint you—with a size twenty-four round brush in my hand as you coat the bristles."

Leaning down beside my ear, he asks me, "What do you think, Gemma? Do you like being *painted* this way?"

All I can think is that being painted by him feels a lot like being *fucked* by him, but he already knows that.

"Phillipe," I beg.

He thrusts the brush back up inside of me, and my hips start to flex against his sinful hand. I turn my head, so our mouths are almost touching. I feel myself getting impossibly wetter, and he licks his lips as his hand shifts again.

"This is wrong," I say, panting.

He grins demonically, nibbling my lip. "All the best things are," he agrees. He drags the brush out from my confused and needy body, and then he pushes it back up inside of me again. "Now, close your eyes, Gemma, and go with it. Who cares if it's wrong? How does it feel?"

I have no words for him as I stand there, grinding down on the brush that is now deep inside of me. All I can do is what he told me—*feel*.

He starts to thrust it in and out of me, quicker with each movement, and that's when I hear him softly humming the strings of *Pachelbel's Canon in D* in my ear. Everything about the situation is fucked up.

What he's doing and how I'm responding is beyond fucked up, but there's not one thing I can do when he bites my ear. I scream out my shockingly intense and inappropriate climax. Once again, I find myself unsure and ashamed of how I'm left feeling.

* * *

Phillipe took me back to the chateau after my performance and told me how moved he was when he watched me play. I could tell by the way he spoke to me that something was different.

He was touching and talking to me as though he had never seen me before. Maybe he hadn't.

My mother always told me that I came alive when I was on stage. Maybe that's what he saw.

"I knew you'd be amazing tonight, but, Chantel, I have no words." He paused and sighed. "You were simply breathtaking."

I kissed him softly. "Well, I don't want you to stop breathing."

His lips covered mine in an almost desperate kiss. When he pulled away, he stroked a hand down my cheek. "I don't plan to, not for a very long time, and neither will you."

He kissed me again, and almost as though he couldn't stand to be still, he lifted me off the ground, twirling me around as I laughed. He slowly lowered me down his body. "Will you come and stay with me, Chantel?"

Automatically, I went to say yes, *but he kissed me before I could even make a sound.*

"Don't say no, please. Tell me you'll move in with me? Let me see you when you awake. Let me be inspired every time I turn a corner, and you're there."

Laughing at his eagerness, I stroked my fingers over his impossibly high cheekbone. "My parents and Beau wouldn't understand why I would choose to stay here in France or why I would move in with you, a man I have just barely met."

He kissed my mouth, and I felt myself sliding under the waves again.

I asked him, "Is this wrong? Are we crazy?"

This time, his lips pressed against my forehead. He whispered, "Probably. But who cares? How does it make you feel?"

My answer was simple. It made me feel complete.

The next day I moved into the chateau.

Chapter Nine

Want

Day 8

I am ashamed to admit that I hid for two whole days. As I am lying here in bed, I continue to find myself reflecting on everything that happened that day up in his studio. *With a paintbrush, no less.*

I'm still trying to understand all that took place, but what it ultimately comes down to is that I invited Phillipe Tibideau into my body.

Well, in actuality, there was no inviting. It was more of a hostile takeover. He took over my senses, including any common sense I possessed before arriving here.

Reaching up to my mouth, I touch my lips and remember his on mine as he played my body so expertly out in the vineyard only a couple of days before.

One thing is certain. My judgment becomes compromised when it comes to Phillipe, and I have no immediate idea on how to stop myself from wanting to be compromised over and over again.

Today though, I want some answers from him. I want to know why people thought their relationship was unhealthy. *Why did the world turn against a man that only months earlier they had revered?*

The obvious answer seems too simple. There has to be more to it because the man I am coming to know doesn't fit with all that I have read.

Why wouldn't he defend himself publicly? Why wouldn't he save his name?

Twice now, I sat in a dark room—a room that for all intents and purposes is cut off from the world—and he blindfolded me. He had every opportunity to do as he pleased, yet he didn't touch me while in pose.

No, he waited until my sight was restored, and my attention was focused, focused solely on him before he…*what? Seduces me? Tempts me? Destroys me?*

That is the word that my mind keeps returning to—*destroyed*. That is the word that has been thrown around and used in conjunction with his name, but I don't feel destroyed. I feel alive. *I feel needy and hungry.*

Lying here with just my thoughts for comfort, I'm shocked to discover that I feel no shame in what we did, even though I probably should. In the face of reflection, I'm craving what I am seeing instead of running from it.

Suddenly, I understand Chantel's words because the wave has come, and I feel it pulling me under.

* * *

Want ~

This morning, I awoke to an empty bed, or to be more precise, an empty mattress.

Phillipe had decided that since we were spending so many hours in the studio, we should just bring a mattress up here. So, two days ago, he'd done just that and hauled his huge mattress up into the studio. It had all been very romantic when he'd placed it beneath the window. Kissing me, he had pulled me down onto it and told me that now he could touch me under the stars, just like he'd touched me under the sun.

That was not all that happened. This morning, I discovered what it means to truly want another. Want in every way that the word can be used. To need, crave, and desire another.

Phillipe had gotten up early. I could tell because there was no sun warming my skin, like it had every other morning. Rolling over, I reached my hand across the pillow beside me. I noticed that it had already cooled, so he'd been up for a while.

That was a shame because I had wanted him to make love to me this morning. I was restless.

Sitting up in the makeshift bed, I held the sheet to my breasts and called out to him. "Phillipe?"

When I got no answer, I lay back down and shut my eyes, waiting a few minutes before calling out for him again. "Phillipe?" This time, he responded from the foot of the mattress, surprising me with his sudden nearness.

"Yes?"

"Oh, there you are." I responded as, I felt the sheet being tugged on at my feet.

"Let go, Chantel," he instructed, his voice darkly persuasive.

Releasing my grip, I almost moaned as he pulled it away from my body. It slid down in a silky caress until I was left lying there naked, save for the beginning of the morning sun that was warming my body as it finally started to rise.

"Where were you?" I asked.

I waited for him to climb up my body, for his lips to find mine, but this time, it didn't come. He wasn't there.

"Phillipe?"

"I'm still here," he assured me. He offered up no other words.

When the intensity of the silence started to unnerve me a little, I questioned, "What are you doing?

And, if you aren't coming over here, can I have the sheet back?"

He chuckled low and deep. "No."

"No?" I queried.

I gasped when his warm hands circled my ankles and pulled me down the bed. My legs were now hanging over the end of the mattress, and they were spread wide enough that I could feel him kneeling between them.

I moved to sit up and touch him, but he told me, "No."

He placed a palm between my breasts, pushing me back onto the mattress. His hand slowly slid up to the base of my neck.

"No?" I asked again, like this was some kind of new erotic game we were playing. It was like a push and pull of want.

His big palm slid back down the center of my body, as his fingertips circled my navel before tracing a direct line down to my spread thighs.

"I want to slide my tongue between your legs and taste you. Can I do that?" he murmured as he dipped his finger down to flirt with my swollen folds.

"Yes."

I moaned as the tip of his finger pushed into my greedy pussy. I had woken up wanting him, and now, there he was, touching me the way he always did. He touched me in a way that made me think I was losing my mind.

"Will you let me paint you like this today?"

I swallowed and squeezed my eyes shut. Trying to gain purchase, I raised my right foot to the edge of the mattress, lifting my pelvis closer to his hand. I needed him deeper inside of me. I needed more.

He stopped touching me between my thighs and moved to grip my ankle.

"What's this?" he asked. He raised my leg and nipped at my anklebone. "Where do you think you're going?"

"I need—" I panted and moved my hands to my breasts.

As I started to rub my palms over my nipples, he groaned.

"So do I," he whispered.

Before I could even think about what was happening, he tugged me down, pulling me fully off the mattress, so I was straddling and kneeling over his naked lap. I could feel his steely hard cock now pressed between our bodies as I gripped his shoulders. I arched my hips closer to him, imploring him to come inside of me.

"I was going to take it slow this morning, Beauty." He growled in my ear as his hands stroked up my back.

One of them found its way into my hair, gripping it and tugging it, so my neck was bared to him. His lips found the spot right at the base of my throat, and he sucked on it hard, the sting of pain making my pelvis flex and buck, seeking what was throbbing between us.

"I was going to take it slow and easy, but I can't," he explained.

He shifted me, raising me up a little. I felt him reach down between us, and then the tip of his cock was there, pressing up against my drenched gate.

"I just fucking can't." He moaned into my chest as he pulled my body down.

His cock delved deep inside of me.

"Fuck." He groaned, holding me still on top of him.

My arms were wrapped around his neck, and my breasts had to be close to his mouth. When he told me to open my eyes, I felt his breath tickle across my nipples.

"What do you see?" he asked.

At first, I wasn't sure what he meant.

As he held me tight against his body, my breathing accelerated. My arms and thighs were now firmly wrapped around him, securing my pussy's grip on his frustrated hard cock.

"What do you mean?" I moaned. I was desperate now to move and satisfy this hunger.

"I mean, tell me what you see, the way you see it, in here." He emphasized his meaning by kissing my temple.

That was when it hit me. I knew exactly what he wanted me to do, and I wanted to do it. Smiling, I released my hold around his neck, bringing my hands up to his face where I started at his hairline. I smoothed my fingertips along his forehead and spoke to him as I went along.

"I see you frowning, maybe from concentration because your cock is in me, and you want to move..." I stopped when I heard his breath leave on a low groan. Then, I added, "Hard."

"Jesus." He cursed.

I felt my wet tight heat contract, fisting him as he throbbed inside of me. Bringing my hands down to trace lightly over his nose, I told him how sexy and strong I knew his face would be. As my fingers reached his lips, I stopped and leaned down, my tongue following the path of my finger.

In a low breath of air, I told him, "Your lips are sexy. The top one is thinner than the bottom, and it has a dip here in the center, like a bow. But it's this bottom lip that I dream about. This is what I imagine biting as you thrust into me over and over again. Your lips are perfect, and they drive me out of my mind every time you put them on me."

The anguished sound that rumbled from his throat thrilled me. I felt his hands slide down my back where he began tracing those imaginary marks on my skin again. F-holes, hmm. *Suddenly, I thought about his fingers and where they had flirted before, but he nipped on my fingertips, bringing my attention back to my task.*

"Where was I?" I questioned softly. I felt those same lips smirk against my fingers.

"I'm not sure, you naughty woman. You disappeared for a moment."

Feeling seductive and playful, I leaned over and whispered in his ear, "Yes. I was thinking about F-holes."

"Fuck me, Chantel. Hurry up."

I laughed softly at the sexual power I possessed. His hips shifted again, as he held on to his control, which I have to now admit was pretty impressive.

Going back to the game at hand, I traced my fingers down over his neck. "I see a strong neck with a sexy bump here, and I know that's what makes your voice so sinful and deep. Just hearing you say the word paint *makes me wet."*

"Really?"

"Hmm," I responded. I rocked my hips on his, feeling his shaft slide deeper.

Knowing that I was not going to be able to hold on much longer, I moved my hands over. "Strong shoulders and arms are wrapped around me. Your chest is solid, and it makes me want to bite it. Down here..." I paused as I smoothed my palm down his body, all the way to where he was nestled deep inside of me. "Down here, I see you and can feel you, hard, veiny, and throbbing, as you sit here so patiently. Your entire body is tense, and you feel like if I even breathe wrong, you might explode inside of me." Once again, I tightened my inner core around him, and I heard his harsh breath. "I see you taking me fast and hard any second now, and I can't wait."

That was when he moved. His whole body grew taut and tense as his muscles bunched, and I found myself lifted and pressed flat on my back as he wedged his cock even deeper inside of me.

"Guess you breathed wrong then because I can't wait another second to fuck you," he rasped out against my mouth as his hips took control of him.

It was as though he gave himself permission to let go, and everything came crashing down. He pushed my knees up high against my breasts. I couldn't be sure, but I thought he was kneeling as he thrust into me one time after another, each a little harder and a little deeper, stripping away any coherent thoughts I had left.

"You're so fucking unbelievable. How are you real?" he demanded with a forceful thrust. "Let me tell you what I see, Beauty."

His palms pressed my legs high and wide against my body, and on each solid flex of his hips, I felt my breasts shift and move.

"I see your eyes—those beautiful but frustrating eyes—looking up at me and offering everything I fucking want. I'm going to take it." He growled out in a voice I hardly recognized. "I'm going to take everything you're offering and more. I see your body laid out before me. You are open, vulnerable, and so fucking sexy that I can't help but want to own it."

My breath was out of control at this stage. His words and movements seemed to be stealing from me something I would never get back as his mouth touched mine. His lips, those sensual full lips, sucked my bottom lip into his mouth, nibbling on it before he bit it gently.

"I see you and I becoming one."

With my legs pulled up between his chest and mine, he drove his hips hard as I arched up.

"Now! I want you now!" I screamed out. As I heard him chuckle, I added boldly, "And don't tell me no."

"I wouldn't dream of it," he responded against my mouth.

His lips left mine, and his hands gripped my shins. He fucked me hard, just as I had predicted he would.

I'd heard about people falling in love, and I'd heard about lust. What I had never heard of was this all-consuming need to be inside another human being.

I felt this desperate compulsion to become one with him.

This was desire. This was to crave. This was what it felt like to want.

* * *

Closing the journal, I shut my eyes in a desperate attempt to control my breathing.

It is becoming increasingly clear to me that Chantel was just as enamored by Phillipe as he was by her. If this last journal entry was anything to go by, the relationship seemed to have taken a turn for Chantel after she moved in. That's when things started to get intense. It also appeared to be the moment when he changed and started to become more mysterious—well, to me anyway.

Another question I want answered is, *What happened that morning?*

Something had happened—that I'm certain of. Something had happened before he'd gone to lay down with Chantel. Something that had made him react in a needy way.

Yes, that's it. I stand, moving to the window, as I think about that for a moment. He seemed needy that morning with Chantel, almost as though he needed her to want him, and in the end, she did. *More than she ever had before.*

A knock on the bedroom door startles me out of my thoughts. I make my way over to it, pulling my robe around me. When I find Phillipe on the other side, I'm shocked. He hasn't been anywhere near my room since I arrived, and now, it has been two days since I have seen him.

As usual, the sight of him makes me agitated in some fundamental way. It usually starts with desire, before it quickly morphs into confusion.

He's dressed in jeans today. They seem odd on him because I'm used to seeing him in his usual black slacks, but they look good paired with the blue hoodie he's pulled on. His appearance is throwing me off-guard. Today, he just looks so normal, everyday All-American, but there's nothing normal or everyday about this man. He exudes the sensuality of his father's heritage as easily as he breathes.

His eyes track down over me, and I'm made very aware of what I'm not wearing. *My armor.* My business clothes.

"Good morning, Gemma. I thought I would come and get you myself. It seems you've been avoiding me," he greets as he steps forward, not waiting for an invitation of any kind.

Then again, this is his house. Why should he wait?

"Morning," I mutter.

I turn and watch him move farther into my room. I tightly clutch the robe around my body, and I have to actually stop myself from laughing at my own ridiculousness. The man has seen me naked. He's touched me naked.

"Was there something you needed?" I ask, waiting for him to face me.

When he gets to the bed, he finally turns and sits on the mattress with rumpled sheets. I don't know why, but seeing him sitting there, looking so ordinary, I find that I'm more nervous than I was the last time I was in his studio. At least, *that* Phillipe, I understand. *That* Phillipe, I expect.

"Well, there's plenty I *need,* Gemma, but I actually came down here to see if there's anything you need."

How is he able to zero in on the very thing I have been thinking about or wondering?

Lifting my head, I shake it and lie. It seems my best option. "Nope. Nothing," I tell him.

His lips purse, and his eyes narrow. "Are you positive?"

No, I'm not positive, I want to yell. *I have a hundred questions I want to ask you as well as a throbbing clit I want you to take care of,* but I'm determined not to mention any of that.

"You slept in late again this morning," he explains, looking at the clock.

My eyes shift to it as well, and I notice he's right. I told him I would meet him at 9 a.m., and it is now 10:15 a.m.

"Oh, I didn't sleep late. I was reading," I explain.

Too late, I realize his obvious trap. I scold myself internally.

"Oh? And how's that going?" he asks while he stands, moving toward me.

"Good," I answer. I try to be vague, but I know he's too intuitive.

He seems to know me too well, and he knows where I've read up to in the damn journal. When he stops in front of me, he reaches out a hand to stroke my hair. Standing my ground, I refuse to move away, and if I'm honest, I stay because I want him to touch me.

"It was much better than good," he assures me.

"I don't want to know," I tell him. *Lie number two.*

Bringing his free hand up to the other side of my face, he cups my cheeks, gently tugging me forward. I drop my hold on the robe and move my hands up to grip his wrists.

"Yes, you do," he whispers across my lips. "You always have a million questions, so ask me, Gemma. What do you want to know?"

Blinking up into his curious green eyes, I take a deep breath. I decide to take his advice, and I ask him what I want to know.

"Okay, what changed for you that morning?" Before I lose my nerve, I tack on the end, "Why were you so needy?"

His mouth tilts up on the side as he leans in to place a kiss against the corner of my mouth.

"Always asking me things I don't expect, Gemma."

"So, answer me," I press. My eyes stay focused on him, even though he is now extremely close, so keeping focus is becoming difficult.

He strokes one hand down the side of my neck, lowering it into the top of my robe. He pushes it aside, and looks down at what he's revealed. I'm wearing a sheer pastel-pink camisole and little silk boxers that match.

"You expect answers when you're dressed like that?" he asks.

I find myself smiling slightly. I remind him, "You came to my room. Don't try and change the topic. What made you needy that morning?"

His eyes come back up to focus on me. He drops his hands to my waist, pushing me back until I'm up against the door. Stepping in close to me, he places his palms on both sides of my head, caging me in.

"What makes any man needy, Gemma? A hot woman? Perhaps a naked one? Or maybe a woman dressed in pink silky pajamas?"

I shake my head against the door. "No. This felt different. You seemed like you wanted to prove something to her. You made her crazy."

"I didn't *make* her anything," he says in a cold tone.

It's so different from anything I have ever heard that I actually flinch away from him.

"What was that?" he questions me quickly.

"What was what?"

"You just flinched as though I was going to hurt you," he tells me slowly as he lowers his hands from the door.

I watch as his face goes from smoldering and sexy to cool and detached. Instantly, I want to apologize. I want to tell him that I didn't mean it. He can trust me, and I can trust him. *I know I can trust him, don't I?*

Closely, I watch him as he slips his hands into his pockets. He takes a step away from me, now averting his eyes from my body. Sighing, I reach down and wrap my robe around myself. I want to scream and tell him that I didn't mean it, but it's clear he doesn't want to talk about it.

"Can you please move away from the door?" he asks in a surly, gruff tone.

I can feel the distance already starting to spread between us. All the trust and all the moments leading up to this are gone in the blink of an eye.

"Can we talk about this for a minute? I still have questions." I try to appeal to his professional nature.

"Get the fuck out of the way, Gemma!" he yells at me.

Instantly, I move away from the door.

When he reaches it, he grips the handle. Turning his head to me, angry green eyes lock with mine.

"Things changed that morning because I spoke to Beau. He told me her parents were coming to visit. He explained how they wanted to meet me. They didn't trust me and didn't trust my intentions. They were coming to visit, and I knew they wanted to take her away." His voice sounds as though he is feeling it all over again. He sounds destroyed. "I wanted to make sure she didn't want to leave. I needed to make sure she believed in us, *trusted* us. So, I made sure she wanted me just as much as I wanted her."

"She stayed, didn't she?" I ask quickly, knowing he's about to leave because he's still pissed.

"She stayed…until she left," he replies cryptically.

Opening the door, he exits and leaves me standing in my room, wondering how the hell I can fix the trust I just broke.

Chapter Ten
ARMOR

I make my way up to the studio after lunch.

He didn't tell me to meet him there. He didn't invite me to come. But, after what happened this morning, I now have a burning compulsion to see him to set things straight.

As I get the door of the familiar studio, I can hear music floating through the air. The violin definitely holds a new fascination for me, and I can see I am not alone. It is obvious it also pulls at Phillipe in a way that I still don't quite comprehend.

Stepping across the threshold, I look around the room and spot him sitting on a stool behind the large canvas that is propped in its usual spot, up on the easel over by the window.

He hasn't seen me yet, so I'm careful not to make any noise as I make my way farther into the room that is dappled by the sun's rays.

I can see his feet resting on the floor. He's taken off his shoes from this morning, and he's rolled up the bottom of his jeans. His hair looks rumpled and disturbed, and his mouth is pulled into a serious line that makes his entire face look different. He appears annoyed, frustrated, and maybe even a little bit sad.

I know that I ruined whatever trust I had gained when I let my preconceived ideas and opinions of him take hold of me for just a millisecond this morning. Now, as I stand here, watching him move his brush across the smooth surface with his focus aimed intently on what he is doing, I can't help but be disappointed in myself.

I am *always* objective in my job. I have never been one to let other people's opinions influence the way I interview or talk to a potential witness or subject of a story. This morning, though when I had let previously reported stories feed my moment of doubt , I did, and in turn, I lost his trust. It's now imperative that I regain it.

"I know you're standing there, Gemma." His somber voice floats across the silence.

Clasping my hands in front of myself, I make my way farther into the room. I stop behind the canvas, directly in his eye line.

For some reason, I feel the need to whisper. "I didn't want to disturb you."

He stops his brush stroke as his annoyed green eyes rise to meet mine over the top of the painting he is working on. "Well, you have."

I grimace for a moment, telling myself not to let him intimidate me. I'm here to do a job. I can't let an argument of a personal nature come between us. *Us? Is there an* us *now?*

Well, there is certainly a professional *us*. The other day there was a personal moment, but I cannot not let one, slight misunderstanding ruin my chance to tell this story. To take away my opportunity to know what happened, and to let the world know there was more to this tragedy than what we'd all been told. Or, at least, that is what I am hoping to discover.

"Well, I didn't mean to. I just wanted to come and see when you next want to work on the piece."

His eyes leave mine to focus back on what is in front of him.

"What are you working on?" I ask, trying to get him to talk to me. It becomes immediately obvious though that I've said the wrong thing.

"Nothing of importance." He dismisses me coolly, placing the brush on the table beside him. "You want to ask me questions, Gemma? Sit and ask. I'm here, you're here, and that's all that's required, correct?"

I clench my jaw, annoyed at his terse words. I make my way to the small desk I've been working at and pull out the chair. I turn it and sit, facing him. The canvas is between us. I'm frustrated at the obstruction, but I know he wouldn't move it, even if I ask.

"What was the decision behind the name of the second painting in the series, *Armor*?"

I fall silent as the soft sounds of the violin fill the air. I almost ask him to turn it off. *Isn't this hard enough as it is without* her *playing in the background?* I know deep down in the pit of my stomach that it is *she* who is currently providing the somber soundtrack.

"Not where I thought you were going to go," he tells me, shifting his eyes to the painting between us.

I settle back in the chair at his words, and I lift my pen to the pad. "Oh? And what exactly were you expecting?"

As I sit there, waiting for his response, I'm not really sure what I'm even expecting at this stage. I know I'm not going to have to wait long when Phillipe stands and moves around the easel, walking across the space toward me.

I uncross my legs, placing both my hands on my lap, as he stops in front of me. He's close enough that our pants are touching. He's close enough that I have to tilt up my head at an awkward angle to look at him.

"I was expecting you to ask about that day. You know, the one everybody talks about? The one you keep avoiding, even though you keep thinking about it," he accuses softly. He turns, walking away from me, going back in the same direction he came. "You surprise me, Gemma. It seems you already have an image of me all worked out in that pretty little head of yours. So, why not try to confirm it as quickly as possible and be on your merry way?"

Standing up, I throw the notepad onto the chair and take a fuming step forward.

"You know what? You're right, okay? I screwed up. I let other people's views and opinions filter in for a moment, and it clouded my own judgment."

Keeping a close eye on him, I try to remember to breathe as he turns slowly on his bare feet. His eyes narrow on me while he takes a closing step back in my direction.

"And what did other people tell you?"

Swallowing once, I remain silent. I don't know how to tell him some of the things people have said. They're cruel and malicious. I have no desire to repeat them, especially when I don't have any way of knowing if it's true. I can only follow my instincts, and even though they are a little jumpy right now, I find myself needing to believe that they wouldn't lead me astray.

"I don't want to talk about that."

Taking that final step forward, eliminating the space between us, Philippe is now bare toes to booted feet with me. I can feel his body heat emanating from him, and his hair has fallen haphazardly into his eyes. Placing his hands behind his back, he bends forward, almost as though he is about to kiss me.

Instead, he stops a breath away from my mouth. "Well, what would you like to talk about, Gemma?"

Refusing to step back, I tilt up my face to him. "I told you. *Armor,* the second pose you painted of Chan—"

"Shhh," he coaxes, those full lips seductively requesting my silence.

Bringing up his right hand, he places a silencing finger against my lips, and I can feel my heart start to beat in overtime.

"Listen," he tells me.

Closing my mouth, I listen. I suspect he didn't stop me to listen to the music. I think it was more to keep me from saying *her* name out loud. Keeping my eyes on his, I watch in fascination as they seem to cloud over and get darker as the music builds. The tempo climbs toward a breathtaking peak before it crashes over and tumbles back down to the soft strains filtering through the air.

"Incorporating the violin into *Armor* came to me one morning when I saw her right over there," he told me, reaching out to grip my arms.

He turns me, and I'm now facing the open window.

His mouth moves to my ear, his voice deep and hypnotic. "She mustn't have been able to sleep because I remember waking to her standing there, just as she had left my bed, completely naked. Her skin was perfect." He strokes his hands over my shoulders and down my arms. "Pale and soft, and as she stood there, she held her violin to her cheek like she would a lover's hand, like my hand."

I feel myself holding my breath as he paints the scene before us. It's crazy, but I actually feel as though I can see her, almost as though she's here in the room with us.

"Her hair was rumpled from my hands the night before, and when she left it out, it hit her shoulders around here." He demonstrates by touching a finger to my shoulder blade.

"She looked like an angel." He lets out a soft exhale. "Like someone had plucked her from the sky and placed her here in my studio. She didn't seem real."

His breath is warm against my ear and neck as his fingers trail down my arms to my hands where he entwines our fingers gently. I close my eyes and imagine what he is telling me.

"She stood there and played for at least an hour, maybe more. That was the moment, right there. I knew I had to paint her with the violin. It was like an extension of her. What better way to do that than capture her naked as the day she was born with the object that brought her to life?"

As the question fades into the now silent room, I feel him release my hands, and I turn to see him walking back to the painting he was working on. I cross my arms over my chest, feeling cold and alone.

"So why call it *Armor*? If the violin is part of her, why name it as though it's a shield? That painting is so soft. I still don't understand."

I'm confused. Chantel seemed like such a strong individual. She was a woman with a handicap. A lot of people would let that hold them back, but she didn't. No, if anything, she exceeded everyone's expectations. She became an accomplished musician who moved to France and became the model for a now world-renowned artist. That did not seem like a woman who needed protection, yet in the end—

"No, you're looking at it wrong," he tells me from where he has now sitting back down, resuming his painting from earlier. "*Armor* as in the violin *makes* her stronger. This painting represents a quiet inner strength."

I feel my mouth form an O-shape at his explanation.

"She was the strongest woman I have ever known."

As I move over to the door about to leave, I make sure to ask, "When should I come back?"

It's clear he wants to be left alone.

"When you're ready to pose, Gemma. Tonight, we get to see how strong you can be. Or perhaps you think you need to arrive wearing the armor, hmm?"

Annoyed at his reference to my lack of trust and bravery, I say nothing as I turn, leaving him to his paints and his ghosts.

* * *

Handling Things ~

Phillipe convinced me to pose full-side profile nude today.

It had taken some persuasion on his behalf, and in the end, a compromise had been reached.

"Here. How about you sit over here?" he instructed as he took my palm in his.

Laughing softly, I followed to where he led me. "So, tell me again. Why must I first remove all of my clothes to appear strong?"

I heard him move in close to me before his lips touched mine. "Because I like looking at the full picture, and, Chantel, your body is a work of art."

"You just like keeping me naked," I told him as I felt him move away from me.

"Well that, too. Okay, so sit down here. Yeah, that's perfect. Face the wall, so I can capture you from the side. Now, place the bout of Diva on your crossed legs and cradle her curves, so the handle is resting between your breasts. There. That's perfect."

The cool surface of the violin's handle fits nicely against my chest.

"Wow, the way your breasts and hips look from this angle is a thing of beauty."

"I feel kind of ridiculous," I told him, licking my bottom lip as my nipples hardened in the cool morning air. "Are you going to paint me real to life?"

"Of course," he mumbled in the way he always did when he was concentrating on a piece.

"I mean, are you going to paint my nipples hard, like they are right now?"

The room went silent until he cleared his throat. "Stop trying to distract me."

"Is that what I'm doing, Phillipe? Distracting you with my hard nipples?"

He chuckled before making a promise. "If you behave for thirty minutes, I'll let you take a break."

It was funny because when he first told me about this idea he had to paint me, it had been one picture. Now, it had turned into two, but if I knew Phillipe, it would end up being more like ten or eleven. Who knew? Maybe he'd never stop. He was always telling me he could look at me all day.

"Okay, I think I can manage that for thirty minutes."

"Good, good," he answered in that far away voice again.

Around thirty minutes later, he told me I could break pose, so I lowered the violin to the floor gently. I stood and made my way over to where he was, uncaring now of my nudity. When I got there, I felt him make a move to stand. He must have turned to face me because I felt a fingertip trace down the curve of my breast to my straining hard nipple.

"Hmm, I like painting you like this," he told me, fingering my sensitive flesh.

"Will you do something for me?" I asked.

I waited patiently for an answer. He took a moment, but I thought that was because he was too busy playing with my naked breasts.

"Phillipe?"

"Yes, Beauty, anything."

I reached up and gripped his wandering finger. "Can you show me what you've painted?"

"How? Tell me how," he urged.

"Turn around," I instructed. I smiled when I felt him move away from me.

Reaching out, I placed my arms around him and ran my palms down his arms that were left bare from the T-shirt rubbing against my skin. The hair on his arms tickled and brushed against my palms as I stroked down his biceps to his forearms, where I could comfortably reach.

As I stood plastered to his body, my sensitive breasts against his back, I rested my cheek against his shoulder blade. "Now, trace your hands over the paint. Trace me the way you saw me just now."

Closing my eyes, I let his body lead mine as his hands and arms started to move.

Just as his fingertips must have touched the canvas, in a voice that sounded slightly strained, he told me softly, "This will ruin the image. Are you going to sit again tomorrow?"

I grinned into his back, as I turned my head and opened my mouth, biting his shoulder blade gently. "Yes, I'll sit for you again tomorrow, and the next day, and the day after that. I'll sit for you every day for as long as you want me to."

He took a deep breath, and my heart sped up after he replied, "So forever."

Taking my left hand, I ran it back up his arm, and then I removed it, bringing it to his side where I smoothed my palm down over his abdomen to the edge of his shirt. That was when his right hand started to move.

"Here, this is your right shoulder," he told me as he ran his hand over the wet paint.

I stroked my fingers across his lower belly, flirting with the edge of his jeans.

"What are you doing, Chantel?" he questioned as he dropped his hand from the canvas.

I could feel him getting ready to turn and face me, so I requested softly, "No. Don't turn around."

"Why not?" he asked.

Honestly, all I could think of was that I wanted him to experience this just like me.

"I want you to be blind for a moment. Just feel me, hear me."

Moving slightly back from him, I brought my right hand down to join my left under his shirt. He let out a deep breath.

"Do you want me to take my shirt off, just like you?"

"No," I told him right away.

I felt him shift his feet a little wider to get a steadier stance.

"I like rubbing my nipples against the material. It feels so good."

"Christ, Chantel. What the fuck has gotten into you?"

Slowly, I rubbed myself against his back. It was true. The material felt amazing as it abraded my stiff pointy tips. I could already feel my pussy start to moisten.

"I don't know," I confessed.

Reaching the button on his jeans, I undid it, only fumbling a little as I slipped my right hand inside, rubbing my palm against his pulsating cock.

"Oh, fuck yeah." He groaned.

I smiled against his back. "Do you like that?" I asked, just the way he always did with me.

"Hell yes." He groaned again. "Grip it, Chantel. Take me in your hand."

Not wanting to disappoint him, I unzipped his jeans and pushed my other hand inside, freeing him from the confinement of only his denim.

Wrapping my palm around his hot cock, I stroked him slowly from base to tip. His hips flexed and bucked forward, seeking the warm downward slide of my palm. Gliding my hand over his sensitive skin, I turned my face into his back and took another bite of his shoulder as I brought my hand back up in a tight squeeze.

"Yes." He hissed and demanded, "Again."

Removing my hand from him, I told him softly, "Make it wet."

"Huh?" He grunted.

I took great delight in the confusion I could hear in that single distracted noise. Bringing my hand up to where he could see it, I told him again, "Make it wet, Phillipe."

This time, he seemed to get my meaning. He moved to the left, and the next thing I felt was his hand clasping mine with cool liquid. Somehow, I knew it was paint.

"What color?" I questioned.

"Are you fucking serious?" He groaned, his hand moving mine back to his impatient cock. He wrapped our fingers around him, as he punched his hips forward on a tormented growl, letting his head fall back.

"What color, Phillipe?"

"Red," he hissed out. "Fiery fucking red."

"Perfect," I purred against his trembling back, as I resumed my slow torment.

Over and over, I stroked him. Each delicious tug of his stiff member rendered a strained groan from deep inside his chest as his hot palm assisted my movements.

"So fucking good." He cursed as his hips flexed and his muscles bunched, thrusting forward into our palms. His flesh was now burning hot, rubbing against my hand hard.

"Bite me again, just like before," he demanded.

I smiled against him. I teased him, nibbling softly. "Like this?" I reached up now with my free hand, stroking it along his abdominal muscles that were straining with each controlling motion of those powerful hips.

"No," he forced out between his gritted teeth.

"No?"

"Chantel," he told me in warning.

I ran my hand up to his nipple while I rubbed my own against his back. His breathing hitched as he grunted in a voice so husky and deep that I could swear he must have stroked my pussy because it contracted and moistened.

He demanded, "Put your fucking teeth on me, Chantel."

How could I resist that? I couldn't, and I didn't.

Instead, I bit him hard, harder than I would have expected, as I stroked and squeezed his cock as fast and rough as I could. It must have been what he was waiting for because his palm gripped my hand and stilled it as I felt his big body twitch and shudder while he groaned my name.

* * *

Snapping the journal shut, I place it on the bed beside me, annoyed and frustrated. Every word I read from her pulls me deeper into their relationship. The more I read, the more I find myself craving the knowledge. *What is it about them that I find so intriguing? Is it the fact that I am reading something so very private?* I feel as though I am violating their love in some way, yet I can't help myself from wanting to know more. No, I *need* to know more.

Sliding down the bed, I rest my head on the pillow and stare at the ceiling, remembering the image of Phillipe as I saw him only a few days ago. Naked, hard, and stroking himself so violently that I thought he must have been hurting himself. *What did he tell her? Put your fucking teeth in me.*

Fucking hell, that was so damn sexy.

I sit, letting my legs fall over the edge of the bed. He wants to start painting *Armor* tonight. The painting is the second one of the collection, and it's the first full nude shot, where you can see a portion of my front side. I'm not sure how I feel about it.

Standing, I make my way over to the mirror that's in my room, and I stare at my reflection. There, looking back at me, are wide green eyes. Raising my hand, I grip the hairband holding my hair away from my face and pull it out, releasing my blonde hair. It tumbles down around me, so I shake it back from my shoulders, looking at the picture I present. I'm trying to see all that he sees.

Reaching down to the bottom of my top, I lift it and pull it over my head, leaving myself standing in my nude-colored lace bra. Bringing my hand to the right strap, I finger the material and run it down to the curve of my breast, watching the reflection of my nipple as it hardens.

It's strange inspecting myself, seeing my body change as I feel it happen. Moving to unclasp my bra, I take a breath as I pull the cups away from my body and let it fall to the ground. I'm left standing there, naked from the waist up, trying to see myself objectively.

My breasts aren't huge. A small C-cup makes them full enough that I usually have to wear a bra, but sometimes, if I want to dress up for someone special, I can go without.

Below my right arm, where my breast curves out, I have a small beauty mark that I have hated for as long as I can remember. As I stand here now, looking at myself, I find that I don't mind it. I think it adds a certain character to me.

Lifting my hand, I gently brush my red-painted fingertips against my nipple and let out a small gasp. Biting my bottom lip, I watch my fingers in the mirror as I trace them around the sensitive tips. I remember Chantel talking about how good Phillipe's shirt felt against her nipples. *Probably as good as my fingers now feel against mine.*

I pinch and tug them between my thumb and index fingers, pulling the tight little tips. I sigh as I feel my pussy start to moisten. Shocked by my own brazen behavior, I can't seem to tear my eyes away from myself.

That's when something in the room changes, and I feel like I'm going a little crazy. I swear I'm seeing dark hair now, falling over my shoulder. Instead of my red-tipped fingers, I'm seeing long elegant ones with blunt-cut nails tracing over my body.

Feeling my lips part, I watch as the hands in front of me cup my breasts and squeeze. I'm mesmerized by the scene. The hands gliding over my body have morphed into hands I know. They are hands that shock me.

They're hands I have seen before, hands I've studied, hands that have created music I've listened to, and hands I have just read about.

"Ah!" I groan as my nipples are plucked and twisted. They are pinched hard and teased. As my eyes are transfixed on the mirror, I can feel myself becoming increasingly wetter.

"Fuck." I pant as my right breast is squeezed, and my left nipple is pulled. Crossing one leg over the other, I now close my eyes and imagine beautiful, pale talented hands caressing me. I can hear music flowing over me, *violins*, and I can feel my aching wet core clenching with each moment of my pleasure.

Arching my back and pushing my breasts forward, hands now squeeze my supple curves, I swear someone whispers, "Do you like that?"

As my climax crashes into me, I find myself calling out a name I never thought to say in a moment such as this.

"Chantel."

Chapter Eleven
COURAGE

That night, Phillipe stands at the kitchen window with a cup of coffee in his hand, staring out to the lit arbor. He can see Gemma out under the large branches, sitting on the bench he placed down there many months ago.

He wonders about Gemma Harris. *What does she really think about everything she's heard?* She doesn't really give him a good indication of her opinion either way.

One thing he does know is that, although she's attracted to him, there's definitely a wary and suspicious side of her when it comes to who he is. *Oh, she lets me into her body, but there is no way that the woman who flinched away from me this morning trusts me.*

Feeling a frown and a headache coming on, he places his empty cup in the sink, turning to make his way up the stairs. When he reaches the *Rhapsody* painting hanging on the wall, he stops for a moment and allows himself to look over *her*.

Taking in a deep breath, he sighs. As he lets it out softly, he shakes his head. "What am I doing?" he asks out loud. He knows he won't get an answer, but he feels the desire to voice his request. Reaching out, he strokes his finger down the sweet curve of flesh on the canvas before dropping his hand as though the memory burned him. Turning on his heel, he makes his way to the studio.

Tonight, he is painting *Armor*. He is painting strength. He needs to remind himself of that, especially when familiar words keep running through his mind. *Don't let them make a villain out of you.*

She is still in his head.

Spreading the drop cloth out under his easel, he moves to where he wants Gemma to stand and angles a soft spotlight on the area. Everything is ready. All he needs is her. The only problem is that he has no clue which woman he's referring to at that precise moment.

* * *

I glance up to the studio window and watch silently as a light is turned on in the west turret. After what happened this morning, I am unsure of how this evening will go.

I know what Phillipe wants from me. He made that clear earlier today. I am finding it hard to garner the courage I need to actually go up there, remove my top, and stand before him—a man who, for very good reasons, is still annoyed at me.

Standing I look down at the bench and the inscription, *Love looks not with the eyes,* I try not to envy a woman who had eyes she could not see from. Because at this very moment, I would do anything not to have to stand before his perceptive and annoyed gaze.

Oh well, best to get it over with. I make my way inside and upstairs to extend my trust with the hope that he will give his in return.

When I reach the studio, I don't wait for permission. I simply make my way inside, determined to prove to him that I can be strong—*just as strong as Chantel.* As I move through the room, I ask myself, *When did this become a competition to me?* No matter how long I think about that, I still have no answer, and now, the question itself is starting to disturb me. Noticeably, there is no music tonight, just silence. This, for some reason, pleases me.

"You came." His familiar voice travels across the room. "I wasn't sure you would."

Straightening my shoulders, I try to remind myself that he is *not* referring to this afternoon when I brought myself to a spectacular climax, fantasizing about *her. No, that dark secret still remains solely mine.*

I make my way over to where he obviously wants me to stand, and I turn to him. "Of course, I'm here. This is why you invited me to the chateau, correct?"

He tilts his head to the side. Seemingly out of nowhere, he asks, "What's different tonight?"

"Excuse me?" I query, tugging on the bottom of my shirt, a little nervous now.

This man constantly has me questioning myself. It's hard to believe that I ever had a moment where I was comfortable enough to let him inside of my body—unless, of course, I hallucinated that whole episode in the vineyard as well. With the way my mind keeps playing tricks on me, it would not surprise me.

"What is different?" he repeats, moving toward me. His long legs cross the space in no time at all. "You seem defensive tonight, like you're out to prove something…or perhaps you're *hiding* something."

Swallowing hard, I clasp my fingers together, fidgeting with my nails.

"I'm not hiding anything. How absurd," I tell him.

I don't feel he's convinced because those shrewd sage-colored eyes narrow as he licks his bottom lip.

"Maybe I'm defensive because you challenged me this afternoon. *Will you be wearing your armor?* Does that ring a bell?" I snap in a tone far more bitchy than I expect.

His silence is unnerving, and his stare is unwavering as he slowly shakes his head. "No. That's not it. You're hiding something."

Clenching my jaw, I stay stubbornly quiet until he finally turns and walks back to where he set up his paints.

"So, take off all my clothes then? We can't work in sections?" I query, trying to decide what he wants.

"No we can't work in sections. You need to remove it all."

"Can't I leave my pants on until you are ready for that part?" I demand instantly.

One of his eyebrows goes up as he states very calmly, "No, Gemma, you know better. The piece is full nude—unless, of course, you aren't brave enough. I don't understand the problem. I have seen it all before."

I curse my own insecurities. I'm not sure if I'm ready to be so vulnerable and so exposed to him again. I reach down, unbuckle my pants, and unzip them quickly, pushing them to the floor. I kick them to the side with a little more force than necessary.

"I suppose you need these off as well?" I question in a surly tone.

Phillipe looks at my fingers, which are touching the lace of my white panties. "Of course."

I roll my eyes. It figures he would find a way to make me feel like I just asked a stupid question. Reaching down to the bottom of my shirt, I start to unbutton it, when I realize he is still standing there. He patiently watches me with intense eyes, pulling his lips into a pensive line.

I raise my eyes to his and decide to try and lighten the mood by joking. "So, I'm just supposed to bare my soul to you?"

In the blink of an eye, he darkens the moment. "Well, you're asking me to bare mine."

Contemplating his terse reply, I reach back to undo the clip of my bra. "That's true in a sense, but what *you* are doing and what I am about to do are two completely different things.

His eyes have moved, focusing on my breasts and my arms, which are paused behind my back for the moment.

"Yet each of those two things requires an enormous amount of trust," he reminds me.

I can see that he's trying to teach me a lesson—something along the lines of, *you blew my trust this morning by thinking I would hurt you, so take off your shirt, and maybe I'll forgive you.*

"So, Gemma, are you willing to trust me?"

I unhook the bra and slowly lower it, revealing my aching breasts to him. Moving my arm to the side, I drop the piece of lingerie on the floor.

"Yes, I am. Now, my question remains. Are you going to trust me?"

* * *

Courage ~

Tonight didn't go very well.

My parents arrived at my uncle's two nights ago. They had made a "special" trip in order to meet the man I had moved in with. They wanted to meet Phillipe, so we went over to Uncle Beau's home.

I'm so annoyed right now because I feel like it has somehow put a wedge between us. He didn't say much at all when we got home, and right now—well, I don't even know where he is.

He left around ten minutes ago and told me he needed to go for a walk.

He's never just left. I suppose this is our first fight. I keep reassuring myself that couples do that...right?

All I can think about is how upset he was.

"What do you want me to say, Chantel? That did not go well," he told me.

"I'm sure they didn't mean to make it sound the way it did." I tried to reassure him as we made our way into the kitchen, but honestly, I knew that my parents weren't being very welcoming.

"They accused me of brainwashing you, and you just stood there!"

"I did not!" I defended while I tried to convince myself that I didn't.

"I hardly think 'Mom, I wanted to go,' was very convincing, especially after I just told them that I would look after you and I couldn't help but want you close to me." His voice trailed off as if defeated. "How could you let them make you question us, Chantel? They basically told you to leave, and when you said nothing—well, you might as well go and pack your bags."

"Phillipe," I pleaded.

He brushed by me. Suddenly, I felt more alone than I ever had before.

"Yes?"

"Don't leave like this," I begged. I hated that he was feeling this way, and I hated that I couldn't express how I felt.

"I just need to be alone for a while. I'm going for a walk." His voice softened as he asked me, "Will you be here when I get back?"

How could he think to question it? How had I made him question me?

"Of course. Where else would I go?"

I never received an answer. Instead, all I heard was the kitchen door as it slammed shut, making me jump where I stood. Why hadn't I told my parents everything I felt? I didn't understand my own reluctance and that annoyed me. Maybe it was because I didn't want them to judge me—judge me like they had him. That didn't seem fair.

It makes me wonder what kind of coward I am. I'm an adult. I'm a grown woman who found a man she loves. How dare they make me question that and how dare I let them make me.

I need to find him. I need to go and find him and bring him back.

Bring him back to me, to us, and to the world we belong in. I need him to come back and paint me as I am—strong, courageous, and brave.

Armor—that's what I need when I deal with my parents from now on. I need a suit of armor and the courage to stand behind my convictions to fight for what I want. And, what I want is Phillipe.

* * *

I can feel my bare nipples harden in the cool air. They almost seem to be begging for attention, like they remember what they received earlier, and they want it again. I slip my fingers into my panties and slide them down over my hips, all the while, keeping my eyes on the silent man across from me.

I concentrate on Phillipe as he makes his way to the shelves on the wall. He crouches down to reach into the bottom. I'm so focused on his broad back and amazing ass that I don't even notice what he is holding in his hand until he stands. It's an old music case.

Almost instantaneously, it feels as though the oxygen in the room has been removed. I can't breathe as he stops at the desk just a few feet from me. He gently places the case down. Immediately, I know what is in there. He doesn't have to tell me. As I stand there silently staring at him, my brain is screaming, *Why? Why on earth does he have Chantel's violin? How?*

It has been reported that the astronomically expensive Stradivarius, which had been passed down for years through the Rosenberg family, was never recovered. It is still reported as missing to this day.

I have no idea how he has it, but I know that the instrument inside that case is a violin. I know it is Diva.

I'm also very aware of what he's going to ask me to do. I have seen the collection and studied each piece for hours on end. None of that matters though, as the locks on the old music case are flicked open.

As he lifts the lid, my eyes are automatically drawn to the contents, like a moth to a flame. This right here is the other piece in the huge, distorted puzzle that is them, and it is about to be handed to me.

He reaches into the case, which is lined with what looks like red silk. He lovingly—yes, lovingly is the only way I can describe the way he is touching the instrument—cradles Chantel's Stradivarius as he removes it from its resting place.

My mouth falls open as he turns and walks toward me. He's cradling it as though it is his child. When he holds it out to me, I look at him as if he is insane, and I begin shaking my head.

"Apparently, *I* am going to trust you. Here, take this."

Looking at the violin he's now handing to me, I am very aware, all of a sudden, that I 'm standing here naked. And yet somehow, that is not the most bizarre part of this equation. No, the most bizarre part is the fact that he thinks I can and will be responsible for hanging on to an instrument that is not only worth more than a million dollars but is also reportedly a missing family heirloom. Not to mention, it means more to him than the entire house we are both standing in.

Shaking my head again, I raise my eyes from the beautiful Diva. "No. I can't use that to model with."

"Here. You need it to model with," he tells me, pushing it closer to me.

I literally step away from him, refusing to take a hold of what I essentially know to be his heart.

"No." I refuse again. "Don't you have a spare one?" I realize how stupid that sounds but so does the fact that he wants me to hold *her* violin.

He steps closer to me and reaches out. He takes my right hand in a firm grip and tugs me to him. Placing the neck of it in my hand, I have no choice but to close my fingers around it tightly. I'm afraid I might drop it, smashing it into little pieces.

"See, it won't hurt you," he reassures as he steps in closer. "You seem spooked tonight. That's what it is." Bending down until our noses are almost touching, he asks, "What happened this afternoon, Gemma?"

Denial falls smoothly off my tongue. "Nothing happened."

"You're lying."

Raising my head, I bring the violin up close to my body. "How do you want me to hold this?"

Strong, nimble fingers grip my wrist where my pulse is beating a rapid tattoo. "Once you are seated facing the wall, cross your legs, rest the bottom on your calves, and let the handle nestle between these beautiful breasts of yours." As he finishes that provocative statement, he reaches up to run the back of his fingers gently over the curve of one of the breasts in question.

I gasp. They are still sensitive from earlier. My eyes move up to meet his. As he repeats the move, I clamp my bottom lip between my teeth.

That's when a seductive grin appears. "I like teeth," he tells me before turning on his heel, making his way back to the easel. He's letting me know that, all along, he's been aware of the sensual journal entry I read earlier, and he knows, somehow, that I'm hiding a secret.

What he doesn't know is that secret involves a dark-haired woman with talented hands. My secret involves the woman he so obsessively loved, a woman he himself has admitted to wanting close by *at all times.*

Well, that woman has crept into my mind. Somehow, she has stolen my very sanity because now I want her hands on me. *I begged for her to touch me* until I, too, lost myself in the beauty of a fantasy—a fantasy I still don't fully understand.

* * *

She is aroused. As she sits there holding the violin, Phillipe can tell that Gemma is one-hundred percent aroused. Her breasts are beautifully flushed, and her nipples are nice and tight.

When he handed her the violin, her eyes dilated, and he could have sworn that he could smell her arousal and he is reminded of the passage she must have been up to. A moment in time that had literally changed him as a person.

He wants to talk to her about what she read.

Once he is behind the easel, he looks over to where she sits. The violin's handle is resting against her skin, and her hands are holding it with so much care that he can't help but feel moved by her attentiveness.

"So, tell me, Gemma. What did you learn this afternoon?"

Her eyes focus on him, so he lowers his on purpose, giving her the space she might need to open up.

"I'm here to ask you questions, not the other way around."

Raising only his eyes, he tells her, "Well, you are being so quiet, so I'm trying to start an open forum."

"Well, I don't need one," she tells him firmly. "If you weren't so disagreeable this afternoon, I wouldn't feel this way."

"And how do you feel?"

"Confused," she admits immediately.

"What are you confused about?" He genuinely wants to know.

"You. Her. Both of you together," she tells him, licking her lips.

She shifts where she is sitting, and he wonders for a moment if she is aroused by what she just said. *I believe she is.*

"What is it about us together that's confusing to you?"

"I don't know." She quickly adds, "That's a lie, and I promised myself I wouldn't do that."

"What? Lie?"

"Yes." She nods. "You seem so different through her eyes."

Silence stretches between them as the weight of her words float across the air.

"Interesting choice of words. How do I seem different?"

He watches her red fingertips caress the side of the violin as she continues looking down at it.

"With her, you seem…happy."

Phillipe acknowledges that with a nod. He explains simply, "I was happy, happier than I had ever been. I guess it showed." He stops and asks, "What do I seem to be now?"

Gemma turns her head and looks at him with narrowed eyes. "Angry, sad, hurt."

Placing his brush on the easel, he moves over to her. He's tired of not being able to do what he wants, and right now, he wants to touch.

"Angry?" he asks, stopping and crouching down before her.

She raises her eyes to his. "Yes, that day I saw you, you were in your room and..."

Phillipe cocks his head and waits. *Let her say it.*

"And you were hurting yourself. Why? Why are you hurting and punishing yourself if you didn't do anything to be sorry for? I don't understand. I'm confused."

Reaching out a finger, Phillipe traces the pad of it against the turgid tip of her ripe breast.

"Have you ever had a moment of passion that was so deep and so fucking perfect that you know you will never have it again?" he asks.

Gemma's eyes move to his lips before shifting back to his eyes.

"Have you?" he presses.

She shakes her head as she returns the question. "Have you?"

Phillipe feels the side of his mouth pull up into an ironic smirk. "Yes, and no matter what I do, I can't seem to capture it again."

* * *

I'm holding the violin so tight that I start to think I might accidentally crush it. *What is he trying to tell me?* He is so close to me that I can smell the scent that always seems to cling to him. It's making my head spin.

"I don't understand." I finally manage to push out of my mouth.

His right hand moves to stroke my hair, gently tracing it to the tip where he twirls it around his finger. His heated stare wanders all over my face but never dips below my neck. I can't explain why, but it makes me even more aroused that he doesn't feel the need to outright stare at the obvious. It's almost as if he has memorized it already.

Dropping the ends of my hair, Phillipe stands and walks around my body, tracing the tip of his finger against my shoulders, until he's behind me where he kneels down. I can feel the fabric of his clothes pressed against my back and bare skin.

"What I mean, Gemma, is that I've experienced a moment so perfect that it remains unequaled."

I think about that for a minute as a shiver runs down my spine, starting where his warm fingertips are touching the base of my neck.

"So, what you're saying is that because the moment was perfect, you can't feel that pleasure anymore?" I try to make sense of his words while his fingers trace across the curve of my shoulder and move down my arm.

"What do you think I mean?" he queries, his mouth now joining his fingers on my left shoulder.

My fingers tighten against the violin as I dare myself to say it. *Just do it. Don't be a coward.* "I think you have been ruined since the night Chantel took you in her hands and pleasured you. I think you have trouble doing that on your own now, so instead, you punish yourself. You hurt yourself, trying to get where you want to go, and you get frustrated because you can't."

As my speech comes to a definite end, his fingers stop tracing, and his mouth stops the lazy kisses. He lowers down on his knees behind me as his hands smooth around my waist and move down between my thighs to cup my aching sex. All the while, I am clutching her violin, just as she once did. The only difference in this scenario is that I know I am using it as a shield. Against what though, I have no clue.

Removing his hands from between my legs, he strokes his palms up my thighs to run his fingers over mine where I still hold the violin. He traces each finger, slipping in between, and then his mouth is by my ear.

"What makes you think I don't get there? And, let's be clear here, Gemma. Say exactly what you mean."

Taking a breath, I feel my breasts rise on each side of Diva, reminding me that *she's* here in the room again. "The morning I saw you."

"Yes?" He breathes softly.

"You didn't—"

"Didn't what, Gemma?"

Looking back over my shoulder, my eyes connect with his. "Come. You didn't come."

"But, in the vineyard, inside of you, I came," he reminds me.

I feel my core clench, and I have to shift because there is no way to tighten my naked thighs with my legs crossed as they are.

"Yes, but you were with me, not by yourself."

His left hand traces back down to my leg to my inner thigh. "I like you like this. Your legs are already open for me." He growls.

I once again shift mindlessly.

With a wicked smooth voice, he questions, "Do you know your inner thighs are wet?"

I nod silently, trying to remind myself I am asking him something. "So, why do you hurt yourself?"

I feel his fingers slide between my legs, moving up to touch my pouty wet lips. I shiver as my mouth parts on a moan.

"Because I deserve it," he tells me.

My fingers hold the violin in place as I look down to see his right hand tracing the strings now, almost as reverently as he's stroking me between my thighs.

"Why?" I sigh, wanting to part my legs further for him. "Why would you think that? You didn't—"

"Shh." He hums as he has before, while his hand on the strings comes down to where I am cradling the violin. "Give me this," he instructs.

I let go of Diva. He accepts it and leaves me abruptly. I take the moment to stand and face him. I'm completely naked and quivering with need as he places Diva in her case. As he turns, my eyes can't help but fall to below his waist. He's as aroused as I am, and I can feel the tension in the room like it's a live wire.

"Tell me what happened this afternoon."

He completely catches me off-guard. Shaking my head, I refuse. Instead of answering, I take my hand and press it down between my legs, trying to ease the ache. His eyes glance done at the apex of my legs before they move back up to my eyes.

"This portrait for Chantel and me was about regaining trust and finding strength, yet you *still* hold yourself back from me, Gemma," he explains, stalking toward me.

I step back as he moves forward, and my naked back bumps up against cool, rough bricks. I have nowhere to go, and he's a solid unmovable force in front of me. I'm achingly aroused, and at the same time, I find myself fighting the instinct to take flight and run.

"You want me to trust you and tell you why I do something, yet you won't tell me what happened to you this afternoon," he continues.

I open my mouth to lie, but I find his index finger up against my lips.

"Don't tell me it was nothing because I don't believe you."

Blinking up at him, I remain pinned to the burnt copper bricks, like a trapped butterfly. Removing his finger from my lips, he opens his palm and places it on my chest at the base of my throat where I know he can feel my pulse beating nervously against his fingertips.

"Do you trust me, Gemma?"

I have no idea. I want to. I don't have any reason not to, but as his eyes narrow and methodically trace down over my nakedness, I find I can't answer him.

My needy body is responding to every word he's saying while my mind is screaming at me to get out of here. It's telling me over and over that he's playing with me, yet my weeping sex is yelling at me to shut the hell up and let him have me.

His hand grips my shoulder, gently pulling me forward an inch, and he turns me so I'm now facing the wall.

"Stay? Or run?" he questions mimicking the thoughts in my head. "Trust me or trust them?"

Trust them? Who? The public? The people outside of the world I now find myself immersed in.

I really want to ask him, but I don't have the chance because he's urging me closer to the wall.

Unrelenting, he instructs, "Put your hands up on the wall, Gemma."

Thoroughly confused and shaking, I raise my hands, placing them palms flat against the wall. It feels as though I have no choice but to obey him, and then he's all up on me.

His hands smooth up my naked back on both sides of my spine to my shoulders where he squeezes them for a moment, right before his fingers twist into my hair, tightly gripping it. I gasp at the unexpected bite of pain.

"You don't know if you should trust me, do you?" His big body crowds in against me, pushing his hard cock through his pants against my ass. "That's probably smart. You're trembling."

He's right. I am.

"You're trying to scare me," I whisper.

"I'm trying to warn you," he admits.

If it's possible, his voice dips lower, so low that I can feel it stroke between my thighs.

"I'm not what you want, Gemma. You seem to be confused and struggling to understand who I am, but shouldn't you be questioning yourself? Why would *you* want someone like *me*?"

I squirm against him and try to fight against the grip in my hair.

"Let me go," I tell him. I want to leave and get away from him and the words coming from his mouth. He is hitting too close to home.

"I would..." He pauses for a moment and I hear a belt unbuckling. I know what he's about to do. My body wants it, but my head is telling me to *get the fuck out.*

"But I don't want to," he whispers.

Swallowing, I try as hard as I can to push back off the wall.

"I don't want this," I deny feebly. I feel his hand loosen my hair. "Let me go, Phillipe."

I think he's about to do as I've asked until he moves. His whole body is flush up against me, and I move slightly. My breasts are pressed against the chilled wall while his hands trap mine at my sides. His body is wrapped up close behind, like he's trying to crawl inside of me.

"You're lying again," he rasps into my ear.

His voice is edgy and almost sinister in its frustration, but what frightens me the most is that I can't explain why it makes my soaked pussy clench so hard that I almost come.

Releasing my arms, his hands slide around both sides of my hips and cover my bare mound. Pressing my hot cheek against the wall, I start to pant as I try to sound believable, needing to convince him and myself. "I'm not. I don't want this right now."

But, I moan as one of his hands slides down between my thighs, and I feel his hard, hot cock throbbing insistently against my ass crack.

"Yes, you do. You just don't want to admit it," he persists.

As he voices one of my biggest fears, I feel two of his fingers slide down over my distended clit through my soaking wet lips. Shifting a little, I bring my legs together, and I feel his mouth on my shoulder.

"No. Keep them apart, Gemma, so I can get inside of you."

Biting my bottom lip to stop myself from screaming, I leave them where they are, but still, those clever fingertips start to push up into me.

"Okay then, have it your way. Drenched." He groans. "Absolutely drenched."

I find myself finally giving in, embarrassed by the way my traitorous body is responding to this man — a man I don't want to need right this minute. He moves back and pulls my hips away from the wall, tilting my ass up toward him.

In a voice I hardly recognize, he tells me, "Your body is begging for me to fuck it, Gemma, and I think your mind is too."

I can't help myself from responding. "I think you're already doing that."

"What?" he quietly demands.

"Fucking with my mind."

I feel him dip his legs a little. His cock begins sliding through my hot, wet folds from behind, pushing through to meet where his hand is stroking my clit. I wish I could see down between my legs because I know he is also touching the tip of his own cock as it slides back and forth, teasing my entrance with the promise of a good hard fuck.

"Hmm, your ass is perfect," he states, stroking a warm palm across my cheeks. The tips of his fingers are on my crack, and they grip tight, gently pulling my cheeks apart. "So fucking perfect."

My breathing is out of control now as my hands support me against the wall. My breasts are swaying with each torturous slide of his cock between my needy pussy lips, and all I can think about is what he's looking at. Closing my eyes on a moan of my own, I wait for his next move.

"All I am telling you, Gemma, is that maybe you should heed what the stories have told you. Maybe you should run. Run far away from me."

I'm about to respond when his cock suddenly penetrates me with a long hard thrust. I gasp and bite my lip as he growls and lets go of my ass to grip my hip.

"But, for right now, it's too fucking late," he enlightens me, punctuating each word with a hard thrust.

His left hand moves to my ass, and his finger strokes over the dark pucker he's looking at.

"Right now, you're mine, just like *she* was mine. I'm going to pull you under and drown you in me until you can't forget."

His words are darkly disturbing. They're too close to everything I have read. It's too close to everything I have heard or been told about.

He flexes his hips, and his cock strokes deep inside of me. All I can do for the immediate moment is brace myself and hold on for the storm.

After all, if I am going to drown, this isn't such a bad way to go.

Isn't that *the biggest mindfuck of all?*

Chapter Twelve
BROKEN TRUST

Day 11

Broken Trust ~

Today, I was on a mission—a mission to rectify a wrong.

It had been three days, and still, Phillipe remained aloof.

He had returned from his walk the other night and told me everything was fine, but it hadn't been. He hadn't even been back to paint. It was almost as though he had distanced himself from me, and I had felt it as acutely as I would if I had lost a limb.

When I awoke this morning, he had already left the mattress we share up in the studio. I could hear the soft strands of a violin playing from a recording I had given him, so I knew he was somewhere in the room with me.

"Phillipe?" I called out. I waited for a response but not for long.

"Yes?" he replied, his deep voice sliding over me like a caress.

I felt the side of the mattress beside me dip.

Reaching across the pillow, I touched his fingers with mine. "Will you take me to town today?"

There was silence, except for the music floating around us as I felt his fingers squeeze mine.

"Of course."

When I sat up, I let the sheet fall down to my waist, hoping to invoke some kind of reaction from him. Instead of the reaction I was hoping for, he let go of my hand, and I felt the mattress shift as he moved away.

"Phillipe?" I called, hating that my voice cracked.

"Yes, Chantel?"

Faced with the moment to tell him anything, anything that might bring him back to me, I found that I was not as brave as I wanted to be, so I remained silent.

"What time do you want to leave?" he asked.

I could tell he was walking away, moving toward the door.

"As soon as I get dressed?" I asked softly.

"Okay. I'll be back in a little bit."

"Phillipe?"

"Yes, Chantel?" Again, his voice was patient but detached.

I wanted to scream at him.

"I don't want to be anywhere but with you. You know that, right?"

I never got an answer. He'd already left the room.

* * *

Several days later, I pull out my laptop and place the journal beside me in bed. I haven't been sleeping very well. Too many questions and too many thoughts keep swirling through my mind, and I can't seem to block them out, not even by shutting my eyes.

I still can't quite wrap my mind around what exactly happened a few nights before.

Things have changed. *Phillipe* has changed, and for the first time in his presence, I feel frightened. Up until now, I have been wary, suspicious, and careful around him, but I have never felt the overwhelming need to protect myself from him as I had that night. *Right on the cusp of that fear is also the sharp jagged edge of persistent desire.*

It's been days, and I know he's avoiding me. Still, I can feel my body starting to throb at the thought of him.

Annoyed at myself and my traitorous body that seems to be continually betraying me, I turn on my laptop and lean back against the headboard, settling in to do something I told myself I would not do while I was here. I search the name *Phillipe Tibideau.*

* * *

He came and got me several minutes later, just like he had said he would. Once again though, he was silent. I hated the silence because, like anyone else, I couldn't see his face to gauge his mood.

He took my hand as we were about to head downstairs.

"Phillipe, talk to me," I insisted.

He stopped, and I could feel him turn to face me.

"What do you want me to say, Chantel?" he asked.

"I don't know, but not talking to me isn't going to fix things," I explained, trying to get through to him.

"I can't explain how I feel," he softly told me.

I stepped closer to where I knew he was standing, and I raised my hand. He took my palm and placed it on his cheek.

"Tell me?" I whispered.

"No, Chantel. I'm okay," he assured me, his voice strained.

"You're not. You're hurting. Tell me why. Is it because of my parents? I already told you—"

"No," he replied, placing a finger to my lips. "No, it's not your parents. It's me."

"I don't understand," I responded, moving my hand slowly.

That was when I felt both of his hands on my face, cupping my cheeks. As he leaned down and placed his mouth by my ear, I could feel his breath on my face.

He exhaled a soft gust of air. "I don't want to scare you."

"You are scaring me. You're not talking to me. You aren't painting. You've pulled away."

"No," he sighed, his lips still against my ear. "No, Chantel, it's the other way around."

"I don't understand."

"You don't understand what it is I feel for you, and I'm scared to tell you. I'm scared it will make you run far away and never come back," he confessed, placing one of his hands on my chest.

"Nothing could make me leave," I stressed, turning my head to where his mouth had been by my ear.

"Nothing?" he asked.

Somehow, I knew his eyes were on me.

"Nothing," I reaffirmed.

"I can't stop the ache in my chest, Chantel." He paused for a moment.

I made a move to speak, but he continued before I could utter a single sound.

"When your parents said they want you to think about moving back to America, I felt like someone had pulled my heart out of my chest."

"But—"

"Literally, it felt like someone reached in and ripped my heart out of my chest. I shouldn't feel this possessive of someone. I know that in here," he explains, tapping my head. "But, here in my heart and in my soul…Chantel, I don't know what's happened to me. I'm all twisted and consumed in my need with these fucked-up thoughts. If you leave, I wouldn't know what to do."

"I'm not leaving you." I tried to get through to him, but he wasn't in the frame of mind to listen.

"Hearing them talk about you returning in several months made me crazy. I can't let you go. You know that, right? I need you here."

"I want and need to be here, Phillipe. Please," I pleaded, "listen to what I'm telling you. Come back to me. Be strong with me. Trust me."

"My heart aches for you," he confessed, his voice dropping down, quiet and low. "I would die for you, and that terrifies me."

I felt a shiver slide over my spine as I cradled his face in my palms. I had no words.

I was his.

* * *

Opening one of the articles my search revealed, I try not to flinch as the headline glares at me in accusation.

Blind Obsession

Tragic Accident or Tragic Betrayal?

By Michael London

I skim through the story and find myself cringing at certain questions from the journalist.

As my eyes continue down through the article, I see that it only gets worse. Words such as *tragic, horrifying,* and *deceptive* are littered throughout the whole piece.

Disgusted and annoyed at myself, I snap the laptop shut and push it away from my lap.

What am I doing? I have been here long enough to know that if he wanted to hurt me, he would have. Right?

Even though Phillipe is warning me to leave and my brain is agreeing, for some reason, I know that I won't. On the tail end of that realization is a startling one—*I can't.*

Not only am I determined to stay here to get this story and get it right, but I am also held here because of Phillipe and Chantel themselves.

Separately, they are fascinating individuals, both artistic in nature and both passionate about the other. Together, however, they are an irresistible force.

If it isn't her written words, pulling me deeper into their relationship, it is his melodic retelling of their times together, hypnotizing me and inviting me into their lives.

Her music haunts me whenever I allow myself to play it. Before I came here, I made sure I was familiar with Chantel Rosenberg but not like this. Now, it feels as though she is a part of me.

It's his paintings that move me more than everything else. They evoke a sensual side in me that I don't yet fully understand. All I know is that when I look at them I feel things that I've never felt before. *He* makes me feel things I've never felt before. *What is it about Chateau Tibideau?* It's like I arrived one way, and I know deep down in my soul that I will leave another.

As I get up from the bed, determined to go and find Phillipe, I am left wondering if that is how Chantel felt as well.

* * *

When he arrives at the studio, Phillipe is more than a little shocked to see that Gemma is already there. She is standing where she was at their last meeting several days before, but this time, she is holding a towel around her body.

It is immediately obvious to Phillipe that her mood is different. He isn't surprised, considering the previous turn of events. He knows that he shouldn't have pushed her the way he did the other night. The further she delved into Chantel's journal, and by default his own life, the more he felt himself slipping. He is being dragged into his own desolate abyss, and he knows if she stays, he is going to pull her in, too.

So, the best thing he can do for Gemma is warn her and make her want to leave. Maybe then, they can just forget about this whole asinine idea.

What he doesn't expect is to find her up here this morning, already disrobed, save for the towel, watching him as he walks into the room.

"Morning," he tells her.

Her eyes follow his every move. She doesn't say a word. She just keeps her gaze focused and her shoulders straight.

Ahh, so that's how we are going to play today.

She's annoyed with him and more than a little wary, but she isn't giving an inch. She has decided to show up and give him strength.

"So, you're not talking to me, Gemma? That's not very mature, especially since I haven't seen you for three days," he muses.

Her green eyes narrow.

"Fair enough. Silence, it is," Phillipe concedes, stepping behind the easel. "The violin is in the case."

He tracks her movements as she walks over and unsnaps the case with one hand. Her aggravation only increases as she clutches the towel between her breasts while reaching in to lift the violin.

"You're angry at me."

With no response to his statement, he contemplates her honey-toned back as she makes her way to the spot illuminated by the soft light. After she situates herself, she removes the towel, revealing her smooth curvaceous breasts and hips. She has also pulled her hair into a high bun, wrapped with a red ribbon.

The loud color against her light hair is erotically sensual. It stands out like a warning sign. *One that I should heed myself,* he thinks. He has a feeling that Gemma is the final act in this life, which he's already labeled a tragedy.

As she lowers herself into position, raising the violin to the same pose from only days earlier, Phillipe decides to leave her in her silence. If she wants to work that way, so be it, but he has to wonder if she knows just how loud that silence can actually be.

* * *

I didn't come to the studio today with the intention of not talking to him. It just happened. When I arrived, I noticed he wasn't up here yet. So, I got a towel and stripped off my clothes, determined to have the upper hand this time.

Too many times, this man has caught me off-guard, and I have to believe that is why I am allowing him to mess with my mind.

Maybe if I am the one to call the shots, if *I* am the one who holds the control, I won't feel like I am constantly treading water around him. As it stands now though, I always feel like I am trying to keep my head above the inevitable force of the crashing waves, and it feels hopeless. He is dragging me under, just as he said he would, and I am letting him. *Not today though. Today, I want to watch and study him for a change.*

There's more to this story, and I will *not* let him drive me away until I get what I came for.

"So, you aren't talking to me? Maybe I should just talk then, hmm?" he queries across the empty space.

I close my eyes as his low chuckle fills the tense silence, and I hate that my nipples peak and harden at his voice.

"Your nipples just got hard, Gemma. What are you thinking about?"

Refusing to rise to the bait, I grip the violin, siting as still as humanly possible.

"Well, maybe I should guess," he continues.

I find vindication when I discover that he can't seem to stand the silence. I feel as though I'm making him slightly uncomfortable, and I find that I like it.

"Maybe you're thinking about the other night?" he questions.

I open my eyes, turning to lock them with his. I refuse to look away first.

At this moment, all I can see of him are his green eyes peering at me over the canvas. He's sitting on a stool, so his hair is also visible, but I can't see below his nose. Although it's somewhat intimidating to be looked at like an object, I realize that I don't mind being the object of *his* intense perusal.

"Is that it?" he queries in the absence of an answer. He raises a questioning brow. "So, I'm right? I'd love to know what *you* think happened up here that night. You want to know what I think happened?"

Closing my eyes and turning back to face the wall, I block out his all-knowing stare from my vision and let his voice drift over me.

"I think you woke up."

My head turns, and my eyes snap open at that. *Damn him.*

He lowers his eyes. "I think you finally saw me. Didn't you, Gemma?"

Staring over to where he's sitting focused on the painting in front of him, I will him to raise his eyes to mine, and he does.

"What did you do? Run upstairs afterward and look up every article ever written on me? If that's the case, I wouldn't talk to me either." He stands and places his paintbrush down. "Well, you've seen me, Gemma. Maybe it's time you saw her."

I feel my eyes widen when I wonder what he means. I'm curious, so I finally speak. "How?"

He turns his head to face me. "Ahh, so now you speak?"

Heedless of my nudity, I stand and move to place the violin back in its case. It's obvious he's finished for the moment. Turning to him, I cross my arms over my chest, responding more from a natural reaction than one to cover myself.

"How?" I repeat, refusing to rise to his bait.

Realizing I am not going to answer his last question, he tilts his head to the side and steps out from behind the easel. Today, he's wearing jeans with a rip at the knee and a black fitted, long-sleeved sweater. He looks dark and sinful, and I can't help but find him sexy.

He walks over to me slowly. "Do you want to see *Armor*?"

I blink and lick my lips, giving myself time to think. I've seen *Armor* many times, but I have a feeling he means something more. *Maybe the original?* I can't help it. I'm just as curious as he expects me to be.

Somehow, he knows how I feel about her. He's worked it out. He knows I'm just as intrigued by Chantel as he was. So, I give him the only possible answer there could be.

"Yes."

* * *

Wrapping the towel around myself, I follow him out of the studio and down the stairs. I steal a quick peek at the hanging picture and keep walking because he is moving fast.

In fact, he is walking so quickly that I almost miss the fact that he makes a sharp right at the end of the hall to the left of the stairs. Making my way down in the direction he headed, I look at the walls and catch sight of several paintings I have not yet seen. I want to stop and look at them, but I find that am more intrigued about what is at the end of the hall.

I haven't been down to this end of the chateau. Usually, the large wooden door is closed, locking it off from the rest of the occupants. My mind suddenly catches up. *This is where his bedroom is.* I was standing outside of this part of the house that morning I saw him through his open window.

Just as I get to the end of the hall, he appears from around the corner. I stop immediately, slightly shocked because I didn't expect him to come back from where he went.

"It's down here," he tells me.

All of a sudden, every single fear I have determinedly pushed aside into the little you-are-crazy box comes flooding back.

"Down where?" I ask hesitantly.

Smiling so slow and iniquitous, he lifts a hand, crooking a finger at me.

"Come with me, Gemma," he invites.

His tone is so seductive he's managed to make me forget I'm apprehensive and the fact that I'm standing in just a towel. I feel as though he's hypnotizing me.

"What's down there?" I probe, cursing the fact that my voice is trembling.

Nothing prepares me for the answer he gives.

"Chantel."

* * *

Phillipe can tell by the look on her face that she's about to flee.

Gemma's eyes have widened, and her breathing has picked up to rapid pants.

"I don't understand," she tells him, clutching the towel to her breasts.

He takes a step toward her and holds out his hand. "You don't have to. Come with me, Gemma."

Her eyes move from his hand to his face. Considering all the tumultuous emotions that are currently running through him, Phillipe makes sure that his expression gives nothing away. When she reaches out and places her shaking palm into his, he's shocked by the trust she is now extending to him.

He wraps his fingers around hers and squeezes them. When he tugs her toward him, she is hesitant, but she moves forward.

He lowers his mouth down to her ear, teasing her softly. "You want to see this, Gemma. I know you do."

She turns her head, so their eyes meet, and he can see the curiosity burning there.

"How do you know?" she questions, seeming desperate in her need for an answer.

"Because, like me, you find her fascinating. You're consumed by her, aren't you? I can see it every time I talk about her." He pauses, moving his head so their lips are now touching. "It's okay,

Gemma. I did whatever I had to, just to be near her. I wanted her with every breath I took."

* * *

I *can't* breathe. My heart is pumping and my head is roaring from the rapid blood flow. As he stands there, whispering dark seductive words against my lips, I feel like I will pass out from the lack of oxygen.

That's when I am offered a reprieve.

Phillipe removes his lips from mine and takes a small step back, still holding my hand. He pulls me forward with each backward step he takes. He stops at the large wooden door, much like the one blocking this part of the house, and he reaches back to twist the knob.

I wait as it slowly swings open, and he is moving again. He turns, keeping my hand in his own, as he walks through the entryway.

Where the hell is he taking me? The thought is screaming in my mind.

As I cross the threshold, I watch as he descends down a dark staircase, and immediately, I have visions of words from articles—*tragic, horrifying, deceptive*. Instead of doing the smart thing and leaving, I follow him *blindly* down into the darkness.

Chapter Thirteen
Ménage à Trois

He stood in water, hip deep, as rain hit the back of his neck where his wet shirt clung to him. All he felt was numb.

"Wake up," he pleaded. "Come on. It's time to wake up."

Eyes of gray opened. Eyes that held his soul focused as a small smile touched lips of red.

***

As I follow Phillipe one step at a time down the dark stone stairwell, I can't help but wonder at my sanity. I can feel my hand as it trembles in his.

Again, I ask, "What's down here, Phillipe?"

He stops halfway down the stairs and turns to look back at me. "I told you."

I want to scream at him, *I know Chantel is not down there. So, what the fuck are you talking about?* Instead, I remain quiet and continue following him.

When we reach the landing, I can feel him turn to face me in the dark.

"Wait here," he instructs.

I stand exactly where he has left me, not knowing what I might run into if I happen to move.

It's cold down here, I think as I look around, trying to make out what I can. Obviously, we have gone downstairs, which in turn means we are underground. As quickly as that thought enters my head, it is chased by the fear of something horrific happening to me, that I stupidly pushed aside earlier.

I'm about to say his name when suddenly the room is illuminated.

My eyes squint as they adjust to the change, and as they do, a wide, empty space comes into focus. Immediately, I'm aware of several large white boards. Each cut into rectangular lengths, they are mounted all around the walls at different heights. *Blank canvases?*

"Acoustic room, Gemma." His explanation drifts across the expansive room.

After that announcement, silence follows as my brain catches up.

"This was her music room," he adds.

I let my eyes look up to the ceiling, and I see the strange placement of white boards placed there. The room is bare. There is nothing down here, just the panels on the wall and a shelf holding a sound system with what looks like CDs. The thick carpet beneath my feet, which I assume is also for sound absorption, paired with the boards on the walls make the room look odd. As I step farther into the space, I feel as though she is calling out to me, almost as if the echo of her is here in the room, bouncing off of the walls.

Before I knew what was down here, I feared him. Now that I *know* what's down here, I fear myself.

Bringing my eyes back to his, I ask, "Why didn't you just tell me that? Why did you try and frighten me?"

That's when he moves. He is in front of me before I can say another word. Gripping my naked shoulders in his palms, his green eyes roam all over my face.

"Don't you see, Gemma?" His voice is strained, stressing the importance of his words. "You let *them* scare you."

I try to understand what he is telling me. *Them*. There's that word again.

"Who is *them*?" I ask this time, determined to get an answer.

His eyes narrow as he drops his hands from me. "Everyone else," he mumbles as he turns away from me.

I watch him as he moves across the bright white space. As Phillipe disappears through a door on the other side, I'm left wondering if I am supposed to follow.

Making my way across firm carpet, I reach the small door where he has exited.

Stepping through the entryway, I notice right away that this room is different. It's just as large. I assume that these rooms use to be the wine cellars. Phillipe must have converted a different space for that though. As I move farther into the room, stepping onto hardwood floor, my eyes are drawn to the paintings hanging up on the far brick wall.

There, directly in front of me, are what I can only assume are the originals from Phillipe's series. The six pieces he painted of Chantel are displayed at the opposite end of the dimly lit room. Each one is larger than life, and each one is illuminated with a picture light.

They are resplendent, and I am enraptured.

* * *

Phillipe watches Gemma from the far right corner of the space. He has purposefully left the room in shadows, so he could gauge her reaction unnoticed, wanting to witness the moment she first looks upon the collection.

He knows that seeing it in person for the first time is always a shock to the system. Many have described it as breathtaking, and now, it is revered as haunting.

To him though, it will always be beauty.

Six portraits, each thirty-six inches by twenty-four, line the far brick wall in silent repose. Each one is lit by a picture light secured above the frame, and each of them holds him ensnared whenever he comes down to look upon them.

Right now, however, Phillipe finds himself intrigued by a petite blonde shrouded in a white towel. She hasn't seen him since she stepped into the room. As she makes her way closer to the paintings, he can sense her fascination with what is before her.

"It hurts to look at her, doesn't it?" he asks, watching as she turns to look at him over her shoulder.

He pushes himself away from the wall and makes his way toward her. Gemma keeps her wary eyes locked to his as he moves closer. When he finally stops beside her, shoulder to shoulder, he looks down to where she has turned her head to peer at him.

"She would play her violin in the room next door, and I would come down here to sketch," he explains.

Gemma turns her head back to stare at the paintings on the wall. "These are simply magnificent,

Phillipe," she whispers in awe. She takes a step closer before looking at him over her shoulder. "May I?"

Phillipe nods once and remains where he is. He tries to remind himself that there is no reason he should feel guilty about being bound by one woman who is becoming entranced by another.

* * *

"Guilty?" her voice seeped into his mind. "What are you guilty of?"

"Everything," he confessed as he stroked a hand down her cheek.

"Do you see the lights over there?" she asked.

He closed his eyes, blocking out what she was telling him.

"You don't see lights over there, Chantel. You can't see anything," he told her gently.

"Just like you can't be guilty," she whispered.

He watched her wet lips part on a soft sigh.

"Don't let them make a villain out of you. Don't let them break you."

Leaning down, he pressed his lips to her wet ones, knowing what she was trying to tell him, but the truth was the lights were there.

He raised his mouth from hers and looked into her sightless eyes. "You can't break a man that's already broken."

* * *

I can't believe that I am standing in a room with the original six pieces from *The Blind Vision Collection.* I move as close as I dare, and I turn to look over my shoulder at the artist—a man so complicated that I am starting to realize I haven't even begun to scratch the surface.

He's watching *me* as I look at *her,* and I find that I like it. His eyes glance over my naked shoulders, and he frowns before quietly turning to walk away.

"I'll be back in a minute, Gemma. Take your time," he informs me as he exits out into the music room.

Left alone with Chantel, I turn back to face the paintings. I move over in front of *Armor,* the same image I have been posing for. It's easy to see that Phillipe was fascinated with her by the way he made the light fall upon her, creating shadows along each sensuous curve of her body.

Each stroke was executed with such care and love that I feel as if I am witnessing it being painted. He's captured the luminescence of her skin with such perfection that I can't help but move closer. Once again drawn to her in a way I've yet to understand or make sense of, I stroke my fingers down her arm.

From the slope of her breasts down to her tight hard nipples, her skin almost glows, making her appear ethereal in nature, but it's also the darkness he's captured in the pose that's so eloquent in its meaning. It's as though you can't tell where she ends and the shadows begin. You can only see what he has decided to show you.

She appears strong and brave as she holds the one thing that makes her formidable in her own right, and that's the Stradivarius.

I don't realize how caught up in the painting I've become until I hear a thud behind me. Snatching my hand back as if I were just burned, I turn to see that Phillipe is back, and he's carrying a wooden chair. He places it right behind a small plush rug, the only covering on the wooden floors.

"What do you think?" he asks, moving to sit.

I find I have no words for him. *How do you tell someone that his creations are the most painful and beautiful objects you have ever looked upon?*

Instead of talking, I stand motionless in my towel and wait for him to do something, *anything*.

"Come here, Gemma," he commands quietly.

I don't know what I'm feeling at this moment. As I look at him sitting there in the low lights with his slightly spread jean-clad legs and his dark hair brushing the collar of his sweater, I find myself moving toward him. *I want to touch him, and I want him to touch me.*

Slowly, I walk to where he is sitting, facing *Armor*. I stop before him as his eyes move up the white towel, over my breasts, and finally rest on my face.

Once again, he raises his hand, and in a gesture that is now familiar, he crooks his finger. "Come closer, Gemma."

Like a dream in the night, I find I have no choice.

* * *

As Gemma stands before him, Phillipe can see *her* behind Gemma, and that's all it takes for his desire to magnify.

Raising his eyes to Gemma, who is now staring down at him, he brings his legs together. Softly, he invites, "Sit with me."

He watches as she lets her eyes fall to his lap, and then she glances back to his face. He places his hand on his thigh. Coaxing suggestively, he says, "Turn around, Gemma, and sit here on my lap. Tell me what you see."

He isn't sure if she will do as he asks. She licks her lips and pivots on her heel. He lets out a deep breath as she sits down on his lap, her towel-covered ass firmly seated on his thighs. Raising his hands, he places them on her waist and pulls her back against him until her sweet curves are molded to his front.

Lowering his chin to her shoulder, he looks at *Armor*. He repeats his original request, "Tell me what you see when you look at her."

He feels her take in a breath of air, before she releases it softly before wriggling a little closer.

He reaches across her waist with his left hand. "Sit still, Gemma, and tell me what you see."

"I see Chantel," she finally replies.

"Yes, so do I. What else do you see?"

"I see her violin. I see Diva."

At the mention of the violin's name as though it is an actual person, Phillipe feels a small grin tug at the corner of his mouth. He takes the side of the towel in his fingers and pulls it away, leaving her body on full display.

She moves automatically, trying to cover herself, but he drops the towel's edge and shifts his arm back to hold her in place.

"Shhh, don't hide. There's no one here."

"You're here," she points out.

Phillipe chuckles sinfully before he gently bites her naked shoulder. "Yes, but I've been looking at your beautiful breasts for the past few hours,

Gemma. So, what's the problem?" he queries. "Is it her?"

Breathing a little harder, she asks, "Who?"

Phillipe lifts his head and licks her earlobe. "*Her*."

* * *

I close my eyes, trying to remind myself that *she* is not really in the room with us.

"No, that's ridiculous."

"Is it?" he questions.

His teeth nip my lobe. I can feel my pussy clench every time he licks and flicks the soft skin of my ear.

"Yes. Why would I care that the paintings are here?" I ask, trying to convince myself as well as him.

He shifts his arm that's wrapped around my waist, and his hot palm slides down to my bare thigh. Slowly, his hand slides between my legs, and I watch, mesmerized, as he gently tugs on one of my thighs. Like a puppet on a string, my legs part until they are splayed wide on both sides of his.

As I lean my back against his front, resting my head against his shoulder, he slides that same hand up my thigh until his fingers finally graze my soaked core.

"Oh, Gemma, you are very, *very* wet. Look."

He inhales deeply and raises his fingers, so I can see them glistening from just one touch between my thighs.

"So, what is it that has you so excited, Miss Harris?"

I moan at the formality he adds to my name, reminding me how inappropriate this kind of relationship is with him. Returning his strong fingers to the warmth between my legs, he rubs against my swollen clit.

"Is it me?" he murmurs.

I push my hips up to him. I know he isn't going to stop there.

When he pushes the tips of his fingers inside of me, he asks the forbidden, "Is it her?"

I clamp my bottom lip between my teeth and moan loudly.

"Ahh, now we're getting somewhere." His conclusion slides over me.

His other hand comes around me, and I watch as his palm cups my right breast. He squeezes and caresses it while his other fingers slowly push deeper into my aching body. As I'm leaning back against him, spreading my legs wider, I am completely aroused by the sight of the most erotic scene I have ever been a part of.

"Look at her, Gemma," he instructs.

I'm having a hard time tearing my eyes away from his hands while they play over my needy body.

"Now, tell me what you *feel*. What do you feel when you look at her?"

I close my eyes, trying to find some sort of anchor to hold me steady, as he tells me, "Wake up, Gemma. Open your eyes."

My heavy eyelids open, and I find myself now staring at the image of Chantel in *Armor*.

His seductive voice asks again, "How do you feel?"

"Hot," I answer softly.

"I can't hear you, Gemma. Louder," he tells me while his fingers rub over my hard nipple.

"Hot. It makes me feel hot," I repeat louder. I arch out my chest, chasing his fingers as they move over my skin.

"What else?"

Looking at the painting hanging in front of us, I let my eyes run over her. I confess, "Needy. She makes me feel needy."

He groans in my ear as his fingers once again push deep between my wet folds. "You're so fucking turned on. I think she makes you wet. Doesn't she?"

Squeezing my eyes shut, I wait for his firm fingers to retreat, so they'll give me that delicious high when they slide back into my greedy demanding body.

His hand stills as he asks quietly, "What happened yesterday, Gemma?"

Stiffening in his arms, I feel my thighs tighten. I try to get a grip to pull myself away, but there's nothing I can do. His fingers are sliding between my hot swollen lips while the other hand is pulling and twisting my nipple.

"Stop," I say, panting.

"No."

God help me, my slick cunt clenches in response to his refusal.

"Tell me," he demands, like a dog with a bone.

Between gritted teeth, I answer, "No."

His long fingers brush my clit gently. "Are you ashamed?"

Shaking my head, I arch my hips, my entire body begging for release.

"Did it have something to do with her?" he persists.

I cry out when he tightly pinches my nipple.

"Did it?"

I don't answer. I can't. Instead, I bring one of my hands up to my neglected breast and start to pull and twist the straining peak.

"Yes, Gemma," he urges with a deep groan. "Touch yourself. Feel me touch you, and look at us while your body sings. It is singing, Gemma. It's weeping and crying all over my fingers."

Flexing up my hips, I finally feel his long fingers push deep into my tight, wet core, and I cry out, pinching my nipple hard.

"Oh yes Gemma, fuck my fingers. God, you're fucking beautiful," he whispers.

This time, he seems far away. As I turn my head against his shoulder, I see his eyes on the painting in front of us. I know I should be upset that he is looking at her while his fingers are thrusting inside of me, but it turns me on even more. Knowing that he is touching me while fantasizing about her makes my body quiver and clench uncontrollably.

I finally give him what he wants. "Her," I confess, my breath brushing over his cheek.

He turns his head, so his eyes are once again locked with mine. As I look from his eyes to his lips, I feel his hand flex between my thighs while his fingers slide out only to push back in hard.

"What about her?" he asks, his eyes dilating.

I can feel his cock pushing insistently against my ass, and I grind against it as I move my hips to meet each thrust of his fingers. Almost cruelly, he pinches my nipple, and I still my hips, biting my bottom lip to control the scream I feel building.

"What about her, Gemma?" he demands.

I decide now is as good a time as any to confess my sins and have them washed away. "I had a fantasy."

Our eyes never waver as he slowly pulls his long fingers from me. Forcefully, he pushes them back inside, making me groan, but I stay focused on him.

"What kind of fantasy, Gemma?" he questions, his voice gruff. His mouth is stretched tight in a grimace.

I close my eyes, remembering the thought of her, while I tweak my nipple. "She was touching me."

Before anything else can leave my mouth, he removes his hands, gently pushing me away, and I stumble to move. I'm terrified I've gone too far, but before I know it, he's pulling me down to the rug on the floor. I feel the plush material against my back as he throws the towel, which has been our only barrier, behind us.

Looking up, I cautiously study him while he sits back on his knees. As he unbuttons and unzips his jeans, he looks above me to the paintings hanging all around us on the wall. I raise my legs up and slowly spread them in invitation. When his eyes finally come back to me, he can see everything that I'm offering. Pushing down the denim, I notice he's naked beneath, and I feel my pussy clench at the sight of his thick, veiny cock when it's finally freed.

Breathing hard, I lock my eyes with his fiery ones while he crawls up my body.

He places his palms on both sides of my head. "I'm all fucking wrong for you," he rasps in my ear.

The smooth, hard tip of his shaft pushes against my soaked slit, seeking entry.

I turn my head, so my lips are now against his ear. I tell him the only truth I feel right at this moment, "I don't care."

He rears back slightly and thrusts his strong hips forward, pushing his pulsating cock deep inside of me.

As he moves his large body over me, I open my eyes and tilt my head back to look up at the paintings on the wall. As my eyes come back to the tortured man moving above and inside of me I notice that he, too, has his eyes on the woman above us, and I can't help but think he is right.

Phillipe, Chantel, and I—we are three.

Chapter Fourteen
ACQUIESCE

Day 12

Acquiesce ~

It was a beautiful day today. We spent all morning down in the arbor.

Phillipe had asked me to come outside with him for a while, and he'd requested that I bring Diva with me.

"It's the perfect time to pose for me. Penny won't be back today so she won't be shocked."

"Shocked?" I asked with a small laugh.

"Yes, to be shocked."

I felt him shift his weight as he leaned down over me where I was still lying in bed.

"Now, why would she be shocked if we're outside in the arbor?"

He pressed his lips to mine, and I giggled as his hair fell forward, tickling my face.

"Because you won't be wearing anything but the sun."

"I won't?"

His smile curved against my mouth. "No, you won't, unless it's me."

As he moved away, I sat up, chasing his movement across the bed.

His hand touched my cheek as he invited, "Come with me, Chantel. Let's go outside in the sun."

* * *

The following morning, after reading through one of the entries, I close the journal and get up, making my way to bathroom. Looking myself over in the mirror, I realize that I'm having trouble recognizing the face that is staring back at me.

Before I arrived here in France at the chateau, I knew exactly what I wanted to do with my life. I knew where I was going and exactly how I was planning to get there, and a few weeks ago, Phillipe Tibideau was just another part of that future progression toward my dream.

Now, I'm finding that the longer I stay here surrounded by memories of *her* and moments with him, I feel myself changing. Everything I thought I knew suddenly seems so unclear.

Originally, I came here intending to uncover Phillipe's secrets.

Now that I'm here, I'm finding my feelings are changing, and I'm discovering that I'm not so eager to share.

Shaking my head, I reach up, running my hands through my hair. Pushing it away from my face, I hold it in a ponytail and turn my head, glancing at my side profile. I smile, trying to see what he sees when my face pulls a certain way when out of the corner of my eye, I swear that I see movement. Dropping my hands quickly, I turn but find nothing.

My heart is racing, and as I stand frozen in the small tiled room, I feel as though *she* is here. Ever since last night in his showroom, I've felt her more intensely than ever before. I look over to the space where I thought I saw something. Even though I know how ridiculous the notion is, I can't help but wonder what she thinks of me.

* * *

Picking me up, he carried me down the stairs and led us outside into the warmth of the sun. We laughed the whole way, and he kissed my nose as I rested my head against his shoulder.

"So, what do you plan to do with all these paintings?" I asked.

He finally set me down on my feet. "I don't know," he replied, moving around me.

I turned in the direction where I thought he had moved. "What do you mean you don't know? You told me you wanted to touch the world. What happened to that man?"

Warm palms pressed through the thin fabric of my shirt as he wrapped his arms around my waist. His lips nuzzled into my neck as he gently kissed it.

"He met you."

Lifting my hands, I stroked my fingers through his silky hair. It was longer than usual, and I loved running my hands through it, feeling the soft texture against my fingertips.

"So, you met me and abandoned your dream? I don't like the idea of that."

"No, Chantel. I met you and decided that I didn't need to touch the world." He rested his stubbled cheek to mine. "I just need to touch you.*"*

* * *

Moving back out to the bed, I sit and pick up her journal again to continue where I have left off.

It's clear she was in love with him. I can feel it in every entry she typed, but she had yet to say it.

I think she would be the kind of person who would type it over and over, but then it occurs to me that words weren't her way. *No, they're mine.* Music was her way of showing how she felt.

Reaching down, I pick up the photo album from my workbag and flip through it to the print copy of *Acquiesce.* At first glance, this painting of a young woman, marked only with two bold F-holes, sitting in the grass with a white sheet surrounding her appears the most simple.

Acquiesce means to submit or comply silently.

The label for this piece is so unusual that I've always wondered why he called it that, but again, she too used that same word for her journal entry. Perhaps it's the fact that she willingly removed her clothes and posed in the sunlight, doing it all without protest.

They each give me such similar yet uniquely individual points of view. They merge together to harmonize in a symphony so evocative that I feel it altering my very soul with each separate movement being played.

* * *

"Here. Sit right here," he told me, slowly leading me backward.

I felt a wooden bench of some kind touch the back of my legs. I smiled and asked, "When did you move this down here?"

"I just dragged it over this morning. It's from the vineyard. The men use it during lunches, but it will work perfectly for today…until I'm ready to get you down in the grass," he explained.

He lightly pushed on my shoulders, and I sat down without protest.

"Will you play while I set up?"

I placed my violin case beside me. "Of course. What would you like me to play?"

"Anything," he replied as his fingers traced the line of my jaw.

I reached over to my case and unsnapped the locks. Feeling around the familiar silk, I found Diva's neck and gripped her firmly before lifting her to my shoulder. Time to show him what we can do, *I thought as I lifted her to my shoulder, getting ready to start playing.*

"Wait."

His voice halted me, and I lowered her from my shoulder.

"What are you going to play?"

Smiling confidently, I knew this piece was one that often shocked people with its slow and, at times, methodical vibe, but then there was that moment—that amazing shift when Diva would take control and at a hellacious speed, the piece would turn to cool arctic fury.

Standing, I raised my violin once more to my shoulder. "Vivaldi 'Winter.' It's from—"

"The Four Seasons," *he finished for me.*

"Yes. You know it?"

"I do, and I would love to hear you play."

I closed my eyes and began.

* * *

I know Vivaldi. I know I've heard this piece, but now, I find myself searching for it. When I locate it online, I hit play and move to the window in my room. Looking down below to the vineyards and the arbor, I close my eyes as the music begins softly.

I picture her standing there under the large trees among the grass, her hair gently blowing in the breeze, as she serenades Phillipe in the sunlight.

That moment was her *I love you*. It didn't matter if she never told him. Every time she stood in front of him and shared a piece of her soul, she also offered up a piece of her heart.

Two passionate people, two insanely talented people, were so consumed in their own world that they couldn't understand that the world around them would not fathom such a union. For those moments in time, it didn't matter. For *this* moment, when she stood down there under the trees and played for him, I knew he had to be in complete awe of her.

I have only heard her play through recordings, and I am always moved and enamored by her at the end of each piece. To have her standing in front of me, eyes closed with fingers swift and sure, I can't even begin to comprehend the feelings she would have evoked.

She is the mystery that is wrapped tightly around the man I am trying so desperately to unravel.

* * *

As I finished the piece, I could feel my heartbeat thunder through my chest. It was always this way after I had performed, but knowing Phillipe was standing somewhere close by made the experience even more arousing and somehow more exhilarating.

"Phenomenal," he said from behind me.

Turning around from where I now stood, I felt his hands on my face. "You are absolutely without question surreal, like a dream."

As his breath washed over my face, he entreated, "God, don't ever let me wake." Right before his mouth crashed down on mine, and I opened to him immediately.

I could feel the desperate and soul-consuming passion he was holding on to as he reached down to my hand, taking Diva from me. I relinquished my hold, and when his lips left mine, I waited. He moved a little, presumably to place her down, and then he was back.

He straddled the bench I was on and took my mouth with his own. His tongue slid between my lips, and as it rubbed up against mine, I moaned and reached up to clutch his shoulders. He angled his head as his hands smoothed down my sides to move under the bottom of my shirt.

I smiled against his hungry lips. "Is this where you take off all my clothes?"

His shoulders relaxed, and he laughed, the intensity of the moment now eased. "I don't think I will get anything done, but I'm going to try. I want to wrap a white sheet around your waist and add the F-holes again."

His fingers gripped the edge of my shirt. "Lift your arms."

Without question, I acquiesced as he removed my top.

Standing, he moved away from the bench. "I wish you could see all that I do. Then, you could tell by my face just how much I love you. You take my breath away."

I removed my pants and panties, and stood before him proudly. My breasts rose, like an oblation to him, as I replied with my heart in my hands, "Love looks not with the eyes, but with the mind, and, therefore, is winged cupid blind. I don't need to see you, Phillipe, to know you feel as I do."

* * *

I close my eyes as the final strands of *Winter* float over me, and I find that I have tears running down my cheeks. Reaching up, I brush them away and wonder at myself.

Last night, I wanted Phillipe with a hunger that I never knew. I felt like he was right there with me. *But is he? Or is he always with her?*

I'm finding it increasingly harder to believe that anyone would come between the two of them, yet last night, I felt as though he *invited* me in. As he laid down with me in the gallery, he took me with such force and passion that I felt him hours after.

The most disturbing realization to come from last night is that now I can feel her, too.

* * *

Lying in his bed, Phillipe closes his eyes and lets the smooth sounds of the violin float over and calm him. His mind keeps running over last night with Gemma, and no matter which way he looks at it, his continual surrender to his lust feels like betrayal. His betrayal is so deep and painful that it aches like an open wound.

He knows his desire for Gemma is growing. It will likely continue that way, but he can't seem to shake the overwhelming *need* he still holds for Chantel. *She* is still everywhere, and no matter what his body is craving, his mind cannot and *would* not deny her.

In the studio is where he feels her the most, but that's expected.

That was their world. No one touched them there. No one tried to come between them.

Up in his studio, there is just him, and there is just her.

* * *

"I know you're watching me," Chantel mumbled.

He smiled as her gray eyes slowly opened.

"And how would you know that?"

"Because I can feel you," she told him.

She shifted, so she was lying on her side, just like he was as he watched her.

"I've always been able to feel you, right from the beginning."

He reached out and ran a hand down her hair. "I remember. You looked right up at me. I thought you were beautiful. I needed to talk to you."

She raised her hand, and he reached for it, bringing it up to rest palm open on his chest.

"You feel my heartbeat?" he asked.

She nodded and tapped her finger. "It's so strong that I could use this like a metronome and keep time when I play."

"It beats for you."

"As mine does for you."

He reached across the bed, pulling her closer to his side under the sheets, until their legs were entwined and their noses brushed.

"I want you to tell me everything, and I want to tell you everything," he expressed as eager as a child.

She grinned against his mouth as her eyes shut, and she brought her free hand up to trace her fingers down over his cheek and jaw.

"Everything?" she questioned, and kissed his mouth.

"Yes, everything," he implored.

"I love you. That is the beginning, and that is the end. That is everything."

He rolled her over, so she was lying on her back. He followed until he was above her, hands on both sides of her dark hair. He touched the strands gently and looked down into the loving eyes peering up at him. Her eyes were so beautiful that they stole his breath.

Leaning down, he pressed his lips to hers, kissing her reverently. Her eyelids fluttered closed, and he felt her thighs part slowly, allowing him to slide sensually between her legs. When his cock brushed up against her warm mound, her mouth parted against his lips as she sighed.

Her breath was becoming his, their souls becoming one.

"You, Chantel. You are everything," he told her as he brushed his fingertips across her lowered lids. He closed his eyes and rocked his hips, pressing himself lovingly against her.

"Your lips," he whispered. "Your eyes, your talented fingers, and your perfect soul. All of that is everything I want, and everything I need."

Bringing one hand down her body, he traced her warm hip as she lifted up, allowing his hand to move under to her curvy ass. Squeezing it gently, he raised her hips and pushed against her.

"Let me inside." Gently biting her bottom lip, he pleaded, "Let me inside, and never let me go."

She arched up, her body wrapped in sunlight, and her thighs squeezed his hips tight while she pushed her wet folds against his pulsating desire. Rocking against her, he felt her juices as they coated the tip of his hard cock. She was so ready, and her body was so needy that she cried out as he teased her with a gentle push, only giving her an inch before sliding back out of her completely.

Her ripe lips parted on a sigh as she arched up once more, pleading silently with her body. So, again, he slid inside her heat. This time, he pushed a little deeper and a little harder. As he retreated from her body, he felt her greedy pussy gripping him tightly.

Her neck strained back on his pillow, and the sheer eroticism of the moment crashed down over him.

"Phillipe," she moaned.

He couldn't help but bring his free hand up to her face, tracing her parted lips with his fingers, while his other hand lifted her hips, tilting them and once again positioning them for his smooth slide inside her tight warm center.

She gently sucked his finger into her mouth and swirled her tongue around his fingertip, teasing him, much like his cock was teasing her body. She bit down and raised her hips, letting him know that she was done playing.

Removing his finger, he placed his hand by her head, palm flat on the soft mattress, and he squeezed her ass where his other hand was holding her.

Leaning down, he kissed her mouth. He told her, "I love you," right before he thrust his cock deep inside her, feeling her warmth as it flooded over his hard, sensitive skin.

Bracing himself, he slowly moved inside of her, slowly, like the beginning of a beautiful orchestral piece. He started out steady and calm. As her mouth parted and her thighs tightened around his waist, his hips moved faster, and the fury was upon them as they crashed down to earth.

Each entwined in one another, and each bathed in the other's love.

* * *

No, he thinks as he stands and moves to the window, looking out at the arbor.

He can't keep Gemma. To pretend otherwise would not be fair. While she is here though, while she is here with them, maybe they can share her for just a little longer.

Chapter Fifteen
REQUIEM

Day 12

I find Phillipe up in his studio later that afternoon. Making my way inside the room, I move over to the desk, placing my laptop down and opening it.

He's sitting where I found him the first day I arrived at the chateau. Dressed in the same dark pants and a black turtleneck, his sensual eyes are stunning in contrast. I lean up against the desk and take a moment to really look at him.

"Are we going to discuss what happened?" I ask, taking this moment to try and make sense of everything I'm feeling and possibly everything he is.

"What is it you feel needs discussing, Gemma?"

"Stop it," I tell him, moving forward.

I take a step closer to where he is seated, and that's when he pushes up from the chair and moves in my direction, meeting me halfway. Looking up at him, I'm struck for the first time in days as to just how incredibly attractive Phillipe really is. His dark hair looks like he's pushed it away from his face, but a few strands have fallen forward, flirting with his lashes.

"Stop what?" he questions in a voice I'm starting to dream about.

"Stop trying to intimidate me. I want to know you," I tell him, taking that final step to him. It's a shock to me when he takes a retreating one back.

"You don't know what you want, Gemma," he informs me darkly, those mysterious eyes narrowing.

"I seemed to know what I wanted last night. Wouldn't you say?"

He shakes his head in disagreement as I move again, taking one step forward to his step back.

"You didn't know what you wanted last night."

"Didn't I?" I query, starting to get annoyed. I need him to open up to me. I want him to trust me, and the only way I can see that happening is for me to trust him.

"I knew exactly what I wanted last night. I wanted you," I explain. I watch his mouth pull into a grimace, but I'm not finished yet. "And I wanted her. I *still* want her."

As my words penetrate his mind, he looks me over before allowing those hot eyes to come back and land on my face.

"You don't know what you're saying right now. Would you listen to yourself?"

Straightening my shoulders, I lift my chin. "How about you listen to me? I know exactly what I just said, and I know exactly what I'm feeling. I'll admit that I don't have the first idea why or how it is that I want her, but I do, just as much as I want you."

Finally, he stops moving backward and takes a step toward me. He reaches out to grip my shoulders tightly. "Do you hear what you're telling me?"

I lick my lips as his voice skates along my spine, touching every nerve. I shiver with anticipation.

"Yes," I reply on a breathy sigh. "I'm sick and tired of hiding it from you. You know what I'm reading, you know what you're telling me, and I'm placing my trust in you. I'm giving my *body* to you." Swallowing deeply, I try to regain my slipping composure. "I don't know what it is you see, and I don't know what you're feeling, but when you bring *her* between us, something happens inside of me."

I watch almost in slow motion as he reaches out a hand and fingers my hard, tight nipple.

"See? I'm not lying, Phillipe. You and Chantel have done something to me." I shiver as I confess, "And I want you to do it over and over."

* * *

As Phillipe stands there, listening to the words that are tumbling from Gemma's mouth, he's trying to tell himself that this is *not* a good idea. Not only is she going to be there temporarily, she is also a journalist, a reporter who is writing a story on him.

None of this can end well. She wants him to touch her, to break her down, and to crawl inside of her. She wants *Chantel.*

He knows she has been struggling to understand her feelings when it comes to the paintings, as well as her reactions to him, but to stand in front of him...*to confess her perversion?* Well, he knows there's no way he can walk away from that. If anything, it makes him want to slide deeper inside of her to indulge in her debauchery.

"Honesty," he commands gruffly, removing his hand from her nipple to touch her chin.

She doesn't flinch. In fact, she doesn't even blink.

"If we go where you want to go, Gemma, if we get deep inside this head of yours, you have to give me honesty."

Her eyes dilate, and her lips part.

"Do you understand?"

"Yes," she whispers, breathing slowly.

"You need to tell me what you're thinking—*all* the time."

She nods as Phillipe moves his free hand to her waist. He wraps his arm around her, pulling her forward. "And if you want to scream her name out when my cock is fucking you, you scream it, right into my ear."

* * *

I can feel the inner muscles of my soaked pussy spasm and clench at his dark suggestion. *How is it that with just a few simple suggestive words this man has reduced me to a quivering pile of flesh and bones?*

"Can you be that honest, Gemma? Can you let yourself go and be that raw?"

Quickly, I agree, afraid he's going to change his mind—*or that I will.*

"We will see," he muses, letting me go. "*Acquiesce* seems to be a perfect fit for you today, but it's too cold outside. So, let's go down to the music room. You can pose there."

He turns on his heel and walks away from me. I tell myself to move, to follow him, but for the moment, I'm stuck where I'm standing, wondering what I just agreed to.

* * *

As I finally make my way out of the studio, I head downstairs.

Passing by the painting of *Rhapsody*, or at least a print of it, I'm reminded of the first time I saw it only weeks earlier. It still calls out to me, except now, instead of stopping to examine it, I find myself rushing past it to get to her music room where *he* is waiting for me. As I descend the stone stairs, I realize that I'm no longer frightened of what's below. I'm anxious and extremely aroused.

I know what we discussed just moments ago affected him, and I understand his need to digest what I was truly saying to him.

When I reach the bottom step and turn, I'm greeted by bright lights. My eyes move around the odd room until I see him standing with his back against the wall.

He's watching me quietly. "Come in."

"Said the spider to the fly?" I ask, stepping forward.

I see that he's moved a wooden bench into the center of the room.

"*Acquiesce* means to submit or comply silently. Did you know that?" he inquires smoothly.

"Yes," I manage to say as I walk closer to him.

He, too, has moved and is now waiting for me on the other side of the bench.

Finally, I stop opposite him. "Where are your paints?"

"Upstairs," he informs, his hands moving to his belt buckle.

Licking my lips slowly, I raise my eyes to his again. "Then, how are you going to paint me?"

I'm trying to focus on his face, but the soft snick and clink of metal is distracting me, so once again, my eyes fall to his waist.

"I'm not. The whole idea of painting you was to gain your trust. Obviously, I have it since you told me upstairs I can do whatever I want to you." His low voice stops as my eyes return to his. "Over and over again."

I swallow before asking, "Why the bench?"

"I still want you to feel her, Gemma, to understand her."

That's when he reaches across the space to take a handful of my shirt, pulling me forward. I stumble, my shins lightly hitting the wood, as I'm held in a somewhat awkward pose.

"Now, I know *you* trust me. It's time to see if *I* can trust you."

I feel my eyes widen, wondering just what he has in mind.

"I'm going to let go of your blouse, and I want you to take one step back, bend over, and place your palms on the bench. Can you do that, Gemma? Can you submit and comply silently?"

Blinking slowly, I feel my head starting to spin. He's seducing me. I can feel him slowly sliding over me, searching for a way to slip past my defenses, and this time, I'm aware of it. This time, I want to be seduced.

As he lets go of my shirt, he straightens, and I do as requested. I step back and bend over. I place my hands on the bench, leaving my ass pointing out.

I comply, and I do it all silently.

* * *

Phillipe watches as Gemma takes a step back. Eyes locked with his, she bends at the waist to do as he requested.

Her blonde hair has been left free today, and it falls like a curtain down both sides of her face, That just wouldn't do. He wants to see her face. Moving away from her, he notices when she lifts her head to watch him.

Making his way over to the elaborate sound and recording system, he turns it on and selects the piece he is searching for. Hitting play, he looks back to see Gemma with her neck crooked and her head raised. Her eyes are focused on him.

"Have you ever heard *Lux Aeterna* from *Requiem for a Dream,* Gemma?" he asks, reaching down to undo the top button of his pants.

* * *

My eyes are transfixed on him as the eerie piano begins to play over and over, and there *she* is. Chantel has entered the room with us.

The music and violin is filtering in from all around us, and it's chilling. The intensely desperate melody floats around me, and it's feeding some dark fucked-up part of my brain. I can see he's undoing his pants. When he's walking toward me, I know what he's about to do.

I feel my whole body tremble with the startling realization that, as much as I want it, I'm terrified I'm going to end up craving him and the darkness that swirls around him, like the thickening air before a storm.

The violin starts to pick up tempo as he stops in front of me. He reaches out to brush my hair back from the right side of my face, tightly gripping it behind my head.

I raise my eyes to his, which are now looking down upon me. "Open your mouth, Gemma."

Immediately, my mouth falls open, and the words *submit* and *comply* run through my mind. My eyes are now level with his open pants. I watch with complete focus as he pushes them down from his hips, so his thick cock comes into view.

With his free hand, he strokes himself roughly over and over to the strands and rhythm of the violin as it begins again. I realize he's placed the music on repeat.

Swallowing deeply in anticipation, I follow each rough stroke of his fist, and I feel myself becoming increasingly wetter. This is exactly what I have been waiting to see, ever since witnessing it just over a week ago. Raising my eyes to him again, he gives me a smirk that is so knowing in its sensuality that I almost come from that alone.

"Do you want to suck my cock, Gemma?"

I close my eyes, listening to the violin and his voice, as his hand grips my hair tighter.

"Yes," I reply, opening my mouth to him.

"Yes?" he asks me again.

This time, he steps forward to place the head of his cock against my parted lips. I can taste the salty fluid of his desire coating his smooth, bulbous tip.

I flick my tongue out, tasting him, right before I lean forward, intending to take him inside my mouth.

The hand in my hair tightens as he tells me, "Not yet. Wait for it. Close your eyes, Gemma."

His voice finds its way somehow to my brain, and once again, I submit.

"Now, listen to her. Listen to the passion in each movement of her bow as she strokes it across the strings."

I listen as each note and chord is played with more passion the further into the piece it goes. His hand tugs on my hair, and I open my eyes to look up into his fiery green ones.

"Now, Gemma, put your lips around me and suck me as eagerly as she once did."

Moisture floods my pussy at the thought of *her* mouth wrapped around the flesh I'm about to suck. Opening my mouth, I gently slide him between my lips against my tongue. His hand tightens in my hair as the music pulsates and pounds through my ears, and his hips flex as his shaft starts to fuck my mouth hard.

I brace myself with my palms on the bench, but as he tugs my hair, the pain bites into me. I lose balance and shift forward a little, causing his cock to slide all the way to the back of my throat. He grunts and pulls out as I cough a little in reflex, but before I can say anything, my mouth is full again, and the piece has started over.

He's slowed his hips down and is sliding his shaft back and forth between my swollen lips. As I raise my eyes to his tortured ones, his hips pick up movement as the music does.

He imparts darkly, "You're the complete opposite of her, but you're so fucking stunning in your own way, just like she was, Gemma. Your lips…your lips are pink though where hers were red.

I listen as he becomes a victim of his own seduction, and I watch as he closes his eyes on a groan, stilling his body and hips. I mold the lips he's describing around him and take as much of him as I can inside my hot mouth.

Both of his hands come up to hold the sides of my head as he starts again, and this time, I'm ready as he pushes into my mouth like he'll never have another chance.

Furiously, he tries to find release, but as I have seen once before, he can't.

Pulling away from me, he curses loudly over the tragic music and tells me harshly, "Don't move."

My arms are trembling as they continue supporting me, and my legs feel as though they are about to collapse as the piano starts over, *Lux Aeterna* beginning once again.

He moves behind me, and his hands slide around the waist of my pants, undoing the buttons and zipper. He tears them apart, pulling my pants along with my panties down my hips. My naked ass and achingly aroused pussy are now on display to him.

His hands grip my hips, and without so much as a warning, his cock thrusts hard inside of me, pounding into me from behind.

"This is the sweetest fucking torture." He groans, sinking into my soaking core.

I shift my feet to get a sturdier stance, and using my hands for leverage, I push myself back against him.

"That's it, Gemma. Fuck *me*," he demands, moving against me with one solid thrust after the other.

I feel a finger tracing the crack of my ass. He dips it down to where his cock is furiously fucking me and swirls it around my juices before bringing it back to trace my rim with his lubed fingertip.

"Oh god." I moan as the tip of his finger pushes against my tight rear hole.

"*She* liked this, Gemma. She loved when I pushed my finger inside of her here."

I feel his finger slip past the tight ring, but there's no discomfort because my body is wound up from his insistent pounding.

As he thrusts deep one final time, pushing his finger all the way into me, he tells me darkly, "And she loved it even more when I fucked her here."

That's all it takes for me to scream, and true to what he said earlier, the name that leaves my mouth is hers.

Chapter Sixteen

FEAR

Fear ~

Today, I discovered that Phillipe was hiding something from me. It was funny how you could be close to someone and not sense something so very obvious.

Over the last couple of months, I had posed, and Phillipe had painted. When we first had started out, he had told me that he wanted to touch the world and share beauty and emotion with it. Now, he seemed to be keeping the paintings close, keeping me close, and I wanted to know what was holding him back.

I couldn't help but wonder if it was fear of the critics or fear of the unknown. Either way, I was determined to make him see what I knew the rest of the world would see. I'd found him down in the arbor this afternoon, and I'd finally gotten to the bottom of things.

"How long have you been out here?" I asked as my cane hit the bench.

"An hour or so," he replied.

I could tell he'd stopped whatever it was he was doing.

"Are you finishing up Acquiesce*?"*

I could hear the crunch of the gravel as he moved, and then his large hand took mine, entwining our fingers.

"Yes, I just finished it now. I was trying to get the background just right."

Nodding, I smiled, knowing what a perfectionist he really was, before I decided to just ask him what was on my mind. "When are you going to take the pieces to that little gallery we talked about?"

His fingers squeezed mine, as he released my hand. I felt him turn and walk away from me.

"Phillipe?" I queried quietly. Something was definitely bothering him, and I wanted to know what it was. "Talk to me. Why don't you want to go to town? That's all you've talked about since we first started."

As the silence stretched between us, I moved to the bench, sitting down. "Will you tell me what's going on, please? Why won't you call the gallery owner?"

"I don't think I want to anymore," he mumbled.

My mouth dropped open in shock. "What do you mean you don't want to? That's all you've ever wanted." I paused, trying to work out what might have changed his mind. "Is it me? Do you want a different model? I won't be offended."

Before I knew it, I felt him sit beside me, taking my hands.

"Are you crazy, Chantel? No," he answered, bringing my knuckles up to his lips.

"Then what?" I questioned, taking my hand and running it up through his hair. "Tell me."

He turned his face so his lips touched the center of my palm. "I'm scared," he confessed.

My heart clenched as I tried to understand this complex man I was hopelessly in love with. "Of what?"

"The world."

Laughing a little, I shook my head. "That doesn't make sense. Only months ago, you wanted to conquer it."

There was silence for a moment, and I could hear his breathing. One steady breath in, and one long breath out. "Months ago, I had nothing to lose."

I blinked as I continued to thread my fingers through his hair, luxuriating in the thickness of it. "And now you do?"

"Yes," he told me as she leaned forward, laying his lips on mine. "Now, I have you."

"Yes, you do. I'm not going anywhere." I gripped his hair, tugging on it. I felt him relax as he let me pull his head up. "Is that what you're worried about? That I'm going to go somewhere?"

I felt a brush of air as his fingers came forward to touch my cheek.

"Where would I go, you crazy man?" I asked him before I promised. "I will only be as far as your heart lets me go."

With his hands cupping my cheeks, he moved in and whispered against my mouth, "They won't understand."

"Who won't?"

"The world, your parents—they won't understand what I see when I look at you, how I feel when you play, or the way that I love all of the simple things that makes you whole." He continued to confess almost desperately, "Some might even say it's wrong."

Turning my body to face where I knew he was seated, I told him, "I don't care about everyone else. I care about you, and I care about me. Do you feel like this is wrong?"

"No," he replied, letting out a deep breath.

Reaching up, I stroked the shell of his ear. "Then, that's all that matters. Share this with the world. They need to see it. They need to see me as you do."

Phillipe Tibideau had one fear, and I planned to help him conquer it by never leaving.

* * *

As I sit here on a soft chair that Phillipe moved into the corner of the music room, I look at him over the journal I'm now reading. It has been a little over two hours since we've been down here.

After the soul-destroying way he took me earlier, I'm finding it hard to concentrate on anything other than the man who is sitting directly across from me as he sketches my portrait.

At first, I rejected the idea because I wasn't sure if I was ready to be studied so closely, especially after having him inside my body so intimately.

Who knows what he would see on my face?

His voice intrudes into my thoughts. "What did you just read? You look...pensive."

Lowering my eyes to the page again, I read the last line to him. "Share this with the world. They need to see it. They need to see me as you do."

I raise my eyes back to his to see that he has stopped sketching. His thoughtful gaze comes up to meet mine. Frowning, I decide to just ask him what I want to know.

"Do you think they did?"

He answers my question with one of his own. "Do I think they did what?"

"You're doing it again," I point out, lowering the journal.

"What can I say? I don't like journalists, but this you already know." He blows out a breath and raises a hand to run it through his hair.

"Do you really think that I'm going to write something terrible about you?" I question, genuinely curious.

Shaking his head, he moves the sketchpad as he crosses his ankle over his knee.

"I don't know, Gemma. For all I know, you might go home and write a story about how I seduced and clouded your mind."

"Would it kill you to *trust* me?" I snap, closing the journal in complete annoyance.

"No," he states calmly. Those green eyes are now frigid as they connect with mine. "But it might kill you."

* * *

Phillipe watches as Gemma digests his words.

Her shoulders straighten. "You can't scare me away."

Raising a brow, he nods. "Okay."

"You can't," she repeats.

"*Okay,*" he stresses slowly.

He starts sketching again. He knows she's watching him, studying his responses. Nothing makes him more uncomfortable than someone watching his every move. It's ironic since he used to wish that one person in particular could watch him—*just once.*

"So? Do you think the world ever saw her the way that you did?" Gemma tenaciously asks.

Gritting his teeth, he peers at her through the hair that has fallen forward over his eyes. "No, I don't think that they did," he finally answers, "but I think you do."

He can tell she isn't expecting that answer because her head tilts to the side.

"What do you mean?"

Continuing to sketch, he looks at her blonde hair that is now messy from his hands. The long, soft strands are still ruffled from where he held her still as he pushed his cock between her hungry lips. He can't help the stiffening between his thighs.

"I mean you *see* her, Gemma. Every time you look at her, you see her as I did. They didn't, and they still don't."

She nods, signaling she understands, as she sits up in the chair, leaning forward to rest her hands on her knees.

He knows that she is about to ask a question he doesn't want to answer.

"*Why* do you think they don't get it? Why didn't they see what you do? Or, for that matter, what I do?"

He wondered if she was prepared for the answer he would or, in a sense, wouldn't give.

"Because they were too busy looking at *me* and how I looked at her," he states. He knows he's talking to her in riddles, but he also understands this is the best way to explain it.

"I don't understand," she tells him, frowning.

"Haven't you noticed the things that your colleagues have written about me, Gemma?" he asks, his voice full of venom. "They were all so busy writing about *my* obsession and *my* perversion of the poor, little blind woman that no one bothered to get to know her. No one bothered to look closer."

She blinks, trying to comprehend, and then she swallows, taking a moment before she responds. "I'm looking closer," she finally whispers.

Phillipe stands and walks over to where she is seated. Looking down at her, he asks, "And what do you see?"

Licking her lips Gemma stands, wanting to keep them on even footing, and keeping her eyes on him the whole time. "I see a man who is broken from an experience he couldn't control. I see *you* in a way that *they* didn't."

Phillipe shakes his head. "God, you're so naive. I'm not just broken. I'm twisted inside my own fucking nightmare that never goes away. I'm fucked on the inside. You're only *seeing* what I want to show you." Agitated, he firmly grasps the sides of her face. "There's a part of you, Gemma, that's so fucking sweet, and I want to steal that part of you, even though I know I shouldn't."

Moving his hands, he cups the back of her neck, tugging her in close to him. She raises her hands, placing them on his chest. Leaning down, he presses his lips to hers.

He grimly elaborates, "They said I took something beautiful and destroyed it. Slowly, image after image depicted a tale of seductive debauchery. People ate that shit up. They loved it. Until, of course, they got their biggest story: *An alluring mixture of dark eroticism that is now enhanced by its devastatingly haunting sadness. The angels must be weeping.*" He pauses, letting out a deep breath. "*She* was the fucking angel. That's what no one understood."

* * *

Parting my lips against his, I feel his breath slide inside of me, and I can sense the tension rolling off of him in waves.

"Why then? Why didn't you tell everyone they were wrong? Why did you make it seem like she wasn't allowed to talk anyone? *Why* keep her hidden?"

His eyes narrow as he drops his hand from my neck. He takes a step away, distancing himself. "She didn't *want* to be in the public eye. That was *her* choice. I respected it, but no one understood that. They all just assumed that I brainwashed her, leading her astray and making her strip down, so I could have my wicked way with her." His whole body seems to be vibrating with tension. "What do you think, Gemma? Was she brainwashed? Should the story of her innocence be retold?"

Shaking my head, I move a step closer to him. "No," I tell him simply. "I think she was in just as deep as you were. The way she wrote about you showed the level of her own desperation. She was enamored with you."

"And what about you?" he demands quietly.

He moves, so we are now toe to toe. He looks down at my upturned face.

I raise my hand, placing it on his strong, solid chest. "I'm entangled with both of you. If the way you wanted her was perverse in anyway, then I am guilty, too. I'm guilty of wanting you both with a hunger that I've never had before. Maybe *you* are the common denominator, but now, I'm just as much a part of this equation as she was. Phillipe, no one is brainwashing me."

His mouth pulls into a tight grimace. "Well, maybe you're the fool, Gemma, because the public—the people outside of here that you dedicate your life to informing—is just waiting for me to fuck up."

Reaching out, he grabs my shoulders and squeezes them tightly. He pulls me in to crush his mouth down onto mine. I gasp at the brutal and violent fury behind our kiss as I feel the familiar stirrings of hot desire sliding between my thighs. Just as quickly as it began, he pulls back, pushing me away from him.

"You have no fucking idea what they did and what they still do to me or to her. Isn't it enough that my heart has already been ripped out of my fucking chest? Why does the world think it's okay to walk all over a memory that has already been destroyed?"

I try desperately to think of a response, any response, but before I can find any suitable words, he turns and leaves the room. I'm left standing in *her* music room. It's just me with an echo of her.

* * *

Phillipe finally took the paintings to the gallery today. They were thrilled to sign him, and they wanted to display his series immediately—well, the first three anyway. He told me that he wants me to sit for three more. He said that the gallery was going to feature him and that journalists would be coming to write pieces on him for the local newspaper and for a national magazine.

This was it. I knew it as soon as he told me. This was the moment when his life would change.

I just left him in the studio to come down here to type. I asked him to set my typewriter outside in the arbor. It was so peaceful here at night. There was no noise, except for the sounds of the wind as it whistled through the branches. I needed to think about some things.

He asked me if I would go with him to his opening night at the gallery. I was reluctant. I knew it was silly of me because I should be proud of what he and I had done, but there was something so intimate about those paintings.

Each one of them meant so much more than just a naked pose. They were a part of him and a part of me, and I didn't know if I wanted to stand there and listen to them being analyzed.

However, I felt like a hypocrite because I told him to get out there to let the world see his vision, but this was his dream, not mine.

I'm happy in the shadows this time. I'm content to stand behind the man I love and watch him rise to the greatness I know he has in him.

I just hope he understands my decision and doesn't end up resenting me.

* * *

Shutting the journal, I stand and make my way out of the music room. Heading up the stairs, I can't help but think, *Why didn't Phillipe just show people her journal? Or at least parts of it?* It would be more than obvious that she was the one who didn't want to be on display. He really had nothing to do with her decision to remain unknown at all. As it stood though, Chantel, he, and I are the only ones who know that.

I reach the top of the stairs and turn to make my way down the hall. That's when I spot him. Catching a quick glance out of the corner of my eye, I see him in his bedroom, the one he was in that morning several weeks ago. This time, he's sitting on the bed with his legs spread apart, his elbows resting on his knees. His shoulders are slumped forward, and his head is resting in his hands. He is painfully gripping his hair.

Stopping at the entrance with the journal in my right hand, I clear my throat and watch as his tortured eyes come up to meet mine. Without saying a word, I make my way into his room.

I'm aware that this is not the room *they* slept in. As my eyes shift to the mattress he is sitting on, I wonder if it is the same one he so eagerly pulled up to his studio a lifetime ago.

Placing the journal on a chest of drawers against the wall, I'm aware of his eyes tracking my every move. I know he's raw right now, thinking of her and the way people turned their relationship into something ugly. I find myself wanting to give him something back. I want to give *her* back to him.

Moving forward, I take a deep breath and stop when I'm standing before him. He releases his hair and drops his hands down as he looks up at me.

Without a word, I reach out to replace his hands with mine, stroking them through his hair. I tip his head back gently and can see he's about to talk.

"Shh," I tell him. This time, I'm determined to be the one in control of the situation. "Let me?" I question the complicated man before me.

His eyes darken as he nods, leaning his head into my palms. Taking that as his consent, I release his hair and take a step back. I undo my pants and push them, along with my panties, off my hips. Kicking them to the side, I move to undo my shirt. I feel the heat of his eyes on me as I hear the same snick and clink of the metal from earlier when he releases his belt buckle.

When I'm completely nude and standing before him, his mouth opens, and he licks his full, sensual bottom lip. His eyes don't stray when he stands slowly to push his pants down his hips. He removes his sweater, and I can't get enough of him as he bares his body to me. Our eyes collide. Staring deeply, I witness the moment when his shattered soul comes into focus.

As he drops his final piece of clothing on the floor, he sits back on the edge of the mattress. Feeling my heart fluttering in my chest like a trapped butterfly, I step closer to him—the man whom I have now become one-hundred percent consumed by. He's stolen a part of me, and I don't even know which part it is. *My sanity? My passion? Or maybe my heart?* All I know is that I want him like I need my next breath.

When I reach him, I climb up as close as I can on his lap, straddling his waist. I wrap my arms around his neck as I press my lips gently against his.

I plead softly, "Let me see you." Pushing his shoulders gently, I whisper, "Lay back and let me see you the way *she* did."

His eyes cloud over at the mention of Chantel. As he remains silent, I reach out with my right hand and trace his cheekbone.

"Let me give her back to you."

Heavy lust-filled eyes blink at me as he slowly lies back, his mouthwatering abdominal muscles rippling with the controlled move. He places his hands up behind his head while his sinful mouth parts open. I feel my pussy flood with moisture.

From his full, thick chestnut hair to his sexy eyes that are looking up at me, filled with desire and passion, he truly is a work of art. His sculptured jaw clenches tightly as I touch his stubble that feels prickly against my fingertips. As I continue brushing my fingers against his cheek, I watch those sexy eyes close while a sigh escapes his mouth.

How long has it been since someone touched him gently? I wonder, stroking my fingers down his jaw to the dip in his chin. When I get there, I tug it a little with my thumb and index finger, and his eyes open while he further parts his mouth for me. I lean down over him and touch his bottom lip with mine in a gentle kiss.

"What are you doing, Gemma?"

Nipping his lip, I look into his eyes and ask him a question I'm not sure he'll answer. "Will you tell me how she was when she was with you like this?"

His mouth tips up in a sad smile as he lowers his arms from behind his head. Warm hands cup my naked waist, pulling me to him, and he arches his hips toward mine.

"She was sensual," he describes, his voice strained.

I sit up on his thighs, reaching down between us, and I grip his throbbing cock in my palm. His eyes look down at my busy hands.

I can't believe some of the thoughts that are coming into my mind, eventually making their way past my lips. "Did she like to touch you?" I ask.

"Yes, she used her hands to teach me, to know me, and to learn what I liked." He moans as he flexes his hips, pushing himself into my palm.

I can feel my breasts sway as he shifts, and I move with him. Stroking my fist along his tight, hot flesh, I watch as he sucks in a deep breath.

Reaching my other hand forward, I stroke my fingers up one side of the V-shape from his lower abdomen. With every touch of my hand, flirting and tracing along his body, his rippling muscles bunch and tighten with each movement of his hips.

"She was a very lucky woman," I murmur as I rock my wet, aching pussy against him. "She had a true work of art to touch."

I watch him bite his lip hard while his hips push and pull his shaft into and then out of my palm.

"*She* was the work of art," he corrects me, eyes locked with mine.

Before I know what I'm saying, it comes out of my mouth. "I bet when you two fucked, it was sexy as hell." Without thinking, I add, "I would have liked to watch that."

"Fuck." He groans, shifting his hips. He begins fucking my palm violently, as he reaches down to the hand I have wrapped around his thick length. He wraps his fingers around mine, forming a tight fist. "Put me inside of you, Gemma. I want to watch your face as you slide down onto my cock."

I can't do anything at this moment but obey him.

Lifting myself up onto my knees on both sides of his hips, my grip moves with his to the base of his shaft, holding it firmly, as I lower my soaked core down onto his wide, thick tip.

Raising my eyes, I keep them locked to his green ones as he sinks deep inside me, inch after delicious hard inch.

When I'm fully seated with my ass on his thighs, he removes his hand and gently touches my clit.

"When I was inside of her, nothing else existed," he confesses.

He surprises me when he sits up and wraps his arms around my waist, pulling my hips and pelvis harder to him. As he slides in deeper, he nuzzles my neck. "And when I'm inside of you, *she's* starting not to exist." He groans as he turns, laying me on the bed.

Bracing his arms on both sides of me, his devastated eyes meet mine, and I can't help but think he is punishing us with every furious stroke.

Touching the hollow of his neck, I part my lips on a moan, arching my back.

"I can't fucking resist you. I keep trying." He curses. "God help me, but I can't stop myself."

Closing my eyes, I grip his bulging biceps as he thrusts into me time and time again, searching for that elusive edge while chasing a fading ghost. I'm left wondering just how far away from his heart he would let her go.

Chapter Seventeen
MINE

"I dreamed about you last night," Chantel whispered across his cheek.

He could feel those talented fingers of hers stroking through his hair. "Was it a good dream?"

"Hmm," she murmured absently and started to hum a melody.

"What is that?" he asked as he rolled her over to lay on top of him, watching as her soft raven hair fell down to conceal them from the outside world.

*"*Air *by Johann Sebastian Bach."*

He closed his eyes and listened blindly. When she finished humming, she kissed his mouth gently. He opened his eyes while running his hand up her naked spine.

"It's beautiful. What made you think of it this morning?"

"It was playing in my dream. You were there, and we were lying in the sun, letting it warm our skin."

He traced his hands down to her ass and cupped it gently. "Strange dream."

"But peaceful."

* * *

Phillipe runs his palm through his hair as Gemma lies with her ear to his chest. He slipped out of her body only minutes earlier, and now, he felt himself slipping from the reality of the moment. As he lie on his back, staring at the ceiling, he can hear *Air* being hummed in his ear, and in his arms, he is imagining a woman he can no longer touch.

"Do you always think about her?" Gemma asks, tearing him from his illusion.

"Yes," he replies stoically.

Gemma falls silent as her fingers stroke along his ribs and chest. "Do you ever stop?"

Phillipe squeezes his eyes shut, feeling his own deception mocking him. "I stopped when I was inside of you."

He feels her push up against his chest, but he can't bring himself to look into her eyes.

"You won't even look at me?" she asks.

Grimacing, Phillipe is disgusted with himself and the delusions he's clinging to.

It's bad enough he has given in, letting Gemma touch him in a way he never would have allowed weeks earlier when she arrived. With each stroke of her hand and each question she asks, he feels himself losing *her*, and he refuses to let go.

Moving his eyes from the ceiling, he brings them down to meet green eyes still clouded with lust. She's still feeling that glow from the euphoria you get from having someone touch you so deep inside that you don't know where the other person ends and you begin. For him, that euphoria is forever out of reach. It died a long time ago.

"You need to leave, Gemma."

Keeping a cool tone his face remains impassive. "This doesn't change anything, and I want to be alone."

Gemma scrambles off of him and scoots away. He watches her climb over the bed to pick up her clothes, and she silently puts them on one piece at a time.

"You don't want to be alone," she accuses from across the room. "You want to be with *her*."

Turning his head on the pillow, Phillipe looks into Gemma's annoyed eyes. "Well, you knew that all along, didn't you?"

Her jaw tightens, and her eyes narrow. Spinning on her heel, she marches to the dresser and picks up the journal she placed there. Without another word, she slams the door on her way out. Finally left alone, he confesses his sins to *her*.

* * *

Marching upstairs to my room, I'm more than annoyed. I'm pissed off at him, at myself, and at *her*. *Damn it!* Is all I can think as I throw her journal on the bed.

Moving straight into the bathroom, I turn the faucets on, feeling the need to wash the afternoon away. The man is so infuriating and complicated to the extreme.

One minute, he's silent, involved, and right there in the moment with *me.* I'm sure of it. It's, the minute we stop touching, the second that connection breaks, *she's* there, filling his head, getting into his mind, and telling him what to feel.

"Well, fuck you!" I curse at her.

I realize how stupid I must seem. I'm standing in the tiny bathroom, taking my clothes off, and cursing at nothing. *I'm going crazy.*

Pulling the shower curtain back with much more force than necessary, I step into the tub and turn, closing my eyes. Tipping my head back under the spray, I feel the warm water stream down over my face. I bring my hands up to my hair and push my fingers back through the wet strands. Closing my eyes, I start to picture Phillipe as he was earlier, lying across the bed. I imagine him rigid, naked, and hard, his muscles rippling with every breath he took.

Lowering one hand, I slide it down to my breast and squeeze it tight. My other hand closes around my throat where I place a slight pressure on myself while the water now glides down my skin and across my lips. Music filters through my mind as the hand at my breast trails down my torso, stopping between my thighs. I squeeze my sensitive flesh and part my lips on a sigh as the haunting melody of *Lux Aeterna* repeats over in my mind. Pushing my fingers deep into my needy pussy, I can't be sure why that song stays with me while I picture his tortured eyes and hear his angry words.

That's when I start to imagine the melody getting louder, more forceful, like the way it was playing this afternoon in *her* music room when he was in my mouth and on my tongue. As the fantasy takes over, I thrust my fingers in and out of my body. The water pools around my hand before it slides down my inner thighs, mixing with my own juices.

Suddenly, it's there, I feel it again—that second elusive presence. I'm not alone. I stop moving and open my eyes, sensing that I'm being watched. I feel like she's here. As my eyes try to focus through the water, I notice a dark shadow pass before me. A shiver skates up my spine, and I hear the word *mine.*

* * *

Possession ~

We started a new painting today, and Phillipe named it Rhapsody. I liked this one. It was my favorite so far.

"So, you want me naked with Diva across my ass cheek?" I asked.

He laughed. "Yes. Perfect."

I shook my head at him and raised a brow. "Kind of an odd place to put a violin, don't you think?"

His fingers ran down my bare arm. "It's an odd place to want to put a lot of things," he replied sensually. His voice was so deep that it slid down my spine, creating a pool of moisture between my thighs.

Sexy, sexy man, I thought. "I know what you want to put there," I told him.

Reaching out to touch his waist, I moved my fingers below. He was wearing loose cotton pants, and they did nothing to conceal the hard cock he now had pulsating between his thighs.

"Hmm," he murmured. He stepped closer. "When you're ready and not a moment sooner."

Licking my lips, I blinked. "What if I'm ready now?"

His lips pressed hard against mine. "You're not."

"I'm not?" I questioned.

His arms wrapped around my waist as his nose brushed against mine. He shook his head. "No, you're not."

Closing my eyes, I asked, "How do you know?"

His fingertips touched my closed eyelids. "Because you won't have to ask or tell me. It'll just happen." He assured me, his mouth was by my ear. "It will happen, Beauty, and then I'll have all of you."

I shivered as I turned my face toward his. "Do you want to start painting now or later?"

His arms unwound from around my waist as he moved away from me. "Let's start now, and then I want to show you something."

Smiling in his direction, I started to remove my top.

He sighed. "This is the best part."

"It is?" I teased as I undid my pants and pushed them off.

"Yes. When you take off your clothes for me, it shows so much trust and faith. You're so warm and naked. It makes me so fucking hard that I want to sink deep inside of you and never leave."

As I stood completely bared to him, I turned and looked over my shoulder in his direction. "Maybe it's not me who isn't ready."

There was a long silent pause and before I knew it his large palms were on my shoulders, and his hot mouth was by my ear. "What on earth do you mean by that, Chantel?"

Shivering, I pushed my hips back toward him, so his cotton-covered cock was pressing insistently against my ass crack. "Maybe you're worried if you take me there, you'll never be able to leave," I suggested, pushing his desperation and fueling his obsession. I wanted him dark. I enjoyed having him want me as much as his next breath.

"Is that what you think? That I'm scared?"

His sinuous voice slid inside of me. I felt goose bumps rise along my skin.

"I think you're worried that you won't ever escape me," I confirmed.

He chuckled darkly, wrapping one large arm around my waist. He pressed a big palm against my naked mound before pulling my ass tight against his thick shaft.

"When I get inside of you, you will be mine," he told me and bit my earlobe.

I reached my hand behind my head to grip the back of his and turned to meet his mouth with my own as I whispered against his lips, "Or maybe you'll be mine."

* * *

Dropping the journal as though it physically burned me, I look around the silent room I'm sitting in. The bedroom is empty, except for me, the bed, and the small desk, but right at this moment, I feel like it's occupied by more.

Taking a deep breath, I stand, moving to the window. I feel like I'm losing my mind. *Is it coincidental that I heard the word* mine *while I was in the shower? Did I accidentally flip to that page and subconsciously see it there in her typed print?*

I have no clue, but as I stand by the window, I spot Phillipe walking down the gravel path toward the lit arbor. That's when it hits me that I need to get away from here. However, if I do that, I will lose the story of a lifetime, but if I stay, I might end up losing something much more valuable, like my sanity.

Watching him closely, I notice he's carrying something in his hand. He's wearing a long dark coat, and his hair looks wet. *Maybe he washed* me *from him as well.* He stops in front of the bench, and he does something I never would have expected. He moves down to one knee and places a single red rose on it.

I can't help but hold my breath as he reaches forward and traces his fingers over the inscription there. *Love looks not with the eyes. Oh, how very appropriate that statement is,* I think as I turn away from the heartbreaking moment.

Watching him down there, in what I can only guess is an apology of some sort, I realize I'm not only in danger of losing my sanity but my heart as well. That's when it occurs to me that I want him, and I want him to be *mine.*

***

As Phillipe kneels before the bench and traces his fingers over the inscription, he closes his eyes and thinks of *her*. How very true these words—*Love looks not with the eyes but with the mind*—seem today, and so be it. He can't see her anymore, but she's the one constant on his mind, especially tonight. Tonight, he let her go for just a few moments, and she completely disappeared. She left him, and he let her slip away.

Now, he has to get her back though. He can hear her humming in his mind, and he can feel her all around him as he kneels there. In the place where she once found such peace, he offers up his apology.

How could I have abandoned us? Even in a moment of selfish pleasure, he *always* keeps her there, involving her somehow, but this time, he let her go. He failed her. Right on the heels of that self-deprecating thought, he reminds himself that she, too, failed him.

Placing the rose on the stone bench, he closes his eyes and utters a soft accusation. "You lied."

He doesn't expect an answer. He doesn't understand his need to lash out, but it's bubbling inside of him. He's angry at himself, which in turn fills him with an undesirable urge to scream or hit something.

"You lied to me!" He loudly curses out again. "You told me never…" he criticizes.

He closes his eyes as pure anguish threatens to overwhelm him. He pictures her face the first day he took her down to the music room. He's reminded of that moment of complete joy, an expression he'll never see again, and it calms him, easing his anxious heart.

Closing his eyes, he takes a deep breath. "You told me that you'd never leave, and you lied," he admonishes her gently.

* * *

"Where are you taking me?" I asked.

Phillipe took my hand and tugged it. We seemed to be going in the direction of the hallway near the stairs.

"I have a surprise for you," he explained.

I could hear the joy in his voice.

"Ooh, I like surprises."

"I'll keep that in mind." He promised, making me think of all things sexual.

"What kind of surprise?"

He stopped abruptly, forcing me to run into his side. "Well, if I tell you, it won't be a surprise. Will it?"

Reaching around his body, I moved my hand to touch him.

He moved quickly. "That won't work, Miss Rosenberg."

I pursed my lips. "Okay, fine. I only wanted to touch you. Take me and surprise me."

Before I knew it, his mouth was on mine. He pushed me backward until I felt a wall behind me.

"Stop, Phillipe!" I shrieked and giggled. "Penelope might—"

"By now, Penelope knows to just turn around and walk away." He growled playfully, nipping my chin.

"What?" I asked after a breathy sigh. "How many times has Penelope walked in?"

Phillipe laughed now, and the deep timbre of it made his chest vibrate against mine. "Oh, too many to count."

"Like when?" I demanded, slightly horrified by the thought.

"Hmm, the other day down in the kitchen."

"What?" I shouted, remembering how he'd lifted me up onto the counter.

He grinned against my mouth while one of his large palms stroked my thigh.

"Lift your leg, Chantel. Put it around my waist."

I complied because I didn't have the will to say *no* to him, but I was otherwise not deterred. "She walked in on us in the kitchen?"

He unbuttoned and parted my pants before his hand slipped inside. As he found his way into my panties, his fingers slid down between my wet lips.

He groaned against my mouth. "Yes, but you still had your top on."

Blinking, I let my head fall back against the wall. I pushed my hips out to him, and I thought of what he just told me. "Just my top? I had my top on the whole time."

He laughed mischievously, as his teeth bit my bottom lip while his thumb brushed over my clit.

"Oh god!" I moaned, arching against his hand.

"Well, you had your panties on," he stated softly.

His index finger flirted with my soaked core. I sighed and closed my eyes, ready to really let go.

That's when he smirked against my mouth and added, "They were just around your ankles."

Mortified, I moved my head away from him, but he chased me and had the advantage of sight. His hungry lips captured mine. His tongue pushed deep inside my mouth while two of his long fingers thrust inside my pussy.

Hearing his groan deep in his throat, I wrapped my arms around his neck as he hoisted me up. His free hand moved under my ass, pulling me toward him tightly, so I was wedged between the wall and his fingers pushing deep inside of me. He dragged his mouth away from mine.

In a voice that sounded strained and stretched beyond its limits, he said, "God, Chantel, your hungry little cunt is always so eager."

Closing my eyes, I listened as his words washed over me. He started to rhythmically move his fingers in and out of me.

"Yes, Beauty, surrender. That's right," he murmured with his lips on my ear. "Give yourself to me."

I opened my eyes while he continued to finger me.

"Your eyes are so fucking beautiful. Keep them on me. Keep them where my voice is, and I'll tell you everything you would see."

Parting my lips, I focused on his voice and let him take me over.

"You'd see a man who can't keep his eyes away from you and can't keep his hands off of you. You'd see someone who wants to be your lover…" He punctuated his last word with a deep thrust of his fingers. "Your friend…" With another thrust, the sounds of his fingers pushing through my slick soaked folds filled the space. "Your confidant…" His mouth was at my ear, and he bit the lobe before his fingers started fucking me fast and hard. "Your everything, Chantel. I'll be everything you need."

His lips were on mine and his hips were moving as if he were inside of me, and in a sense, he was. He crawled deep into my soul and staked his claim.

"You would see I am yours, and you are mine."

With that, I felt my body clasp around his fingers, and I screamed his name, the intensity of it echoing down the hall for anyone to hear.

I never did get my surprise, but what I did get, I planned to hang on to forever.

Chapter Eighteen
FLEUVE SAUVAGE DE FLEURS

Day 13

I did everything I could to avoid seeing Phillipe today. In all honesty, I'm not ready to face him after the way he so coolly dismissed me last night. My pride is still wounded, and I know the best thing for me is avoidance. Instead of sitting for him, I have spent the day organizing my notes and typing up some key pointers on my laptop.

Having just awoken from a nap, I stare at the ceiling in silence as I lie in bed. As the sun disappears and the night begins to engulf the chateau, I get up and start to wrap up for the day. Yesterday evening took a lot out of me, not only physically but mentally. I'm actually starting to believe that I'm *seeing* and *hearing* things. I'm tired, and it's becoming more and more obvious that I'm far too close to the man at the center of this story.

A loud knock startles me from my troubling thoughts, so I temporarily shelve them. Making my way to the door, I straighten the red blouse, and I open the door to a sober-looking Phillipe. He changed from yesterday's jeans, and he is now back in all black. He's wearing black slacks and a black button-up shirt with long sleeves. The coat I saw him in earlier is hanging over his arm, and he has one palm on the doorjamb.

He looks down at me with piercing green eyes. "Evening, Gemma."

Raising my eyes to his, I somehow find my voice. "Good evening."

Taking his palm off the jamb, he steps forward. I automatically step aside to let him into the small space that I have been occupying since I arrived nearly two weeks earlier.

I watch his broad shoulders as he advances toward the window. When he reaches it and looks out, I know the view he will see. I instantly feel guilty, as though he'll know that I watched him down in the arbor earlier this afternoon.

He clasps his hands behind his back, his coat wedged between his wrist and his back. Without turning, he informs me, "We're going for a walk. I suggest you put on some shoes."

Looking down at my bare feet, I wonder when he even looked down to see that I was without.

"Where are we going?" I question quietly.

As he turns to face me, I move over to the small closet and bend down to grab my shoes.

"You have a very nice ass, Gemma."

My spine stiffens as I straighten and glare at him. "Don't."

Raising an inquiring brow, he makes his way to me, arms still behind his back. "Don't what? Look at your ass or say that it's nice?"

Shaking my head, I brush past him to pick up my jacket. I'm not going to let him do this to me again, so he can just walk away when he's finished. Instead, I do the mature thing and ignore him.

"Are we going?" I ask pointedly.

His eyes run over me as he nods. "Lead on, Miss Harris," he replies and moves to the open door. Making my way past him with my head held high, I cringe when he whispers, "and I'll keep my eyes on the rear."

* * *

Phillipe keeps a close eye on Gemma as she practically runs down the stairs to the front door. When she gets there, she wrenches it open and goes outside. She has left her hair out this evening, and as he moves closer, he can see the foyer lights shining off it, making it look like spun gold. Her hair appears so rich and luxurious that he wants to reach out and run his fingers through it. Considering the rigid way she's standing with the determined look on her face, he should take the opportunity to do so, just to see her reaction.

When he reaches her on the front step, he looks down at her annoyed expression and suggests, "Let's walk."

Moving forward and passing her, he buttons his dark coat up the center of his body.

The wind is howling tonight, so he pulls up the collar on his coat and slides his hands into the pockets, looking over to Gemma as she zips up her jacket.

"Where are we going?" she asks again, following behind him.

Looking over his shoulder, he tells her, "To the river."

* * *

"I didn't even know there was a river here," Chantel told him, smiling, as she held his hand tightly.

Today, he decided to take her down there to have lunch. Running down the back of his property, the secluded area was always so peaceful.

"Well, now you know. It's just a little bit of a walk. You don't mind, do you?"

She gripped the crook of his arm. "You'll guide me?"

Reaching around with his free hand to touch her bottom lip, he told her, "Every step of the way."

* * *

He's taking me down to the river. *The river.* That's all I can think as I follow silently, the darkness now mocking my uncertainty and me. I don't know what I'm feeling as I watch him stride along the dirt path between the rows of grapes.

I know all about this river and about what happened here, and eventually, I know that I would need to ask him questions regarding it. The one thing I don't count on is him taking me down to it, and I'm not quite sure how I feel about that.

"You're very quiet back there. Are you okay?" His voice cuts through the cool night air.

"I'm fine," I tell him, trying to show bravery in the face of complete consternation.

He stops on the path, just a few feet ahead of me, and turns around. In the inky blackness that's surrounding me, I can't make out his details exactly, but I know his eyes are fixated on mine. As I draw closer toward him, I try to appear much more courageous than I am.

"Are you sure? Because usually you are much more chatty."

That makes bravery a little easier because all I feel at that statement is annoyance. "I'm a journalist, remember? It's my job to be chatty and ask questions."

I finally stop in front of him. As I look up into his perceptive eyes, his mouth pulls into a grim line. The wind is whipping around us, and I can feel my hair ruffling in the breeze as his shifts and falls down over his eyes.

"Yet you haven't asked me one."

I blink, trying to push everything I have heard, read, and been told out from my mind, so I can start fresh. I need to start blank and let *him* tell me the story, but first, I find myself asking something I do not expect. "Do you still feel her here?"

The silence that follows my question is so discernible that I can almost reach out and touch it. I hear his feet shift as he bends slowly, lowering his face to within inches of mine. His tormented expression comes into sharp focus through the night.

Quietly, he asks, "Do you?"

Licking my lips, I nod once. "Yes, I feel like she's here."

"Right now?"

He is still staring at me, revealing his curiosity. *Did he think he was the only one?*

"No, earlier," I admit as the wind wraps around me before it wails through the vines.

"But not now." He agrees before he instructs, "Close your eyes."

I swallow deeply and do as he's asked.

"Listen to the wind, Gemma."

I hear it whistle as it shuffles the leaves on the ground.

"What do you hear?" he questions in a whisper.

I can tell he's moving. I keep my eyes shut and listen as the wind gusts again. This time, it seems to be an almost mournful sound as it blows through the branches, filtering into my mind.

"What do you hear?"

Insistently, his hypnotic voice slides over me. As the question is repeated, directly in my ear this time, I flinch at his proximity. "I hear the wind."

His warm lips press against the lobe of my ear. "And how does it sound?"

How did it sound? I don't know. I listen closely as it whips up once more, resembling a scream through the air. The sound is as chilling as it is heart wrenching, and it leaves me with goose bumps on my flesh. I'm unsure if those are from him at my ear or from what I'm feeling. "Sad. It sounds sad."

Without warning, his mouth is gone. Moving around me, he starts walking again. I follow after him as he murmurs, "She's here."

* * *

"Tell me what's here," Chantel asked softly.

"Why are you whispering?" he questioned.

He let go of her hand and moved toward the mossy bank.

"I don't know. It feels like I should."

Chuckling, he turned toward her. "Well, it is peaceful. I'll give you that."

"Yes," she whispered, stepping toward him. "All I can hear is the water. Maybe the water and the birds? Is that what's moving around above me?"

He looked up into the tree branches above her head and spotted the little yellowhammers chirping as they jumped from branch to branch.

"Yes, it's those little yellow birds I told you about."

As she reached out toward him, he met her hand halfway, entwining their fingers.

"Are they happy? They seem happy."

Pulling her into his embrace, he wrapped her arms around him behind his back. She tilted her face up toward him. As the fading sunlight touched her cheeks, he thought she looked like an angel.

"Yes, they're happy."

A smile tipped her ripe red lips as she admitted, "Good, so am I."

* * *

Phillipe can hear the leaves crunching beneath Gemma's feet as she gets closer. He has just made it through the clearing and is now down by the rapid water. He can't quite bring himself to look at the river, but just hearing it flow over the snagged branches and large boulders brings him peace that he doesn't yet understand.

"Is this where—"

"Yes," he answers before she can finish her question.

They both know what she was going to say. Voicing it merely acts like a knife in an already painful and gaping wound. Any noise from leaves underfoot disappear, and he knows that she has come to a standstill. He waits patiently, knowing that anything that needs to be said has to begin with her. He's too raw to initiate anything.

"Did it happen at night?" she asks, her voice quiet but steady behind the difficult question.

"Not at first," he replies. "It was a beautiful day. It was the best we'd had for months," he explains, turning to look back at Gemma. He can barely make her out, but what he can see is that she has her arms wrapped around her waist as though she is holding herself together.

"How?" she finally whispers.

That's when he moves. Making his way toward her, he notices she's cautiously monitoring his every step. He wonders about what she's thinking. *Does she want to run? Is she scared?*

How ironic is it that the last woman he brought down here was completely at ease with him. She trusted him with her very life and trusted him not to fail. And yet, fail her, he had.

However, right now, standing before him is a woman who let him inside of her body and trusted him with her care, yet she looks like she's ready to bolt at the first wrong move he might make.

Walking around her, he notices she does everything but physically dig her heels into the grass to keep from moving. When he stops behind her, he places his palms on her shoulders, feeling her stiffen.

"I thought you knew how, Gemma," he rasps into her ear. "You read the papers. You watch the television. What do they say happened?"

* * *

I take a deep breath as I focus on the water that is moving at a startling pace before me. It's only a few feet from us, but as his hands firmly hold my shoulders, I can't help but think he can easily make me—

No, that's ridiculous! I remind myself.

This man has held me, touched me, and been inside my body. He would never do something like that, yet that is exactly what everyone is determined to sell to the world. *Could this man, Phillipe, really have done what the stories claim?*

I'm so busy thinking about all the frightening and very real possibilities behind the statements I have read regarding this man that I don't realize his mouth is by my ear again.

"What do they say happened, Gemma?"

I don't want to answer. I don't want to voice the terrible things I have read, and somewhere in the fearful part of my mind, maybe I don't want to give him ideas.

"Tell me," he demands, more forceful this time.

"They say you were involved," I divulge, shying away from the details.

"Gemma, Gemma, *Gemma,*" he admonishes. "That's not all they say. You know it, and I know it."

Tightly gripping my own waist, I tell him the truth he is tenaciously searching for. It's ugly when it slips past my lips. "They say you brought her down here. They say it was your fault."

His fingers tense on my shoulders and on an anguished rush of air, he answers, "They were right."

* * *

"Phillipe! Really? Here?"

Chantel giggled as he started to undo the buttons on her shirt.

"Why not here? It's quiet and peaceful. You're here. I'm here."

"Kiss me."

Laughing, she grasped his hands, tugging him closer.

Lowering his head, he pressed his mouth to hers. "Always."

* * *

Phillipe turns his nose into Gemma's hair and takes a deep breath. She smells sweet and spicy. As he grips her shoulders, listening to her breathing accelerate, he knows she is scared.

He isn't sure what she's scared of, but he knows fear is starting to trickle through her veins, making its way up her spine.

"Nothing is as beautiful or peaceful as watching the purity of an untainted soul leave the world," he murmurs, placing his lips against Gemma's cool cheek. "She looked right at me, *right* at me. Do you know what she told me?"

Gemma turns her head, and her eyes meet his. She mouths, "No."

"She told me she saw lights." He closes his eyes, releasing Gemma's shoulders. "She was blind, and even *she* was seeing the fucking lights. I told her not to look at them, Gemma," he explains, feeling the desperation behind every word leaving his mouth. "I told her, but she didn't listen to me."

Jamming his hands back into his pockets, he moves around her and makes his way back to the edge of the water. This time, he makes himself look at the swirling current.

"The first day we ever came down here, we had a picnic. It was beautiful—a perfect moment and a perfect day. So, of course, I wanted to come back. I wanted to paint her here, but the second time we came back, things changed."

Leaves crunch, and then she is beside him. Gemma reaches out and takes his hand with hers. The wind picks up and ruffles through their hair. Phillipe closes his eyes as he pictures *her* beside him instead.

"I wanted to paint you. You told me I could, so I brought you back here. That was the day you went away."

* * *

I hold Phillipe's hand, trying to extend my sympathies. I try to show that he can trust me as he stands beside me, talking to a woman who is no longer here. In that moment, as the wind picks up and swirls around us both, I look out across the water to the opposite bank. I stop and focus on a shadow. No, maybe it's a figure. It stands there, looking back at us. It's quietly judging, quietly watching.

Shaking my head, I turn to see Phillipe has his eyes closed, and his mouth is pulled tight. I don't understand much of what has happened to me in the past few days, but one thing I know for certain is that he is still with her and *she* is still with him.

And me? Well, I'm caught somewhere in between.

Chapter Nineteen
RHAPSODY

Day 17

Adagio for Strings is a piece I am familiar with. I remember watching it once on a tribute to 9/11, and ever since, it has moved me. Today, it once again moves me for different reasons.

During that evening by the river, we agreed to a few days of respite before making our way back to the chateau in complete silence. Consequently, I lie in my bed, unable to sleep for the rest of the night.

Time doesn't stand still though, and it is slowly creeping by. No matter how painful it might be, we need to move forward.

I make my way into the studio this morning to see Phillipe over by the window. That's when I hear the weeping sounds of the violin. Stepping into the space I now ironically feel the most comfortable in, he turns, and as our eyes meet, the expression I receive is pained and tired. It's almost the exact replica of mine.

"I want you to paint me," I tell him as I step closer.

I've thought about this for the last few days. Running it through my mind, I have tried to figure out the best way to connect with him. Obviously, it isn't by talking things out face to face, and it occurs to me that the most I have ever gotten out of him is when he's painting me.

"Why?" he asks, shaking me from my thoughts.

As he moves closer, I notice that he's dressed today in the usual black pants with my favorite hunter green sweater, and he looks devastating.

I find myself talking, just for something to do. "I think it gives me a better idea of who she was. This isn't a question of me trusting you anymore. It's to help me understand how you saw her."

When he stops directly in front of me, I look up into his troubled eyes and beseech him, "I *need* to understand, Phillipe."

Tilting his head to the side as though he's studying me, his eyes narrow as he nods once.

"Okay, Gemma. Then, we start *Rhapsody* today."

Immediately, I picture the image in my mind. I have been captivated by it since my first day here in the chateau, and it isn't one that I am likely to ever forget. Then again, none of them are ones that I would ever lose sight of.

"This music is beautiful. Did she have a favorite?" I murmur.

He brushes by me and makes his way to the stereo, abruptly ending the melancholy piece.

"Yes, she did," he explains, crouching down to remove the violin case. Looking over his shoulder, he reminds me softly, "You have to be naked, Gemma, so please take off your clothes."

Swallowing my next question, I nod and start to unbutton my long-sleeved ivory blouse. Tugging it out of my pants, I keep my eyes on him as he moves to place the case on the desk.

The silence is starting to become suffocating, so I ask, "What piece was her favorite?"

His eyes rise to meet mine as he unlocks the latches of the case. I already know he isn't going to tell me. When he looks away to pick up Diva from her resting place, I try to remind myself that he'll tell me when he's ready.

Removing my pants, I'm now left in my bra and panties. I reach back and unsnap my bra hooks as he walks toward me with the violin in his hand. Keeping my eyes on him, I remove the lacy fabric from my aching breasts, and as the cool air hits my skin, I feel my nipples harden. Raising my arm to the side, I drop it on the floor.

"Turn around," he instructs.

His voice is so somber that I swear I can feel it stealing a part of me, saddening my heart. Silently, I turn away from him.

He orders quietly, "Remove your panties."

I reach into the sides of the thin material and bend to push them down, realizing he has a perfect view of my naked ass—an ass he commented on only yesterday.

"Reach behind yourself with your left arm, Gemma."

Slowly, I do as requested. Knowing he is going to place the violin in my hands, I'm nervous because I know how much this violin is worth, not only in the monetary sense but in the emotional one as well.

When I feel the wood, cool against my palm, I clutch it gently with one hand around the neck.

All of a sudden, his mouth is by my ear. "Very good. There's just one more thing."

As he walks away from me, my eyes are trained on the easel and covered piece of artwork still sitting on the opposite side of the room.

"What is that?" I ask, nodding in the direction of the easel. I wonder if he'll tell me what he's working on.

Instead of answering my question, he replies, "This."

I feel the cool slide of paint on the left side of my lower back. I'm not sure if he's intentionally avoiding my question or if he really does misunderstand me, but right now, I know he is adding F-holes to my skin. After the first one is complete, he switches to the right side, and I can feel the cool bristles of the brush as he paints the matching symbol.

"There."

I look over my shoulder. "But there are no F-holes in this painting."

Disturbed, clouded eyes rise to mine. "No, but there were on the model that posed for me. Now, you're perfect."

"But not her."

"No, you are definitely not *her*." He pauses and licks his lower lip. Nodding slightly, he instructs, "Eyes forward, Gemma."

Silently, I do as I'm told.

* * *

Phillipe stands behind his easel and looks over to the woman once again standing in the middle of his studio, gently holding Diva across her lovely left ass cheek.

The night down by the river was painful. There is no other way to describe it. In fact, he was ready to tell Gemma that the deal is off, so she should just go home. Taking her down there and telling her only parts of the story was so emotionally crippling that he can't imagine how he'll ever tell her the whole sordid tale.

When she arrived in his studio this morning and he turned to see her stepping through the door, something about her pulled at him. Maybe it is the expression on her face.

Yes, she looks tired. She probably didn't get much more sleep than he had, but the sheer determination and look of understanding in her eyes now makes him realize that if anyone can tell this story the way it needs to be told then it's going to be Gemma Harris.

* * *

"You look lovely like this," he told Chantel.

From the middle of her spine, he traced a finger up her back to just below her hairline. As she dropped her head forward, he smiled slowly to himself as she let out a long sigh.

"You've been standing here for a little over an hour." Reaching out, he squeezed her shoulders,

massaging away some of the tension from them. "Maybe we should break."

Chantel turned, and he connected with gray eyes that saw nothing, but that didn't stop a sensuous smile from touching her lips.

"Maybe we should."

Reaching for her left hand, he took the violin that had been covering her round bottom.

"Let me have this."

He leaned to the side, placing it in the case lying open on the small empty desk, and then he was back. She still had her back to him, and her head was now tipped forward, leaving her elegant neck bare. Moving in close behind her naked body, he wrapped his arms around her waist and laid his lips at the top of her spine.

"Let me relax you."

In response, Chantel let out a deep breath. "Yes."

* * *

As he stands there now, looking at Gemma waiting before him nude and in pose, he wonders what she is thinking about while he focuses on someone else.

"What made you decide to paint her this way? Why did you name it *Rhapsody*?"

Well, there's his answer. Ever the professional, Gemma's always thinking of new things to ask him.

"Rhapsody," he repeats, taking a minute to mull over the word. "Well, the definition I always liked for it is *an ecstatic expression of feeling or enthusiasm*."

There's complete silence while he runs the brush over the canvas.

"But the picture seems so still," she mutters, more to herself than as a response to Phillipe.

"Yes, it does. Doesn't it? It was what came after the painting was captured that inspired the name."

* * *

Biting the gentle curve of her neck, he cupped her breasts and squeezed while she pushed her back against his chest. A piece she had recorded for him just the other day, Adagio for Strings, *was playing. It was his favorite.*

"Hmm, your breasts are the perfect size for my palms."

She raised her hands to place them over his.

"Show me," she moaned, entwining their fingers.

He nipped her neck and kissed her just below her ear before he started to move his right hand. Slowly, he slid their palms down her body.

"You have perfect breasts with smooth skin like satin. I could touch you all day and never grow tired of it."

Their fingers traced her ribs and moved down over the gentle curve of her abdomen where he dipped his finger, flirting with the small indentation. Her breathing became more rapid as he gently squeezed her left breast.

"Show me where you want my hand," he demanded, his voice dipping low. He was finding it difficult to even think. All the blood left in his brain was now making a speedy descent to his rapidly rising cock.

God, all she had to do was be in the room with him, and he became insane with lust. It was rare that they could be anywhere for less than thirty minutes before he'd have her stripped, naked, and beneath him. He'd decided that was exactly the way he liked her—screaming his name.

"Down here," she sighed, directing his hand to her warm mound where she pulled his fingers between her thighs.

At the first feeling of moisture on his fingertips, he groaned in her ear and pressed his steel-hard erection against her naked ass.

"Take your clothes off, Phillipe," she requested. "I want to feel your skin on mine."

Releasing her hands, he stepped back, making quick work of removing his clothes, before he moved back. Standing so close to her, his cock immediately wedged itself into her enticing ass crack. Grinding against her, he wrapped his arms around her waist. With his left hand cupping her breast again, his right hand took hers and pulled it back down between her deliciously juicy thighs.

"Now, where were we? Here?" he asked.

He ran their index fingers through her soaked folds. Her head fell back on his shoulder as she widened her stance for him.

"Yes." She sighed.

"Feel good?"

She moaned a little louder while he moved their fingers to play with her hard little clit. "Yes."

"It's so ripe and swollen, like a plump little berry." He exhaled, letting out a deep breath. "I want to devour it before I push my tongue deep inside of you."

Her eyes opened as she turned her head in his direction. As her mouth parted, a ragged breath escaping, he locked his eyes with hers even though he knew she saw nothing.

During moments just like this, he almost believed she saw everything, and that was when she told him something that almost brought him to his knees.

"I want your mouth wherever you want to put it."

Taking her lips in a fierce kiss, Phillipe turned her in his arms and lifted her up against his hard thick shaft. Her legs wrapped around his waist as he walked over to the mattress under the window. Mouths still fused together, he stopped when his toes touched the base of their makeshift bed. Her tongue was twisting and flirting with his. Every time she pushed it deeper, she gripped his shoulders and pulled herself closer, rubbing her wet core against his cock.

His hands cupped her ass and tugged her closer. First putting a knee on the mattress, he slowly lowered them to the bed. Following her down, he never released her mouth from the hot tempestuous kiss she had him engaged in. When he was firmly pressed against her, he couldn't help the drive to thrust into her. He flexed his hips, using the force to push into her hard, and then he pulled out of her, dragging his cock against her mound.

Finally, she leaned back from the kiss, licking her top lip. "Come up here."

Looking down at her, he grinned, touching her lips with a finger. "I am up here."

She shook her head against the pillow. With both hands, she reached down between their bodies and fisted his cock.

"This. Bring this up here and then come."

He groaned and thrust into her tight grip. He leaned down and kissed her mouth only to feel her bite his lip.

"I want you to come in my mouth. I want to taste you."

"Christ, Chantel." He cursed. "Are you sure?"

A sinful smile appeared as she reached up to his face, bringing him back to her. When his mouth was against hers, she told him, "Yes, I want to taste you on my tongue as you slide inside my soul."

Grunting low, he closed his eyes and moved away from her. As she released his throbbing hardness, he straddled her waist.

Gruffly, he instructed, "Scoot down the bed."

As she followed his command, her breasts swayed. Leaning down, he couldn't help himself from taking one of her ripe nipples between his lips. She reached out, clasping his head, as she arched up into his mouth. He bit the hard little tip before progressing to her upper body. Gently, he tapped her lips with the wet tip of his cock.

"Open your mouth, Beauty."

Without question, she obeyed, and he slid deep between her warm, wet lips.

"Fucking hell." He cursed as he shifted.

Putting his fists down onto the mattress to brace himself, he raised his hips. He lifted himself up on shaky arms as he slowly brought his hips back down to push farther into her mouth. Closing his eyes, he tried to imagine how she was feeling.

With his cock plunging between her lips, he could hear her breathing in and out through her nose. Her talented fingers were on his hips and ass as she pulled him closer, taking him deeper down her throat until her nose was against his skin. He could feel her breath tickling around him with each inhale and exhale.

"That's it, Chantel. Suck me deep." He growled as he slowly pulled away from her deep-throated squeeze. "That's a fucking pretty sight." He grunted while he

looked down his body, watching when the tip of his cock slid out of her mouth as she leaned her head back.

Through aroused, unseeing eyes, she pulled his hips back toward her. She pleaded, "More."

When she took him in once again, her left hand moved to the crack of his ass. He closed his eyes as he tried to control himself. As she sucked vigorously on his engorged flesh, erotic noises started to fill the room and his head. There was nothing he could do to stop his hips from picking up pace. As her finger now skirted along the sensitive skin of his ass, his hands white-knuckled the sheets, and his knees sank into the mattress.

Shaking his head and trying to hang on to some semblance of control, he groaned loudly as her finger dragged down his ass to his tight balls where she tickled over the sensitive skin.

Biting his bottom lip, he started to fuck her mouth in earnest now.

As much as he wanted this to be gentle and sweet, she was tapping into a part of him that he couldn't control. Closing his eyes, he could feel the climax skating along his spine, knocking for release.

"Fuck! Yes! Harder!" he roared, not really having a clue what he wanted harder. Her mouth? Her fingers? Or to get even farther down her amazing fucking throat?

Somehow, she knew. Right as the climax was about to slam into him, she slid a finger past his tight ring into his ass while she clamped her lips around his cock. He shouted her name as he came so hard that he thought he would pass out from the sheer force of ecstasy.

"Jesus Christ, Chantel." He sent up a prayer and slowly slipped out of her mouth as he slid his body down hers. When he was in line with her mouth, he took it in a kiss so erotic and decadent that he thought he might come a second time just from tasting himself on her mouth, lips, and tongue.

She smelled and tasted like him. Now, as she arched her hips toward him, he knew he wanted to return the favor.

Pulling back, he whispered, "That was the most religious fucking experience I have ever had and I will never listen to this piece, what's it called again?"

"Adagio for Strings." *She informed on a sigh.*

"I will never be able to listen to this piece without thinking of you, right at this very moment."

She smiled and laughed softly before curving her back. She was aching, and he needed to tend to her.

"Do you need me, Chantel? Do you want to see heaven?"

Closing her eyes, she nodded and widened her legs. Phillipe scooted off the edge of the mattress to kneel on the floor between her spread thighs. Damn, she's soaked. *Her thighs were glistening from her excitement. He reached out and ran his finger through it, bringing it to his mouth for a taste.*

"You're aching. Aren't you, Chantel? Did having me in your mouth turn you on?"

Leaning forward, he took a deep breath, inhaling her sweet and spicy arousal. "I think it did because your pussy is so wet that it's dripping all over your thighs."

Turning his head, he placed a kiss on her knee. He heard her whimper as he flattened his tongue to lick and kiss his way up her left thigh. When he reached her lush, wet center, he leaned in so close that his nose bumped her clit. Taking one of her pouty lips between his own, he sucked on it, savoring her delicious juices. When her taste hit his tongue, it went straight to his cock, which was making it rise and harden again.

"Put your legs over my shoulders, Chantel."

Although languid in movement, she obeyed immediately. With her heels brushing against his back, he gripped her ass and tugged her right to the edge of the pillow-top mattress.

"I want to taste you now while you slide over my tongue and come for me."

He lapped at her sopping wet cunt. She raised her hips and reached down, gripping his hair in her hands, as he licked and sucked on her sensitive flesh.

"Phillipe." She moaned.

He stiffened his agile tongue and held her in place as he started to tongue fuck her toward her orgasm. He knew it wouldn't take long. He brought his finger to where his mouth was busy devouring her sweet pussy, lubricating it with her own sweet juices. Mimicking her movements that took him to the edge, he moved the wet digit down to the tight little virgin hole that was currently spread apart in this position.

"Hmm. Yes, Chantel." He hummed against her aching sex. "You're a naughty little tease, pushing your finger into my ass earlier. Was that a hint, Chantel?"

Shaking her head back and forth, she lifted her hips, trying to get his mouth back into action.

"No?" he questioned. He pressed the tip of his finger on her hot little rosette.

"No, I just wanted to— " She panted.

"You wanted to get up my ass?" he asked as he licked her hot center again.

"Phillipe!" she screamed.

"Ahh, there's the ecstatic enthusiasm. Hmm, pure rhapsody."

Suddenly, her knees tightened around his ears, and her hips bucked up as he sucked her clit hard between his lips while pushing his finger deep into her tight, hot ass. She screamed his name so loudly as she came that his ears were actually ringing.

As the somber violins continued to play well after the ringing had subsided, Philippe knew exactly what he was going to call this painting of her—Rhapsody.

* * *

"Are we done then?" I ask, looking at Phillipe over my shoulder.

It has been at least an hour since I have been standing here naked and somewhat cold. It has been dead silent for at least half of it. I decided to leave it that way because it seemed he just needed some space today.

"Yes, we can be done, Gemma. Is your shoulder bothering you?"

He seems far away and distant. I know he's thinking of *her*.

"No, it isn't. I'm just a little cold."

His eyes come up from the canvas, and as he looks over at me, he nods. I see a look in his eyes that, under any other circumstances, I would think is arousal, but I know that look is not for me. That realization makes me feel more than naked. *I feel vulnerable.*

Slowly, I bring the violin to my front, and I move to the case, placing the instrument gently on the red silk. He says nothing as I go through the motions of putting on my clothes, item by item. Although he's here, I know he has left the room somehow. He's not with me.

Moving toward the door, I stop before I leave. "Do you mind if I go downstairs tonight to look at the paintings?"

I don't really know what to expect, but he nods once.

Looking over to me, he quietly says, "While you're here, Gemma, you can go wherever you like."

I give him my thanks and turn to leave the studio. Making my way down the main curved staircase, I stop to look at the painting hanging on the wall. *Rhapsody* depicts the very replica of the pose I was in only moments earlier.

This time, I don't hesitate to reach out and stroke the curve of her right cheek. I trace my fingers over the F-holes in the violin, the same pattern that is now dry paint on my skin. She really was beautiful with her otherworldly flawless skin. It is easy for me to see the appeal.

Shaking my head, I make my way down into the kitchen. As I stand at the window, staring out on the vineyards, I can hear Phillipe's voice playing over in my mind.

While you are here, Gemma, you can go wherever you like.

Yes, I can go anywhere, just not into his heart.

Chapter Twenty
ALONE

Alone ~

Throughout my whole life, I had been comfortable being alone. It had never really bothered me until he left me standing on my own tonight. It was then that I realized I had never really known what it was like to be truly by myself. Ironically, this occurred when I was surrounded by a room full of people.

Phillipe's paintings took off. Saying a few people purchased them was putting it too lightly.

In the past two months, prints of his paintings had been replicated and sold around the world. From the exposure afforded by that little art gallery and first newspaper article, the media had courted and hounded Phillipe, trying to get a piece of him ever since. In fact, just the other night on the radio, I heard an announcer jokingly discuss the talent that had propelled him into the spotlight. She'd laughed and went on to say that the ladies of the world thanked him for his skills because now they could admire his smoldering good looks.

For once in my life, I truly hated the fact that I could not see what the world sees.

Tonight, as I stood in a room full of beautiful women—of that, I had no doubt—I let my insecurities slip between us.

His success was both amazing and completely unreal. If I was being honest, the level of success he'd reached in such a short amount of time—not to mention the fact that thousands of people now had pictures of me in their homes—was slightly mind-blowing. I had known all along that he would succeed. He had been so passionate about everything he did that it had made sense that his paintings also evoked such a strong reaction.

But, tonight, he wanted me to go to a gala with him. So far, I had declined every invitation, realizing that people wanted to know all about the woman behind the paintings. After all, in a recent interview, one reporter had asked if I was, in fact, real or a figment of his imagination. He had assured the man that I was very real.

Now, he was asking me to confirm it. How could I refuse?

* * *

I tightly clutch the journal to my breasts as I make my way downstairs. I cling to it as if loosening my grip on it might lose my place or, even worse, the words might vanish. It amazes me that Chantel was so reluctant to be in the spotlight only because she seemed so comfortable there when playing Diva and posing for Phillipe.

I know it had to do with the content of the paintings, but really, there is nothing to be ashamed of. Like she wrote, Phillipe Tibideau's work propelled him into the spotlight, and his brooding dark looks made him a solid favorite when it came to magazine sales. One minute, no one heard of him, and suddenly, he was everywhere, not only with his paintings but as the man himself.

He is the enigmatic, mysterious artist, who is undeniably attractive, and he is the man who every woman wants to pose for, but he wants none of that. He only wants *her*.

It all begins and consequently ends with Chantel Rosenberg.

* * *

The gala was at 7:30 p.m.

I was sitting up in the studio, waiting on him. He'd left around twenty minutes ago to get ready while I had done the same.

I was dressed in red silk. Phillipe had picked an evening gown the color of Diva's velvet violin case. He'd told me that my complexion and my dark hair reminded him of Snow White.

It was ironic because we would be tested tonight. Our foundation would be shaken, and for a minute, I would forgot who we were.

Someone would offer up temptation, a whisper of doubt, but it wouldn't come in the form of an apple. No, it would come in the form of something much worse. For the first time ever, I would doubt Phillipe, and with doubt trickling through my veins, I would feel like I had nothing else in the world.

For that moment in time, I would feel completely alone.

* * *

I finally reach the bottom of the stairs and step into the music room. I move over to the light switch I saw him turn on the other day. The bright lights illuminate the stark white space with the odd-shaped boards on the walls. This is the first time I have been in here alone, and I am almost positive that I can sense her presence here, feeling it stronger than before.

Making my way over to the sound system, I look at the rows of CDs. Each label is different: *CR-Canon in D, CR-Requiem for a Dream (Lux Aeterna), CR-Vivaldi, Four Seasons (Winter).* This is her collection. *This* is her.

I look through all of them until one in the back under a stack of books catches my eye. Pulling it out, I read the label, *CR-Air.* I haven't heard this one yet, and I'm curious. That's one of my favorite classical pieces, and Chantel was a musical genius. The fact that she learned to play each of these pieces by ear just makes her even more incredible to me.

Putting the CD in the player, I hit play and wait for the music to begin. Instead of the sweeping strains of the violin, I hear a hell of a lot more than I anticipate.

Suddenly, the room is full of happy laughter. From every corner of the room, a female voice now surrounds me. I stiffen automatically, knowing it is *her*.

"Really, Phillipe? Give me Diva. Let me play." Her voice filters through the speakers.

Reaching up, I clutch my throat. My very own breath leaves me, but nothing prepares me for the deep rumble that follows.

"Come and get it."

"No, you wanted to hear my favorite piece. Remember?"

"Yes, but now, I want you to come here."

"Well, too bad. You can't always get what you want."

Straining with every fiber of my being, I listen to every single second of this intimate moment caught in time. There's a shuffling noise, and then his voice. The sound is now so familiar, yet in this particular moment caught in time, it's so completely foreign as it drifts over me.

"Play for me."

She starts playing.

The room fills with one of the most famous melodies in the world. With absolute clarity, the piece permeates the air so smoothly that there isn't one part that feels rushed or mechanical. As each rise ebbs and flows seamlessly, it is almost surreal that I find myself likening it to the tides of water flowing downstream.

Chantel plays the piece with such passion that I can only sum it up as this: If the notion of *sublime* were to take musical form, *this* is what you would hear.

* * *

Phillipe has been gone all afternoon. After Gemma left, he decided that he wanted some time to think. *Things are not going as planned*. Originally, he wanted Gemma to come to the chateau, read the journal, ask her questions, and write her story.

However, like the way everything else seems to be turning out for him as of late, it is not going according to plan. Instead, he's finding Gemma extremely hard to resist, especially when she's imitating or replicating Chantel. In his mind, it's becoming more and more difficult to differentiate between the two. Both women seem to be merging into one, and it's now almost impossible for him to stay away.

This evening, he makes the decision to go to her. He knows that Gemma has gone back down to study the paintings, and he has a feeling that he will find her there.

As he makes his way down the stairs, he can hear music playing. *Air,* he thinks immediately. Stopping two steps from the bottom, he leans against the wall and closes his eyes, remembering that day. He knows that, at the beginning of the recording, he captured *her* for a moment.

When she first left him, he sat down in the showroom with that particular piece playing on a continuous loop. *But now?*

He remembers he hid it away because it's been months since he's heard her play this.

Taking the last two steps, he expects to see Gemma standing in the empty space, but she's nowhere to be found. Obviously, she left the music playing before moving to the showroom.

Deciding to leave it on, he makes his way across the room to the door leading to the dimly lit area. When he steps through, he sees Gemma standing directly in front of the painting labeled *Sacred*.

She has her hands behind her back, and he can see the journal between her fingers. He must have made some kind of noise because she turns to face him.

"Gemma." He nods in acknowledgment.

She responds in kind with a slight nod and serious eyes. "Phillipe."

"How was your afternoon?" he inquires as he moves closer.

"I spent it down in the arbor reading."

His eyes move to the journal before looking back to hers.

"Oh? What did you learn today?"

"So far, not much. She's writing about the night she went to the gala with you." Gemma hesitates. When he doesn't make any move to respond, she foolishly continues. "Isn't that the night the press first wrote about her?"

Keeping his eyes trained on her, he nods again. "Yes, it was. Do you remember what they said, Gemma?"

A frown forms as she thinks about that question for a moment. In stark detail, he witnesses as each emotion crosses her delicate features when they enter her mind.

"Yes."

He narrows his eyes, knowing he just put her on guard. "You do, don't you? What is it they said?" he asks.

His voice is deceptively calm, but his eyes are giving him away. There's a storm brewing inside of him, and he knows that she can sense it.

* * *

Licking my lips nervously, I square my shoulders as though I am heading into battle. "They said that you broke the ambassador's nose and ribs in a jealous fit of rage."

He moves abruptly, looming down directly in front of me. Gripping my shoulders tight, he hauls me up against him, and the journal falls from my hands.

"I was jealous, Gemma. I should have fucking killed him that night." He growls out, his tone sinister.

I don't know what's wrong with me, but I can't look away. He's so magnificent in his rage that I can't help but stare up at him as I see the truth of his words in his eyes.

"Do you know why I didn't?" he questions quietly.

At this stage, I know my eyes have to be as wide as saucers. I stand mute, not having the ability to voice the question that I am dying to ask, but it doesn't matter. He's going to tell me anyway.

"Because I was afraid I'd hurt her as well," he explains harshly. He pushes back from me and turns, pacing across the space. "She just fucking stood there, Gemma!"

His rage is absolutely palpable. I can feel it rolling off of him in waves. He's still so very angry over what took place all those months ago. I feel as though he is reliving it right before my eyes.

As quietly as possible, I move back a step, not seeing any means of escape at this moment. I'm not really sure what I should do, so I revert back to my questions.

"What was she supposed to do?"

Turning swiftly, he pins me with angry eyes. "She was supposed to tell him to fuck off. She was *supposed* to tell him that she was mine, just like I told Susanna!"

Quickly, in my mind, I flip through the many articles that I had read, trying to catch up. I need to remember all the details.

Coming up short, I question, "Susanna?"

Shaking his head, he starts to laugh malevolently. I frown, not understanding the rapid shift in his mood.

"Yes, Susanna, the tall blonde the press splashed all over the goddamn place. She was much like you, Gemma. She was the fuckable blonde that *he* told her I was fucking."

I let the details, as confusing as they were, seep into my mind. "He told Chantel you were sleeping with Susanna?"

Slowly, Phillipe starts to make his way toward me. I take another step back, and my back meets the wall. Beside my shoulder, I feel the frame of the painting, and I know I am trapped. *I am trapped between him and her.* When he's finally toe to toe with me, he leans down, so our noses almost touch.

"The good ambassador told Chantel that I had been fucking Susanna for months. He then went on to describe in detail what she looked like, where we went, and how often we did so."

I swallow slowly, before I ask a question that I'm not sure I want the reaction to. "Were you?"

His angry green eyes skewer me before he moves to the left, placing his mouth by my ear. "The only blonde I have fucked in the last three years, Gemma, is standing with me now, pinned to the wall, and probably getting wet."

His teeth bite down on my lobe as I take another deep breath. I'm embarrassed that he is right. *I am wet. His rage is beautiful. It terrifies me. It impassions me.*

"*She* let *him* touch her," he says, emphasizing each word angrily.

Turning my head against the wall, my eyes connect with his. We are so close that I can see the flecks of gold and brown around his irises.

"I can't imagine that she would let anyone touch her after you," I confess, knowing that I'm going to have the same problem.

"It wasn't her body that he touched, Gemma."

I blink once and focus back on his hypnotic stare.

"It was her mind."

My breathing accelerates. Any notion I had about wanting to get away has now been replaced with lust. *I want him.* I want to reach out and stroke him to ease his pain, but his eyes are wild. I'm almost afraid of the wrath I might unleash if I make the slightest misstep.

"Let me tell you what she wrote in *that* journal entry, Gemma," he explains. His left hand rises to cup my right breast. I arch into his grasp when he leans in to me, whispering so harshly that his mouth burns against my ear. "She typed about how we arrived at the gala."

Squeezing my breast, his hand moves a little, so his fingers are at the buttons running down the center of my chest.

"She typed that I *left* her. She said I left her standing in a room full of people, and she felt more alone than she ever had."

While he's talking, his talented fingers slide inside my blouse, and he shifts back to look down at me. Bringing up his right hand, he grabs the other side of my blouse as his angry eyes start to heat.

"She wrote that she had never felt more disconnected from me than in *that* fucking room."

As the curse leaves his lips, he rips my blouse apart. The buttons pop away from the fabric, falling around us as he places his right palm flat on my chest over my heart.

"Your heart is beating fast, Gemma," he informs me, moving in close.

He's so close that I have to lean my head back on the wall to look up at him.

"Are you turned on? Scared? Or both?"

Swallowing deeply, I open my mouth and ask, "Why did you leave her?"

Calculating eyes meet mine and narrow. He reaches down my body and starts to undo my pants.

"I want to fuck you," he tells me.

I know what he's doing, and I'm determined to make him talk. "Why did you leave her, Phillipe?"

His jaw clenches, as he looks to my left, staring at the image of Chantel hanging in silence.

"Shut up." He growls as he pulls down the zipper of my pants.

Belatedly, I realize that I can't. I'm finally breaking through, pushing him into a place he doesn't want to go, and I'm relentless. Like a bloodhound, I can smell when I'm close.

I stop his busy hands. "Tell me."

Glaring at me fiercely, he hisses, "Fuck you."

I shake my head against the wall. I know he's lost. He's not thinking about anything now, except losing himself. The only way he thinks he can purge the memory is by fucking it away.

"So what, Phillipe? Are you going to rip down my pants and fuck me against the wall right beside her?"

His eyes flame, and his breathing increases. Twisted as it is, I find that I'm getting off on his fury. The angrier he gets, the more aroused I become.

"You're going to fuck the blonde right in front of *her* to finally prove that she had a right to be angry."

His fist slams against the wall near my head next to the side of the frame. "Shut the fuck up, Gemma!"

Reaching out to press my hand against his pants, I grip his cock hard.

"Is that why you hurt yourself? Do you think you let her down that night?" Squeezing him a little tighter, I glare right back at him. "If she were here, would I even exist to you?"

Licking his lips, his eyes blaze into mine. "You already know the answer to that."

"And you want to fuck me anyway. Why?"

Tearing my pants apart roughly, he pushes my hand away from him, slamming it up against the wall beside my head.

"Because I can't fucking help myself."

Taking my mouth with all the violence I can see swirling in his eyes, I can feel his teeth on my lower lip. He bites it right before thrusting his tongue deep inside. Moaning against his lips, I arch my hips toward him, trying to get him closer. I raise my free hand to touch his side, but he clutches it, securing it on the opposite side of my head.

He tears his mouth away from mine, and I tremble at the lust I see burning in his eyes.

"Now what, Gemma? You got anything else you want to say?"

Panting hard, my breasts strain against the fabric of my bra as I think about my next question. I can tell that he thinks he's won. He thinks that he's pushed me beyond my questioning but not this time. This time, I want to know. This time, I want an answer.

"I want to know why you left her."

Releasing my hands immediately as though I'm a hot flame, he steps away from me and drops his eyes to where I'm propped up against the wall half undressed. With my eyes locked on his, he looks beside me, his eyes trailing over *her* in the *Sacred* pose.

I feel my own anger rise. "Why did you fucking leave her, Phillipe?"

Bringing his eyes back to mine, he swallows and simply replies, "I wanted to see if I could."

Making it crystal clear that he has no problem doing so with me, he walks quietly out of the room.

* * *

Left standing in the shadows while the music from the next room still filters through, I reach out and clasp both sides of my blouse, covering my body, as I crouch down to pull my pants back up. I can feel tears threatening to spill.

I can't believe that I have let him reduce me to this—*a person who is aroused by anger, a person who almost willingly let a man have sex with me just to find release.* I hate what is happening to me, yet I can't stop myself.

Sucking in a breath of air, I try to compose myself. Running a shaky hand through my hair, I step away from the wall. I walk over to the journal lying on the floor and bend down to pick it up. Out of the corner of my eye, I see something move in the shadows.

Somewhere deep inside of me, I know that if she were to be anywhere, it would be here, but thinking it and feeling it are two different things. Gripping the leather-bound book, I stand and turn to face the wall. The six images hanging there silently mock me.

"He wasn't with her that night," I say aloud.

I shake my head at myself. *What the hell am I doing? Now, I'm reassuring her?*

I can't explain why, but it feels imperative for her to know this. So, like a fucking crazy person, I whisper, "He couldn't even be with me."

I turn and start to make my way out. Just as I reach the door joining the music room, I hear her laugh coming from the still playing CD and I swear I hear, *He already was.*

Chapter Twenty-One
Possess

Like the hounds of hell are after me, I run up the stairs two at a time. I turn sharply into the hall, heading back up to my piece of privacy in this place. When I start to make my way past *his* room, the door swings open. He reaches out and grabs my arm, pulling me inside.

As I'm tugged into the pitch dark, I hear the door slam, as my back is thrown against it. I can't see anything. I've gone from a brightly lit space to complete inky darkness. All I can hear is breathing—*his breathing and mine.* Without a sound uttered, I feel his hands reach down my body to grip the journal I'm still hanging on to.

"Give it to me," he demands softly.

I relinquish my hold, and I hear a soft thump. I know he has dropped it on the floor. I can barely make him out in front of me, so I can't see the expression on his face, but the mood in the room is tense. *I'm disturbed, and he's explosive.*

His fingers start to trace down, whisper soft, from my temples to my cheekbones. He reaches my jaw, and then his mouth is there. Lips to skin, he presses a soft gentle kiss to the right side of my jaw. His touch is in direct contrast to the waves of agitation I feel rolling off of him. As he shifts, a small burst of air ruffles my hair. He's planted his palms on both sides of my head. I can feel my traitorous body pulsating as my pussy starts to throb.

I'm turned on. This mysterious and intimidating man has me pinned to his bedroom door, surrounded by shadows, and I can't help but want him inside of me.

"If you want to leave, leave now."

The warning in his voice rumbles over my tightly strung nerves. When I make no move to go, he lets out a chuckle that's low, disturbing, and God help me, sexier than anything I have ever heard.

"In that case, while you're in here, you are mine."

I can't help the needy sigh that leaves me as his mouth moves above mine. His warm breath floats across my lips.

"Do you want to be mine?"

I close my eyes. *He's fucking with me now.* I know I can't be his. He knows he can't offer that to me, but he seems to like playing this fucked-up game. When I don't respond, that wicked chuckle escapes again as he brings one of his hands down to tug apart my ripped blouse. His warm palm cups my breast and squeezes it tightly.

"Spread your legs," he commands gruffly.

The hand at my breast slides down my body to palm my aching mound, pressing firmly against it.

"Are you ready for me, Gemma? Did arguing with me make your pussy wet? It made my cock hard, and now, I want to put it in you. What do you think about that?"

Pushing my hips out to him, I bite my bottom lip in an attempt to keep my mouth shut. It's almost embarrassing how ready I am. While his strong hand grinds my covered flesh, he lowers his head, brushing his lips on my ear.

"Now then, no one is in here to watch me fuck the blonde. So, what do you say, Gemma? Are you going to let me get in between your long, sexy legs?"

I moan and feel my lips part as his arm wraps around my waist and his hand rubs over my ass. He tugs my body forward, pushing his hard cock against me.

"Or maybe you want me here, hmm?"

I feel my heart accelerate at the implication.

"No answers from you? You were so talkative only minutes ago. What happened?"

Refusing to answer, I reach out with determined hands. I smooth them up and over his shoulders where I grip him, drawing him down to me. His mouth opens over mine, and immediately, his tongue is inside my mouth. I grasp his shoulders tightly, feeling my body weep as his tongue rubs against my own sinuously.

I'm going crazy. I want this man to possess me. I want him inside of me. I want him any way I can get him.

Feeling his sweater under my hands, I find I'm getting frustrated because I want skin. *I want him.* Pulling my mouth from his, I pant. "Take this off."

Releasing me, he steps back as I remain propped against the door. Not wanting to waste any time, I undo my pants and push them off along with my panties. After stepping out of them, I stand back up, and he's there in front of me. He gets as close to me as possible, and I feel his naked body on mine. His engorged length presses into my stomach while his hands move back up to frame both sides of my head. He dips his legs and drags his cock back and forth against me.

My hands move up to his shoulders again, gripping hard, while I grind my needy body against him. That's when I feel his hands move under my ass, clutching each cheek tightly, as he hauls me up. My legs automatically wrap around his waist.

"Yes," he hisses out. "Wrap those long, glorious legs around me, Gemma. Hold on tight."

I do as I'm told and cling my arms around his shoulders and my legs around his waist. My sensitive breasts crush against him as he pivots and walks us through the darkness to the bed, where he lays me down across the soft mattress. Following me, he presses me into the pillow top. Bracing his hands on the sides of my head, he pushes himself up while grinding his stiff shaft against me.

"I can smell your arousal, Gemma. You smell fucking delicious." Leaning down over me, he whispers against my mouth, "Let me taste."

My lips part as I nod.

"No. Bring it to me. Offer yourself."

I can hear ringing in my ears as the blood rushes through my head while the erotic request penetrates my lust-addled brain. Slowly, I reach down between our bodies, stopping at the apex of my thighs.

"Like this?" I ask. I find myself anxious to please him, so he can ease my ache.

"Yes, Gemma, bring it to me."

Dipping my fingers through my own juices, I coat my fingers and bring them up to his face. I watch in a trance as he slowly lowers himself. Resting on his left side, he takes my wrist firmly and lifts my fingers to his mouth.

My chest is heaving now in anticipation of what he is about to do. I can't take my eyes away from him. He opens his mouth and sucks the tips of my wet fingers between his sensual lips. My mouth parts at the sheer decadence of the act. As a moan slips free, I raise my aching hips while he sucks two of my fingers deep into his mouth. He swirls his tongue around them, cleaning my very essence from my fingers.

Being this close, I can now see his eyes through the darkness. His gaze penetrates me as he starts to rub his weeping shaft against my thigh. I'm so wet that I can feel the moisture dripping from my body as it trickles down to my ass crack. I'm locked in the most erotic battle of wills I have ever been in.

Finally, he releases my fingers free from his mouth, creating a sexy popping noise. His whole body moves up and over me again until his lips are on mine. His tongue pushes inside my mouth, and I can taste myself all over him.

Groaning loudly, I plant my feet on the bed and raise my hips up to him. He grinds down, but he makes no attempt to enter me. As he thrusts over and over, I can feel his cock as it leaks warm, sticky pre-cum on my skin.

"Roll over, Gemma." He groans as he braces his weight on his arms, lifting himself up.

Blinking at him, I hesitate for a moment as his left hand moves between my thighs. Moaning loudly, I arch up and push my hips against his hand, seeking penetration.

"Roll over," he demands again, removing his hand.

Not seeing any other option for release, I do as he asked. I turn over onto my stomach, settling my right cheek on the soft comforter. Immediately, I feel his body covering me from head to toe.

His warm cock nestles into the crack of my ass as his left hand rests on the mattress. I can feel his solid chest pressed firmly against my back and shoulder blades. His large thighs straddle over mine, and I can feel the hair from them tickling my outer thighs.

Rubbing my aching flesh on the mattress, I try to find some kind of satisfaction against the soft material, but nothing is easing me. That's when his teeth skim over the skin joining my shoulder and neck. My hips buck back and wedge his heavy throbbing length farther between my ass cheeks.

"Ahh, yes, Gemma."

His voice creeps into my ear and skates down over my spine, causing goose bumps to rise over my flesh.

"I want *this,*" he tells me as he pushes his erection back and forth between my cheeks.

I know what he wants. I've never had a man there. The thought terrifies me, but at the same time, it turns me on more than I care to admit. In fact, the thought alone has my pussy clenching and my ass cheeks flexing.

Shifting my hips up, I try to bring my hand under my body, so I can ease myself in some way. Before I get my arm fully under me, Phillipe grips my wrist and pulls it out, placing it by my head. I can see it being held down by his large palm, and the entrapment turns me on even more.

"No, no. I get your pussy, Gemma," he informs me darkly. He moves in close to my ear. "I get your pussy and..." He thrusts his hips, driving that steel-like shaft against me. "I get your ass."

Whimpering, I raise my hips as he scoots away from me. He releases my hand, and I feel the absence of his body more acutely than ever before. Quickly, his hands are back, gripping my hips. He tugs me up until I'm on my hands and knees in the center of his bed.

"Yes, just like that," he murmurs, his hot breath against my ass. "Spread your knees a little."

I do as requested, hearing him groan.

"Nothing is going to stop me from getting inside of you, Gemma. Nothing." He promises.

His mouth is on my thigh, his tongue lapping up the slick path that my juices have created. He moves his sinful mouth closer and closer to the part of my body that is weeping with need for him. Fisting the mattress tightly, I push back as his tongue swipes across my swollen lips. He licks a little harder the second time, as his tongue dips inside of me and my desperate moan splits through the silence.

"Phillipe!" I cry out.

Instead of a response, I feel his mouth leave the space between my thighs right before his fingers grasp my hips. His insistent cock kisses my pussy, as slowly, inch by delicious inch, he slides into my wet center. When his hips are finally flush against my ass, he stops and waits. I try to push back, but he holds me still.

"Not yet," he instructs while his fingers trace over the curve of my spine. "Jesus, you're perfect."

Panting heavily, I can feel my breasts swaying and aching as he plays my body as expertly as someone would an instrument. Finally, he grips me and starts to move. Gradually at first, he pulls his cock from me, before he rocks forward, slamming back into me hard. I cry out and hold on to the comforter. Again, he stops, fully seated in my pulsating core. His fingers repeat their motion on my spine, flirting down my back, but this time, they don't stop at the end of my tailbone. They continue their path to my ass and push against my rear entrance.

Before I can question or get comfortable with the notion, the fingers are gone, and he's pulling out of me and slamming back inside, making me forget everything but the deep penetration of him at this angle.

"Oh fuck." He grunts as he impales me over and over.

My whole body jerks forward with each strong thrust of those hips. Moaning and shoving my hips back against him, I find everything in my mind is gone. All thoughts have disappeared. In their place, pure instinct fills me with the need to fuck and demand to be fucked. Like an animal, I find myself thrusting back on the cock that is dominating my every feeling at this moment. When his finger returns to my ass, I feel the tip of it pushing inside, and all I can do is strain back against him harder.

Instead of being frightened, I'm even more turned on, knowing that I am giving him what he wants, and the thought of what he's seeing as he fucks me and fingers my ass further seduces me.

"Gemma, your ass is so tight. It's so fucking warm."

He stills inside my soaked and well-used cunt as he leans over and grabs my hair. Jerking my head back, he makes me look at him over my shoulder. His eyes are almost glowing in the darkness, and the feral lust on his face ignites my own fever pitch desire. As he watches me, flexing his hips slightly, he pushes his finger deep inside me, and I scream out.

"Yes." He groans and starts to fuck me again. "Yes, Gemma, I'm going to take you. I'm going to fuck your ass hard, and you're going to love every fucking moment of it," he promises darkly as he releases my hair.

My head falls forward, and I brace my hands on the bed as he hammers into my moist depths. Abruptly, he pulls out completely.

The shock and loss of his fullness makes me cry out. "Phillipe!"

There's no response in the darkness, the only sounds coming from my harsh breathing. I can't even hear him over my labored breaths, but then he's back. His lips are against my ass cheek as his teeth nip and bite the tender skin there.

Making his way to my crack, his hands come up to grip both cheeks, pulling them apart to spread me wide. Ashamed but aroused, I groan and lower my head and upper body to the mattress, leaving my hips in the air. I'm on display, and he can see everything.

"Oh yes, you are fucking delicious," he tells me before swiping his hot, wet tongue over my quivering hole.

"Oh god." I gasp, feeling my pussy clench and gush.

"Ahh." He chuckles sensually against my exposed flesh, his hot breath whispering across my most vulnerable skin. "You like that." He states as he continues to swipe his moist tongue against me.

Closing my eyes, I try to forget what he is seeing and just go with the sensation. I feel one of his fingers right there beside his tongue, and as it pushes into my back passage, I find myself grinding back toward him. My body is greedy for anything he will give me.

"That's right, Gemma, take my finger into you. Suck it in deep."

His voice is as hypnotic as his finger and mouth. As he starts fucking me with his long digit, his mouth bites my ass cheek, as his tongue dips down to lick where his finger is penetrating me. I can hear my whimpers of pleasure and frustration, and I don't even understand what it is I want.

More? Do I really want him to fuck me there? Where his finger is? These are the lust-crazed thoughts I'm having as a second finger pushes inside of me, stretching me wider. I wince through the bite of pain and concentrate on his mouth, focusing on my need to climax.

I'm so wet and achy that I feel like I'm going to soak the entire mattress. As his fingers continue to stretch me for his final penetration, his mouth moves down lower. Suddenly, his tongue is at my pussy, lapping up my juices. Furiously rocking my hips back, I fuck his face, pushing his tongue deeper into my hungry body, as his fingers thrust farther into my ass.

"Ahh…oh." I moan. High on desire, I start begging. "Phillipe? Please. Phillipe!"

After a final lap on my slick folds, he drags his tongue up, flicking it across my hole that is currently stretched and I feel a third digit push in slowly.

I scream at the sharp sting of pain. "Fuck!"

When all three fingers are fully inside of me, he licks around them and bites my ass cheek hard.

"You ready, Gemma? Show me you're ready," he whispers against my flesh.

I think about how I am supposed to do that. As he leaves his fingers snug and still inside of me, my body begins to grow accustomed to the foreign feeling, and I find I have this insatiable need to move. Pushing back on his hand, I start to rock my hips against his fingers, and I can feel them moving in and out of me.

He curses darkly. "You've fucking destroyed me. First, she did, and now, you are."

I don't have a voice at this moment. Honestly, nothing in my brain is functioning, except my unanswered need, so I don't answer him. He removes his fingers, and I whimper at the loss until I feel his throbbing tip resting against my now stretched hole.

Clutching my left hip with one hand, he strokes his other palm up my spine to my hair, gripping it tightly, and I wince at the pain. That sensation is quickly replaced when his cock pushes inside of me, and a burning sensation begins in my ass.

Biting my lip, I try to pull away.

He coaxes me softly. "Shh, Gemma. Concentrate on that juicy pussy of yours. Fight through the pain, and believe me, your body will explode from the pleasure."

Taking a deep breath, I try to get use to the burn as he moves again, and I feel him slide farther into my back passage, stretching me even wider. When he pulls my hair hard, the delicious bite of pain surrounding me couples with the throbbing ache between my thighs.

Finally, after what seems like hours, I feel his hips against my ass, and I know he is firmly lodged deep inside of me. I'm so full of his cock that I can barely breathe without feeling him throb inside my body. Holding me steady, he waits motionless behind me, letting me grow accustomed to his girth.

My empty core clenches, trying to grasp onto something, *anything,* to ease the ache. When it clenches a second time, I groan and push back on him. He sucks in a deep breath before he leans down to reach under me, brushing a finger across my hard clit.

Screaming out his name, I feel the room start to spin as he bites my neck.

"It's so fucking hot inside of you that I might have to just stay here."

Moaning, delirious with my own pleasure, I know that I'm selling my soul to him at this very moment. I know I have passed the line from light to dark, but as I push back on him, feeling him rub my clit again, I find that I like it.

"How does it feel, Gemma?" he asks. He shifts his hips, gently thrusting his cock. "How does it feel, knowing my cock is inside your tight little ass? Do you know how it feels to me?"

I shake my head as he moves back, holding on to my hips.

"It makes me lose myself, Gemma. It makes me feel like I've crawled inside of you, and now, I have all of you. *You're mine.*"

He pulls out of me and drives back inside roughly.

"Fuck!" I scream.

He starts to pound into me, fucking my ass relentlessly, as his fingers punish my hips. I know that I'll have bruises tomorrow, but at this stage, I don't care. I'm pushing back against him, loving the sinful feel of his cock every time he plunges deeper into my dark, hot hole.

"Yes, Gemma. Fuck me. Fuck me hard and make me forget."

As I mindlessly obey, I know he's not the only one forgetting. I've lost my mind. As his hand snakes around me, his fingers penetrate my pussy, and I'm crazed with lust. I bite my bottom lip to prevent an agonized scream, but I find I can't hold it in.

"Now!" I demand hoarsely. "Now. Fuck, Phillipe! Now!"

Moving his hand, he pinches my clit hard and plows his cock into me. That's when I feel it. His hot, sticky come shoots up inside of me, plunging into the deep, dark places clouding my very soul.

Phillipe is right. He now possesses me.

Chapter Twenty-Two

MARKED

Phillipe wakes up an hour or so later to the melodic tune of *Air* running through his mind. In the darkness, he closes his eyes and feels *her* there. It's almost as though he can smell her if he concentrates hard enough. *Just close your eyes and think of her,* he tells himself, but it isn't as easy this time.

No, this time, a blonde with big guileless eyes, a perfect mouth, and a delicious ass keeps crashing into his thoughts. Squeezing his eyes shut, he tries to deny any kind of feelings he has for Gemma. *There's no room left in my heart for her. Is there?*

Yes. I'm gone.

Phillipe's eyes snap open, thinking he heard her. He swears he sees her when he calls her name. "Chantel?"

Hearing a shuffling sound over by the door, his eyes narrow as they try to adjust in the darkness afforded to him by the heavy drapes he pulled closed. There, on the floor by the locked door, is the figure of a woman.

She's naked with her hair falling down over her shoulders. She has her arms wrapped around her raised legs that are crossed at the ankles as she holds her knees close to her chest.

She looks frightened. Chantel looks scared.

Pushing the covers aside, Phillipe moves his legs over the edge and gets out of the bed. Mindless of his nudity, he makes his way toward her.

Holding out his hand, he coos to her, "It's okay, Beauty. I'm here."

He hears a quick intake of air as goose bumps break out across his exposed flesh. His heart starts to pound as he moves closer to the motionless figure on the ground. She has her face turned up to him, and as he approaches, she doesn't move. *Air* continues to float around him. *It's her favorite.*

"Chantel?" he whispers again.

This time, there's slight movement. *She's coming back to me. I haven't lost her.*

The woman before him shifts. She rises to her knees as he sinks to his.

She takes his hand in hers before she replies, "Gemma."

* * *

Holding my breath, I kneel there before the man I just gave myself to completely. He is lost. He's in some kind of hallucination where he can't even see me. He is seeing, feeling, and remembering *her*. As I hold his hand in mine, I realize that he is shaking.

"Gemma?" he questions.

Squeezing his fingers tightly, I rise up on my knees, so I am now face to face with him. Placing my free palm to his cheek, he closes his eyes as he leans his face into my hand.

"Yes, it's Gemma," I softly reveal.

There's silence all around us, except for our breathing.

"I thought…" His voice sounds miles away even though he is kneeling right before me. "I thought she was here. I heard her," he confesses.

I swallow slowly. I try to decide if what I'm about to admit is better for him or just something that will make me feel less crazy. "She was."

Haunted green eyes move to mine. The darkness still surrounds us, but he is close enough that I can make out the sadness and dejection in his eyes.

"That's why I woke up," I whisper. I run my fingers up through his hair. "She was here only minutes ago."

Scooting forward on my knees, I release his hand and bring my hands up to cup his face in both my palms now.

"Give her to me, Phillipe," I entreat softly.

His weary eyes search my features. He raises his hand to my chest where he places it over my heart. The warmth that radiates from him seems to seep through my skin, touching my soul.

"Will you look after her?"

Tears start to fill my eyes as I nod slowly. "Give her to me, and I will take care of her."

He swallows deeply, his Adam's apple moving, as he closes his eyes and removes his palm. "Where's the journal?"

My breath catches as I look around the room. I spot it on the floor where he dropped it earlier. Moving away from him, I reach out to pick it up. As I touch the leather cover, I feel a shock hit my fingers. Deep down inside, as crazy as it seems, I know it is *her*. I know she's just as frightened as the both of us. Refusing to be sidelined, I grab the journal and turn around, only to find he's moved back to the bed.

He's sitting on the edge of it. He's naked, save for the sheet he has now pulled over to cover himself. I make my way over to him through the shadows. When I am standing before him, I stop as he looks up at me with eyes full of sorrow.

He admits, "I would have done anything to swap places with her. I begged him, you know."

Gritting my teeth, I try not to let my tears get the better of me. My fingers tighten on the journal as he reaches out to take it from me.

"On the day she left, I made deal after deal with him to take me instead."

I release the journal as I keep my eyes on his.

"He didn't listen."

* * *

Marked ~

"How could you have left me tonight, Phillipe?" I yelled as we made our way into the studio.

"Excuse me? I think if anyone left anyone, it would be you when you left me to have an all-night cozy chat with the ambassador."

Fuming, I turned away from him. He is being so unreasonable. *"He told me things."*

"I know what he told you, Chantel!" he boomed.

I felt it rattle my very bones. Phillipe was furious. I had never seen him this way.

Tonight had gone completely wrong. We had arrived at the gala, went inside, and then we had been separated. People had wanted to speak to him. That was understandable. I had disappeared into a corner, a place where I felt the most comfortable, but I hadn't remained alone for long. No, not five minutes after I had retreated to my own space, I had felt someone behind me.

Spinning back to where I knew Phillipe was, I asked him pointedly, "And what am I supposed to believe? You just left me standing there tonight! You didn't introduce me to anyone—"

"You didn't want me to! Jesus, Chantel, make up your fucking mind!"

"Was she there?" I asked him softly, feeling my jealousy clawing at me like a vicious animal.

"Who?"

"Don't treat me like a fucking idiot!"

"No. No, she wasn't even there."

Swallowing back my irrational tears, tears of anger and unwarranted jealousy, I spun away from him. "Just go away. Leave me alone."

I heard movement, and then his hands were on my shoulders, spinning me back to him. I knew he was up in my face because I could feel his breath, warm and intoxicating, as it floated over my lips.

"I wanted to kill him tonight," he confessed dangerously.

I believed him.

"You almost did," I pointed out. "Leave me alone, Phillipe."

"No." He growled out, gripping my shoulders tightly.

"Are you going to hurt me, too?" I asked him.

I knew it was a low blow. Automatically, his big hands released me.

"I'd never."

Blinking at him, I lowered my head. "Yet you have."

* * *

Looking down at Phillipe, I notice his left hand is clenched into a fist.

"You know you didn't hurt her that night, right?" I try to reassure him.

Eyes full of remorse come up to meet mine. "I betrayed her trust that night."

"But you told me you didn't go with Susanna. I believe that. She would have, too."

Shaking his head, he grimaces as he lowers his eyes to the page. "Not in that way, Gemma."

* * *

He has finally left me alone for a moment. He's given me time to think. He's so all-consuming all the time. Everything about him binds me. Everything about him makes me love him.

Even as he was continually punching the ambassador, all I could think was, He is doing this for me, and I love him.

I don't know what I feel. I think it is love. It steals every fiber of who I am and wraps around me like a tight fist. It makes me burn with jealous rage, and it also makes cry at the thought of loss.

I've realized that I don't know how to be without him. I don't want to know. I want him to take me and mark me. Does that sound absurd?

Maybe but that's how I feel. I want it to be just him and me. I want him to own me.

Here with me—that's where I want him to be. I want to be with him in this little room where we sleep and forget about the rest of the world. Forget about the fame. Forget about the stupid paintings! They are the reasons for everything that happened tonight.

Those stupid paintings! I wish he'd never painted them.

Now, the world wants him, and he wants the world.

I just want him.

* * *

"Phillipe, she was angry. We always say or write things when we're angry."

Closing his eyes, he places the journal by him on the bed.

I'm disappointed. I want to know more. I want to know what else she wrote.

Spreading his legs apart, he beckons me forward. Moving closer, I step between his naked thighs as he raises his hands to my hips. Leaning forward, he places his mouth against my stomach, just above my navel. I take a deep breath and bring my hands to his hair. Threading my fingers through it, I brush his hair softly and lean his head back, so his face is upturned with his eyes focused on mine.

"She loved you completely. Even when she was angry, she wrote that she loved you."

Blinking slowly, he remains silent.

I confess softly, "She was intoxicated, just as I am."

Nestling his head forward, he flicks his tongue against the small indentation in my tummy. Against my flesh, he reveals, "God help me, so am I, Gemma."

* * *

He didn't leave me alone for long. He came back, not even ten minutes later, and hugged me in his arms.

"Don't be angry at me," he begged.

There was no way I could stay annoyed.

Wrapping my arms around him, I admitted, "I'm scared."

He pulled back from me to kiss my forehead. "What are you scared of?"

Taking a deep breath, I decided to be honest because he was always honest with me. "I'm scared of losing you. Sometimes, I wish I'd never told you to go to the gallery."

I closed my eyes as he stroked my hair.

"Nothing, Chantel, nothing will ever take me away from you."

Tears formed in my eyes, and I tried to blink them away. I tried to hide them from him.

"Will you do something for me?" he asked.

Raising a hand, I swiped my eye and nodded. "Yes. What is it?"

"Come to town with me."

"Phillipe, it's nearly 1 a.m."

"It doesn't matter. This place stays open late." He paused as he took my hand in his. "Trust me?"

I smiled tremulously at him. "I trust you."

* * *

I can feel Phillipe's teeth as he nibbles around my navel. He moves back, and the sheet falls away to reveal his interested cock.

"Come up here," he instructs gruffly.

I wrap my arms around his neck and straddle his thighs, wedging his shaft between us. He strokes his hands up my back and down to my ass.

"Are you sore?"

I nod slightly with a smile. "A little."

His fingers flirt with the crack of my ass, and finally, a small smile flirts with the corner of his mouth. "Was it worth it?"

Running my hands through his hair, I wriggle closer to him as he clenches his jaw.

"Yes, it was worth it."

He leans forward, and I'm captivated as his avaricious mouth sucks my nipple between his moist lips. Arching toward him, I marvel at the gentleness that is pouring from him as his hands caress my back, pulling me closer. Something's different. He seems calm, like he's almost at peace for the first time. He seems content to be sitting here with me on his lap as he torments my aching hard tip.

I take joy in this moment of solace he's finding with me in his arms. I feel like I'm finally touching the man I ache to own.

* * *

"Phillipe, will you tell me where we are going?" I asked.

He pulled the car to a stop, and I waited patiently as he came around to open my door.

"Come on," he told me. He was almost as enthusiastic as a child.

My head was spinning with ideas as to where we were. This night was so crazy and so full of different emotions. He took my hand and guided me out of the car. I followed as we moved across the pavement, wanting to know what had him so excited when I heard an electric ding-dong, signaling that we had arrived.

"Phillipe?" I asked again in a hushed whisper, pulling on his hand. "Where are we?"

That was when I heard the insistent buzzing in the background. The noise was foreign. It was nothing I had ever heard before.

"Ahh, Phillipe," a deep voice greeted us.

"Marcus, hi."

"Is this she?" The smooth French accent floated across the air.

"Yes, this is Chantel."

I remained still, knowing I was being inspected, and I hated it.

"Phillipe?" I questioned again.

I felt him turn toward me, and he took both my hands in his.

"I'm sorry. This is Marcus. I met him at the gallery a couple of days ago. He is a tattoo artist."

Pulling my hands back, I raised an eyebrow. Phillipe saw the questions all over my face because he chuckled low and deep. He moved to me and wrapped his arms around my waist.

His breath brushing by my ear, he told me, "Trust me. He is going to tattoo me, not you."

I thought about that for a moment, and before I knew what I was saying, I told him softly, "I want one."

Phillipe laughed. He thought I was joking, but I wasn't.

"I'm not kidding. I want one."

"I didn't bring you here to mark you. I want your *mark on me."*

Rising up on my tiptoes, I kissed his mouth. "You're already on my heart, and you're already in my soul. Now, I want you on my body."

His lips curved against mine. "Do you even know what you want?"

Surprisingly, I did. It was amazingly obvious.

So, I told him simply, "F-holes."

* * *

Phillipe looks up at Gemma as she straddles his thighs, running her fingers through his hair. Her eyes are focused on him as she moves slowly. Rocking her hips gently against him, she presses her belly and mound against his impatient cock.

She is simply breathtaking. He hasn't let himself see it before. He doesn't want to admit it, but as she sits there open to him, vulnerable in her emotions, he sees her for the first time. Bringing his hands up from her waist, he traces her ribs to cup the sides of her breasts. She arches into his palms and pushes her hips forward.

Her eyes never leave his as he plays with her plump, aching flesh. When her mouth parts, he expects a sigh, but as he is coming to find with Gemma, nothing is ever what he expects.

"What about you?" she questions quietly.

Closing his eyes, he lowers his right hand down between her thighs and touches her wet pussy. He feels her thighs tighten around his as she rises up, allowing his fingers between her moist folds. She grips his hair as she moves gently against both of his hands.

"What about me?" he replies, continuing to watch her pleasure herself.

Licking her lips, she pants softly. "She got F-holes. Her parents made sure to tell the whole world what a disgrace that was."

Phillipe winces as Gemma leans forward, putting her mouth to his. "Stop thinking that they were right. She *wanted* it. She wanted all of this."

Phillipe removes his hand from between her thighs. He twists them both around, so Gemma is now lying under him.

"Did she? Do you mean I didn't brainwash her? I didn't make her lose the ability to think for herself? Do you mean I haven't made *you* lose the ability to think for yourself?"

Phillipe watches as Gemma's blonde hair moves across his pillow as she shakes her head.

"No. Don't you see? I can't stay away, just as she couldn't. Why do you continue to do this to yourself? Why won't you look at what's in front of you?"

Sliding over her, he drags his shaft through her wet slit. "And what's that?"

Phillipe lets her pull him down.

She explains, "Chantel and me. *We* are what's in front of you."

Her lips part as he penetrates her with the tip of his cock.

"Open your eyes and see us."

As she finishes that statement, he thrusts deep inside her tight, warm core, vowing that he will never leave.

* * *

I knew he was shocked. As he stood behind me speechless, I knew he was shocked with all that he saw.

"They're flawless," he finally stated, almost reverently.

"So, they look good?"

"They look perfect. It's like you should have been born with them."

I felt his fingers reach out to touch the surrounding skin.

"Oh no. No, Phillipe. Do not touch, not for a while," Marcus told him seriously.

I smiled to myself as Phillipe came around in front of me.

"Your parents will kill me."

"How will they ever know? And, Phillipe, I'm an adult."

"They already hate me. This will just make them hate me more."

Reaching out, I traced his mouth with my fingers as I reiterated, "I don't care what they think, and neither should you. When are you going to understand that the only thing that is important is right here in front of you?" I paused and kissed his mouth. "Stop worrying about what everybody else thinks and open your eyes. See me."

He gripped my fingers, and I felt him nod. "I do. I promise."

Stroking a finger down his impossibly high cheekbone, I told him softly, "The only thing worse than being blind is having sight but no vision."

As we stood there in the tattoo shop, I could have sworn that I felt a tear under my finger, but before I could comment, he pulled away.

"Marcus?" his voice rumbled over my skin.

"Yes, Phillipe?"

"I want that—what she just said—I want her words marked on my body."

* * *

As I lie silently, face to face with Phillipe, I run my palm over his chest.

"So, you had a quote tattooed on you?"

I watch with a small burst of happiness as a smug little grin pulls at his mouth. It's an expression that has been gone for so long that it takes me off-guard with its appearance.

"Yes."

Biting my lip, I remove my hand, but he quickly reaches out and pulls it back. This is the first time that he has voluntarily let me touch every part of him—not only with my hands, but also with my mind and body. He's letting me reach parts of him that I never have before. I feel we have crossed a line. He's finally letting me in.

"Where? I haven't seen it, and I've seen you..." I pause, feeling ridiculous in my shyness.

"You've seen me what, Gemma?"

"Naked. I've seen you naked."

Looking down our bodies, he then brings his eyes back to me and raises his brows, wiggling them playfully. "So, it would seem."

"Are you going to tell me?" I ask, wondering where on earth it can be. I let me eyes run down his arms and across his chest. They skate over his rigid abs and softening cock. *Nope, there's not a tattoo in sight.*

"Always full of questions." He muses as he reaches out to play with the ends of my hair.

"And *you* are always deflecting them."

"I find that the less I say to journalists, the less I have to worry about."

I narrow my eyes at him, hating that he has mentioned my profession.

"But when I look at you, I no longer see a journalist," he informs thoughtfully.

I don't know why, but this confession pleases me. I feel my heart start to flutter in my chest as I watch his eyes track over me.

"What do you see?" I ask. I'm curious as always.

His hand reaches out, and he brushes my nipple with his finger. "I see me, I see her, and I see you. When I look at you Gemma, I see *us*."

Moving in close, I ask again, "Where is it, Phillipe?"

His beautiful green eyes slide close, and he rolls over onto his side to his stomach. Across the top of his back in script reads *The only thing worse than being blind is having sight but no vision.*

I trace my fingertip across the words before I lean down over him and place my lips to his skin. *How have I not seen this before?* Well, the answer is simple really. He never wanted to show me.

In the silence that now surrounds us, he lies face down on the mattress with me pressed close to his skin. I finally feel that he has let me in. He has shown me a truth, and now, I have *vision.*

Chapter Twenty-Three

CONFESSION

Day 18

As I stand in the shower with my eyes shut the next morning, I think back to the night before. Phillipe let me stay all night. He pulled me in close and held me steady as I listened to his heartbeat. *Thump, thump, thump.*

The steady rhythm lulled me to sleep while my mind was playing trick after trick on me. One moment we were alone, and the next I swore I could see haunted gray eyes staring at me. As I laid there, I squeezed him tight and vowed nothing could make me leave.

Running my hands through my hair, I try to understand where my head is. The only problem is that it's becoming more difficult with every passing hour and every disappearing day.

I have an article to write first and foremost, but my want and need to touch and be touched by this man is pushing that aside. I'm starting to discover a part of myself that I didn't know existed.

Drive, desire, passion—these are all things I know I possess. They are what got me to the chateau in the first place. I have pushed myself to succeed and be recognized in this competitive field. *But now?* Now, as I'm standing here with the water washing over my aching body from an intense night, I don't know where I begin and he ends. I have no idea which side of me—journalist or woman—will win.

Either way, I need to get up to that studio. I have questions—from the journalist *and* the woman—that I want answered.

* * *

Phillipe wakes up as soon as Gemma slips from his bed. The sheets automatically cool as she dresses in silence. She picks up the journal right before leaving his room during the early hours of dawn.

As he is lying there alone and in complete silence, he tries to hear *her*. He waits for a sign to prove that she is there with him, but nothing comes.

Realizing that sleep eludes him, he heads to the studio to work on the half-finished piece waiting for him. *What the hell do I think I am doing?* He asked himself that same question last night when he stroked a hand down warm naked flesh.

He isn't being fair to Gemma. He knows that, but he also knows that he doesn't have the desire or strength to continue saying *no. So, why should I?* She knows who he is. Gemma knows what happened, yet she still trusts him to hold her all night while she sleeps entwined with him. *When was the last time I had the complete trust of a woman?* Well, he knows the answer to that question.

Pulling the cover from the canvas in the far corner, Phillipe looks at the floating figure. Midway down the piece, a beautiful white gown extends up toward the surface beyond the sinking body. With her arms falling away and legs pointed to her watery grave, the picture mocks him while the absolute silence is killing him.

* * *

Stepping into the studio, I immediately spot Phillipe over by the window.

His arms are behind his back. He's wearing a blue sweater with the sleeves rolled up to his elbows and black wool pants that cling to the muscles of his legs and ass. Even from behind, he's magnificent.

"Good morning," I say, announcing my arrival.

He looks over his shoulder at me, and his mouth tips up at the corner. "Morning, Gemma. You look well rested."

Smiling, I move farther into the room, walking toward the small desk. "I am. Thank you."

Without a word, he nods before looking back out the window. I try to gauge his mood, but once again, I find that I'm having trouble pinpointing it. Pulling the chair away from the desk, I sit and wait for him to turn. It doesn't take long, but before he does, I notice when he takes a deep breath.

Finally, when he is facing me, I look him over in the way a woman who spent the night with him would. Up until this moment, I haven't allowed myself that privilege. Yes, I have been with him many times, but this is the first morning I feel as though I have permission to enjoy the afterglow, basking in the memories of our shared intimacy. So, that's exactly what I do.

"You showered," he comments, turning away from where he is standing.

Keeping my eyes on him, I follow his sinuous stride as he prowls toward me. His eyes are on mine, and his sensual mouth is pulled tight.

"Yes," I finally answer.

I lick my lips in anticipation. The full force of this man is potent. From the way his eyes are focused with his full attention on me, I feel like a hand has reached out and stroked me between my thighs.

When he stops before me, he instructs seductively, "Stand up, Gemma."

Without hesitation, I do as requested, noticing a slight twitch to his mouth. My heart is hammering in my chest as his eyes move to where my blouse parts at my neck. I wonder if he can see my thumping pulse.

He places his large palm at the base of my throat, so his fingers are caressing my neck, and his thumb is at the hollow of my throat.

Should I be scared? Probably. Am I? Not in the least.

"You smell fresh and…" He pauses as his eyes run over my face. "Moist."

Swallowing, I can feel his thumb as he presses it a little firmer against my throat.

"Frightened?" he questions.

His deep voice slides down to join the imaginary fingers in my panties.

"No." I smile, hoping he feels as aroused as I do by his seduction. "Turned on."

His free hand comes out to wrap around my waist, and he tugs me close to him. "Yes, so am I, Gemma. I keep thinking about how hot and tight your ass was last night."

A low moan rips from my throat as his large palm strokes over the ass in discussion. Before I can think or stop myself, I'm confessing all the longing and all the emotions that have built up inside of me.

"It's yours—all of it." Panting now, my desire and need for him override my common sense, making me say things I know he is not ready to hear. "Take me, Phillipe. *Love* me. I am yours."

Slowly, I feel the arm around me loosen, so I reach down to grab it, trying to keep it around me.

"No! No, don't let go," I beg him, not even embarrassed at how needy I sound. "I didn't mean it that way," I say in a rush.

His eyes, only seconds ago full of desire, now slide close, and his mouth grimaces as he releases me completely.

"Let go, Gemma," he instructs firmly.

Feeling my heartbeats skip and falter from the ache of him pulling away, I blink rapidly and turn my head away from him. I'm humiliated. He's still so close, and I can smell his skin. He hasn't made a move to shift away from me, but he's placed an emotional barrier between us like a ten-foot brick wall. Biting my bottom lip to keep myself from either crying or screaming, I steel my resolve against him.

He demands firmly, "Look at me."

I hear him, but I refuse to comply. Instantly, his hand and thumb are at my chin, and he turns my head back to face him. I know I have tears in my eyes because his face is blurry. Still abusing my lip, I'm furious with myself for pushing and angry with him for leading me on.

"What is it you really think you are feeling, Gemma?"

Clenching my teeth, I try to pull my face from his grasp, but he doesn't let go.

"Love? I don't think so. Lust? Infatuation?" he asks.

I remain mute.

Instead, I feel a tear finally spill forth, sliding down my cheek. Moving my hand, I swipe it away. When he reaches out to grip my wrist, I become infuriated.

"Let me go!" I demand, attempting to twist my arm away from him.

Releasing my chin, he pulls my arm back behind me and gathers me up close to him. My breasts press against his chest as I feel a second tear slip free down my cheek.

"I can't let you go, Gemma," he rasps fiercely, leaning forward. "That's the whole fucking problem."

Suddenly, I can't stand the thought of his mouth on mine. I have my pride, and he just walked all over it. As I turn my head to the side, I'm shocked when I feel his tongue against my skin. He licks the tears from my cheek, and then his mouth is at my ear.

"Trust me, I'm not what you want, Gemma. I'm not what you *need*," he whispers, stressing his last word. "Don't waste your time loving me."

Moving back to face him, I find myself staring into intense green eyes that are pleading with me to understand.

"But you're who I have come to love," I confess, finally allowing my head to catch up to my heart.

His eyes search my face, like he's trying to find something, before he releases me abruptly. Walking away, he mutters, "Then, you are a fool."

Crossing my arms over my chest, I watch him stop at the easel in the corner. I have to agree with him. I am the biggest fool of all.

* * *

Phillipe knows he's being purposefully cruel, but Gemma—sweet Gemma with the wide innocent eyes—thinks of him as Chantel once did. They believe he is a man worthy of being placed high up on a pedestal. He already toppled from that lofty pedestal months ago, and he still has the broken bones to prove it. The last thing he needs is to be placed back up there only for him to fall again.

When he reaches the other side of the room, he turns back to face the woman who is watching him with a mixture of love and hate etched across her face. He wonders about his self-destructive behavior.

He knew last night how Gemma felt about him. There was no other reason for her to let him touch her and possess her in such a way. *But love? Where does she get the absurd notion that I'm capable of loving anything anymore? I'm not even capable of loving myself, let alone someone else.*

Bracing himself for whatever she's about to do, he asks cautiously, "Do you wish to continue?"

Raising her hand to her face, she wipes the remaining tears from her cheeks and squares her shoulders. She glances toward the window and takes several deep breaths. Every time her chest rises, Phillipe curses himself for wanting to touch her. He wants to place his ear on her chest to hear the proof that she is alive, but he won't do that to her. He *can't* do that to her because he's barely breathing himself. To drag her down with him would be the cruelest twist of all.

"Continue what?" Her voice floats across the space to him.

"The paintings, Gemma. What else would I mean?"

She shifts, wrapping her arms around her waist.

Defensively? Maybe. Protectively seemed more likely though. She is back to protecting herself against him.

"There are only two left," Phillipe explains.

She continues staring out the window, looking anywhere but at him.

"*Sacred* and *Deceptive*."

All of a sudden, she turns back to face him, focusing her eyes on his. Cool and devoid of emotion, she tells him calmly, "I'll be back here tonight at 6:00 p.m. We will do *Sacred* since that's the ground I just apparently walked all over."

Then, without another word, he watches her leave the studio.

* * *

Sacred ~

There are moments in your life when you know you are in exactly the right place at the right time.

This morning, as I was lying beside Phillipe on my stomach, I knew that I had one of those moments.

As the sun warmed my skin, his fingers traced my tattoo for what felt like hours, and his mouth was against mine, kissing and nibbling.

I finally opened my eyes.

"Good morning," he murmured.

I smiled at him and arched my back into his touch.

"You like this?" he asked.

His fingers once again moved over the F-holes that had been permanently marked on my skin. Nodding, I scooted in closer to him turning my head. His mouth found mine in a sweet morning kiss that made my heart speed up and pound against my rib cage.

"In the sunlight, your skin is almost iridescent. Did you know that?"

Feeling a full smile appear on my mouth, I was thrilled when he joined in the joyous moment as he kissed me again.

"I can't stop touching you," he told me, his fingers dipping down to flirt with the curve of my ass.

Nipping his bottom lip, I pushed my tummy and pelvis on the mattress as I felt his cock start to stir against the side of my leg.

"Who's asking you to?"

I felt him sigh, and his breath floated across my lips. He let his index finger slide deeper between my dark crack.

"No one?" he asked as though it were a question.

"That's right. No one. Certainly, not me."

His lips moved, and I felt them on my shoulder. He bit it gently as he shifted, rolling me to my side.

In this position, I could feel the sun hitting my naked breasts and belly while his warm strong chest pressed against my back and his throbbing shaft nestled into the cleft of my ass. One of his hands wrapped around my waist, and his large palm brushed along my exposed mound before he slid his hand down to my thigh.

"Lift this back here," he instructed.

Moving my leg back, he propped it up on his thigh, exposing myself to him. His fingers traced down my inner thigh to where my pussy was now spread open for his playful fingers. They dipped and slid through my wetness, and all the while, I could feel his hips shifting and pushing that strong cock to my crack.

"I don't want to leave today," he confessed, nibbling my ear.

"You need to go to the States. It's only going to be for three days," I replied through ragged breaths.

He brushed my clit with his fingers. "I don't want to leave you."

Pushing my hips back, I looked over my shoulder to where I knew he was. "Take me?"

Flexing his pelvis forward, he thrust his fingers up into me. "I'm going to. Have patience, Chantel."

Shaking my head, I pushed back again with my ass. "Take me here."

His whole body stilled as I wriggled against the fingers that were deep inside of me.

That's when he seemed to find his voice again. "You sure?"

Reaching for my sun-warmed breasts, I smiled at his hesitation. He was usually so confident. To catch him off-guard showed me just how much he treasured this gift.

Pinching my nipples, I replied, "Yes, Phillipe. I want to feel you everywhere before I feel you nowhere."

I heard a pained groan rumble into my ear as his chest vibrated against my back, and his hand moved as he slowly dragged his wet fingers out of my clingy body.

Shifting behind me, he brought up his fingers and pressed down on my bottom lip. "Taste how excited you are, Chantel. Taste how excited you are to be mine."

Groaning, I took his fingers into my mouth, sucking on them, while rubbing my ass against him.

He pulled me in tight. "Goddamn it." He growled. "What you're giving me is sacred."

I felt a tear fall from my eye at the beauty of the moment and at the thought of not touching him for days.

"I love you," he told me over and over. "You are perfection."

As I rocked against him, I knew this was our moment, the exact right place I was supposed to be in.

We were sacred.

* * *

Who am I kidding? I think, throwing the offending journal on the bed. I can't write this piece anymore. I'm too involved. All of my professional detachment is gone, and all I'm left with is this emotional mess, who is currently curled up on a bed, hating a ghost.

When I first arrived, he was a stranger, and *she* was a figment of my imagination that I put together from pictures and articles. *But now?* Now, she is just as real as he is, and with every word she typed, I feel her touching a part of me that I don't understand.

I don't *want* to love either one of them, yet I know that is exactly what has happened. Somewhere between Chantel telling me why she loved him and learning for myself that he was too hard not to love, I have fallen deeply for a man who I barely know and who doesn't want me. He touches me with every look he gives me, and she touches me with every word she tells me.

I feel as though my heart is being pulled in two separate directions, yet neither direction is the right path for me to choose. She is no longer here, but he won't let her go. *So, where does that leave me? Well, that's easy. I'm left alone.*

Chapter Twenty-Four
DREAMS

Sleep is not my friend tonight. Getting out of bed, I make my way over to the window and look out at the inky sky. The wind is whipping and howling through the vines, and I can almost feel the breeze as it seems to surround and penetrate me. Wrapping my arms across my chest, I take a deep breath before I whisper her name.

"Chantel?" I call, expecting no answer in return. "Help me," I plead into the empty night sky.

Shaking my head, I try to remind myself that she isn't real—*well, not anymore. So, why the hell am I trying to communicate with her? Next thing I know, I'll start a séance.*

Moving back from the window, I pick up the journal and climb back into bed to let her communicate with me in a way I know she can.

* * *

Dreams ~

I keep having the strangest dream.

*This is the third night that I've had it, and I have to think that it means something. Right? It always starts with music—*Air *by Johann Sebastian Bach. That doesn't surprise me or feel strange though.*

I love that piece. I have always found it so peaceful to both listen to and play, so dreaming about it seems natural. In fact, when I was a little girl, I had dreams about all the pieces I was learning by ear. It was probably because I had to play them over and over to get them right.

That's not what makes this dream odd. No, it's what comes after it.

It always starts the same with music floating all around me. I'm there, but I can also see myself. Yes, I can actually see, *which is a completely unreal situation, even without all the other factors.*

I'm down by the river. I believe it has to be the river at the back of the chateau because Phillipe is there as well, and I can see him, too. I don't know if how I picture him is accurate, but he takes my breath away every time, so much so that I want to stay in my dream just so I can look at him.

He's tall—that I already know. His brown hair blows gently across his eyes every time the wind shifts directions, and his eyes—wow, those green eyes of his are stunning. When he is looking at me, and he is *looking at me in the dream, his gaze is sensual and intense.*

He gestures me forward, raising a long arm with his palm open toward me. Without hesitation, I place my hand in his, and our hands lock right together. His hand holds mine and protects it, just like how he protects me.

"Come," he requests softly, his voice calming me the way it always does.

As I take a step toward him, I feel the soft grass beneath my feet as it tickles my toes. Glancing down, I wiggle them and smile at the fact that I can actually see my toes.

Looking back up at him, he is also smiling, and again, I'm mesmerized by the sight of him. He is beautiful. His lips are perfect, full and soft, and I know exactly how they feel against every inch of my body. As I move toward him, I can see his eyes looking me over from head to toe.

"If we wade out just a little, it will be perfect," he tells me.

I nod my agreement, trusting him implicitly. I know what he wants from me, and I want to do this for him.

Stepping closer, I feel my long white dress move and flutter between my ankles as I cross the bank to the edge of the water. There is a slight breeze in the air, but I can't hear it. All I can hear is Air *by Johann Sebastian Bach and the sounds of birds floating through the branches. Little yellow birds chirp and hop from branch to branch above me. In just the way he described them, they are happy.*

"I went and bought a secondhand violin today," he informs me, holding my hand.

I can feel the water lapping at my toes, and I giggle softly. "Well, that's good because I was not going to bring Diva in here with me."

This is the part of the dream that I love the most. He bends down, and I see his eyes. They are full of love, virtually shining with it, as he smiles right before his lips softly and reverently touch mine. I don't ever close my eyes in my dream because I am afraid of what might happen if I do. When I open them back up, he might be gone, and I might not be able to see him.

Instead, I slide my hands through his thick hair and squeeze gently as I hear and feel a rumble vibrate through him. When he pulls back from me, he runs a hand down my loose hair and asks me the same question one more time, even though he has asked me one hundred times already.

"Are you sure you don't mind being in the water?"

I release his hand and step forward, the cool water engulfing my ankles. As I look back over my shoulder, I smile and reassure him. "Not in the least."

* * *

Closing the journal gently, I sit on my bed in shock. *Premonition,* I think automatically. Chantel had a premonition of what was going to happen. There is more to this journal entry, but I want to—no, I *need* to understand what I am reading.

Grabbing my laptop off the desk, I sit down and open up a search engine. Frantically, I type into the bar, *Chantel Rosenberg,* and it reveals more than 5,820,000 results. Scrolling down, my eyes roam over the salacious headlines and look for an article with some kind of substance. *There it is!*

Clicking it open, I search through the keywords I am seeing: *chateau, despicable, Phillipe, sinful.* That's when, I find exactly what I am looking for.

Today, we are saddened to learn about the shocking death of one of our own on foreign soil.

Miss Chantel Rosenberg, live-in girlfriend to world-renowned artist Phillipe Tibideau, was found dead yesterday at 1:30 p.m., lying seemingly peaceful on the bank of the Fleuve Sauvage de Fleurs (Wildflower River) in Bordeaux, France.

The French authorities have reported that when they arrived, they found a shocked and somewhat disengaged Mr. Tibideau and a motionless Miss Rosenberg, who was reportedly wearing a long white dress.

One of the policemen went on record. He stated, "Elle a ressemble a un ange," which translates to "She looked like an angel."

Full details are still unknown at the time of this release.

As I stare at the screen, I feel a shiver skate up my spine, making my flesh break out in goose bumps.

She had a premonition.

* * *

"Is this far enough?" I ask, looking over my shoulder to where Phillipe is standing.

He's watching me carefully, and I can feel the water lapping around my upper thighs. I can sense that he is a little bit worried, but at the same time, I know he has no reason to be.

"Would you quit worrying? I've been swimming for years. Plus, the water is only up to my thighs."

I watch as a shaky smile touches his lips, and he nods at me. It's a gesture I know he must do all the time because it seems so second nature to him, but to me, each time I see it, I enjoy it more. After all, this is only the third time I have actually seen it.

"Okay, can you float?" he asks.

Giggling, I tip my head back, and, I find I am blinded by the sun as it warms my face.

That's when the dream shifts. It changes mood and alters its course. As I focus once again, Phillipe is by me in the middle of the river, but I can't see him. Everything is dark, and my vision is gone. I can feel him beside me, holding my head between his palms, while the music continues to float around us.

I can still feel the sun on my face as I inquire softly, "Phillipe?"

His hands tighten in my hair as he mumbles something.

"Phillipe?" I call again, feeling my heart start to flutter in my chest. I can feel myself becoming frightened.

Then, I hear him reassure me, attempting to calm me. "I'm right here."

"What's going on? What happened?"

The water gently laps against my temples, trickling into my ears a little. I start to realize the rest of my body is submerged. My arms are floating, and my legs…my legs feel as though they are being pulled down. My legs are—

"Stuck," his voice confirms. "You're stuck."

* * *

Shaking my head, I get up from my bed and put the journal aside. I don't know if I can finish this. I don't know if I can read whatever it is she wrote next. Making my way into the bathroom, I sit on the edge of the tub as I fill it. Maybe a soothing soak in the tub and some relaxation will help to get my mind where it needs to be, so I can finish what I feel will be a disturbing precursor to her final moments.

Standing, I quickly undress and climb into the tub, lying back in the fragrant warm water. Closing my eyes, I start to picture Chantel as she saw herself in her dream with a long white dress, floating around her ankles, and her hair left down, like mine is now.

Sliding farther down into the tub, the water laps gently against my ears as it surrounds my head, making my hair float down around my cheeks. Slowly, I lower my hands to my sides and close my eyes, letting the dark take me under. There is no sound in the bathroom, no *Air* by Johann Sebastian Bach floating around me. I hear only the rush of blood that is pumping through my ears as I lie still and silent in the tub.

"Gemma."

I hear my name spoken softly as though whispered directly in my ear.

I ignore it, knowing I am imagining things. Once again, I'm trying to get inside her mind, while she is trying to get inside of mine.

"Gemma."

I hear my name again, a little louder this time.

Taking a breath, I lower my head deeper into the tub. I'm determined to block her out. I'm determined to feel as she felt. The warm water completely envelopes my ears and starts to creep up onto my cheeks as I struggle to remind myself that I am in control. *I can sit up at any time,* I think to myself, but my heart is choosing to ignore my common sense as it starts to pound anxiously.

"Gemma."

My name is called again.

"Go away," I reply, feeling the water touch my chin.

Not a minute later, a hand grasps my shoulder. My eyes snap open, and I see gray eyes staring down at me and a face curtained by raven black hair. My heart viciously thumps inside my chest, making my head spin, as I try to clear my addled brain. As my vision clears, the image above me morphs until Phillipe is standing there, shaking my shoulder.

"Gemma!" he calls desperately.

I swallow, sitting up abruptly, and find myself returning to the present. Blinking rapidly, I bring up my hand and swipe away the water from my cheeks.

"What are you doing in here?" I demand.

Now that I am finally coherent, I can see he is in a panic. His eyes are wide. His hand, still gripping my shoulder, is shaking. Quickly, he releases me and steps back to lean against the counter.

He explains, "You were calling out."

Belatedly, I remember that I am sitting in a bathtub, and haphazardly, I try to cover myself.

"I was?"

Nodding slowly, he remains silent.

"What was I calling?"

His eyes move to my hands that are now cupping my breasts. As he takes a step toward me, I scramble back in the tub to the wall, making the water slosh around me where I land, not an inch away from where I was just sitting.

As he looks down at me, I'm aware of the hard bulge that has formed behind his zipper. My eyes move to his hands as he reaches down to unbutton and unzip his pants.

Shaking my head, I tell him softly, "No, Phillipe."

He doesn't heed my request though because he quickly pushes his pants and underwear down and off his hips. He reaches for the hem of his sweater, tugging it up over his head. My traitorous pussy clenches at the sight of him naked and hard before me. Lowering my arm from my breasts, I sit in awe of the body he has just put on display for me.

Looking down at where I am seated, he lets his arms come to rest by his sides, palms facing me.

He asks, "No?"

My breathing increases and the water I am sitting in now feels like it's starting to boil because looking at him has me overheating.

"What was I calling?" I ask him again. I'm determined that if he wants something, wants *this* from me, then he needs to give me something in return.

Reaching around to the front of his body, he takes his cock in his hand and starts to stroke himself. My mouth parts as I watch the decadent act taking place not more than a few feet from me. Unable to resist the seductive allure of him, I find myself moving to kneel before him in the tub. With a large palm, he cups the back of my wet hair, drawing me forward. Licking my lips, I look up at him.

One more time, I ask again, "What was I calling?"

Gritting his teeth, he finally replies, "Chantel. You were calling out her name."

His hand tightens in my hair as he brings my lips closer to his pulsating shaft. With eyes raised to him, I let out a deep breath, teasing his sensitive skin.

"That's because I was thinking about her."

His head falls back, and the muscles and veins in his neck start to strain as his taut body trembles. His pleasure at just my breath on his flesh is intoxicating. He's making me feel like a queen as I kneel before him.

Finally, he releases his grip on his cock, and I replace his hand with my own, grasping at the base of his shaft. Leaning forward, I lick the wet tip of his desire, and I delight at the deep groan that rumbles from his throat. Encouraged by the hand fisting in my hair, I part my lips and take him inside my mouth.

He might have had a problem admitting his feelings for me earlier, but when it comes to physical action, I own Phillipe Tibideau right now, just like he owns me.

Rubbing my tongue against the underside of his cock, I suck him between my lips and drag my mouth up his throbbing length. He's not letting me get away that quick though. His second hand grips my hair, and his hips thrust as he slides in deep. He's so deep that I have to concentrate on not choking from his sheer size. Grunting softly, he starts to move, fucking my mouth over and over, as my free hand holds on to the edge of the tub.

I can feel my core clenching with each sensuous stroke he makes into my mouth, and this time, as I raise my eyes, I see him looking down at me. He's watching his cock, glistening with a combination of my saliva and his pre-cum, as it pulls out from between my wet lips. It's messy and dirty, and I love every minute of it.

He clenches his jaw, and I see it twitch. As I feel his fingers tighten in my hair, I watch as his eyes dilate. He's gone, and he's lost. This time, it's in me, and I bask in the high I get from that. Tears start to leak out of the corner of my eyes from the sheer force of his thrusts and the raw emotions that are riding me hard. I'm shocked when his hands leave my head, reaching down to grab my shoulders.

As his cock slips free of my mouth, he pulls me from the tub, and a gasp emerges from my throat. My wet body is hauled out, and I'm turned around to be propped up on the bathroom counter.

Leaning back against the cool mirror, I stare into the eyes of a man who looks like he's about to crack, and I want to be the one who pushes him. Smiling seductively, I run my eyes over him as I slowly part my legs and reach down between my wet thighs, running my fingers over my clit. His eyes follow the move, and his mouth parts as he unconsciously licks his lips.

"Wider," he instructs gruffly, reaching down to fist his cock.

Spreading my legs more, I notice when his hand starts to move faster.

"I'm going to fuck you in a minute, Gemma, and it's going to be hard." He punctuates his sentence with another rough stroke. "If you don't want that, then shut those sexy thighs and get the fuck out of here."

I take my bottom lip between my teeth, and instead of leaving, I push my finger inside myself in invitation. His nostrils flare as his fisting quickens. Bringing my hand to my mouth, I suck my finger between my lips, and before I know it, he snaps.

His hand leaves his cock to grab my wrist tightly. His other hand wraps around my waist and tugs me to the edge of the counter as he wedges his naked body between my thighs.

"Do it again," he insists roughly.

While he watches intently, I reach down between our very close bodies and push my finger back inside myself. I arch forward, bringing me only an inch away from his mouth, and my lips open on a sigh.

Opening my eyes, I smirk as I move my hand. My now wet finger traces up his cock that's pulsating between my splayed thighs before I bring up my hand to tap it against his lower lip.

He bites the tip of it. "This doesn't change anything, Gemma."

I push my finger into his mouth, and as he sucks it clean, I place my mouth by his ear.

"Of course not. Why would it?"

Pulling his head away, he shifts a little, so his cock is finally touching the opening of my weeping folds.

"Indeed," he mumbles.

He flexes his hips, filling me with one hard thrust. Reaching around me, he clutches my ass cheeks with his big hands and pulls me toward him even closer, burrowing deeper into my soaked center.

"Un-fucking-believable." He groans as he starts to move, one slow pull out and one solid stroke back in. "A fucking fist—your pussy is like a fucking tight fist."

I wrap my arms around his neck, and as he starts to pick up pace, I can't help the whimper that turns to a loud moan. Biting my lip, I arch my breasts into his chest and start to roll my hips into his.

Not having a clue what possesses me, I lean up, so my mouth is by his ear. As he starts to pump faster, I whisper *her* name into his ear.

"Chantel." I moan softly. "Is that what you would say?"

It seems as if his game has rubbed off on me, and I delight in the reaction I'm receiving. His hands grip my ass tighter as a growl emerges from his chest.

"When you were deep inside of her, Phillipe, did you scream out her name or whisper it softly in her ear? *Chantel*."

I taunt him again and again, making him groan. Pulling away from me sharply, he turns his head to the side, locking eyes with mine.

"What fucking game are you playing?" he demands.

Narrowing my eyes, I tighten my inner muscles and watch his eyes dilate further. "You don't want me, so I'm giving you her."

Shaking his head, he tries to pull out, but I tightly wrap my legs around his hips, tugging him back.

"No! You started this. You fucking finish it."

I watch as his jaw ticks, and I feel his cock twitch inside of me. Leaning in to me, he flicks my lower lip with his tongue, and then he bites me hard. Gasping, I pull my mouth from his.

"So, that's what you want, Gemma? You want me to fuck you and call out for *her*? Is that what *you* were doing all alone in here? Were you going to fuck yourself and think about her?"

While pushing hard against his hips, I'm frustrated out of my mind. I feel tears starting to slide down my cheeks. "None of your fucking business."

Sage eyes full of anger and desire narrow as he nods slightly. Like a hard punch to my gut, I'm reminded of her journal entry and the fact that him nodding is a move that is second nature to him.

"Fine. Have it your way," he grits out on a harsh whisper as he proceeds to fucking rail me.

Over and over, he fucks me harder than I ever thought possible. As I claw my nails into his skin, I'm captivated by the ferocious power he's unleashing. As he stiffens, my pussy clamps around him tight.

He looks me right in the eye and screams out her name at the top of his lungs. "Chantel!"

* * *

The dream always ends there. That is when I awake.

It's a strange dream, and I have to wonder what it means.

Stuck. You're stuck.

Does he mean with him? Does he mean here in France?

Dreams are odd, strange things. It's a good thing that is all they are—just dreams.

Chapter Twenty-Five
SACRED

Phillipe looks over to where Gemma is kneeling naked on the floor with her arms wrapped around her waist. He can see her fingers against her back as the violin is propped up behind her.

The *Sacred* pose now resonates in the deepest parts of him. Depicting a woman's smooth skin, she's stripped bare of everything, except for her violin and her soul.

When he walked by Gemma's room earlier tonight, he heard her calling out Chantel's name. He didn't know what to think. At first, he stood frozen by the door while the name he cherished floated through the air. He thought he had imagined it until it was repeated over again.

Deciding to go in and investigate, he was shocked to see the bedroom empty, especially when he expected Gemma to be lying in bed. All that greeted him though was an unmade bed with rumpled sheets and her laptop open, displaying that horribly tragic article. The words pointed at him like an accusatory finger.

That was when he heard it again. Chantel's name was almost moaned this time. As he followed it to the bathroom, he found Gemma halfway submerged in the tub of water. Moving quickly to her, Phillipe felt his stomach plummet as his heart picked up at a rapid tattoo pace.

No, no, no! was his initial thought as she laid there, unmoving and silent. Automatically, he reached out, watching the blonde hair floating around her face change to black as he was hurled back to that day. That terrible day was forever etched into his mind with such alarming detail that he felt like it was an image carved on the insides of his eyelids.

Blinking rapidly as his frantic heartbeats increased, he grasped her naked shoulder. When he touched it, feeling her warm skin, he allowed his breathing to somewhat calm. *She's alive.* As that thought registered in his mind, she opened her eyes to stare up at him.

"Phillipe?"

Looking away from the spot he has now painted over several times, he notices Gemma is looking at him over her shoulder.

"Yes?" he replies absentmindedly. He tries to bring himself back to the present with the woman who is here.

"You said something. I was just asking what you meant."

Frowning, he shakes his head. After placing the paintbrush down, he runs a hand through his hair. "I'm sorry. I don't remember."

He concentrates as Gemma's eyes narrow on him. He knows that she wants more from him. Every time he touches her, he feels her whole body open, wanting to give herself to him. Instead of returning the gesture though, he just continues to take. He takes her mind, and he takes her body. He also knows that, at some point in between, she has also handed him her heart.

Repeatedly, he reminded her that there was no way he could be what she wanted. He was still spoken for. He was damaged, and he was still *hers*.

"That's okay," she says from across the room.

She stands and turns to pick up the sweater that she left on the desk. It's the same desk that he moved up here for a journalist only weeks ago. Weeks ago, he specifically requested that journalist to be Gemma Harris.

After she pulls the blue wool over her head, she steps into her pants. He quietly watches as she gets dressed. *If things were only different,* Phillipe thinks to himself. If she had been first for him, maybe he wouldn't be where he was today. Maybe he'd be happy, and maybe, he could have made her happy.

She crosses the space to where he is standing and moves around the easel. That's when he hears her take a shocked deep breath. Looking at her, he sees the questions flooding in her eyes.

"What? Why..." She stutters and then stops. Licking her lips, she straightens her shoulders. "That's not me," she points out.

Phillipe turns away from the full force of her accusation and reaches out to trace his fingers over the canvas. He doesn't care that the paint smears and smudges. His fingers move over the *dark* hair that is pulled into a loose bun at the nape of a luminescent neck.

"No," he confesses, "but when I look at you, *she* is all I see."

* * *

Trying not to lose hold of the tight grip I have on my emotions, I bite my bottom lip and nod.

"All of them?" I question, needing to know. I need to know if he painted *her* in every single one of the images he made me pose for.

He turns on the wooden stool he is seated on, and haunted eyes stare up at me. He replies softly, "All of them."

I nod, and without a word, I pivot on my heel, wanting to leave the space. I *need* to get away.

Just as I reach the door, I hear him whisper, "I'm sorry."

As I turn around, ready to forgive him, I notice his hand is on the canvas, and I realize that it isn't me he is apologizing to.

Picking up the journal from the table by the door, I quickly flee the scene. I can't even begin to hold back my emotions while I run down the stairs. I glance swiftly at the woman who hangs silently as the center of attention. She's the center of importance in this house. I feel the tears welling in my eyes. I know that I'm fighting a losing battle, yet I keep throwing myself down on the sword. Constantly, I give myself to him, and continually, he denies me for her.

As I push open the back door, I'm relieved to see that night has settled in because the darkness is the exact place where I want to be. Picking up my coat and a small flashlight, I head out. Following the little dirt path he led me down a couple of nights before, I make my way through the rows of vines as I reach up to wipe the tears from my face.

When am I going to fucking learn? The pain caused by his confession continues to pummel me in waves. *She is all I see.* His words repeat in my mind as the memory of his tortured expression tears at my heart. *Why can't I just let him go?* It has only been a few weeks. Days before this, I didn't even know who Phillipe Tibideau really was. In fact, the thought of knowing him intimidated me. *But now?* Now, the thought of *not* knowing him slays me.

As I make the final turn in the bend, the Fleuve Sauvage de Fleurs comes into view. I slow my pace and notice the moon is casting a beautiful glow across the running water.

Gradually, I move toward the edge of the bank. I can hear the yellowhammers chirping in the branches above, just like she did. As I get to the edge of the river, I sit down and open her journal. Closing my eyes for a minute, I pause, listening to the sounds around me. There aren't many. It's extremely peaceful. I hear only the running water, the birds, and the occasional croak of a full-bellied toad. Opening my eyes to stare up at the sky, I search for peace or comfort of some kind before I look down at the writing before me.

If I can't have him, then I am determined to hear from the one woman who did.

* * *

Perceptions ~

I spoke to my mother today.

She called me because one of our family friends had let my parents know that they had read an article about their daughter and how she had inspired an artist. Naturally, my parents had then looked up the artist and the collection online.

It always amazes me that two people can be put in a room with the exact same object or image, and as they stand there and study it, they will undoubtedly arrive at two very different conclusions.

Especially when it comes to my relationship with Phillipe.

"Chantel, honey, I think it's time you came home. Don't you?"

"No, Mom, I don't think I need to come home. I'm an adult, and I am happy here."

In all fairness, she had started out calmly. It wasn't until she had mentioned the reason for her call that I got annoyed.

"How can you be happy, posing naked for a man all day, Chantel? Is that your definition of a productive life now?"

"I do not pose naked all day for a man, Mom." I paused, taking a breath, as I paced around the studio.

Phillipe went to town when I received the call. I was starting to wish I had gone with him.

"Mary Beth called me today, and she told me she had read all about you and The Blind Vision Collection. *Chantel, honestly, the paintings are obscene."*

Shaking my head, I tried to remind myself that she was my mother, so of course, seeing those pictures shocked her. The poses were intimate. They were nude. Her reaction was normal, especially coming from a parental point of view.

"He is using you, Chantel."

That was not parental. That was cruel and unfair.

"He has a name. It is Phillipe. You met him once, but apparently, you can't even be bothered to remember that. He is not using me, Mom, and even if he was, maybe I want to be used."

"Chantel!"

"What?" I demanded into the phone. I was angered on behalf of the man who so lovingly touched me and looked after me. I was angered for a man who was not here to defend himself. "He has never done anything but love me, Mom."

She lowered her voice, and I could tell that she was either trying to keep herself under control or she was trying to hide the conversation from someone.

"What he has done is take your gift—your love of music—and destroyed it. He's defiled it and you, Chantel Rosenberg. The fact that your uncle allowed you to meet him in the first place and that you have allowed all of this is abhorrent!" Her breath heaved through the phone until

she finally let out a quick disgusted breath. "Well, obviously, he's manipulated you."

Gripping the phone tightly, I gritted my teeth and spat back, more irate than I had ever been before. "Phillipe has not in any way manipulated me, Mother. He asked, and I said yes. It was nothing more and nothing less."

There was a frosty silence before she said, "What he has done is take a vulnerable girl who was lost and seduced her into a relationship that is disgusting and depraved. It should be a crime!"

Squeezing my eyes shut, I took a breath. Almost as though my brain understood what I wanted to say better than my heart, I told her calmly, "I am a woman. I am a grown woman who fell in love with a man. I was never lost, Mother, but if I was, I am glad that Phillipe is the one who found me. There is nothing sick, nothing depraved, and certainly nothing criminal about the way we love one another. It is not my fault that when you look at the images, you see something unhealthy and disgusting. That's all on you." I closed my eyes, and before ending the call, I said, "Until you can understand that, do not call me again."

After I hung up, I felt tears escape my eyes.

I wasn't crying for my mother or for myself. I was crying for the man I loved. I was crying at the realization that anyone could think he was anything other than good.

* * *

Phillipe suspected he would find her down by the river.

As he steps around the final small bend, he spots her. She is close to the edge with a tiny light pointing to the journal she holds in her lap. The sun set around fifteen minutes earlier, and as she switches off the light, he knows that she is done for the moment. Uncertain as to what she is going to do next, she surprises him when she places the book beside her on the grass and lies down.

Closing his eyes, images started to flash before him—*the sun, the rain, and then the night.*

Shaking his head to dislodge the thoughts, he steps forward. As the leaves crunch beneath his feet, Gemma turns swiftly, pinning him with her stare.

"You scared me," she accuses quietly across the empty space.

Phillipe understands that. Right now, Gemma is as consumed as he is. That's what this place does. That's what *she* did.

"I'm sorry."

He follows her movements as she turns back to lie down again, staring up at the sky. Making himself walk over to where she is, he sits and looks down at her in her silence. When he realizes that he wants to reach out and touch her, he makes himself look away. Instead, he focuses on one of the trees on the opposite side of the river, where he always saw *her* standing.

"Will you tell me?" Gemma asks softly.

Taking a deep breath, he feels anguish splintering through his chest. Reaching up, he clutches the sweater covering his heart as he feels tears gather in his eyes. Swallowing deeply, he tries to form the words but finds nothing will come. Gemma's small palm slips into his free one.

Turning, he looks to where she is sitting up beside him. He brokenly confesses, "I don't know if I can."

Compassionate eyes hold his while she reaches across them both, placing her other hand against his heart.

"Will you try?"

* * *

I can feel his sorrow as if it is my own as I grip his hand tightly. The hand he clutches around his sweater is locked against his chest. As he turns his head and eyes away from mine, I remove my palm but continue to hold his hand.

"I wanted to paint her here," he starts softly.

Holding my breath, I try not to make a sound. I don't want him to stop, but I have no idea if I'll be able to handle what he is about to tell me.

"It was a beautiful day. The sun was out, and it was warm, not like now." He stops for a moment and frowns.

He licks his lips nervously before continuing. "I had this idea. It was a vision of her." He releases his grip over his sweater and drops his hand into his lap. "I always thought she was so…" He stutters here, and a shudder racks him as he continues holding my hand. "*Ethereal.* She was always so ethereal-looking. Her skin was so white and perfect."

Turning his head, he pins me with his stare, and I notice for the first time that his eyes have tears in them.

"She was perfect." Shaking his head, he looks back to the water or across it in the darkness.

"I asked her if she would mind posing in the water."

Laughing a little, he squeezes my hand again. My heart thumps harder at every word that is coming from his mouth.

"She smiled and asked if she had to be naked. I told her, 'No, I want you to be in a dress, a white dress.'"

The tight grip he has on my hand loosens, and I feel him slipping away from me. I try to think of something, *anything,* to keep him talking in the moment.

I ask, "So, you wanted her in a white dress? Why?"

This time, when his eyes meet mine, they look tortured. They look haunted as he turns back to face the water.

Out into the empty darkness, he whispers, "I wanted to paint her as I saw her, like my own gift from God. I wanted her to look like an angel."

I try to imagine how he is feeling, but I find I have no words. Instead, we sit silently for I don't know how long on the grassy bank of the Fleuve Sauvage de Fleurs. I can feel her presence in a way I never have before.

His angel is here.

Chapter Twenty-Six
DECEPTIVE

Day 19

Deceptive ~

Perceptually misleading—that is how I have always seen myself.

People always tend to label me or make assumptions about who I am. I suppose that's what happens when you're different or have a handicap.

I woke up this morning to Phillipe curled behind me, his arms wrapped around my waist and his mouth against my neck. He told me a few days ago that he was done with the collection. He said Sacred *was the final image, and he already sent it to town.*

He was wrong. I knew I wanted him to paint one more picture.

I wanted him to paint Deceptive.

I wanted him to paint me from my perspective.

* * *

Stepping into the studio the next morning, I find him over in the chair I first saw him in weeks ago. Not one word is spoken as I move to the easel that is still set up where he left it yesterday. Steeling myself against what I'm going to see, I tell my heart to calm down.

I can feel his eyes tracking me. Instead of feeling uneasy like I did during that first meeting, I feel aware, and I feel loss. *I feel the loss of a man I want and know I can never have.* Turning to face the *Sacred* image, I am once again shocked by the knowledge that he never painted me in any of these replicas. It was always *her*. This time, I don't back away from the recreation of her he has so painstakingly painted. No, this time, I reach out and trace my fingers down the violin.

"She truly is beautiful, not only her, but Diva, too." I whisper to him, trying to let him know that I'm okay with this. I want him to know that I am resolved to the fact that I can never be her and that I can never have him, but my words are met only with the heavy weight of sobering silence.

I let my eyes travel over all the tiny details he has remembered, focusing on the position of her hands and the scratches on the violin. It is terrifying in its brilliance, and I know that each and every image he has recently painted is a perfect replica of the originals that are hanging in memory two floors below.

"There are no F-holes on any of the paintings after *Solitary* and *Acquiesce*. Why is that?" I realize belatedly and look over to him.

His shifts and his elbows move to rest on the arms of the chair. His fingers form a steeple in front of his mouth, covering the lower half of his face. Still, he says nothing.

There's absolute silence.

"Why?" I question him again. I turn my eyes back to the image. Examining it, I theorize out loud. "Diva's there, and *she* is naked. She is special. Her image to you is sacred, yet Diva is covering her. Why are there no F-holes?"

Blinking slowly, I trace my fingers over her again, scouring my brain. I am desperately trying to think of why. *Why didn't he include her tattoos, not only here, but on any of the final four?* I am so involved in my own thoughts that I don't even notice when he moves. His shadow falls over me from the opposite side of the canvas, alerting me of his nearby presence.

Lifting my eyes to his, clearly confused, I ask again, "Why are there no F-holes?"

"It is not my fault that when you look at the images, you see something unhealthy and disgusting. That's all on you," he recites her journal verbatim.

Everything slowly starts to fall into place. The pieces I couldn't fit together from just moments before join as one.

"You were there that day," I accuse softly.

His eyes lock with mine, unashamed at what he has just revealed to me.

"That day she argued with her mother, you were there, listening to her. Why?" Shaking my head, I ask a different question. "Why didn't you tell her you knew about the argument? What significance did it make to leave them off?" I finally stop my rapid-fire questions and stare at him, anticipating an explanation. I pause, allowing him time to explain this strange revelation, so it makes sense to me.

Closing his eyes, he turns, pushing his hands into his pockets. Slowly, he moves to the open window and stops. I stand impatiently where I am, having learned that it is best to wait for Phillipe to talk than to push him.

"I could tell when I first met her parents months earlier that they didn't approve of me or of us."

Clearing his throat, he looks at me over his shoulder. I frown and as he pauses before continuing.

"They thought I had seduced her. Her father told me so the first time I met him. He didn't understand that she was a woman. She was a grown adult woman who had feelings and desires. All he saw was the little handicapped girl he had raised."

Turning to face me fully now, he leans back against the window, and his hair falls forward as the wind catches it.

"They didn't want to let her go. I understood that." He paused again, and his eyes pinned me with the force of his intensity. "I don't want to either."

Glancing down at the image before me, I lick my lips and move away from it, walking around the easel to stand in front of it. I leave nothing between him and me—*well, nothing except for her*.

"That doesn't explain why you left them off," I point out, being persistent as ever.

Closing his eyes, he shakes his head. "After *Solitary*, since she had permanently tattooed herself, I decided that I could give them this. I could leave her untarnished for them."

I realize that I'm fidgeting with my hands, so I clasp them in front of my body and tilt my head to the side.

"When I came back from town and heard her on the phone, I knew it was her mother. She was shaking with anger at whatever her mother was saying, but I could also tell by the flush on her face that some of what she was hearing was ringing true with her."

I find myself captivated by his story and also baffled by the thought of him believing the tale he was telling me. Before I can voice my reasoning, he continues.

"I decided not to add them out of respect—respect for her parents, respect for her, and respect for the music I defiled. After all, *I* turned her and her music into something lurid and depraved."

Eyes full of conviction challenge me as I narrow my own and step toward him.

"You are so wrong," I stress.

He straightens and stands tall, freeing himself away from the window and wall.

"She wasn't embarrassed, not at all. Didn't you hear and read what she wrote about you?"

As I stop before him, I let my eyes search the face I have now grown so passionate about. *How can he not see what I see?* He's so wrapped up in her and all that he thinks he did that he doesn't even see what she left behind to show him.

Taking a huge risk, I reach up and gently cup his cheek. He doesn't move, except for his jaw tightening beneath my palm.

"She loved you, Phillipe. She was so proud to have those marks on her skin. She wasn't embarrassed at all."

His nostrils flare as he leans down, so we are eye to eye.

"You weren't there. She was agitated, and she looked humiliated."

Shaking my head, I stare into his eyes to get my point across. "Well, we all know that looks can be deceiving. Don't we?"

* * *

"You want me to paint you how?" he asked me again, sounding slightly confused.

"I want you to paint me looking at a wall covered with sheet music," I stated again.

There was a long silence in the room.

Finally, he spoke again. "What do you mean? As in, you reading the music? You don't use sheet music."

I had thought about this many times. The whole emotion behind the piece that I wanted him to convey was one of deception, not really seeing what was in front of you. What better way to show that than me staring at sheets of music on the wall? For years, I had learned to play by ear, and for years, people had never really seen me as the woman I am.

"I was thinking of a white room, like my acoustic room. Instead of the sound boards, it will have sheets of music everywhere. It will represent that sometimes what is

front of you and what you are seeing isn't really so. It can, in fact, be quite deceptive."

Stillness wrapped around me as the room went silent.

A minute passed before he said, "I want to understand why you feel this way. Do you feel..." He paused. "Like I don't see the real you?"

I took a deep breath and shook my head. "Oh no! Phillipe, god no. See, that's the whole point of the piece. I want to call it Deceptive. *I want it to make people think."*

His hand cupped my cheek, and his lips pressed against my own.

"Who do you think doesn't understand you?"

"Everyone," I replied quickly before shaking my head. "No, that's not true. My parents, people who don't take the time to know me, the ones who find out I'm blind and make a split-second judgment."

I opened my eyes and looked to where I thought he would be. I strain to see, trying to remember everything about my dream from just the night before.

"I want them to see what they think I am but wonder at the title."

"Deceptive," he muttered against my mouth.

His warm breath brushed my lips as he tried out the title. Parting my own, I sighed, and his tongue entered my mouth. He kissed me deeply before pulling back.

"Truer words have never been spoken. You are so much more than they all know."

"I love you," I told him.

His hands trembled where they cupped my face. "And I love you."

* * *

Phillipe reaches up and covers Gemma's hand where she still has it pressed to his cheek. Slowly, he moves it until her open palm is against his mouth.

Keeping his eyes on hers, he kisses there. "Thank you." He can see her eyes beginning to fill with water as she blinks, trying to keep her emotions in check.

Shaking her head, she replies, "I didn't do anything."

"You have done far more than you know," he whispers against her soft skin.

"No," she whispers. She moves her hand down his neck, stroking her fingers across his chest. "Don't do that yet."

"Don't do what?"

He reaches up, intent on removing her hands, but she's not having it. Instead, she removes her hands and steps forward. Boldly, she reaches under his sweater to touch the button of his pants.

"I feel like you're saying good-bye to me," she explains, her fingers slipping inside his trousers to undo the top button.

Phillipe takes a deep breath as she slowly lowers the zipper and she looks up at him with wide eyes. He tightly grips the wrist at his waist as his heart picks up at what he's about to do. Taking her hand, he loses the will to speak as she drops to her knees before him. She leans up to blow a warm breath of air against his now painfully hard cock. He's trying to tell her something, but words are failing him as he looks down to see her sizing him up like her next meal.

"Gemma," he says, trying to stop her again.

"Shh," she replies. Looking up at him, she parts his pants. "Let me."

Closing his eyes, Phillipe lets his head fall back. *This is a bad idea for so many reasons.* He's just finding it hard to come up with one.

"You shouldn't," he tells her.

As he reaches down to grip her hair, she dips her hands inside and gently pulls him free. Leaning forward, she touches the tip of him with her tongue and looks up at him.

"But I want to."

"Gemma, this doesn't change or help anything," he stresses.

This time, he releases her hair as she takes the head of his cock into her warm mouth.

"Jesus. No!"

Looking down, he watches as her blonde head moves down over his hard-as-hell shaft, and he feels a shiver skate up his spine. *I shouldn't be doing this. I brought her here to tell her this is done. It is over.* He didn't intend to have her down on her knees, essentially bringing him to his.

Knowing this will break her but not seeing any other way to do it, he reaches down and grabs her arms, pulling her away from his hungry body.

"Stop!" He growls, pulling her close.

He takes her lips brutally. Spearing his tongue deep into her mouth, he pummels it over and over as if he would die without the taste of her. He knows he has to let her go, so after one last sweep of her warm mouth, he pushes her away. He fists his cock hard, tugging it, as he stands there, staring at her. She's panting, her mouth parted, as her eyes latch onto his angry throbbing shaft as she tries to move back to him.

"You don't want to do that," he warns. He steps away with his hands on his frustrated body, keeping his eyes on her.

"Why? Let me ease you," she pleads, reaching out a soft gentle hand.

Knowing he needs to crush this right this second, he quickly grips her wrist and pulls her forward. Wrapping her fingers around his aching flesh, he curses.

In a voice so thick and full of gravel that he almost has a hard time getting it out, he tells her, "You came here, Gemma. You came here and listened. Now, it's time to go."

"Stop." She shakes her head. "We aren't done yet. There's still more I have to ask." She pauses, pulling her hand away. Rushing on, she says, "There's more you need to tell me."

Phillipe tilts his head while he stuffs his unsatisfied cock back into his pants. "What more do you need to know, Gemma? I sent the last two pictures, *Sacred* and *Deceptive,* to the gallery owner two weeks before!" He leaves his explanation hanging there. Both of them know what he's referring to when he mentions *before.*

"Those paintings completed the final six that then became *The Blind Vision Collection*. That's the whole reason why you came here."

Putting her hand on her mouth, she takes a step back, realizing the enormity of what he's finally telling her.

"No. No! I came here to learn about *you,* not your damn paintings. I already knew about them!" she yells at him.

Resolving himself to her reaction, he steps forward and grasps her shoulders, drawing her body in close to him. He crushes his mouth down onto hers again. She gasps and parts her lips, allowing him to push inside. Stealing one more brutal kiss, he wants to ease the desperate, frantic realization of loss flooding her as she stands there, trembling in his arms. As he moves away, letting her go, he looks down into eyes filled with hurt and confusion.

"The story has *ended,* Gemma. There's nothing left to say."

Wrapping her arms around her waist, she looks like she'll fall apart at any moment.

"So, that's it? After everything? After every *single* thing I have read and sat through, you don't even trust me to tell me what fucking happened?"

Getting up in her space, he leans down until they are nose to nose.

"Yes. Isn't that just too fucking bad? *This* is all you're getting."

With that, he storms past her, leaving her broken and bereft, just like he is.

* * *

I feel empty, like he's ripped my heart from my chest and left with it clutched in his fist. As I stand in the center of the studio, I can't comprehend everything that just happened. One minute, we were talking about the final two paintings. I was reassuring him. He thanked me, and then his mood completely shifted.

Breathing hard, I rub my forehead, still clutching my waist with my arm. *Oh god, it hurts.* I didn't think it would hurt so much as he pulled further and further away from me, but it does.

Closing my eyes for a moment, I make myself take several breaths to calm down. My head is still ringing with his angry words. Instead of worrying about my stupid fucking article, all I'm doing is thinking about how he doesn't trust me.

Finally, when I have my emotions somewhat in check, I open my eyes slowly and shake my hands by my side. Turning to leave the studio to go back to my room to start packing, my eyes fall to the large painting that had been sitting covered in the studio corner the whole time I have been here. This time, it is facing me, and *this* time, there is no cloth covering it. Raising my hand, I cover my mouth as it falls open with a silent gasp.

There, before me, is a painting I have never seen. My body trembles, and my skin breaks out in goose bumps as at the image sinks into my brain, passing through all my anger and all my hurt.

Walking toward the large canvas, I am once again captivated and entranced by his work. I swallow, feeling my heart pounding in my chest. It's beating so fast that I'm surprised I can't see it thumping against my shirt.

She is in the center of the canvas. Even in death—because death is what I see—she is beautiful. It's immediately obvious what this image is depicting, and as I get closer, I feel like she's behind me, urging me forward.

She's in the water. Her beautiful white dress floats toward the surface as her lifeless body seemingly floats in repose. Arms, legs, and hair point down to her final resting place.

With a trembling hand, I run my fingers down her arm and touch her hand gently. As I let my eyes take in all that I am seeing, they are drawn to the ray of light, shining through the water from above, as it casts a glow over her as she finds peace. I'm spellbound by Diva. The very instrument that brought her to life is floating down with her as the sun hits the bout of the violin. It makes complete sense that it is there, lingering near her, even in death.

Biting my bottom lip to keep myself from sobbing, I can feel the tears streaming down my face as my shoulders shake. I remove my hand from her palm and raise it to cover my mouth again as I let myself feel the pain of each agonizing stroke he made.

Stepping back slowly, I realize something else through all of the sadness and pain. He does trust me. *This is him trusting me.* I can feel it just as strongly as I can feel her presence here with me. She's sharing in my moment of clarity and insight. I realize this is *him* trusting me with *her*.

Wiping the tears away from my face, I turn to go and find him. I'm determined to tell him that I understand now. I have everything I need. I know how incredibly wrong they all were.

After her death, Chantel's parents had been the most vocal of his accusers. They pointed to him as the man who had brainwashed, manipulated, and trapped their poor *blind* daughter who had no knowledge of his wicked ways.

What irony it is that their daughter saw life and love more clearly than either of them did. Nothing about Chantel was explored. No one asked how she felt. No one looked beyond the surface. Everyone saw the finality of her life and made assumptions.

I now know that assuming was the biggest deception of all.

Chapter Twenty-Seven
TRUTH

I race down the stairs and grab my coat from the rack by the door. Heading outside, I know exactly where he is—the river. He's got to be down by the river.

Stopping for a moment, I look to the sky and feel the warmth of the sun as it beams down over my face. It's just turned noon, and there isn't a cloud in sight. It's cool, but there's no wind. The air is still.

Zipping my coat, I start to make my way to the small path through the vineyards, and as I get closer, I find myself picking up pace until I'm jogging. Reaching the last bend in the path, I make the turn and spot him immediately.

He's over by the edge of the water with his back to me. As usual, he's wearing his long dark coat. The collar has been turned up against his neck. His hands are clasped and drawn into tight fists behind his back.

I realize that I'm holding myself as still as a statue. I'm barely even breathing, not wanting to disturb him. I try to think of some way to let him know that I'm there without startling him. I'm surprised when his deep voice reaches between the empty space.

"I know you're there, Gemma."

Swallowing and shaking my hands out by my legs, I tell myself, *Move. Put one foot in front of the other and move. Go to him.*

Just as I make that first step, he mumbles, "I always know you're there."

That's when I feel myself falter. My foolish heart starts to thump at the idea that he notices me until I remind myself of everything he's told me and everything he's done over the last few days. *He sees me only because of her.*

Compelling myself to move again, I manage to make it as far as a couple of feet behind him, but I lose my nerve and stop. I wait patiently for him to either acknowledge me or pretend I don't exist. I know that no matter which option he chooses, it will cripple me in some fundamental way.

It feels like hours are passing by as I stand there on the bank of the *Fleuve Sauvage de Fleurs,* staring at the strong shoulders shrouded in black wool, but in actuality, it's not much longer than several minutes.

His voice finally breaks through the thick silence. "It was a day just like today, you know. Only, it was warmer."

I don't question which day he's talking about because I already know.

"There was not a cloud in sight," he tells me. Following that statement, he lets out a small laugh. "I had this idea to paint her here in the water."

Looking over his shoulder, our eyes connect. He's waiting for me to comment. Perhaps he wants me to make some kind of accusatory statement, but he won't get that from me. I know he has done nothing wrong. When it's clear that I'm not going to say anything, he once again turns back to face the running river.

"The weather was perfect. The sun was up, bringing you warmth when you stepped outside. It was blue. The sky was such a brilliant shade of blue that day. I didn't think to check the weather that day. Pretty fucking stupid of me since I knew the water table had risen with all the rain we had received."

I shift my feet slightly, looking up at the cloudless sky, and I realize that it looks exactly as he is describing from that day. *The sky is a brilliant shade of blue.*

"It was around two thirty in the afternoon when we came down here. I clothed her as I wanted to paint her. She wore a white dress that flowed down to her toes. Her beautiful..." Pausing, he seems to be trying to gather himself before continuing. "Her beautiful hair was left out. I wanted it to float around her."

Shaking his head at himself, I know somewhere deep inside he's villainizing his actions. He's blaming himself for bringing her down here, blaming himself for dressing her, and blaming himself for ultimately letting her go.

* * *

Over and over, he watches the scene playing out in his mind. As he stands there by the river where she finally let go, leaving him, he closes his eyes and sees every detail with startling clarity.

* * *

Chantel stepped out of the chateau.

"You look like an angel," he told her as he moved toward her and looked her over. He had bought the dress the other day when he'd been in town. It had been hanging in the window of a little boutique, and as soon as he had seen it, he'd visualized her wearing it while somehow floating. She had then told him about her dream. It wasn't until they had gone down to the river when he had realized he wanted to paint her in the water.

She laughed. "An angel?"

He reached out to take her hands in his own.

Entwining their fingers, Chantel smirked. "I think I proved last night that I'm no angel."

Pulling her forward, he leaned down, unable to resist, and pressed his lips to hers. After kissing her gently, he smiled. "And let's not forget this morning."

Leaning her head away from his, she arched an eyebrow. "Oh, that was you?"

"Oh yes, Chantel." He let his eyes move to her plump red lips. "That was me deep, deep inside of you as you screamed my name."

Letting her head fall back, she parted those lips as she basked in the warmth of the sun. "Hmmm, that's because you set me on fire."

He wrapped his arms around her waist. "Don't start that. I want to get down to the river before we lose the light."

Sighing dramatically, she shook her head. "Fine, Mr. Artiste. Lead the way."

Taking her hand, he guided her down the small dirt path through the rows of vines. As they rounded the bend, he let go of her hand and moved forward until he realized that she had stopped.

"You okay?"

Chantel nodded as she tilted her head to the side. "Yellowhammers, right?"

He looked up above them, and sure enough, there were several little birds chirping and jumping through the branches.

"Yes," he confirmed and laughed. "How did you know that?"

Instead of answering him, she just smiled and bent down.

"What are you doing?"

"Taking my sandals off," she replied as though he should already know this. "I want to feel the grass." She paused for a moment. "There is grass, right? That day we came down here, I think I remember— "

Laughing, he answered, "Yes, there's grass. It's extremely green and lush right now. There are no stickers either. Your dainty little feet will be safe."

He watched as she kicked off her sandals and let her toes sink into the long green blades. Clasping her hands in front of her, she smiled in his direction, and for a moment, he was struck with just how incredibly special she was.

This woman was not only beautiful on the outside. She also had everything good and pure inside of her that seemed to find a way to touch people. Whether through her music or just the way she stood there now guileless, trusting, and serene, she had a way. In a place so untouched, he couldn't imagine a better scene to capture her true essence.

"Come," he invited, watching as she moved toward his voice.

With each step she took, she seemed to delight in the grass tickling her toes. Her smile beamed as she moved closer. When she finally reached him, he took the hand that was by her side.

"If we wade out just a little bit, it will be perfect."

Nodding in agreement, she squeezed his hand and turned, moving toward the water's edge.

"I went and bought a secondhand violin today" he told her.

He noticed that she was looking down to where the water was now lapping at her bare toes.

Giggling, she looked back to where she heard his voice. "Well, that's good because I was not going to bring Diva in here with me."

He couldn't help but smile as she stood there with her feet in the water and a grin on her face. God, he loved her, and tonight, he was going to ask her to be his forever.

As she reached up and ran her nimble fingers through his hair, he closed his eyes and groaned from the pleasure of her touch. Who knew he would ever feel such peace at the hands of another human being? What a gift she had, and each time she touched him, she reminded him of the bond and pull they had with one another. When he opened his eyes, he saw that she was staring right back at him almost as though she could see him, and he knew that she felt it, too.

Pulling back gently, he ran a hand down her hair. He asked her one more time, "Are you sure you don't mind being in the water?"

She released his hand, and he felt the absence of it as acutely as he would a missing limb. When her ankles were submerged, she turned back to him and smiled.

"Not in the least."

He moved and kicked off his own shoes. He'd worn shorts today, knowing that he would have to wade out into the river. Moving in behind her, he placed his hands on her shoulders. "You okay?"

Laughing, she nodded. "Yes, Phillipe, I'm fine. Let's go."

As they both walked out into the water, he could feel the cool liquid creeping up his calves. Her dress was starting to rise and float to the top.

She gasped softly. "Oh! It's cool."

Gently, he squeezed her shoulders. "Want to leave?"

"No, it's already starting to feel nice."

"Okay, let's go out a little bit farther," he told her.

As they continued, he could feel some branches that must have fallen into the river. They brushed his legs as they moved farther out.

When the water lapped around the top of her legs, he stopped her. "Here. This will be perfect."

She turned in his arms and grinned up at him. "Hmm, I like this. Maybe we should strip and go for a swim."

"If we strip, we will never leave. Okay, I'm going back to the edge. Are you alright here by yourself?"

Sighing, she arched a brow. "I'm fine. It's only to my thighs, and I'm pretty sure I can rest against this huge boulder if I get tired." She paused as she reached her hand into the water. With a mischievous grin, she lifted her hand to splash him. "Go already, or the sun will go down."

"I'll get you for that," he promised as he started making his way back to the bank. "And Chantel? Move away from the boulder. I need you to float, not sit on the rock like a mermaid."

When he got to the edge, he turned around to face her. She was standing almost at the halfway point between the two banks, and the water was moving slowly around her, shifting the white dress back and forth as it floated on the surface.

He smiled to himself, knowing his vision would be perfect, but at the same time, he felt a niggling of fear because she was out there on her own.

"Is this far enough?" she called out.

He didn't answer right away as he was starting to second-guess himself. He was about to go to her and bring her back in, when on a loud shout, she told him.

"Would you quit worrying? I know you're worrying, Phillipe! I've been swimming for years, plus it's only up to my thighs."

Smiling at her smart little mouth and the constant reminder she kept giving him, he nodded slightly as if she could see him.

"Okay fine. Can you float?"

Nodding, she lowered herself into the water. "Yes, I can float."

As she stretched out, he looked up to the sky and noticed that several clouds had started to shift in overhead. Damn it!

Wondering how much time they had before they lost the light, he picked up his sketchpad and started to draw. Her dress drifted all around her as she held out her arms to the sides of her body. He sketched her for a solid thirty minutes. He captured the outline of her hair, the yards of material, and the water. He figured he'd fill in the violin and other details tomorrow.

He couldn't help adding her lips though. They were parted, and she looked peaceful as she lay there in the water. As he shaded from her hip down to her legs, he noticed her ankles had started to fall beneath the water. She was getting tired.

Smiling, he figured that she didn't even realize it. Ha, and she thought she could float.

"Chantel," he called out to her.

When he got no answer, he placed the charcoal on the sketchpad and called out again. He figured that the water was covering her ears or she had zoned out as she lay relaxed in the warm afternoon sun.

"Chantel!"

He was about to stand and go to her when a fat raindrop hit the page he was working on. Looking up to the sky, he saw the clouds were darkening and moving now at a more rapid pace. Placing the pad on the ground, he stood and made his way out into the water.

He didn't know if he was imagining it, but it seemed like the current had picked up. Chantel was exactly where he had left her, but he knew he was right about the current because her dress was now shifting much more with the water that was streaming all around her.

When he got closer, he called her name again, feeling that the water was now to his waist. It had definitely risen in the last thirty minutes. All of a sudden, that slither of fear started to slide back in.

"Chantel!" he called more frantic than only seconds before.

This time, she turned her head toward him just as he reached her. She smiled, and he felt the weight lift from his heart as she moved to raise herself. That was when she faltered slightly.

The expression on her face shifted, turning to one of confusion. "Phillipe?" she questioned.

Moving quickly, he made it to her side and reached out to grip her shoulder, trying to help her get upright. He watched as she seemed to be pulling on her foot, straining to move it. She attempted to place her other foot on the bottom to stand herself up, but she failed. The water sloshed around her. As her foot was swept up, she was thrown on her back again.

What the hell is going on? *He felt his heart start to pound in time with the speed of the now rapidly falling rain.*

"Phillipe?" she called again.

This time, he could tell she was starting to panic.

Not knowing what to do, he moved around to where her head was resting above the water. As she continued to float, he reached out to grip her head with his hands.

"I'm right here." He tried to reassure her as he looked around them. He was feeling anything but calm.

"My foot…the boulder. I don't understand what happened."

He looked down her body where her arms were lying beside her. Her one leg was floating, and the other was now fully submerged as the water still moved all around them.

"Stuck," he told her, not believing the words coming out of his mouth. "You're stuck."

Feeling the rain hitting him on the back of his neck, he was shocked when she opened her mouth and smiled.

"It's raining."

He knew that she didn't understand yet. She hadn't put it all together the way he had, but as she lay there, letting the rain water hit her face, he couldn't bring himself to say anything.

"Can you float here for a minute, Beauty? I want to see if I can get your leg free," he whispered, hoping he sounded a hell of a lot calmer than he felt.

"Yes," she responded. Almost as though it was an afterthought, she added, "I can't touch the bottom anymore."

He tried to control his shaking voice. "I know. Let me check out your leg, okay?"

"Okay."

Moving to where her leg was pulling down under the water, he told himself it was as simple as getting down there and getting her free. As he looked over to where her head lay half in the water with the rain falling down around her, he closed his eyes and sent out a prayer, hoping that he would be able to fix it whatever he found beneath the surface.

When he opened his eyes, he took a deep breath and dove under the water. With the clouds covering the sun and the rain hitting the surface, seeing what he was looking for was a difficult fucking task. Finally, he zeroed in on the problem.

Her foot and dress was wedged between not one but two boulders under the surface. Fuck! This is not fucking good. *Swimming over to it, he grabbed the material and yanked it hard, feeling her also try and pull at it from above. The fucker wouldn't budge.* Fuck!

Feeling his breath leaving him, he pushed himself from the bottom back up to the surface. When his head broke free, he took a gasping gulp of air and watched as she craned her head up toward him.

"Still stuck?" she asked softly.

Moving quickly up to the side of her head, he tried to calm his breathing as the rain now beat down on them. Reaching out, he stroked his hand over her hair, pushing the hopeless words from his mouth. "Yes, you're still stuck."

"It's raining harder, Phillipe."

This time, he knew that she realized what was going on.

"Yeah, it fucking is." His voice cracked over the admission. He took a moment and reminded himself that panicking would not do either of them any good. "I'm going to try again in just a second. We'll get you free. Don't worry," he said, trying to convince her as well as himself.

She nodded, but he could tell her mind was starting to wonder.

"The water…it's getting faster," she stated almost factually.

Biting his lip to keep in the curse he wanted to scream, he instead agreed. "Yes, it's getting faster." Before she could say anything else, he told her, "Now, you just keep floating, okay? I'm going to go back down and try again. We'll get this." He moved to her feet and reaffirmed his vow. "I will fucking get this."

Chantel didn't answer, but as he looked back to where she lay, she closed her eyes to the rain falling steadily down upon them. Quickly, he dove back down and took a hold of her calf. Pulling as hard as his body would let him, he tried to make her foot shift just a little, but nothing happened. His lungs were burning, her foot was still stuck, and nothing had changed. Absolutely fucking nothing changed.

As soon as he surfaced, on a rushed and ragged breath, he said, "I need to go and get help."

He didn't have a clue who he'd get. Penelope wasn't physically able, and anyone else was several miles away.

"No!" she cried out. As her voice cracked, she reached out a hand. "No, don't leave me here."

Wading up to her head, he took her cool hands. "I can't get you free on my own, Chantel. I need *to go and get help."*

"I'm scared, Phillipe. I don't want to be here alone."

Her voice trembled, and he felt as though someone had impaled him with a hot poker.

"Don't leave me here."

That was when he made a decision. He made a promise that he knew would destroy them. "Okay. I won't leave."

"Promise?" she demanded quickly, her voice shaking.

He stroked unsteady fingers down her cheek, and he gripped her hand tightly. "I promise."

The sun had finally been replaced by the moon, and as the rain continued to fall on them, he moved around to where Chantel's head was. Placing his hands beneath the water, he lifted her up so that her head was free of the now rapid current moving quicker with every passing minute. He could feel the water creeping up his body while it lapped above his waist as it covered her entire lower half.

"Phillipe?" she whispered softly.

Looking down, he could see her eyes were open, staring up at him. Battling his tears, he squeezed her head gently as he stood there completely helpless to do anything.

"Yes?" he managed to ask.

"Talk to me," she requested.

Biting his bottom lip he tipped his head back, feeling the rain fall onto his face. How can I possibly talk to her? What am I supposed to say? *She was stuck to the bottom of a river that was fucking rising, and he couldn't do a damn thing about it. A river he had brought her to! A river he had put her in.* I am killing her.

"Phillipe?" she murmured again. "What are you thinking?"

Feeling an uncontrollable sob tear from him, he confessed, "I'm thinking that I should never have brought you here."

She reached back and grasped one of his hands holding her head. She was miraculous. Even in a situation like this, she was comforting him.

"No, don't do that," she told him firmly.

He leaned down and pressed an upside-down kiss to her lips. They were cool from her body now having been in the water for so long. As he felt her mouth part softly beneath his own, his tears fell, joining the moisture already on her cheeks.

"I'm cold," she whispered against his mouth.

Sucking back an anguished sob he straightened his body.

"I know, Beauty," he acknowledged. "I'm so sorry. God, am I sorry."

He felt a shiver rack her body as her eyes closed.

"Shhh, don't do that," she told him.

The rain continued, and the river rose. There was absolutely nothing he could do but hold her and try to calm her. He was fucking useless.

"Don't do what?" he asked as clearly as he could.

"Don't be sorry. You didn't do anything."

He shook his head at the absurdity of that. "I brought you here. I put you in this fucking river, Chantel. Let my guilt take place. Trust me, I deserve it."

Her small teeth—teeth that had once bitten down on him in moments of pleasure—now bit down on her bottom lip to keep from trembling and crying.

"Guilty? What are you guilty of?"

"Everything," he confessed as he stroked a hand down her cheek.

"Do you see the lights over there?" she asked.

Closing his eyes, he blocked out what she was telling him.

"You don't see lights over there, Chantel. You can't see anything," he reminded her gently.

"Just like you can't be guilty," she pointed out gently.

He watched her wet lips part on a soft sigh.

"Don't let them make a villain out of you. Don't let them break you."

Leaning down, he pressed his lips to hers again, knowing what she was trying to tell him, but the truth was the lights were there. They were coming, and it was his fault.

He raised his mouth from hers and looked into sightless eyes. "You can't break a man that's already broken."

Water swirled around them, and as it moved above his waist, he firmly planted his feet and continued holding her. Her lower body pulled her down as he pulled her up. He refused to let her go. His arms were shaking from the rigid position he had been holding for some time now. Still, she lay there calm, almost resigned, as he felt his heart being torn from his chest, knowing he was watching her being pulled away from him.

He cursed God and pleaded with Him to take him instead, but he knew it was pointless. This could only end one way. As he stood there helpless, he knew that was the cruelest fate of all. He knew how this was going to fucking end, and there wasn't a damn thing he could do about it.

She had closed her eyes earlier. He guessed it was around twenty minutes ago. She hadn't opened them or spoken since. He needed to hear her to reassure himself that she was still there, still fighting this losing battle with him.

"Chantel," he urged softly. His throat was sore from silently crying as he gripped her head in his hands, praying he was strong enough to hold her. "Chantel."

He now stood in water chest deep as the rain hit the back of his neck where his wet shirt clung to him. All he felt was numb.

"Wake up," he whispered. "Come on, Beauty. It's time to wake up."

Eyes of gray opened. Eyes that held his soul focused as a small smile touched lips of red.

"You stay with me, okay?" he ordered firmly, trying to keep his voice from trembling.

Those same lips smiled slowly, and he felt his heart crack in two.

"It's too cold. I can't feel my feet anymore."

"That's just because they're numb." He tried to reassure her as a shiver racked her entire body again.

Biting his lip hard, he blinked rapidly, trying to clear his vision to see her clearly.

"I'm not scared, Phillipe, not anymore."

Shaking his head, he finally lost the tight grip he had on his emotions. He let the tears fall down his face as his body shook from the soul-shattering pain it was enduring.

"I'm not scared, not as long as you're here with me." She closed her eyes and whispered, "The water is much higher now. I can feel it against my chin." Suddenly, she cried out, "Diva!"

The name broke free from her cool lips with a surprising burst of force.

"You must take Diva, Phillipe. Don't let them have her. They don't understand…" Her voice faded as the eyes that held his soul pleaded with him. "She is me, and I belong to you."

Swallowing in as much air as he could, he pushed out the only reassurance he could now give. "Don't you worry. I won't let Diva go, and I won't leave you. I'm not going anywhere."

He tried to hold her higher, but he couldn't make her move, not even an inch.

The last thing she whispered was, "Neither am I."

As he stood there for the next thirteen-and-a-half hours, the water rose to his shoulders, far above Chantel's chin, far above where he was able to hold her. Then, it fell away, leaving him cradling her in water up to his thighs.

She left him in a peaceful river that turned out to be the most deceptive place of all.

* * *

I am still standing behind him as the final words leave his mouth. Tears are streaming down my face, and I can feel my heart breaking for the agonizing loss he had suffered. As soon as he turns toward me, his face is etched in sorrow and pain, and his eyes are bloodshot from the tears he's shed while laying his soul bare. I have no words for him, not one. How do you give a tortured man absolution? How do you convince him it was not his fault when he so clearly believes that it was?

As he makes his way to move by me, I reach out and grip his arm. He stops as I turn. Looking up at him, I see an expression so broken that I'm surprised he's still able to breathe.

I offer him the only thing I am able. "She never did leave here that day."

As his eyes search my face, his expression never wavers as he moves away from me.

"Neither did I."

Chapter Twenty-Eight
CONCLUSION

I don't remember how long I sit there on the riverbank, but as the sun begins to set, I feel as though the darkness is engulfing my very soul. *This is it.* I knew that at some stage, this would all be over. I just didn't expect to feel as desolate as I now do, sitting here on the lonely mossy bank.

The river, fluid and seamless as ever, continues to flow silent and strong, breathing life into its inhabitants, yet it remains as a cruel reminder of the life it took away.

Running my hands over my face and through my hair, I make myself stand. I know I can't prolong this for much longer. I need to go back. I have to say good-bye.

Staring out into the night, the inky water swirls and shifts around the rocks. As I look up into the stars, I wonder how Chantel really felt that night.

How does one feel, knowing that her time is running out? Terrified? Angry? Or am I projecting my own feelings? *Was she peaceful?* That's what I like to believe. I wonder if she felt scared. *Did his arms bring her some semblance of comfort? A moment of solace?*

Blinking away the brightness of the stars, I look out once more to where the moon now shines over the trees lining the bank opposite me. As I stand there, I feel her come from out of the shadows. However, this time, I'm not scared. This time, as I stand here looking across the wide body of running water, I feel my heart splinter and crack, wishing I could reach out to her. I wish I could be the one to comfort her. *Am I insane?* Ghosts don't exist. I know that, but my eyes and the feeling I have deep inside my chest won't let it go. Although I might be hallucinating, as I stand here on the bank of the *Fleuve Sauvage de Fleurs,* I can see her.

She is standing by the water, toes touching the cool liquid, as a long white dress flows around her with hair dark as night surrounding her pale beautiful face. As she stares back at me with eyes unseeing, I feel my own heart break for a woman I now love.

* * *

As Phillipe stands in his room, looking out at the old arbor, he tries to remind himself that what he did earlier was necessary. Reliving old wounds frees one's soul, right?

Then, why don't I feel free? Instead, he feels trapped.

Standing down by the river tonight, he felt her there, holding his hand, as he relived the most horrible night of his existence. Once again, she was there comforting him, letting him know that everything would be okay. When Gemma finally let him walk away, he knew that he was leaving them both by the river as broken as he was.

Closing his eyes, he takes a deep breath in and runs a hand up through his hair. This is it. The story has been told, and the tale has now ended. He knows Gemma will be leaving soon. Although he has done everything he can to push her away, he still feels her inside of him almost as strongly as he felt *her*.

When did this story morph? When did it change from a tale of two to a tragedy of three?

Shaking his head at his own selfishness and need to touch another, he berates himself for ever involving Gemma in the first place. When he first decided to grant this glimpse into his private life, he thought he would be smart. He planned to bring in a woman that did not resemble Chantel at all, someone who was the complete opposite of her, so he could look at her and feel nothing. That was not the case.

This independent, curious, and brave woman pushed her way in. She took everything he threw at her and stored it away behind a fierce wall of strength. She listened and shared in his love—his love of art, his love of music, and his love of a woman who was no longer here.

Gemma gave *her* back to him in ways he couldn't understand and would never have suspected possible. As a result, she also witnessed and shared in his agonizing heartache.

Turning away from the window, he moves to the locked closet. Opening it, he stares at the clothes still hanging untouched and cold. At the very end, still in the plastic garment bag, he finds what he was looking for. Avoiding all the other clothing, he reaches in and pulls it out.

Maybe if I do this? Maybe if he gave Gemma this, he can send her away, knowing she would be leaving with all of them, and she wouldn't be alone, like him and, ultimately, *her*.

* * *

When I arrive back at the chateau, I go straight up to my room. I am under no illusions that my time here will continue. There are no more journal entries to be read. There are no more tales to be told. *The story is over*. The problem I'm having is what to do with everything I now knew.

I open the door to the room that has been my sanctuary for the past few weeks. I'm surprised to see that the small bedside lamp is turned on, and my bed is turned back. As I move across the small space, I notice a dress laying out across the bed. Stepping even closer, I spot a small note nestled in the V-neck of the soft material.

Gemma,
I'll be waiting in the showroom.
Phillipe

Reaching out, I trace my finger over the rose trim of the bodice. I take a deep breath and close my eyes for a moment.

I hadn't known what to expect when I arrived here all those days ago. As I scoop up the beautiful ivory gown from the bed, I find I still have no expectations of what I will find down in the showroom where Phillipe is waiting. One thing I do know for certain is that nothing will stop me from finding out.

Showering quickly, I style my hair in a regal notch at the nape of my neck, sweeping my blonde bangs across my forehead. Believing this gown calls for elegance, I am determined to do it justice.

Making my way out into the bathroom, I spot heels that were covered by the gown. Beautiful taupe tips adorned with rose-colored jewels peek out from under the bed.

Sitting on the edge of the bed where I slept, dreamed, and fantasized, I slip my feet into the leather-lined shoes and stretched my legs out in front of me, admiring the sparkling jewels as the light hits them. Taking a deep breath, I stand and look myself over in the mirror by the dresser. I'm struck by the woman who is looking back at me.

She is a stranger, she is a woman who has given her heart away, and she is a woman who will never be the same.

She is now me.

* * *

Phillipe feels her the minute she enters the room.

He's waiting by the corner in the shadows, wanting to give her the time and space to feel whatever it is she needs to feel.

Once again, the room is dimly lit, except for the spotlights on each of the paintings. As Gemma moves into the space, Phillipe is surprised when he feels that the room is now complete with her presence.

Breathtaking. That's how she looks as she steps carefully into the low-lit space. The dress he chose for her cloaks her body like candlelight, and with every step she takes, the satin parts and her long, sensuous leg appears through the clouds of fabric. He is mesmerized.

He notices that she has pulled her hair back to the nape of her neck. Smooth and graceful, her elegance calls to him as she moves farther into the room. She stops before the painting, *Armor*. Watching silently, he is spellbound as she reaches out, and this time, shows no hesitation as she strokes her fingers down Chantel's arm.

Phillipe steps out from the shadows and takes a step toward her, but he finds himself paralyzed as she moves even closer to the painting. Resting her right palm on Chantel's shoulder, she inches in as close as possible and turns her head, laying her cheek against Chantel's breast. Whispering, she asks, "How do I leave him?"

Phillipe holds his breath as she raises her left hand and traces her fingers along Chantel's naked thigh.

"And how do I leave you?" she pleads, sounding confused and desperate.

Stepping back into the shadows, he gives her a moment to say her good-byes. After all, he knows how hard it is to let go of *her*.

* * *

As I stand there, brushing my fingers over her flawless figure, I close my eyes, remembering her words to him. *Don't let them make a villain out of you. Don't let them break you*. It shocks me to my core to know that I am now the *them* in the equation.

Letting my fingers come to a stop against the curvature of her hip, I make a vow to her. "I will *not* villainize him. I'll make sure the whole world knows what happened that night. They will all know that he didn't leave for help because there was no time to go." Stepping back from her, I reach out and stroke my fingers down the silent violin that stands stark and strong against her. "That I promise you."

I turn to look at the door, expecting Phillipe to come through at any moment, but as I stand and wait, he doesn't appear. So, I turn back and take solace in the knowledge that I am not alone.

As I stand here in a room that once frightened and confused me, I feel calm and comforted. Finally, I understand his need to have her here. *She* is his peace. *She* is his sanity. As I gaze upon the six images that torture and sadden the rest of the world, I feel an overwhelming sense of love and acceptance from both the man who painted the images and the woman who posed for them.

Finally, I feel more complete than I ever have before.

* * *

Phillipe doesn't know why he chose to put this particular piece on. As soon as he hits play on the system, the sounds filter through to the room Gemma is standing in. He feels his heart tighten and then release, like he is giving himself permission to continue.

Setting it to play repeatedly, he makes his way into the room to face Gemma who is now turned and looking right at him.

Without a word, he crosses the wide space to stand before her. Finally, he allows his eyes to really take in the woman before him, without comparing her to the woman who hangs in silent repose on the walls beyond them. Tracing his eyes over her, he marvels at the creamy texture of skin that is displayed so magnificently by the deep V-cut of the bodice. It is edged in a dusky rose that reminds him of her sensitive nipples after he's sucked them to a full, pouty point.

Caressing her shoulders are thin straps of satin holding the dress in place. Molding down her sides to tuck in at an extraordinarily narrow waist, the dress bunches on her lower back and falls out into a long flowing train that brushes the ground with each step she takes. His eyes gaze over to the sensuous slit in the gown that runs up the left side of her leg, ending high on her smooth thigh in a peek-a-boo ruffle. It makes him want to reach out and touch her.

In the heels he has given her, she is now almost eye to eye with him, and as she stares wordlessly, he allows himself to care.

Reaching forward, he touches her high cheekbone and closes his eyes. When he opens them, he isn't sure what he expects to see, but he's surprised enough to confess that his vision has finally cleared, allowing him to see *her*.

"Gemma," he whispers, almost affectionately.

* * *

Standing before him, I'm dressed in the clothes he laid out for me. I feel an overwhelming need for him to see *me*. As soon as my name leaves his sensual lips, I take a step closer to him, raising my hand to where his is touching my face.

"Phillipe." I breathe softly, my heart fluttering inside my chest.

He flattens his large palm against my cheek as his eyes run over me as though he is seeing me for the first time. I can hear music floating around us. It's a tune that I haven't heard before, and I want to know what is playing, so I can find it later when I mourn the loss of him. I know that is what he is doing. He is telling me good-bye.

When he appeared in the door, I felt my breath catch in the back of my throat at the sight of him. After the intense and emotional morning we both shared, I didn't know what to expect tonight.

Now, as the beautiful melody begins to fill the air while his eyes move over me, I know he has come here to let me go.

He is no less beautiful today than he was the first time I saw him. In fact, he is almost more so because now I can see and understand the pain that is etched into every line and crease on his face. His stunning green eyes framed by those long brown lashes hold mine as he moves closer. All I can see is the way they looked at me this morning. He was filled with so much pain and sorrow that I wanted to reach out to soothe him, to calm him, and to love him.

"You're devastating," he confesses.

Searching his face, I finally let my eyes connect with his, and I can see the longing there, revealing the emotion he wants to give to me, but I can also see that it is forever trapped behind those haunted eyes.

"Thank you. The dress is beautiful."

I take a swift breath in and hold it as he reaches out to place his free hand on my chest over my heart.

"It's not the dress, Gemma." He tilts his head once again, letting his eyes trace down my body.

I can feel my nipples tightening in response to his silent, hungry perusal. As his eyes make their way back up my figure, they finally stop, focusing where his hand is resting against my chest. I place my palm over his fingers where his touch weighs heavy against my beating heart.

"The story is over," he mutters, focused on our joined hands.

He lowers his fingers from my cheek. Gripping his wrist, I pull his hand from my heart and bring it to my lips. His eyes now move to mine, and as I kiss his knuckles, I don't waver. I let every emotion I am feeling surface until he can see just how much I love him. I can feel the tears gathering in my eyes as he pulls his hand away from me.

His voice, soft and firm, he commands, "Turn around, Gemma."

Licking my lips, I wonder about what he's going to do. *Undress me? Take me on the floor in this very room, like he did that day weeks ago?* I can feel the heat from his body as he steps up close behind me. He wraps a large arm around my waist, smoothing his warm palm against my abdomen in a slow stroke.

Pulling me back against him until my shoulders connect with his chest, I sigh as his mouth moves to my ear.

In that deep smooth voice of his, he explains, "*Méditation* from *Thaïs*."

I try to decipher what he's saying as his warmth radiates through me. I lean my head back, now resting on his shoulder, as I turn to see him looking at me intently.

"This song use to haunt me every time I heard it. It reminded me of her."

His eyes move to the paintings in front of us, and I follow his gaze to the images on display.

"The song seems very sad," I acknowledge softly.

"It used to be..." He confirms and pauses. "Until you. Everything is changing, yet it's still the same...because of you."

His arm loosens from around my waist, and his warmth leaves me. I look over my shoulder to see him standing a step away from me. Turning, I move to him, but he takes another step back.

Stopping, I tilt my head. "Phillipe?"

His jaw clenches as his eyes glance behind me to the wall. He is staring at *her*. This time, I'm not upset by it. This time, I know what he's doing. He's seeking permission. He's trying to decide if being with me will somehow betray her, and he's doing that because he cares. My heart swells right along with the melody as I reach out. This time, he takes my hand in his.

"Phillipe?" I plead, trying to get through to him. I try to make him understand.

His eyes come back to me as I pull him forward. Slowly, he moves, eyes locked with mine.

I place my palm to his cheek. "It's okay," I tell him. Moving forward, I kiss his lips. "I love her, too."

With that whispered confession, his binds seem to break. His large hands grip my waist as he tugs me that final inch closer. I mold my body to his as his hands run up my back. The eyes that now look down at me are full of anguish and agony as I run my hand across his cheek to his hair. Threading my fingers through the silky strands, I feel a shiver rack his body as his eyes slide close.

"Phillipe," I call to him again, keeping him in the moment. "Stay with me. Look at me."

Something in my words break through because those eyes I love open. They focus, and I can't help myself from saying exactly what I'm feeling.

"I love you."

Shaking his head, he clenches his jaw. Those full lips pull into a tight scowl, and for the first time since I met him, he looks unsure and defeated.

Bringing up the hand resting on his shoulder, I touch my index finger to the lips he's pulled tight.

"Does that scare you?" I ask.

He doesn't answer. Instead, he stares down at me, his hands tight on my waist. I tighten my hand in his hair and pull. Those wicked eyes of his finally appear and narrow as his lips part on a ragged breath of air. Suddenly, I know. I've hit it. I've been tiptoeing around the issue, and now, I know that as soon as my foot falls on the landmine, he is going to explode.

"Are you afraid because I love you?"

His eyes run over my hair, my eyes, and finally my mouth.

Licking my lips, I take the final leap. "Or because you love me, too?"

That's when his fingers dig into my waist, and his mouth crashes down onto mine. Strong lips collide with mine. He kisses me in a way designed to punish, but I know it isn't me he's punishing. Grasping his hair, I pull his head forward and rise up on my toes to get as close to him as I can. I hear an anguished groan rumble up through his chest, and I take the painful cry into my mouth.

Closing my eyes, I feel him shaking against me as I grip his shoulder tight. I rub my body up against him, begging him to take what he needs from me.

Hands firm and strong move up the curve of my back to the zipper resting between my shoulder blades. I tremble as he slowly lowers it down my spine. Lifting his mouth from my swollen lips, he keeps his gaze locked with mine. His warm palm slips inside the dress and parts the fabric away from my skin. Without a word, he nudges it gently, so the straps fall from my shoulders. Releasing my hold from him, I take a step back, lowering my arms. Turning around, I present him with my back, waiting for him to pull the dress off of me.

Closing my eyes, I feel the moisture pooling between my thighs. My body shakes in anticipation of his hands on me, but as I stand there staring up at Chantel, I hear footsteps and then the loud crash of a door slamming shut.

That's when the full weight of truth falls over me. As I wrap my arms around my waist in an effort not to shatter into a million pieces, I am left standing in the showroom with the only other woman in the world who lost her heart to Phillipe Tibideau.

Final Impressions

It has been a little more than seven months since I left the chateau. It's been a little more than seven months since I have seen or heard from the man I left behind.

When I returned to the States, I was given a deadline of two months. I had two months to somehow make sense of everything I had learned while staying in Bordeaux, France.

At first, I found it extremely difficult to sit down and write a tale of two people so obviously in love, knowing where the story would eventually lead. However, in the end, I discovered that in writing it down and telling the world, I once again found myself that much closer and connected to them both.

It's Friday night and has just turned 6 p.m., I stand in my room, slipping into a golden cocktail gown I purchased for the evening. As I turn my back to the full-length mirror, I look over my shoulder and let my eyes trail down my spine to my most recent addition. There, on the lower curve of my back, are two perfect F-holes, stark in their inky boldness against my pale skin.

Every Friday evening, I now go out to the local theater to watch the city's orchestra. I have developed quite an intense obsession with classical music. As soon as I returned home from France, I purchased season tickets to the local symphony.

Hiding my secret away from the rest of the world, I zip up the gown. I slip my heels on and make my way to the front door. I reach out and open it to find a short, stocky man standing there with a large rectangular box, resting against the wall.

He glances down at a clipboard he has in his hand and then looks back at me. "Are you Gemma Harris?"

Nodding, I frown and tilt my head. "How can I help you?"

"I was told to deliver this to you," he informs me, holding out the clipboard.

Once again, I find myself looking over to the box marked *Fragile.*

"I didn't order anything," I explain, looking at the work order. Nothing on the page gives me any clue as to what is inside the package.

"Oh, I know, ma'am. This was shipped in late last night from a gallery over in France. We were told to go ahead and deliver it to you as soon as it arrived, no matter the charge." He chuckles. "Looks like someone bought you a very nice gift. Do you want me to bring it inside for you?"

Moving aside, I tell him softly, "You can just put it in here by the door."

Leaning down, he picks up the piece and shuffles it into the foyer. After he places it against my living room wall, he smiles and tips his cap at me. Returning his friendly grin with one of my own, I close the door, locking it tight. Leaning my back up against it, I stare at the rectangular box that is now leaning against the wall inside my small apartment.

A gallery in France? It has to be from him. Of course, it is. *Who else do I know that lives in France that would send me—well, send me what? A painting?*

Forgetting all about the symphony, I kneel down in front of the box and run my hand over the brown surface. When I realize I need scissors, I stand and run into the kitchen. After returning to the mysterious box, I cut through the binding and slice through the tape.

When I finally rip apart the cardboard, I'm greeted with a lot of bubble wrap. Untangling and unwrapping, I tear through the padding at record speed. When I finally get to the framed image, I'm almost relieved that it's facing the wrong way.

I kneel back down in front of the painting as my heart races a million miles an hour. *What am I going to see when I turn it around? Is it a painting of* her? *Maybe it's one of the prints. A copy of one of the six?* I have no clue.

As I reach out to turn it, I notice a small envelope down in the left corner. It's taped to the back of the frame. Scrawled across the smooth white paper is my name in the same handwriting painted on the plaque by his house.

I take the envelope and open it. Pulling out the small card inside, I flip it over. I find I'm holding my breath as I stare down at the words printed so eloquently in black pen.

For the lady we never let go of.

Blind Obsession

You are both mine.

P.

Biting my bottom lip, I can feel the tears threatening to spill over my eyes as I sit reading those words over and over. Leaving that day so many months ago was something that would stay with me for as long as I lived. Pulling the card close to my heart, I let myself think back to that final day at Chateau Tibideau.

* * *

The sun was shining, and the day was perfect.

I remember standing outside the chateau on the gravel drive, waiting for Phillipe to come and say good-bye to me.

I was still raw from the night before when he had walked away from me.

As I look back now, I can understand why he did what he did.

He didn't want to make things harder than they already were. Although how that could have been possible, I wasn't sure. As soon as I felt him move up beside me, my heart cracked and splintered just a fraction more. I looked up at him as he stood there beside me. He was dressed in black wool slacks and a hunter green sweater. His profile was one that I would never forget. Just over his shoulder, I saw the plaque that I had seen on my very first day here. Reaching over, I dared to touch his arm one last time.

He turned his head, looking down at me. His green eyes were distant and devoid of any emotion. The man once again locked himself away, and there was nothing I could do to help him.

Instead, I asked softly, "What does that mean?"

He looked over his shoulder before turning back to me. "Les vrais paradis sont les paradis qu'on a perdus." His voice was so smooth and deep.

I realized in that moment just how much I would miss it. I nodded at him as he turned to look back out at the vineyards.

"It means, The true paradises are paradises we have lost."

Staring up at him, I willed him to look at me one more time, but he did not. Instead, he clasped his hands behind his back, and I felt the dismissal and distance more than I ever had before.

Moving down the steps, I made my way to the small red Toyota that I had rented and climbed inside. I refused to cry in front of him, but as I pulled away, I wiped tears that had finally escaped from my eyes.

As I drove farther down the gravel path, I looked in my rearview mirror to see a haunted man staring back at me and as my gaze moved to the top window, I could have sworn that I once again saw the curtain move. I knew I was leaving him where his heart was—in the chateau that was slowly crumbling into the ground but rested only miles from the place where he'd lost his soul many months before.

I left him there with her.

* * *

I place the card down on the carpet beside me and reach out a trembling hand. Pulling the picture out of the box, I move to grip the other side and turn it to face me. Sitting back on my heels, I stare silently at the image looking back at me.

There, seated on the soft chair that he sat in up in his studio, is me. He painted *me* in the dress I had worn that final night. I had my legs crossed, and I was sitting opposite a mirror.

I move in closer to trace over the image he so patiently and, as far as I can see, lovingly created. That's when I notice the image in the mirror. He painted me looking away from the distorted reflection, but as my eyes zoom in to look at every tiny detail, I notice the hair is darker. In fact, it is black, and the face is slightly different as well. He managed to capture me and *her* in one painting with Diva resting by my feet.

I am entranced, and as my eyes become misty, I grip my hands in my lap and let the tears stream down my cheeks. I cry for everything I learned during my months with him, and as I stare at the painting before me—painted by a man I can tell is so obviously in love—I cry for everything we cannot be.

Wiping the tears from my face, I blink twice, clearing my vision. That's when I see, down in the bottom right corner, one of the most famous signatures in the world scrawled beneath two simple lines.

Love looks not with the eyes
but with the mind.

The very words *she* gave to him. As I sit there alone in my apartment, I let my mind drift a million miles away to the place where I left my heart.

Into the empty room I'm left kneeling in, I whisper, "I love you, too."

Special Thanks

It must be said, as always, a huge thank you to all of my readers. Without you I wouldn't be able to do what I love. So I thank you all from the bottom of my heart and look forward to writing many more stories for you.

Also, a GIANT thank you to all the bloggers who took the time to read and review Blind Obsession. I appreciate everything you do, not only for me, but the Indie Writing Community at large.

Thank you to my wonderful editor Jovana. Your genius cannot be matched and what you did with this story was beautiful. Thank you for working so patiently with me. Your knowledge blows me away.

Finally, it was said to me just recently, by a lady I work with, that we use a small village to get to a point where the book is presentable to the world. So I must thank my fellow villagers – Ninj, Mendy, Brit & Chele. Not only have you been there now through all three of my books, but you are currently working with me on my fourth.

Oh and let me not forget the newest member to the world I inhabit, and she is currently cyber holding my hand and reminding me I *am* really a calm person deep down inside, C. Thank you for reading and critiquing Blind Obsession and pushing me when I needed pushing. I promise a 24 round paintbrush is in the mail!

Xx Ella

About the Author

Ella Frank is the *USA Today* Bestselling author of the Temptation series, including Try, Take, and Trust and is the co-author of the fan-favorite contemporary romance, Sex Addict. Her Exquisite series has been praised as "scorching hot!" and "enticingly sexy!"

Some of her favorite authors include Tiffany Reisz, Kresley Cole, Riley Hart, J.R. Ward, Erika Wilde, Gena Showalter, and Carly Philips.

Made in the USA
Columbia, SC
22 November 2019